THE AMBASSADOR'S SON

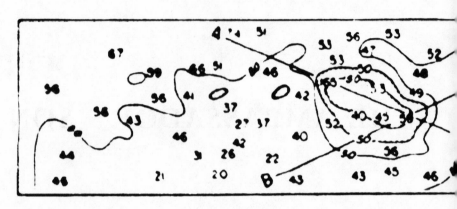

Also by Homer Hickam

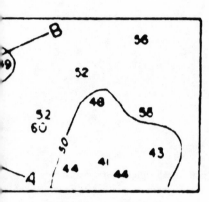

THE
AMBASSADOR'S
SON

Homer Hickam

THOMAS DUNNE BOOKS
ST. MARTIN'S PRESS
NEW YORK

THOMAS DUNNE BOOKS.
An imprint of St. Martin's Press.

www.stmartins.com

Library of Congress Cataloging-in-Publication Data

Hickam, Homer H., 1943–
    The ambassador's son / Homer Hickam.—1st ed.
      p. cm.
    ISBN 0-312-30192-8
    EAN 978-0312-30192-7
    1. World War, 1939–1945—Solomon Islands—Fiction.   2. Kennedy, John F. (John Fitzgerald), 1917–1963—Fiction.   3. Ambassadors—Family relationships—Fiction.
    4. United States, Coast Guard—Fiction.   5. Americans—Solomon Islands—Fiction.
    6. Missing in action—Fiction.   7. Solomon Islands—Fiction.   I. Title.

PS3558.I224A83 2005
813'.54—dc22

2004051312

First Edition: March 2005

10   9   8   7   6   5   4   3   2   1

To Captain Pat Stadt and the crew of the United States Coast Guard cutter *RUSH* (WHEC-723), with gratitude and admiration for your kindness and hospitality as we sailed across the wide, pearl-blue Pacific . . .

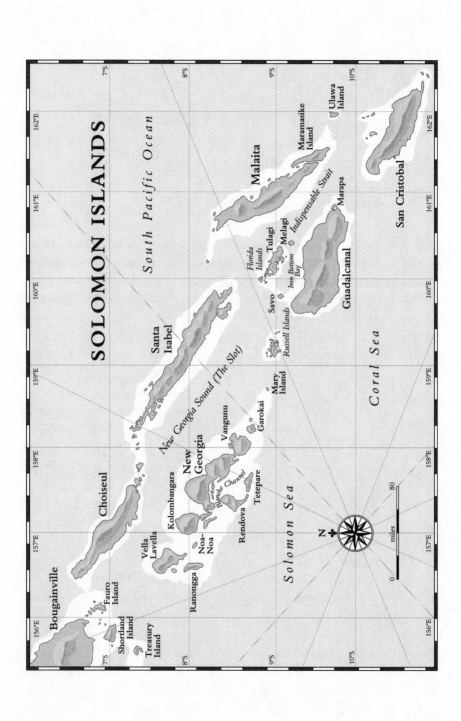

SOLOMON ISLANDS

South Pacific Ocean

Bougainville

Fauro Island

Shortland Island

Treasury Island

Choiseul

Vella Lavella

Ranongga

Kolombangara

Noa-Noa

New Georgia

Rendova

Vangunu

Tetepare

Blanche Channel

Garokai

Mary Island

Santa Isabel

New Georgia Sound (The Slot)

Russell Islands

Savo

Florida Islands

Tulagi

Melagi

Iron Bottom Bay

Guadalcanal

Marapa

Indispensable Strait

Malaita

Maramasike Island

Ulawa Island

San Cristobal

Coral Sea

Solomon Sea

N

miles

0   80

SOME REASONABLY PAINLESS HISTORY FROM THE AUTHOR . . .

This is a story of the strange kinds of love and passion that can sometimes occur during a time of war. When an author writes a love story, his readers rarely demand that he first establish the existence and nature of love. This is also true for passion. They are ancient emotions, instinctively understood by most people. A story of love and passion set during a time of war, however, especially a war as vast and complex as World War II in the Pacific, requires the reader to have some knowledge of that conflict. An author therefore has two choices: to bring forth the historical context of the war through exposition (and the necessary slowing of the action), or by presenting a little history up front. I have chosen for this particular story the latter approach. For those readers too impatient to wait for the further adventures of Josh Thurlow and the women and men who are always complicating his life (see *The Keeper's Son,* Hickam, 2003), or believe they already know the history of the place and times, or simply dislike renderings of history, I think they will eventually get the gist of things by going ahead with chapter 1. For those who want to know a bit more, I shall endeavor to make my history lesson as reasonably painless as possible.

The Solomon Islands, the locale for this story, are a group of subtropical volcanic and coral islands located about a thousand miles northeast of Australia. The Solomons have nearly always been a backwater, both in geography and in history. The indigenous people are not Polynesian, as famously presented in films and onstage in productions of *South Pacific* as adapted from James Michener's fine novel *Tales of the South Pacific.* There are no golden people in the Solomons dispensing flowery leis and free love to all who reach their shores. The native Solomon Islanders are actually an ancient racial mixture of Negroid and Australoid peoples who generally happen to have very dark skins. Until recent times, they were mostly known to the outside world for their tendencies toward headhunting and sporadic cannibalism. They are, of course, otherwise a splendid people but history loves to dwell on the colorful and savage.

In the late nineteenth century, a variety of adventurers, mostly British and Australian, tried to make the Solomons their home. They quickly discovered it was one of the toughest places in the world to live. Tropical diseases and disputes with the local populace resulted in the deaths of many of these colonists and chased most of the others away. Yet a few very hardy types persevered, and by 1942 a small colony of planters, traders, and Christian missionaries still hung on. They might still be there if the Japanese Imperial Army, fresh from an astonishing series of victories across Southeast Asia, had not arrived, first on one island in the chain, then another, always moving south. At the sound of the first distant shot, most of the colonists left with their families, never to return. Only a very few stubbornly remained behind, caught up in the clash between two of the mightiest countries in the world, the United States of America and Imperial Japan, each representing very different concepts of civilization, each determined to win at all costs. In the epic battles that ensued on these insignificant islands, the history of the world would be changed for all time.

Neither of the major combatants who fought in the Solomon Islands initially planned to fight there. Japan's purpose in World War II was to create a vast sphere of economic dominance across China and Southeast Asia. In the Pacific, only one country realistically stood in its way, and that was the United States of America. In 1941, the Japanese government toted up the strength of their naval and ground forces, compared it to what the Americans had in the Pacific, and determined that if they were ever going to attain their dream of dominating the region, now was the time to accomplish a quick knockout of the opposition. The surprise attacks on the United States in Hawaii and the Philippine Islands in December of that year were the result of this calculation (or it might better be called a miscalculation), followed by a surge of Japanese forces across Southeast Asia and thence south to New Guinea, Rabaul, and Bougainville. Almost without a thought, they continued to plunge toward Australia, although it was never clear what they would do when they got there. That was when the Solomon Islands entered Japanese military planning, especially one large island that offered a suitable area for an airstrip from which their bombers could interdict the sea-lanes leading to Australia and New Zealand. That island's name was Guadalcanal.

In June 1942, a little more than a thousand Japanese engineers and Korean laborers were put ashore on Guadalcanal to build an airstrip. A few hundred miles to the south, American forces had established themselves practically overnight in the island group known as the New Hebrides with the idea of slowly building up a force that could defend Australia and New Zealand and then perhaps move cautiously north. When reports came in about the construction of a Japanese airstrip on Guadalcanal, Admiral of the Fleet Ernest J. King decided to put a stop to it.

Although most of the American civilian and military leaders in Washington, D.C., including President Franklin D. Roosevelt, were determined to concentrate on the war in Europe, Admiral King, famously prickly and tough (it was said he shaved with a blowtorch), insisted on forcing the issue against the Japanese in a place where his navy and Marine Corps could reach them. Reluctantly, Roosevelt gave King permission to proceed. In August, the United States Marines arrived in the southern Solomons for what they hoped would be an easy fight against the few Japanese troops guarding the still unfinished airfield on Guadalcanal.

At first, it was a pushover. The Americans came ashore all but unopposed, piling up their goods on the beaches and securing the airfield. The Japanese engineers and the Koreans ran back into the hills. That might have been the end of it except the Japanese military, drunk on victory, refused to give up territory to the enemy even if it was on an island they didn't much need or want. More than anything, they desired to teach the Americans a lesson. Japanese troops, supported by the Imperial Navy, were ordered to retake Guadalcanal.

Thus, with neither side in the contest understanding the intentions or the determination of the other, a brutal seven-month campaign began with the cream of the Japanese military hurled against a rapidly assembled American counterforce of marines, army regulars, and National Guard troops, and what battleships, destroyers, cruisers, PT boats, landing craft, and freighters could be scraped together. The battle for Guadalcanal turned into a bloody slugging match between nearly equal forces. In the end, the Japanese would be utterly defeated and killed nearly to the last man. It is not hyperbole to write that the Japanese were astonished at this result. There were many recriminations in Tokyo. What had the army and navy done wrong? Who was to blame? Certainly it was not possible that the American fighting man might be the equal of the superior Japanese warrior.

A few Japanese politicians, unaffected by the samurai code of Bushido, knew after Guadalcanal that the war was essentially lost, especially considering the battering the Imperial Fleet had suffered at the Battle of Midway.

What Japan had in its inventory was about all it would have to fight the entire war. The Americans, on the other hand, had very quickly implemented a massive and efficient retooling of their entire economy to produce the implements of war. Millions of fresh, well-trained troops were in the pipeline along with massive cargoes of weapons, big and small.

Even with the evidence of ultimate defeat provided by Guadalcanal and the great sea battles, the Japanese refused to face the reality of the situation. Instead, they fashioned another strategy. They would go on the defensive and stop the Americans by demonstrating courage and brutality on a scale they believed Western culture could not imagine nor sustain. They reinforced their positions on the central and northern Solomon Islands, told their men to die bravely and to take as many Americans with them as possible, and waited. They would not have to wait very long. Vice Admiral William Halsey, commander of the American forces in the area, had discerned the enemy's mind and had instituted a straightforward but terrible response best illustrated by a big billboard he had planted on a hillside in Tulagi, the capital of the Solomons, where every American naval vessel and the troops they carried could see it. It said, very simply, ADMIRAL HALSEY SAYS KILL JAPS, KILL JAPS, KILL MORE JAPS.

JUST A LITTLE MORE HISTORY FROM THE AUTHOR . . .

One of the more famous and misunderstood episodes in the battle for the Solomon Islands between the United States and Japan occurred a little past midnight on August 2, 1943, when a PT boat skippered by United States Navy Lieutenant (jg) John Fitzgerald Kennedy, the future president of the United States, was rammed by a Japanese destroyer in the Blackett Strait off the island of New Georgia. After clinging to the wreckage of his shattered boat overnight, Kennedy, at the time an emaciated youth with a bad back, malfunctioning bowels, and probably a touch of malaria, ordered his crew to swim to an island four miles away, only to discover it was but a spit of sand with neither food nor water, save a few coconuts. Aware that the Japanese tended to murder their prisoners by beheading or evisceration, Kennedy and his crew spent the rest of the day hiding behind the bushes that lined the beach and being pelted by bird excrement.

While crouched in the stinking bushes, Kennedy, the second son of Joseph P. Kennedy, the former ambassador to Great Britain, surely must have reviewed in his mind what had led to his present situation. The mission that had sent him out the night before had been the result of a sudden brainstorm by the commander of Kennedy's squadron. Without rehearsal, fifteen boats had sallied forth to form a picket line across the strait between Rendova and New Georgia. Their purpose was to interdict the fast Japanese destroyers nicknamed the Tokyo Express that sped down from the north each night. Strict radio silence was kept, which meant no boat commander knew what the other one was doing. Only a few of the boats had radar, and Kennedy's boat wasn't one of them. When Kennedy saw flashes of light in the darkness, he assumed the action was on. He tried to get into the fight but couldn't find it. He was attempting to get his bearings when something massive struck his boat like a gigantic seagoing meat cleaver, tearing it to pieces and instantly killing two of his men. It was a destroyer of the Tokyo Express.

All the next day, Kennedy and his crew hid in the bushes. One of the crew, the mechanic, was horribly burned. All were hungry and thirsty. As darkness fell, Kennedy was apparently seized by a sudden energy. He announced he was going to swim into the shark-infested waters to signal the PT boats he was certain were searching for them. Nothing anyone could say could keep him from following through on his plan. Carrying a salvaged flashlight, he plunged into the sea.

All night, Kennedy swam, fighting a vicious current and reportedly being visited by hallucinations. The next morning, completely spent and bleeding from numerous coral scratches, he staggered ashore to report failure. After resting a few hours, but not sleeping, Kennedy once more displayed a tremendous reserve of energy. He convinced his reluctant crew to swim to another island several miles away. After an arduous swim, their new island also proved to have neither food nor water except for a few more coconuts. Another miserable night and day passed, during which, it was reported, Kennedy slept very little. Expecting rescue, he kept looking out to sea. When no ships appeared, he began to suspect the truth and bitterly remarked on it to his crew: They had been abandoned.

The next morning, a terribly thirsty, hungry, and sleep-deprived Kennedy tried to convince his men to swim to yet another island. They refused. Finally a fellow officer, along on the mission for a joyride that had turned into a hellish nightmare, agreed to go. After hours of struggling against wicked currents, they managed to reach the island and discovered a small wooden box containing Japanese crackers and candy. It was nearly midnight before they were able to claw their way back with the pitiful food. To Kennedy's surprise, two native Solomon Islanders were waiting for him. They were coast-watchers, men who reported Japanese naval and air movements to the Americans, and had just happened to be paddling by in their dugout canoe when they spotted the forlorn PT boat sailors. Kennedy scratched out a message on a coconut asking for help, and the two men carried it off. The next day, another canoe manned by two more coast-watchers arrived with a message. Their chief, a Britisher named Evans, had contacted Kennedy's PT base, and help was coming. Kennedy was transported via the canoe to an island named Wana-Wana, where Evans lived.

Kennedy arrived at Wana-Wana around midnight, about the same time the *PT-157* from Rendova pulled up to the dock. He climbed aboard the boat and collared its commander. "What the hell took you so long!" he vehemently demanded. Astonished by the verbal attack, the *157* skipper sputtered that everybody thought Kennedy was dead. The next morning, a sullen Kennedy directed the *157* to his crew. They were all transported to Rendova. After hearing Kennedy's story about how he'd been run down by a Japanese destroyer, some of his military superiors were determined to court-martial him for dereliction of duty. How was it possible, they asked, to be rammed by a huge, noisy destroyer on an otherwise quiet night? They muttered that Kennedy and his crew must have been asleep.

What happened during the next two weeks to the future president is not entirely certain. Some historians maintain Kennedy was taken to a naval hospital, although there is no record of it. Others say he brooded at the Lumbari base on Rendova, bitterly waiting for his fate to unfold.

PART I

I form the light, and create darkness. I make peace, and create war. I the LORD do all these things.—Isaiah, chapter 45, verse 7

1

The morning sun was a grinning, red-toothed warrior, come to slay the night. Bloody and quick, it tore through the night-riding clouds sitting on the purplish, rolling sea and flung a silver-white spear across Melagi, abruptly turning the great volcano that dominated the island from gray shadow to the color of bright jade. The night-wet air convulsed in the sudden heat. Steam boiled from the winding jungle hollows like hot smoke, and the feathery leaves of orchids, sitting in the crooks of giant, sodden trees, shook as if in the hands of malevolent spirits. Through the tangled bush, beneath a cloud of squawking birds rising into the fetid sky, a Marine Corps captain determinedly worked his way skyward along the volcano's eastern slope. Trickles of hot sweat carved paths down his face as he swept aside the sticky webs of giant spiders and pushed past vast green leaves, big enough to hide a man. Resolutely he climbed on, his hand on the butt of the forty-five pistol strapped to his waist. He came with an urgent message, and from his high perch on the slope of the ancient volcano, Josh Thurlow sensed something dire was headed his way.

"Another cup of coffee, Skipper?"

The offer came from Millie, cook and medic to Josh's Coast Guard crew. The slim, gray-eyed young man held the pot over Josh's mug and waited for his commander to give him the nod. In Millie's other hand was a bottle of Mount Gay rum. "A little of this, too, sir?"

Josh nodded agreement on both accounts, which Millie, who happened to be a cousin, never doubted would come. He poured the coffee, added two glugs' worth of rum, then went back to his stove, which was one half of an oil drum on welded scrap-iron legs, and his kitchen, which was a bamboo hut that sat beside the opening to a large cave. The cave, about as good a place to live as there was in the Solomon Islands since it was almost dry and almost cool, was known as Thurlow's Cave, and Josh Thurlow took his ease outside it on a rock his boys called Look-it Rock. Far below was a bright green punch bowl valley, collapsed on one side and disgorging a river of grass that flowed inexorably down to an abandoned copra plantation by the sea. The plantation presently served as the headquarters for the 5th Marine Raiders, their hundreds of brown tents and dugouts dotting a muddy plain.

Josh heard singing, borne by the breeze of hot, moist air lifting from the Melagi plantation. The Raiders regularly cursed the Corps for putting their camp on the island they called "Me-soggy," since it rained every day, producing a sticky brown mud that coated everything it touched. Still, if fortified by sufficient drink from their various illegal applejack distilleries, the Raiders could yet sing, though their favorite song was bitter and sad:

> *Bless 'em all, bless 'em all,*
> *The long and the short and the tall,*
> *There'll be no promotion this side of the ocean,*
> *So cheer up my lads, bless 'em all.*

One by one, Josh's boys came out of the cave to go down to the slit trench to do their morning business. As they passed their commander, they gave him their greetings: *G'mornin', Skipper, more rain today, I'm thinking,* or *Cap'n, easy breeze, ain't it?* Josh helloed his boys in turn, agreeing with their estimation of the weather and calling them by their names: Here was sweet-faced Ready O'Neal, the bosun; the gangly identical twins Once and Again Jackson; stubby, owl-faced Stobs Mallory, the radioman; and Fisheye Guthrie, the greasy-haired, fox-faced mechanic. Like Josh, his boys had all been born and raised on the island of Killakeet of the Outer Banks of North Carolina. Escorting the boys as they accomplished their morning duty was Marvin, a small black-and-white terrier, also a native of the Outer Banks. Marvin was smart. That's about all you needed to know about him except not to mess with him when he had a fresh bone.

The last boy out of the cave was Pogo. Pogo was neither a Killakeeter nor even an American but a bushman who'd appeared out of the jungle on Guadalcanal to attach himself to Josh when he and his boys were fighting alongside the Raiders. Pogo had chosen that morning to wear a hawk's feather in his puff of black hair, a necklace of cowrie shells and glass beads about his neck, big wooden plugs in his earlobes, and, for no reason Josh could discern, the stub of a number two pencil through his nose. He also wore a flapping breechcloth the locals called a lap-lap. On this particular day, he had chosen a bright blue lap-lap with a 5th Marine Raiders patch, which was a grinning skull, stitched to its front. "My word, good morning, Mastah Josh," Pogo offered as he trooped past, a grin on his round and mischievous face.

Megapode Dave, whom the boys had adopted since their arrival on Melagi, was a bird that looked as if it might be the offspring of a turkey and a vulture, though not as attractive as either. Dave, according to Pogo, was magic and could answer prayers if he was in the mood. Magic or not, he mostly slept. Now Dave waddled out of the cave on his big splined feet and laboriously climbed Look-it Rock, difficult since he was not designed to be a rock-climbing bird, and cuddled next to Josh for a postsleep nap. Josh idly petted Dave's hard, bony head and worried anew over his belief that something dire was coming toward him and was likely to arrive very soon. He wished for more rum.

The boys returned from their business, ate their breakfasts, and began to clean the cave. Millie brought Josh a pan of scrambled eggs and more coffee with the required dollops of Mount Gay. It was then that Josh decided to read again the letter he had kept in his shirt pocket for the past two days. The letter was from Miss Dosie Crossan of Killakeet Island, who was, until the arrival of the missive, Josh's girlfriend. Now Josh wasn't so sure.

Josh and Dosie had known one another since childhood, but she had gone away from Killakeet as a youngster, and, just a little later, so had he. It was coincidence, or fate, or a curse, that saw them return to their beloved island at about the same time, she to find herself, and he to fight the scourge of German U-boats that suddenly appeared off Killakeet's shores. During that time of adventure and change, Josh and Dosie discovered they were in lust, then love. What might have come of that discovery was interrupted, because Josh was sent off to the far reaches of the Pacific by Secretary of the Navy Frank Knox. Now a year had passed, and maybe Josh hadn't written as often as he should. Dosie, however, was a faithful writer, though it seemed to Josh now she had written one letter too many.

He had another sip of Millie's fine coffee and began to read Dosie's latest, and probably last. The first paragraph of her letter was the good one where Dosie told Josh the news of Killakeet, that his father, the lighthouse keeper, was doing well, as was his brother, who was now the assistant keeper. She also reported that she had placed some flowers on his mother's grave, though for what purpose, other than respect, she didn't say. He got no further with his reading because Dave suddenly erupted with a loud *squawk* and stuck his neck out straight as a finger. Josh followed the megapode's trembling beak and saw a dot in the northern sky over the channel known famously as the Slot, a constriction of the sea that the Japanese Imperial Navy used like a highway.

The dot rapidly grew into an airplane, which, by its raspy muttering, Josh recognized as a twin-engined Japanese bomber known as a Betty. "Stobs!" he bellowed over his shoulder, and the fat-cheeked, flaxen-haired radioman came running, though he nearly tripped over his untied boots. "Call Henderson Field, tell them they got a Betty coming their way. Call the Raiders, too, and tell them to get in their dugouts."

Stobs went off to comply, and Josh went back to Dosie's letter. Bettys were common enough occurrences, but letters were comparatively rare. The next paragraph was the critical one, the one Josh needed to think about. In it, Dosie had written she wanted to be *useful,* that it was only by being *useful* that she could know who she was. She had therefore decided to become a nurse, as *useful* a profession as there might be, and was traveling over to Morehead City for her training. Furthermore, she had quit the Coast Guard Beach Patrol, except for weekends when she still rode her quarter horse named Genie up and down the Killakeet beaches with Rex Stewart, the old Hollywood stuntman, who, by the way, had a new gelding he'd named Jubal Early. She also reported that no U-boats had been spotted for months, but the people still talked about the night the Germans had come ashore and all that had transpired before and afterward.

And then she mentioned a certain young doctor at Morehead City who seemed to have made quite the impression.

He's a handsome boy, was the way she'd written it, *and so gosh-awful smart. I am lucky to be a student nurse under his hand.* Josh read the sentence a second time and thought about the young, handsome doctor's hands, surely with fine, long fingers, capable of plucking out an appendix or stroking a woman's breast with the same tenderness and care. The heat in his face rose, so much so that his cheeks turned a bit rosy even through his deep, leathery tan.

Josh looked up just as the Betty let two bombs go over the Raider camp. He watched them fall until they splashed among some tents and exploded, throwing up big clods of mud and shreds of canvas. He saw no bodies fly through the air, so he supposed the Raiders had heeded Stobs's call and repaired to their coconut-palm-roofed dugouts. The bomber then turned toward Guadalcanal, but it didn't get far before it was surprised by two American P-40s. The big-nosed fighters pounced, guns blazing, and filled the unfortunate Betty full of holes, whereupon it broke apart, crashing into Iron Bottom Bay with one wing left to flutter down like an autumnal leaf. The P-40s did a couple of victory barrel rolls and Dave nearly twisted his neck into a knot trying to keep his eye on them. Dave surely loved airplanes, odd for a bird who couldn't fly.

Ensign Eureka Phimble ambled out of the cave with a cup of Millie's coffee and idly watched the Betty's wing smash into the water and disappear beneath white ripples of salty foam. Then he smirked when he noticed that Josh was reading Dosie's letter again. He and Josh had been together for nearly a decade, beginning their association on the Bering Sea Patrol. Phimble knew all the man's foibles, including that he had always been a fool for women, even on the Bering Sea where there were virtually none. Phimble had been an ordinary seaman then, kept even lower because of his black skin, and Josh an officer, both of them assigned to the cutter *Comanche* commanded by Captain Phineas Falcon, the legendary Arctic brawler. Somehow, maybe because they were both from the Outer Banks, they had become the best of friends, though they often bickered like an old married couple.

Josh took note of Phimble taking note of him. "Dosie's letter," he said, shrugging. Then he added, though he instantly regretted it, "She's fallen for another man."

Phimble tamped down his smirk. "If that was true," he said, "I'd have heard about it from my Talky. I got a letter from her the same day you got one from Dosie, as you might recall. Nary a word except Dosie's going to be a nurse."

"She says that, too. But she's still got herself a new fella."

"She wrote that?"

"Not in so many words."

"Dosie knows lots of words," Phimble answered, with a smile meant to soothe. "She's the kind who'd use them, too, if she had something to say. I think you must be wrong in your assessment."

Before Josh could reply, a Marine Raider by the name of Captain Lester Clooney abruptly appeared out of the bush. Mosquitoes were in a cloud around him, his helmet was askew, and his shirt was soaked with sweat from the exertion of climbing the volcano, and probably a low-grade fever. While Josh and Phimble stared at him, the Raider officer waved the mosquitoes out of his face (a motion known as the Solomons Islands salute), wiped his sweaty brow with a scrap of an old gray towel that was draped around his neck, set his helmet aright, took several long breaths, then looked Josh square in the eye. "Commander Josh Thurlow," he intoned, "you are to report to the office of Colonel Montague Burr of the 5th United States Marine Corps Raiders Battalion. Colonel Burr told me to tell you it had better be *toot sweet,* too, which is French, I think, for you'd best get your butt moving."

Josh now knew the source of his foreboding. Anything to do with Montague Burr was surely dire. Josh eyed the pistol strapped to the captain's waist, and further eyed the hand that was wrapped around its grip. "You aim to use that Huk-killer on me if I don't comply, Lester?"

"The Monkey said if you didn't come, I had permission to shoot you," Clooney replied, using the familiar nickname for the Raider commander.

Josh looked at the pistol held by the malarial marine. "I don't answer to Colonel Montague Burr," he replied in his stubborn manner, "and you can tell him I said so."

After a moment of reflection, Clooney took his hand off his pistol. "Commander, please accept my apologies," he said. "This place does strange things to a man's head. I completely regret my overly aggressive posture. Good morning, Eureka. Good morning, Dave. I'm sorry I didn't greet you until now. I was required first to accomplish my official duty."

Megapode Dave didn't care if he'd been greeted or not, since he had gone back to sleep, worn out from watching air combat. Phimble, however, replied, "Good morning, Captain Clooney. You did an excellent job with your duty, I swan." Phimble, following the Outer Banks tradition, added his estimation of the weather. "Don't look like it'll rain again for another hour. You want some of Millie's coffee?"

"Don't mind if I do," Clooney answered. "As for the rain, I guess it'll rain when it rains, which will be about ten times every day, as you well know. In between, the sun will shine and the steam will rise and the mosquitoes will bite and the mud on Me-soggy will get ever deeper."

Josh folded Dosie's letter, his mind made up on what to do about it. "All right, Lester," he said. "I have one thing to do, and then you and I, we'll go see the Monkey."

Clooney took the mug of coffee brought out by Millie, who had been listening from the cave. "Thank you, Millie. As for you, Josh, you can go see the Monkey by yourself. Otherwise, he's liable to send me with you."

"Send me where?"

"Wherever it is, I don't want to go. I think Colonel Burr's after you because he's got something bad and terrible that he can't trust a stupid jarhead like me to do."

"Then why don't you hide out here for a while, Lester?" Josh suggested, with surprising tenderness, and went inside the cave, where he sat down at the rude table the boys had built from scrap lumber, took up a thoroughly chewed pencil, and wrote on a blank sheet of paper:

Dear Dosie:

I guess you've found somebody what's good enough for you at last. I never much thought I was, anyway. I hope you and your doctor will be happy. Not much else is happening around here. Eureka and all the boys are fine and I am, too. Say hello to Rex and tell him I'd sure like to get old Thunder and ride the beach with him and his new horse.

Good luck, fair winds, and following seas.

Josh

P.S. Thank you for putting flowers on Mama's grave.

Josh put the note in an envelope, sealed it, wrote Dosie's Killakeet address on it, then called for Stobs. "Put this in the bag going out with my reports," he said, and felt satisfied and sad, both at the same time. Then he strapped on his pistol and the razor-sharp Aleut ax he'd carried since his service on the Bering Sea and went over to the crate used for storage of this or that and retrieved a half-full bottle of Mount Gay rum, the last in the inventory. He walked outside and tipped the bottle into Captain Clooney's mug, a generous two glugs. "Have a bit of this, Lester. It'll soften your day."

"It's too early," Clooney protested, though he tossed it back instantly, then whistled out a breath. "Are you going or not?"

"I'm going," Josh replied. And so he handed the rum bottle to Phimble and went on down the volcano to see the Monkey who, just as Clooney predicted, would ask Josh to accomplish a terrible thing even a marine wouldn't do.

2

Every morning, Missus Felicity Markham made an appearance at the Raider camp on Melagi, walking from the old plantation guest house along a well-worn path that led between the few stately coconut palms left standing. Her procession was invariably greeted by a gathering of Raiders and other straphangers, hungry to see an actual white woman, and a damned fine-looking dish at that. Some were even so inspired, they sang "Bless 'em All" to her, while others simply stared, holding their caps in reverence as she passed.

Such devotion might seem to a man just arrived from the outer world as more than the woman warranted. There was nothing even faintly sensuous in the way Felicity Markham walked. She kept her back as straight and her shoulders as square as a parade-field sergeant major, and she held her chin high, aloofly so. She was no great beauty. She had sharp cheekbones, clear blue eyes, concerned lips, and long, thick brown hair she usually kept tied up in a tight bun. She hid her figure, though evidently a fine one, beneath a uniform of baggy culottes and loose cotton blouses. She was also not young, being well into her thirties. Even so, she was one half of an intense fantasy devised by nearly every Raider on Melagi, each of whom had made up a kind of little story in his mind that would eventually see Felicity Markham and him clinging to one another beneath a monkeypod or frangipani or any other kind of tropical tree available at the moment, lost in hot and sweaty love of the most explosive variety.

"Good morning, ma'am," the shaved-headed marines said one by one, tearing off their caps as she and her son, John-Bull, passed through their gauntlet. Felicity heard a few low wolf whistles, which made her frown even though inside she was warmed. Little did they know she had managed a few fantasies of her own about some of them. It had been a very long time since Felicity had embraced a man. The malarial blackwater that had taken her husband, Bryce, had debilitated him for weeks before the final ravages, and that had been now three years ago. In the meantime, no suitable man had presented himself at her plantation on the island of Noa-Noa. Now, there was the war, and a hateful quarantine on Melagi, and the need to remain chaste in a sea of men who might go a bit bonkers if she selected but one of them for her favors.

John-Bull Markham was a ten-year-old imp. Next to his mother, the Raiders thought John-Bull (his real name was John, of course, but the Marines had supplied his nickname) was the finest thing on Melagi. One of the Raiders, a shirtless, muscled brute with a cigarette dangling from his lips and a tattoo of a naked woman fondling a snake on the ham of his right arm, called out, "Hidy, John-Bull. Come on out to the ball field. We're getting up a game."

"Hullo, Elmer," John-Bull answered. "Might I be allowed to bat?"

Elmer grinned around his cigarette. "Sure you can bat. Hit a home run if you want to. Your mama, I'm sure she'd like to come and see you hit a few, too, wouldn't she?"

The other men, armed with razor-sharp K-bar knives strapped to their belts, brass knuckles in their pockets, and the odd Thompson submachine gun on their shoulders, chorused their complete agreement like schoolboys, even though they were all killers by training, trade, and inclination. The plucky little John-Bull reminded them of a time when they had also been boys, a time that now seemed to most of them as if it had been centuries ago. Besides baseball, they had taught John-Bull how to fieldstrip an M-1 rifle, throw a grenade, cut a throat, break an arm, and even call in artillery. Making a pal of the boy was also a way to get close to his mother, or at least so they told themselves.

"Perhaps I will let John come out and play your game later, gentlemen," Felicity said, lengthening her stride. "But now we have our rounds to make."

"She visits the Monkey every day," one of the Raiders said confidentially to a recent arrival. "She wants him to let her leave Melagi and go on up north, don't ask me why."

A redheaded Raider sporting a peeling sunburn on his nose and shoulders said, "She's got a big plantation up there, you twerp. Island called Noa-Noa. I hear it's got like the Taj Mahal for a house and everywhere you look Maries in grass skirts or wearing nothing at all."

"A waterfall, too," another Raider added. "Bathing beauties sitting on the rocks in the lagoon below."

"Playing flutes," a Raider picking his teeth with a K-bar chimed in. Then he took on a beatific expression, as if he could see one of those beauties right before his eyes. "Ain't no mosquitoes there neither," he added. "And there's plants what cures all kinds of sores and stuff, including the clap."

"Well, the clap ain't nothin' any of us have to worry about, not around this place."

"The Monkey ain't never going to let her go, don't matter how great Noa-Noa is," another of the Raiders said. "He likes to keep her around to look at. He might even love her."

"The Monkey, love someone besides himself?" That got a good laugh.

"But who could blame him if he loved a woman like that?" somebody else chirped, and heads were nodded up and down the line.

"She oughta try the chaplain," a visiting sailor, all decked out in starched whites, said. "The Holy Joe's a right square guy. He could help her, maybe."

"Move along, swabbie. This ain't your affair," Elmer growled out of the corner of his mouth. The sailor did, rapidly distancing himself from the dangerous Raiders by going down into a stand of nearby palms where some native Melagians had spread out a blanket to sell poorly fashioned souvenirs, including one shrunken head, which looked suspiciously like nothing more than a carved coconut. He pretended to look at it but actually kept one eye on the woman as she continued on her way down the path. She was a fair package, for certain.

Felicity turned toward the beach along the path that led through some crepe myrtle bushes. "Why are we going this way?" John-Bull asked. "Aren't we to see Colonel Burr?"

"Yes, dear, but I thought we might first visit with Captain McQuaid."

"Oh, good. I like Captain McQuaid. Don't you?"

"He is an interesting man, my dear," Felicity answered in the most neutral voice she could manage.

The truth was Felicity did not like Captain McQuaid at all. He'd charged her twice what was normally asked for a voyage out to Malaita to pick up plantation workers, and for the money, the man had proceeded to blunder his boat, an old steam-driven schooner named *Minerva,* into the only well-marked reef in the Indispensable Strait. There they would have surely sunk if they hadn't been spotted by a passing American landing craft and taken under tow. They had been lucky for the rescue but unlucky for

the destination, it being the island of Melagi, where they had since been ma-
rooned not only by the condition of the *Minerva* but by order of Colonel
Burr. Claiming concern for their health, Burr had ordered Felicity and
John-Bull Markham quarantined on the island "for the duration," which,
since it referred to the war, was likely to be months, if not years.

But Felicity had neither months nor years to be trapped on Melagi. She
had a plantation on Noa-Noa to run, coconuts that might already be rotting, and disaster in the making if she didn't roast them into copra and get
them to market soon. Copra was a by-product of coconuts and used,
among other things, to make soap and a fine lubricating oil. The world
needed both and would pay for it. But it took seven long years before a coconut palm matured, and all a plantation could do was hang on until that
first crop came in. As luck would have it, 1943 was the year Felicity's coconut palms had finally come to maturity. It was also the year the loan she
and Bryce had taken with a bank in Sydney was due.

Felicity found Captain McQuaid sitting on the stump of a palm that
the Raiders had chopped down to build their field fortifications, not realizing they were some of the plantation's finest. The utter waste of war
fairly took Felicity's breath away. She knew that Brion Morrisette, the
owner of the Melagi plantation, had worked his heart out to plant those
trees and see them to maturity. *Brion Morrisette.* The name stirred memo-
ries in Felicity of a time that now seemed impossibly long ago, when all
there were in these remote islands were the black natives and the white
colonists. Together, they'd created their own little world. Some said it was
a brutal world where the planters overworked and abused their boys. Others thought it a brave place where adventurous men and women tried to
carve out a good life while offering a civilizing influence on the natives.
But never mind, what nice parties Morrisette and his missus had once held
on these very grounds! And where were the Morrisettes now? Languishing
in Australia, Felicity supposed, or perhaps even back in England, where
they would likely die when malaria came calling. Malaria was terrible but
survivable in these climes. In the colder places, it was nearly always fatal.

Felicity had malaria, though it had been nearly a year since she had fever.
Malaria was the fate of nearly every white man and woman in the Solomons,
including the children, though John-Bull had so far escaped it, thank God.
If the disease progressed to blackwater, where your urine turned dark and
your fever raged, you simply died. That's what had happened to her husband, after all.

Captain McQuaid seemed lost in himself, staring at his sad little boat.

Felicity knew the schooner not only represented McQuaid's entire fortune but was also the symbol of his probable future. Though a man might have thought his expression morose or even thoughtful, Felicity was a woman and could therefore better discern the true manifestation of his facial features. She knew it was shame that creased that sweaty face, shame for not only running into that wretched coral but for his entire life. She had known it from the moment she had clapped eyes on him when she had paddled out in her little canoe from her plantation to hail him down. Crime had chased Captain McQuaid out here, that much she knew. Most white men living in the Solomons who weren't family men were on the run for one shameful thing or another, and Captain McQuaid was no family man, though likely he had left his polluted seed inside more than one poor black Marie.

"I see you've done nothing to patch your boat, Captain McQuaid," Felicity observed. "A manifestation of your laziness, I presume."

"Thank you, missus," McQuaid replied, tipping his hat. "And good morning to you, too. I shall add your appraisal to my list of many character flaws." He tipped his cap. "Good morning, John."

"Hullo, Captain," John-Bull responded politely, as he had been taught to do with all adults, white or black, then went off to look for shells on the beach.

"Are you ever going to make *Minerva* seaworthy, Captain?" Felicity asked. "I think a plank and a little caulking is all she needs."

"The old girl needs a bit more than that, missus," McQuaid replied dolefully. "Look at the size of that hole. I doubt if she will ever be repaired. Now, please leave me alone. Can't you see I am thoroughly occupied by my misery?"

"You are more than miserable, Captain," Felicity responded. "You are besotted with drink and black women."

"Guilty! Hallelujah and amen!" McQuaid exclaimed, nearly smiling through his gray stubble.

"If you are afraid to go to sea," Felicity continued, unshaken by his outburst, "then let me take the *Minerva* and go myself. My Malaitan boys can crew her. I will pay you a fine price for a short-term lease. Surely you understand, I have copra to harvest, and delay will ruin my business."

"Business?" McQuaid laughed. "Missus, you have no business. Do you not see what is all around you? I should have left the islands months ago. Drink? Aye, there it is. My downfall, surely, that and an infernal optimism, but now I have seen the light. The only business around here is war, missus.

War! A private vessel can no longer operate in these waters. If the Japanese don't sink me, then the Americans will."

Felicity raised her chin. "I did not see any Japanese or Americans around when *you* nearly sank us, Captain. You seemed to do very well simply by running into a reef."

"It was because I was trying to avoid the Japanese and Americans that I struck that bloody reef," McQuaid replied bitterly. "I was going farther south than usual."

"You had a chart."

"Yes, missus. I did. The reef we struck was misplaced on it."

"It was not. You failed to put out a proper watch. I think you are a pathetic little man."

"Yes, you have defined me. I am a pathetic little drunkard who toys with black women and has a boat which cannot float. My fortune is all misfortune."

"You do not appear to be starving."

McQuaid shrugged. "I provide a service to the Americans and they give me food. I look at their charts and tell them where I think there are reefs that aren't on them. For instance, I know of one that isn't where it's supposed to be, as you are well aware."

"That should be worth a stale loaf of bread a fortnight," Felicity said.

"I pity myself for the day I met you," McQuaid replied. "You have been nothing but trouble."

Felicity narrowed her eyes. "You will rot on this island."

McQuaid shrugged. "At least I'll be alive." Then he made another attempt at communicating the present situation by asking a question. "Missus, I am curious. If somehow you were able to harvest it, who do you expect to buy your copra?"

"I will send it to Australia. People must still wash, war or no war, so soap must be made. And palm oil is surely needed for the war effort. One need only try to succeed, Captain. It is an article of faith my husband and I have lived by all these years out here."

Captain McQuaid raised his tangled eyebrows and resisted the temptation to tell the woman that her husband no longer lived anywhere and therefore, their article of faith was as bogus as any other dreams the English and Australian colonists might have had in this terrible place of heat and biting insects and disease and rot and ruin. Instead, he said, in as kind a voice as he could muster, "Well, I wish you well, missus. It is all I can do.

Now, I really must get back to feeling sorry for myself, if you don't mind."

Felicity called for John-Bull. "Come, dear," she said, taking him by the hand. She looked over her shoulder at McQuaid. "I shall pray you find an ounce of courage, Captain."

McQuaid touched his cap, then watched Felicity Markham and her son walk back up the path toward the American camp. He had to hand it to the woman. She was no quitter like most of the plantation owners in the Solomons. At the first whiff of Japanese gunpowder, nearly all of them had absconded. Only the men who had turned coast-watcher remained, them and a few missionaries and this one lone, persistent woman. McQuaid leaned his chin on his hand and remembered how it had been when he'd first come out to the Solomons. It was good, then. The booze flowed across the islands like an endless river. And all those Maries—just for the asking of this chief or that for a small favor, or a twist of tobacco to their husbands, and those sleek black beauties had been his. Of course, he'd barely escaped with his head more than once, but it had all been a wonderful adventure.

With the coming of the damned Americans, things would never be the same. The locals were already infected by the black Americans who were actually whites in chocolate skins who drove the trucks and operated the bulldozers and generators and such on Melagi. Because of the example of these GI coloreds, the bushmen and saltwater boys were beginning to think they might be as good as any man.

McQuaid chuckled to himself. Of course, they were as good as any man and always had been. The trick for the European mastahs and missuses was to keep them ignorant of that fact. "Bloody Americans," he muttered, then subsided on his stump, careless of life. Before him, his schooner and his future seemed to sag under their own weight.

"What's up, Mac?"

Captain McQuaid looked up into the friendly face of an American sailor wearing a tub hat on the back of his head and a great blue tattoo of a dragon on his shirtless chest. McQuaid nodded toward his sad little boat. "There you see my situation," he said.

"Yeah, me and the boys"—the sailor raised his chin toward where two similarly shirtless young and tattooed American sailors stood huddled beneath a leaning palm tree—"have been thinking about your old *Minerva* here. You see, we hear there are girls on some of those islands out there . . ."

"Girls?" McQuaid eyed the young man. "You mean black Maries?"

"Black or green, man in these parts can't be too picky," the sailor answered with a shy smile.

"That is so true," Captain McQuaid replied. "A woman's a woman," he allowed, and rolled his eyes generally seaward.

"Captain, I can see you are a man of some experience," the sailor said, and removed his hat to display his respect. "Let us now get down to cases. See, we'd like to rent your boat . . ."

3

After the battle for Melagi was fought and the last Japanese soldier hunted down and killed (a necessity since none of them would surrender), the Seabees, which was the nickname for the navy construction battalions (CBs), moved onto the island to build a base for the Raiders. The first thing they did was cut down the rows of tall, ruler-straight coconut palms on the old copra plantation. On the resulting grassy prairie, which quickly turned into mud, they erected two rows of gray Quonset huts. Then, after improving the harbor facilities (the Japanese had used it to support seaplanes), they left for the next island. When the Raiders transported their headquarters and logistics units from Guadalcanal, they packed the Quonsets full of supplies they had mostly stolen from the army, then erected hundreds of two-man tents with some larger tents for the officers. Air raid dugouts were added here and there, covered with palm logs, and their camp was complete.

Josh came down from his cave and saw the Raiders slogging along on their various missions, or resting in their tents, or cleaning their weapons, or reading and writing their letters in the shade of the few straggly palms that hadn't been chopped down, or simply biding their time. Some were huddled together, singing their bitter song:

> *We sent for the army to come to Me-soggy,*
> *But General McArthur said no,*
> *I'll tell you the reason, it isn't the season,*
> *Besides you've got no USO.*
>
> *Bless 'em all, bless 'em all . . .*

Everything seemed normal, at least as normal as was possible for men who killed other men for a living and were also afflicted with malaria or dysentery or yaws or general jungle rot, inevitable in these parts. Josh's nose detected the faint odor of something sweetly sour and he deduced that there was an applejack still nearby, probably just within that copse of bushes on the other side of the camp. When he saw with his keen eyes a wisp of wood smoke from the copse, his supposition was confirmed.

The path he was following led past the little swamp on the edge of the camp. Josh was a big man, broad-shouldered, with muscled arms and stout legs supporting a heavy chest, yet he was surprisingly light on his feet and so avoided a six-foot-long crocodile that suddenly pushed out of the water and snapped its jaws at him. "You got to be faster than that, Eleanor," Josh said, recognizing the croc, which was something of a Raider pet and was guarding her eggs. Disappointed she hadn't drawn blood, Eleanor slunk back into the muddy water, with just her pouty eyes showing.

Josh walked on, executing the Solomon Islands salute against a sudden swarm of the tiny, nearly invisible bloodsucking insects everybody called no-see-ums. They were vicious little creatures that especially liked to crawl into a man's eyes to drink his tears before biting his eyelids. Josh had seen a Raider who, drunk from applejack, had fallen asleep on the beach one night. In the morning his face, ravaged by mosquitoes and no-see-ums, was so swollen, it was scarcely recognizable as a human face at all. Although the Raider was rushed off to the clinic on nearby Tulagi, Josh heard later that the man had died. It was a cautionary tale. The Solomons had lots of ways to kill you. The Jap was just one of them.

Josh came to a company command post, a large tent, its sides rolled up to let in the air. Inside the tent were two rows of field tables, with clerks sitting at them doing whatever clerks in the field had to do, collating orders, typing reports, keeping track of who was dead or alive, filling in supply forms, and such. Outside the tent, a dozen men lounged on the grass doing nothing. Their utilities were sweat-stained, and empty ammo pouches were strewn about, but their rifles were close at hand. Most likely, they were just in from some action, probably up in New Georgia, where the Munda airfield, the purpose for the battle there, had recently been captured. Soon, Josh thought, these men would be sneaking into the copse with their canteen cups so as to dull themselves with drink.

Josh recognized one of the resting Raiders, a hatchet-faced gunnery sergeant named Frank Billocks. Josh had fought alongside Billocks in the battle for Wilton's Ridge on Guadalcanal. "How's it going, Gunny?" Josh greeted him. When Billocks didn't reply, Josh thought he hadn't heard him, so he persisted. "You been out contending with the Jap?"

Billocks spat forth a long stream of tobacco juice into the grass. "It ain't my place to tell you where we been, Commander, but I reckon you'll hear it soon enough." Billocks spat again and stared at Josh, a cold dead fish of a stare.

Josh walked on. Anytime a man didn't want to talk, it was best to leave him alone. God only knew what horrible thing Billocks and his men had seen, or done. Josh hoped it wouldn't be too long before the gunny found that copse with the wood smoke. Applejack tasted awful, but it could make you unconscious in short order, and that, Josh perceived, was what Billocks and his boys needed right now.

The old plantation house where Colonel Burr held forth sat back of the beach within a small stand of chinaberry trees. The house was nothing special, a weather-beaten wood frame structure with a rusty tin roof, typical of the plantation houses in the Solomons. Josh climbed the steps to the veranda and went inside, nodding to the colonel's clerk, a gray-haired sergeant, always in need of a shave, who was typing with two fingers on a battered black typewriter. Josh checked the sergeant's sleeve and was pleased to notice the man had regained his stripes. It was a camp joke that Burr periodically had the clerk's stripes removed for this minor offense or that one, only to restore them when his petty anger was exhausted. "Hidy, Captain," the clerk said, using Josh's complimentary rank. "Colonel's got somebody in there right now but shouldn't be long."

"The word I got was to get down here *toot sweet,*" Josh said, implying that he didn't care to wait.

The clerk eyed Josh for a long second. "Well, hell, sir, then why don't you just barge in on the colonel and shake up his day?"

Josh knew poor advice when he heard it, but didn't care. He knocked once on the frame of the office door and let himself in, finding Colonel Burr seated at his big steel desk. The colonel's left hand rested on a mildewed ink blotter, and his right held a flyswatter at full alert. Sitting in a folding chair alongside, balancing a teacup on a bare knob of a knee, was a man Josh recognized as Elrod Vickers, the commander of the British-led coast-watchers in the Solomons.

The colonel eyed Josh and said, "Well, Thurlow, I don't see a hole in you, so I guess Captain Clooney found another way to persuade you to come down from your mountain resort."

"Colonel Burr," Josh said by way of a greeting, then reached across the colonel's desk to shake hands with the thin coast-watcher. "Hello, Elrod. How are things in the bush?"

Vickers responded with a grin revealing his big false teeth. Quinine, the malarial antidote of choice of most of the old Solomon hands, had taken its toll. "Oh, I'm quite out of the bush now, Josh, with the Jap chased north. I am back on Tulagi in my office, only slightly ventilated by shell holes, and attempting to make some sense of what's left of our colonial administration."

"I'm sure you'll have everything wrapped up in triplicate in a shake or two," Josh said, in honest admiration of British bureaucracy.

"One can only hope," Vickers replied in good cheer. "Although I doubt that many of the planters will come back. I suspect this part of the old empire is quite finished. What will come of it I have no idea."

"Maybe the natives will run things," Josh suggested.

Vickers shrugged. "After we're gone, a lot of them will be back to head-hunting and eating the blokes in the next village in a fortnight. But there are some good people here, too. If they can prevail over their more savage brethren, then the Solomons might have a chance."

Colonel Burr growled, "Josh, usually officers take their caps off in my office."

Josh removed his cover. "Didn't mean disrespect, Colonel."

"You are nonetheless an insolent man," Burr replied, then wearily waved Josh to a chair. "But that's neither here nor there considering what's up."

Josh adjusted his big frame on the indicated rusty folding chair. It creaked beneath his bulk as he settled in. He didn't say anything, knowing full well the colonel would get to the subject at hand when he was ready. It didn't take long. Burr put down the flyswatter and leaned forward. "You see, Josh," he said, "there's been a bit of trouble." He chewed over his next words as if they were difficult to get out of his mouth. "I need your help," he said at last, and then took on the gravest expression Josh had yet seen on the colonel's typically grave puss.

Josh nearly laughed. "Colonel, the one thing in this old world I know is you don't need my help. I'm but a Coast Guard doofus on an inspection trip for Secretary Knox that's taken a little longer than expected."

"You're quick to mention Knox," Burr said in an accusing tone.

"He's the only reason I'm out here."

Burr could not argue the point. He knew very well that Josh had been sent to the Solomon Islands by none other than Frank Knox, the secretary of the navy himself, who was, before President Franklin Delano Roosevelt had appointed him to the job, a wealthy industrialist and a Republican to boot. The story Burr had heard was that Josh had saved Knox off a shipwreck in Alaska many years before, and Knox had not forgotten. The secretary had sent Josh to the Pacific with orders to report directly back to him on the situation. Josh and his Killakeet boys had been around ever since, sticking their noses mostly where, as far as Burr was concerned, they had no business.

But now things had changed. Burr clasped his big hands on his desk and said, "Lieutenant David Armistead."

Josh waited for more, but when it didn't come, he said, "I just saw David's gunny outside."

"Doubtlessly, you did not see Lieutenant Armistead with him," Burr replied in a sardonic tone.

"Where is he?"

Vickers leaned forward. "We believe he has gone north."

"On a raid?"

"I'm afraid not. You see—" Vickers stopped speaking, mainly because Burr had raised his hand to stop him.

"You were with Armistead on Wilton's Ridge," Burr said, his cold eyes burrowing into Josh. "What did you think of him?"

"He was steady enough," Josh replied.

"Steady? Is that all you can say about him?"

"He did his duty on the ridge. Some said more than his duty."

"How about you? What do you say?"

"I say every man on the ridge that night did more than his duty. What's this all about, Colonel?"

After an uncomfortable silence, Colonel Burr said, "Let me bring you up to speed on New Georgia, Josh. We've taken the airfield at Munda, so we've declared victory, but nobody's doing cartwheels over this campaign. It was a FUBAR* screw-up from the get-go. Taking the island was supposed to be the army's show. We marines were supposed to use the time to refit after Guadalcanal, but the doggies got themselves bogged down as soon as they hit the beach. A lot of those boys were brave, I'm not saying they weren't, but they were poorly trained and badly led. Jap came close to kicking their tails. A couple of months ago, Regiment asked me to send somebody up there, give the army some advice, and see what otherwise might be done. When

---

*FUBAR, an acronym much beloved by American troops during World War II, meant "f——d up beyond all repair."

Armistead got wind of it, he volunteered. I let him take twelve handpicked men, and they did one helluva job. The army commander Armistead was attached to said if it hadn't been for that boy, he'd still be on the beach."

"David's a good marine," Josh replied. "His men like him because he trains them hard and fights them that way, too. I'll ask you again. What's this about?"

"Plainly put," Burr replied, "it appears Lieutenant Armistead has deserted."

Josh took a moment to absorb Burr's words. "How is that possible?" he finally managed.

Vickers spoke up. "We think he's run off with Todd Whitman's wife."

Josh needed no explanation as to who Todd Whitman was. He was a legend in the South Seas, having organized a remarkable band of warriors on New Georgia. He and his men had been brilliant, both as coastwatchers, spotting the destroyers and cruisers of the Tokyo Express, and also as guerrillas, killing the Jap in flash raids. Admiral Halsey himself had said that the battle for Guadalcanal could not have been won without Whitman's alerts on the activities of the Japanese ships coming down through the Slot. "I didn't know Whitman was married," Josh said, the only thing he could think to say. It was as lame as he felt.

"Oh, he's married, old man," Vickers said. "And to a Marie. Dark as toast but pretty as a peach. A toasted peach, you might say."

Burr tracked a fly that had landed on his desk. He slapped at it with the swatter but missed. The fly flew off, merrily buzzing, only to return for another run past Burr's face. He waved at it with the swatter, then came back to the conversation. "About three weeks ago, Mister Vickers came to me with intelligence that Whitman and his men were trapped by the Japanese on an abandoned plantation."

"The Truax plantation," Vickers supplemented. "Until I received a radio transmission from Whitman, I assumed he was dead. It had been over a month since I'd heard from him."

Burr shot Vickers a look, then continued. "Apparently, the local Japanese commander decided to even the score with Whitman before pulling out of New Georgia. Admiral Halsey thinks the world of Whitman, you know, so I decided to help. I radioed Lieutenant Armistead, told him I was sending up an LCI for transport. He was to send two machine-gun teams to support Whitman. I told him to put his gunny in charge. I also told him to stay with the army and keep the doggies moving. He came back with a request that he lead the gun teams, that the army was moving, and that he'd feel better about it if he went into harm's way, rather than his gunny. How could I turn him down? Any officer of mine who volunteers to fight is going to get my permission. So Sergeant Billocks stayed behind, and Armistead and his teams shipped out. The LCI skipper said he couldn't get too close to the Truax plantation because of Japanese destroyers in the area, so he delivered Armistead a few miles south. Other than the reports from Whitman, that's the last I heard."

"David didn't call in?"

"He didn't take a radio. He left his with Billocks, saying he'd depend on Whitman's gear."

Vickers put in. "That was a mistake. Radio communication with Whitman has been damnably spotty for some time. I heard nothing until three days after Lieutenant Armistead had been landed, although it was still mostly static. Whitman told me Armistead and his weapons teams had arrived after slipping through the Japanese lines. Two days later, I heard from him again, complaining most bitterly. He said Armistead had taken his wife in a canoe and headed north. Then his radio went completely on the fritz. Not a word since."

Josh was incredulous. "A tall white man paddling around in those waters? Why, Jap would have him in ten minutes! Whitman's story is nuts, Colonel. When the Raiders who were with David get back, they'll tell you."

Vickers cleared his throat. "I fear that won't be possible, Commander. Whitman said they were all killed."

Josh took on an expression of complete disbelief. "Colonel, Whitman's reports should be dismissed out of hand."

"I can't dismiss desertion in the face of the enemy, Josh," Burr answered in a surprisingly quiet voice. He pointed skyward. "And there's no way I can sweep this under the rug. This is more than Raider business. There's a great deal of interest on high. Armistead, you see, comes from a very important family."

"David *Roosevelt* Armistead," Josh said, recalling that the lieutenant had once told him his full name. That was on a night both of them had expected to die as Jap had lined up for a final rush on the nasty earthen mound called Wilton's Ridge on Guadalcanal. Just before the charge, Armistead had suddenly waxed nostalgic and started to talk about his family. It had been a curious mix of bitter and joyful recollections of a family that was distant from one another but joined by a common ambition, that he, David Armistead, the only son, would enter politics and rise perhaps even to become president of the United States, just like his cousins Theodore and Franklin.

"His mother's a first cousin of the president," Burr continued, interrupting Josh's recollection. "And on top of that, his father is Howard Armistead, the ambassador to France before the war and now a top adviser in the Roosevelt administration. He's also one of the richest men in the country. Coal mines, natural gas, that kind of thing. One might say he's one of the most powerful—"

The sudden windup of a siren stopped Burr from continuing to list the attributes of the father. He immediately rose from his desk and waved Josh and Vickers along. They followed him outside to a dugout of palm logs and sandbags. After the men climbed inside, the sirens quieted, and an odd muttering could be heard over the Raider camp. "Washing-Machine Charlie," Vickers said. "Brave chaps, those Japanese bomber pilots, coming down here night and day. I'll give them that."

Josh cocked his ear to the stutter of the Japanese bomber, determined it was flying off toward Guadalcanal, and got back to the matter in question. "So why am I here?" Josh asked.

"You are here," Burr replied, "because the only way to find out what really happened to Armistead is for someone to go up to New Georgia, talk to Whitman, then go find the boy, wherever he is. The powers that be think that person ought to be you."

Startled, Josh asked, "Why me? I'm in the Coast Guard. This sounds like Marine Corps business."

Burr either didn't hear Josh's question or preferred not to answer. In any case, he remained silent until Washing-Machine Charlie had wandered off and the siren howled all clear. "Give us a moment, won't you, Elrod?" he asked the coast-watcher.

"Of course, Montague."

Vickers crawled out of the bunker, and Josh and Burr eyed one another for a long second. Then Burr said, "Now, Josh, we all know you're more than a simple Coast Guard officer on an extended inspection trip."

Josh replied, "Then you know more than I do."

Burr smirked, then continued. "After the battle on Wilton's Ridge, Major Wilton did all the paperwork needed to get Armistead the Medal of Honor. But when he asked you to cosign his recommendation, you refused. Why?"

Josh didn't answer. He just looked at Burr and waited him out.

"You're not going to tell me why you think he didn't deserve it?"

"I never said he didn't deserve it."

"By God, Thurlow, you *are* insolent," Burr muttered, then dug into his shirt pocket and brought out an envelope. "This is for you."

Josh took the envelope and opened it, not difficult since it had already been slit open, even though it was addressed to him and was stamped EYES ONLY on the front and back. Josh raised his eyebrows and Burr shrugged. "Admiral Halsey got wind of it," Burr said. "Even diplomatic pouches can be opened by mistake."

Josh was not the least bit surprised that his mail might be read by Bull Halsey, who made it his business to know everything that happened in the South Pacific. The letter was simple and to the point, characteristic of Frank Knox. It asked Josh to find out what had happened to David Armistead and to please bring him home to his parents. That was all there was to it, signed in a flourish by Knox's distinctive hand.

"Now, here's the thing," Burr said, after Josh finished reading and looked up. "Admiral Halsey ordered me to pass along a suggestion to you." Burr took a breath, then said out loud the suggestion of the great admiral.

Josh's reaction was instantaneous. "Colonel, you know I can't do that!"

Burr nodded. "He said you'd say that very thing. He also asked me to say one word to you. I don't know what it means, but here it is. Hypo." Burr watched while Josh's expression turned neutral. "Is that your poker face?" he asked slyly.

"Don't ask me anything, Colonel," Josh replied, and his voice had steel in it. "And never mention that word to anyone else again."

Burr's smile was grim. "Look, Thurlow, you and I disagree about a lot of things, but one thing we both know is that this war is far from won. We've got a lot of battles yet to fight. If the men think their officers are going to desert them . . ." Burr left the thought dangling.

"Tell you what, Colonel," Josh said, after a moment more of contemplation. "I'll go after David, and if he's alive, which I sincerely doubt, I'll bring him back trussed up on a stick if you like. But this suggestion, you can tell Admiral Halsey I won't do it."

"Well, let's leave it as a suggestion," Burr said, "and you can think about it."

Josh had already thought about it. He knew that Bull Halsey and Admiral Nimitz, Halsey's boss, and Secretary Knox and no doubt even President Roosevelt himself had thought about it, too, or the word "Hypo" would have never been allowed to be on the lips of a lowly Raider battalion commander like Burr. Lieutenant David Roosevelt Armistead was an ambassador's son and a close relative of the president of the United States himself. If he had deserted, it wouldn't take long before troops all over the Pacific heard about it, with the newspapers not far behind. The best thing for all in this case would be a dead hero, with a good story, if necessary, as to why he'd left the battlefield. As Burr had quoted Halsey: *In my opinion, any American officer who deserts his men in combat is already dead. Some bastard should find Armistead and make it official.*

Josh now understood very well who the bastard was supposed to be.

4

Deep in thought, the bastard in question walked past the Raider softball field, which consisted of a large rectangle of mud scraped clean by a Seabee bulldozer. The Raiders were having themselves one hell of a game. The ball had been knocked into the bush, requiring the outfield to arm themselves to go hunt for it, lest a Japanese soldier might still be on the loose. While waiting for the patrol to return, the catcher had gotten angry at the batter for hitting the long foul and slapped him up alongside the head with his glove, foolishly neglecting the fact that the batter still held a bat. Typical Marine Corps mayhem had ensued; the catcher's skull was whacked a good one, and every man left on the field engaged in wrestling or fisticuffs until the ball was restored. Near first base, John-Bull Markham was being taught by example the official Marine Corps method of strangling a man. The instructor was the baseman, and he was demonstrating the method on a runner who happened to be caught on base. John-Bull was clearly enjoying the lesson, as he was clapping his hands and jumping up and down with excitement. He'd never seen a man's face quite so blue.

Among the fans lining the field were three natives, wearing only lap-laps and tattoos and sitting on a Seabee bulldozer. One of the men, a huge, muscled ebony giant, was getting lessons on how to run the bulldozer from its operator, an American of African descent. The giant jerked the levers and the bulldozer's blade abruptly lifted, knocking off one of his fellows, a cherubic little man who happened to be sitting on it. This made the giant laugh while the little man crawled away in the mud.

Josh stopped for a moment to observe the fun, and it was then that Felicity Markham caught up with him in long, bold strides. "Wait up, Commander," she said, in a somewhat insistent tone of voice, before softening it to say, "Good day to you." She nodded toward the ball field. "Quite the contest, is it not?"

Josh tipped his cap. "Ma'am. I guess it's typical. At least it allows the Raiders to blow off some steam."

"Those three boys playing with the bulldozer are my Malaitans," she said. "I've hired them to work on my plantation."

"Well, they appear to be blowing off steam, too."

She stuck out her hand. "I don't believe we've ever been formally introduced. I'm Missus Felicity Markham of the Markham plantation on Noa-Noa."

"Josh Thurlow of Killakeet Island, Outer Banks of North Carolina," he said, briefly taking her hand. It felt, even in the rising heat of the day, cool and dry.

Felicity observed the giant at the levers of the bulldozer. "They're getting above themselves," she said in a worried tone. "Especially that one. Arenga's his name. He's what we call out here a pier-head jumper. That means he was hiding in the bush, having committed some foul crime in his village, most likely murder. Captain McQuaid, my recruiter, lay by his village and waited until Arenga came running up the village pier, jumped into the water, and swam out to us. The other two are pier-head jumpers as well. I'm going to have trouble with them, especially now that your Negro Yanks have put foolish ideas into their heads."

"Foolish ideas, ma'am?"

Felicity ignored Josh's disapproving expression. "It is my understanding that you may be going north, Commander, perhaps in the vicinity of Noa-Noa. I wonder if my son and I plus my Malaitans might go along with you."

Astonished, Josh asked, "How did you hear I was going north?"

"Mister Vickers told me."

"I see. I'm sorry, but where I'm headed, you and your boy would be in danger."

Felicity gave Josh a knowing look. "Come now, sir. I've lived in the Solomon Islands for nearly a decade. John and I can take care of ourselves. Mister Vickers tells me that you have an assignment that will—"

Josh interrupted. "Excuse me, ma'am. Vickers shouldn't be telling you about secret military operations."

"Oh, *pshaw*. Secret military operations, indeed. Do I look like a Japanese spy? And even if I were, how would I tell your awful secret? Yell it up to Washing-Machine Charlie? John and I need to go home. Surely, Josh, you know something of why going home is so important."

The Englishwoman's question, philosophical in nature, gave Josh the opportunity to appear to be pondering it while, in fact, he was simply enjoying the close proximity to a real honest-to-God female. It had been a good long while since he'd been within an arm's reach of a woman, and Felicity Markham was a fine-looking female, make no mistake. She had curves, evident even beneath her baggy clothing, that Josh had nearly forgotten existed. He supposed Felicity had more than a little steel in her personality, and God knew she was a plantation bigot, but she surely smelled good, sort of like fresh cream.

For her part, Felicity was not deceived by Josh's apparent pondering. She knew she was being appraised just as she was appraising him. Josh Thurlow, she had absorbed in a moment, was big and rough, and perhaps not so very intelligent, and his nose was a bit crooked, and a ragged scar on his chin was unpleasant to perceive. He also had that square-jawed, conscientious look about him that made some men in bars want to take a swipe at him and others buy him a drink. She wondered what it would feel like to have his strong arms wrapped around her and to snuggle her face into his shoulder and to run her hands through his sandy hair. "Please take me and John home," she said, to break the spell between them. "You'd go home if you could, wouldn't you?"

Josh finally replied in the only way he knew how, with the truth. "There's not a man on this island who wouldn't give his eyeteeth to go home."

"Then please help me."

"I just can't oblige."

"You are on your way to interview Todd Whitman," she said. "Maybe I can give you some background. After all, he was an overseer on our plantation for a while."

"Well, I would be interested in hearing what you know about Whitman," Josh agreed.

Felicity smiled. "I should hope so. It might make all the difference as to whether you find your lieutenant or not. Oh, stop looking at me as if I've stolen the crown jewels. Everybody on Melagi knows about Lieutenant Armistead. I even met the lad once. Though we only shared a greeting, he struck me as a very thoughtful young man. So we have a deal. I will tell you everything I know about Whitman, and you will take me to Noa-Noa."

Now it was Josh's turn to smile, amused by her single-mindedness. "I will not take you to Noa-Noa, but I would appreciate your information anyway."

"Will you at least take my side of it with Colonel Burr?" she asked. "I might be able to arrange other transportation. All you'd have to do is tell him he should let me go."

"What makes you think he would listen to me?"

"Every man has to listen to someone. I think you're the only man on Melagi that makes the slightest impression on Colonel Burr. He has spoken often of you to me."

"Really? What did he say?"

"That you were insolent, but the way he said it, I knew he respected you. Will you take up for me and John?"

Josh gave it some thought and couldn't see why not. "I will tell Colonel Burr today that he should let you go home, Missus Markham, and that's a promise."

"Very well," she said. "I will tell you what I know of Whitman. But I'd prefer to do it out of the hot sun."

Felicity took Josh's arm and led him to the wispy shade of a frangipani tree where there were two crude chairs built from ammunition crates. High in the branches of the tree, a very bright yellow and green bird sang its little song, scarcely noticing a sleeping snake that wasn't sleeping any longer.

Felicity and Josh sat down in the chairs. Felicity said, "Well, here we are. All we need are drinks and we could be at the club."

Josh glanced up into the tree to where the bird was singing, actually more of a cooing. "That's a pretty sound. A pigeon of some sort, I suppose."

"It's a fruit dove," Felicity said without interest. She gazed into Josh's crisp blue eyes and wished she could look into them a little closer. *You are sex-crazed,* she told herself.

Josh looked up again when the fruit dove, which he still couldn't see, stopped cooing in midcoo. A bright yellow feather drifted down. "The first thing you must understand about Todd Whitman," Felicity said, ignoring the feather, "is he's Australian, not English. He arrived here penniless and probably just one step ahead of the law. He was never able to purchase land. No bank would trust him. So he became an overseer for several hardcase plantation owners who couldn't control their workers. He was quick with his fists and knew how to cow any black after mischief. Once, several years back, we were unlucky enough to get a poor lot of boys and had to hire him on ourselves. But he was just too brutal in his methods, so we cashiered him. I suppose you've heard about the great Malaitan insurrection of '34? Whitman was a star player in that one."

There was a rustle in the limbs above, and more yellow and green feathers drifted down. Josh brushed one off his nose. "There's something up there that's killed that bird."

"Probably a sleeping snake, as it is known locally. Frightfully big, but harmless as long as you're not a bird."

"How long do they get?"

"I really have no idea. Now, about the insurrection. It was '34, as I think I mentioned, and the coconut telegraph brought news that the Malaitans in the village of Kopapu had chopped off a white man's head. You can imagine how upset it made all of us. Before long, we were all looking over our shoulders at our houseboys and nut pickers, wondering if some kind of revolt was brewing. Before the officials on Tulagi could look into the matter, several planters organized an expedition, put Whitman in charge, and off they sailed to storm Kopapu. Quite the bloody battle, so the story goes, with the chief killed and about half his men. Some Maries as well, and a few children, too. Whitman and his cronies came into Tulagi with all flags flying as proud as they could be, bringing with them every man in the village left alive. But after the colonial officials investigated, it turned out the story that started the whole thing was utterly wrong. It wasn't a white man who'd gotten his head cut off but an expat villager who'd been living in New Zealand. He'd sneaked in off a trader boat and murdered a Marie he'd thought to marry. Jealousy, no doubt, since she'd married someone else. The old chief had acted according to the law of his village and put the miscreant to death and took his head as an example to others. Whitman and the other men acted according to no one's law, except their own. It was all quietly covered up, of course."

Silence reigned in the frangipani branches although feathers still floated down, like bright yellow and green snowflakes. "Tell me about his wife," Josh suggested while picking a feather off his nose.

Felicity shrugged. "Whitman was seldom invited to any gatherings of the planters. He was too much a rough old cob, and he wasn't a landowner, either. He only married her a few months before the Japanese came. I saw her at a party. I think it was in November 1941. Whitman was invited because we knew war clouds were gathering and everyone knew he could fight. Of course, his wife, being a Marie, was not allowed to come into the house."

"She's the key to this, I suspect," Josh mused. "Is there nothing else you can tell me about her?"

"All I know are rumors."

"I'd be willing to hear them."

"They say she can fight as well as any man. This is unusual, Commander. The Maries of the Solomons are traditionally kept down by their men. They are the homemakers, childbearers, farmers, food gatherers, and providers of sex, but that is the extent of it. For instance, they are never allowed to touch weapons. It is *tabu*. If she's become a warrior, she is a very special woman indeed."

Josh pondered the information. "She doesn't sound like a woman who'd fall for a young marine like David Armistead. And it's hard to imagine that David would fall so hard for her that he would desert his men."

"Love is a very strong emotion, Josh. Especially in emotional times such as war. I wouldn't dismiss it out of hand."

"I suppose I can't dismiss anything at this point," Josh said, then stood and put out his hand. "You've been very helpful. I appreciate it, but I really must be going."

She stood with him, took his hand, then released it. "Will you speak with Colonel Burr concerning my situation?"

"I said I would."

"Why don't you just take John and me along with you?"

"I've already explained why I can't."

"But I would do anything," she said, and her eyes bored into his. "Anything." She felt a bit disgusted with herself as she made her offer, with all its sexual overtones, but a little excited, too.

Josh glanced away, embarrassed for them both. "I guess you English had a good life here," he said. "Before the war, I mean."

Felicity smiled. "I once heard a planter comfort a newcomer after he passed out drunk and a giant cockroach had nearly eaten one of his toes. 'Take it easy, old man,' he said. 'It's only the first ten years out here that's hell.' Well, Josh, I've been in the Solomon Islands for nine years. During that time, I've worked myself quite near to death, been through a typhoon, caught malaria, buried a husband, and now my coconuts are rotting while John and I are caught up in your bloody war. Another year and surely it will all turn into paradise."

Josh never knew what to do with a facetious woman. He tipped his cap to her and said, "I wish you well, ma'am."

"And the same to you, Commander. By the way, when you see Todd Whitman, you might want to ask him about Joe Gimmee."

"And who would that be, ma'am?"

"Just ask him," Felicity answered, then walked away, leaving Josh standing amidst a pile of beautiful yellow and green feathers beneath the frangipani tree. Overhead, still unseen, the sleeping snake, contentedly full, went back to sleep.

5

All was quiet in the Melagi harbor and, for the moment, there was no war but instead a peaceful tropical splendor, a doldrums, a lazy, languid, indolent passivity. Tiny sunbursts glittered on the placid water near the white sandy beach. The fronds of crossed palm trees hung limply. Frigate birds made long, slow circles in a crystal blue sky. Three idle freighters lolled, their reflections so perfect it was as if they were sitting on mirrors. Above it all, Melagi's great misty-green volcano continued its centuries-old slumber.

The peace was shattered when a PBY Catalina amphibian aircraft stuttered to life, its twin engines spouting blue smoke, its propellers spinning into gleaming circles. The Catalina was not a handsome machine. It had a nose that looked like it belonged on a hound dog and a curved tail that had the grace of a ham bone. Its observation windows looked for all the world like fat transparent leeches hitching a ride, and its ungainly wing was nothing but a long metal slab. But plug ugly as they were, pilots and crews loved their Catalinas for perhaps the same reason men love some unattractive women; they are tough old crates that can take a lot of punishment and still go the distance.

The Catalina preparing for takeoff in the Melagi harbor was named the *Darlin' Dosie,* and it belonged to Josh Thurlow and his boys by way of the scrap heap. In the left seat of the *Dosie*'s cockpit, Ensign Eureka Phimble finished his initial checkout, then said, "I didn't have time to gas her up."

Josh tapped on the fuel gauges and squinted at the result. "We've got enough to get to Lumbari."

"We need to make it back, too."

"We'll manage. Fly the plane."

Phimble scrutinized the wind sock on the beach and turned the Catalina to face the wind, what little there was of it. The lolling freighters were dead ahead. Beyond, the island of Guadalcanal was a gray, jagged shadow. "Wish I had more wind," he grumbled. "*Dosie* don't like to fly when there ain't no wind."

"For God's sake, Eureka," Josh replied. "Will you just get on with it?"

"I don't want to have no part of chasing down Lieutenant Armistead. He found himself a woman, leave him alone, I say."

"We've been over this. If he's deserted, somebody has to go after him."

"Why us?"

"Fly the plane, Eureka."

Petulantly, Phimble fire-walled the throttles, but Catalinas never did anything fast, and that especially included taking off. She mushed forward, as if idling across a sea of molasses, while Josh anxiously peered through the cockpit windshield. "Eureka, you do see those freighters in front of us, don't you?"

"Freighters?"

"You're the worst pilot I ever saw," Josh accused.

"You still breathing?"

"Barely."

"Then I ain't yet the worst pilot you ever saw."

Phimble kept his eye on the needle of the airspeed indicator, waiting until it reached the proper tick on the dial. Dosie shook and roared and rattled, but she was picking up some speed. Finally Phimble pulled her wheel back to put her on the step, as Catalina pilots called the last moment before liftoff. *Dosie* obligingly lifted her nose but then settled back down in a mush. The freighters loomed ever larger. In fact, the features of the men on the freighter directly ahead could be discerned quite clearly. Josh noticed that they all had their mouths open, probably using them to scream. And now some of the freighter men were running across her decks.

"You really might want to get us in the air," Josh suggested in a tight voice as sailors began to abandon the freighter from bow to stern, taking their chances with the sharks.

Phimble kept hanging on to the shaking wheel, his face a grim but determined mask. Finally, *Dosie* seemed to pull it all together. She grunted, licked clean of the ocean, and slowly and oh so ponderously rose into the air, a rainbow of water droplets flung off her tail. The bridge of the freighter swept past, so close Josh could have counted the rivets. Ahead was nothing but the air and the ocean and Guadalcanal, which, Josh noted sourly, was still higher than they were. "Eureka, you really *are* the worst pilot I ever saw!"

Phimble grinned a relieved grin, his teeth flashing in the hot white sunlight streaming through the canopy. "You still breathing?"

"Shut up," Josh said, and turned his attention to the turquoise sea ahead, filled with landing craft, barges, and assorted small gray-painted naval vessels churning and chugging back and forth. The stretch of ocean between Melagi and Guadalcanal was called Iron Bottom Bay, its sad title reflecting the vast tonnage of American and Japanese warships resting now in broken death on its deep beige sand. Guadalcanal had been more than a land battle. The sea battle had been long and deadly for both sides.

Millie stuck his head through the hatch. "Was I seeing things or did we almost hit one of them freighters?"

"You're seeing things," Phimble answered.

"No, you weren't," Josh said, "but it don't matter. We're still alive, which Ensign Phimble here thinks is adequate praise for a pilot."

Millie, wise enough to stay out of an argument between two officers, scratched up under his tub cap. "If you say so, sir," he allowed with a bland expression on his thin face, made yellow by the atabrine all the boys took every day. It was supposed to keep them from getting malaria, or so the docs said. The rumor was it also made a man sterile, not that any of them had much opportunity to discover if it was true or not.

"Got any coffee back there?" Josh and Phimble both demanded at the same time.

Millie disappeared aft and quickly returned with two steaming mugs. Phimble took his with one hand and pulled back the wheel with the other so as to barely skim across a Guadalcanal ridgeline, just missing the tops of trees that were left shaking from the prop wash.

"Why didn't you just give them trees a good trim while you was at it?" Josh grumped as he used his hand to wipe away the coffee he'd just spilled down his shirt and on his pants. He considered them a fresh pair of utilities, too; they had been worn only two weeks since their last laundering, which Millie had accomplished in a brackish pond.

Phimble ignored Josh's complaint and turned northwest, putting *Dosie* on a course across the length of the long green island. The sight of it seemed to improve his mood. "There she is, Skipper," he said. "Guadalcanal. I still get goose bumps every time I fly over it. Lot of history down there."

"A lot of dead men, too," Josh said, just to be contrary, although he felt

the same as Phimble. The island had been the location of an incredible series of battles where a lot of brave men had died. Josh and Phimble had
been in the thick of most of it. It was miraculous they were still alive, and
both of them knew it. The toughest night they'd spent had been on the
nasty little hillside called Wilton's Ridge fighting alongside Lieutenant
David Roosevelt Armistead and his platoon of Raiders. Blood had flowed
like a river all night.

Carrying a mug of coffee, Once Jackson came forward and slid between
Josh and Phimble to pass through the hatch that led to the forward gun turret. His brother Again was already in there, manning the thirty-caliber machine gun. Once handed him the mug. "There you go, brother. Keep a
sharp eye."

Again gratefully took the coffee. "I'll stay awake, I reckon. But I could use
some company."

Once gave the request some thought. "How about Marvin?"

"Perfect. I was hoping for some smart conversation."

Aft, the boys were organizing a poker game. Megapode Dave, quite asleep,
was perched inside the port gun blister. Marvin, stationed at the starboard
blister, was looking at Guadalcanal passing below. Once, returning from his
visit with his brother, patted Marvin on his head and made a request. "Marvin, would you be ever so kind as to go forward and spend some time with
Again? He's powerfully lonely."

Marvin seemed to give the request some thought, then jumped down
and trotted forward. Josh and Phimble both patted his little black-and-
white bony head as he passed them to climb into the forward turret. There
were muffled but joyful greetings between the two crewmates.

With the boys settling down forward and aft, and Phimble climbing up
to a reasonable altitude where he wasn't likely to hit anything, Josh slid into
silence and drank his coffee. Gradually his thinking turned to David Armistead and what he'd learned from Gunny Billocks. After talking to Missus
Markham, Josh had sought out the sergeant to get the straight skinny on
what had happened on New Georgia. He'd found Billocks retired to his
tent with an empty canteen that had recently been full of illegal applejack.
That turned out to be a good thing. The alcohol had loosened him up. Billocks pitched his empty canteen into the mud, crossed his legs Indian style,
and told Josh the whole thing.

The battle for New Georgia had been hell, made worse by the inexperi-
ence of the army troops. Billocks told Josh of seeing evidence of panicky
American soldiers attacking each other in the night with knives and shov-

els. Jap had also captured some of the scared army boys and nailed their bodies to trees where the doggies could see them as they came up. A lot of soldiers had taken one look at the bloody remains and run back to the beach. When some of their officers joined them, it had turned into a mob.

"I couldn't blame them, seeing as how bad they was led," Billocks said as he pushed a chaw of Red Man into his cheek. "They were green, Cap'n, green as grass, and they just got pitched into that awful place. Most of that island's rougher than the Canal. You go ten feet back into the bush and you don't even know where you are. Before we saw what was what, some of our boys started catcalling at the soldiers, saying things like one marine's worth a hundred yellow doggies, but Lieutenant Armistead, he stopped all that, said we were veterans, that was the difference. Those boys, he said, they didn't know nothin' and it was up to us to show them how to fight. He found one of their officers who was buggin' out and stopped him, talked to him, you know, the way only Lieutenant Armistead can. He turned that officer around, got some other doggies with him, too. 'Come on, boys,' he said, 'let's all go up there together and see what we can do. You don't go up with us, you'll regret it for the rest of your lives. You won't be able to look your grandkids in the eye.' It worked, blamed if it didn't. Them doggies what came with us fought like marines with the lieutenant out in front of 'em." Billocks shrugged and eyed his now empty canteen. "A lot of them boys ain't never gonna have grandkids now."

Josh's recollection of Billocks's tale was interrupted by a call from Guadalcanal's Henderson Field. "Hey, Eureka, did you forget to file a flight plan again? Where y'all boys goin'?"

"Hey diddle diddle, right up the middle!" Phimble sang.

"Take care, y'all," came the reply. "Let us know if you see them sons of Nips coming our way, you hear?"

"You bet, buddy," Phimble answered. He turned to Josh. "Love them southern boys." Phimble had found his good mood again. Flying *Dosie* tended to do that. "So tell me again, why are we going up to Lumbari?"

"To get us a boat," Josh said.

"Why do we need a boat? We got *Dosie*. She can take us wherever we want to go."

"I suspect we'll need something a mite slower that can poke around."

"Oh yeah. Now I remember," Phimble said, in an ironic tone. "So we can track a man down who's headed somewhere we ain't got no idea."

"But Armistead will be slowed down," Josh replied.

"How so?"

"He's got a woman with him. He might as well have an anchor around his neck."

In the aft compartment, the boys felt the tilt of the Catalina as Phimble turned the battered old bird north. Through the gun blisters, they watched Guadalcanal slide by for a little while, and then they got out the cards for some poker. They'd tried chess to while away the hours when riding in *Dosie,* but she vibrated the board so hard that one time she put Ready O'Neal in check all by herself.

Fisheye, Ready, Once, and Pogo sat cross-legged on the deck and anted up the necessary matchsticks, each deemed worth a dollar. "Five card stud," Ready proposed.

"Why not?" Pogo said happily. It was his favorite game.

Fisheye borrowed ten matchsticks from Ready. "How much do I owe you?" he asked.

Ready, after consulting a notebook taken from his shirt pocket, said, "Eight hundred and twelve dollars."

Fisheye thought about the sum for a moment and said, "I guess I'd better start winning."

"It would help if you paid attention to your cards, "Ready answered. "For instance, you maybe shouldn't bet when your cards ain't worth nothing."

"But it's no fun to just sit here," Fisheye replied reasonably. "I get bored quick, you know that."

"Well, I'll just keep adding to my little book."

Pogo tapped his knuckles on the aluminum deck. "No worry-worry," he said. "You like for playum dis fella?"

"Yeah, we like, Pogo," Ready answered. "Somebody deal."

Once shuffled the cards. "We're missing the ace of spades and the eight of diamonds," he said. "Everybody remember that."

"Fisheye, that means if you need an ace or an eight when you draw to make a pair or something, you've got less of a chance," Ready said.

"Fisheye him one fella loser-man," Pogo laughed.

"Shut up, you damned headhunter," Fisheye swore. "I'll show you who's one fella loser-man. I'll snatch hair belong you, make hoodoo magic, fix you good."

Pogo touched the shark tooth on his necklace to ward off evil. "Fisheye him bastard fella."

"Both of you, shut up," Ready said. "Once, deal the cards."

Once dealt the cards and the hands were played. Before too long, Pogo had the largest pile of matchsticks, while Fisheye had none. "Sell me some more matches, Ready," Fisheye whined.

"Aren't you ever going to learn how to play this game?"

Fisheye shrugged. "I can't be good at everything." He turned and called over his shoulder to Stobs, who was sitting at his radio console. "Hey, Stobs, where are we going and how come?"

It was assumed that Stobs pretty much knew everything since he could listen in on the officers. "We're going up to the Lumbari navy base on Rendova," he said. "We're supposed to get a boat."

"A boat!" Fisheye exclaimed. "That's great! Be good to pull a wrench on a marine engine."

"I hope it's a big boat," Once said. "With a big stern where we could fish with some heavy tackle. I'd like to catch one of them great long sharks that's out here."

"Yeah, it would be good if it had some heavy guns on board, too," Ready said with an enthusiasm appropriate for a former gunner's mate.

"Me like too much big fella boat," Pogo agreed.

Stobs tamped down the excitement. "I don't think we're going to get a destroyer or anything. Maybe a PT boat."

"They got torpedoes!" Ready grinned. "Boy, I'd like to shoot off one of those!"

"What do you know about torpedoes?" Once demanded.

"I know everything I need to know," Ready answered, although he didn't know anything.

Josh picked past the boys, heading for the pee-tube in the aft compartment. "Gentlemen," he said. "Who's winning?"

"Stacka match belong Pogo," Pogo answered proudly.

"You good fella, Pogo," Josh said.

"Why not?" Pogo answered, with a shy smile.

"Sir, are we going to get us a PT boat?" Ready asked.

"That's the plan," Josh answered, not surprised the boys had already picked up on the skinny.

"How come?"

"We need it to find somebody. Do you remember Lieutenant Armistead?" When all the boys nodded affirmatively, even Pogo, Josh said, "He's disappeared up in New Georgia. Some people think he's run off. Looks like it's up to us to find him."

"Which direction did he go?" Fisheye asked.

"Maybe north."

"Toward Jap?"

"Could be."

"How come it's us what's looking for him?"

Josh thought about it for a second, then said, "I guess we volunteered."

After the skipper had moved aft to do his business, the boys sat quietly, their cards drooping in their hands. "I wonder why Lieutenant Armistead wanted to run off?" Ready asked, though he didn't expect an answer.

"And how come he had to run toward Jap?" Once added.

"Does this mean we're going to get killed?" Fisheye wondered.

Since Ready outranked the rest, they all turned toward him. "Some of us, probably," he said, after a moment of contemplation.

"Hey, you old megapode," Fisheye called. At the sound of the name of his species, Dave woke up, looked around, then raised his stubby wings. "You might want to join another outfit," Fisheye told him. "We're a bunch of volunteers. And you know what happens to volunteers!"

"Bless 'em all," Ready said, shaking his head.

Dave, apparently irritated at being startled out of his dreams, stuck out his neck when Josh came back through, nipping him hard on the arm with his strong beak. Josh jerked his arm away, rubbing the rising welt. "What the hell's got into you, Dave?"

Dave didn't answer except to turn his back.

"I guess even megapodes got opinions about some things," Once said, then clammed up lest he have to explain what he meant to the skipper, who didn't much care for opinions except his own.

6

The base for the PT boats was on a tiny key called Lumbari, just a few hundred yards off the main island of Rendova. It consisted of a sagging dock, a few Quonset huts set up on a muddy little hill, and a score or more of battered canvas tents. A rusty tender was tied up at the dock, and alongside it was a half-sunken Higgins PT boat, down by the stern. A rainbow stain of leaking petroleum surrounded the wreck. Other than the tender and the Higgins boat, no other boats were in evidence.

"What a dump," Again said to Marvin as they poked their heads out of the nose hatch to take a look around. The other boys, clustered around the blisters, made similar observations.

Josh climbed out of the side hatch onto the dock and noted a sign that announced:

WELCOME TO PATROL BOAT SQUADRON I
LT. CDR. T. G. WARFIELD, COMMANDING
BENEATH THIS SIGN WALK THE BRAVEST MEN IN THE SOUTH PACIFIC.

"Well, they ain't humble in these parts, that's for sartain," Josh observed.

"Maybe they're telling the truth," Phimble allowed as he tied *Dosie* to a post. "Takes guts to live in a mudhole like this."

"Stay here," Josh told him. "And try to keep the boys out of trouble."

"How could they get into trouble here?"

"You know our boys," Josh said, then walked beneath the sign and up a boardwalk to a Quonset that was, according to a sign tacked over the door, the headquarters of the PT-boat squadron.

Josh knew that Warfield, the commander, was off-island, but the executive officer, informed by Colonel Burr's clerk via radio, was expecting him. Inside the hut, he found a young sailor wearing khaki pants and a skivvy shirt marking on a big white board with a grease pencil. The youngster glanced at Josh, then went back to his marking. Josh perused the chart, then walked to the door designated LT. PERRY CARPENTER, USNR, XO, PATROL BOAT SQUADRON I.

Lieutenant Carpenter proved to be a handsome and trim young man with an Errol Flynn moustache, the very image of a brash and eager PT-boat commander. "Welcome to the forward edge of battle," he said, standing and offering his hand, then waving Josh to a chair. "The message I got said something about you wanting one of our boats. Too bad they've gone north on an operation." Before Josh could ask it, Carpenter provided the answer to his question. "Have no idea when they'll be back. Could be days."

"How long have they been gone?" Josh asked in a polite tone.

"Hasn't been long."

"Since you learned I was coming?"

Carpenter smiled. "More or less."

Josh did not return the smile. "Is it normal for you to send your boats out in daylight? I thought that was against PT-boat procedure."

"Our skippers are resourceful. They'll keep out of sight until they're ready to go to work. Our work is hot and deadly, Commander, and we use our wits to fight the Jap."

"Just for my education," Josh said after a moment of squint-eyed doubting, "how do you keep out of sight a boat with three high-speed props that send out a wake about a mile long?"

Carpenter made a little steeple with his fingers. "During the day, the boys go slow and stay close to shore, stay tucked under overhanging trees, then attack at night. The Tokyo Express operates only after dark, anyhoo. We're seriously disrupting the Jap's plans in these waters with our tactics."

Carpenter, of course, was spouting nonsense, and Josh knew it. For the most part, Japanese destroyers had simply brushed aside the PTs. It wasn't the fault of the PT crews, who were often brave to the point of foolhardiness. They simply had the wrong boats and armament for the job they'd been given. Josh said, "Let's cut the bull, Lieutenant. I know you've hidden your boats from me, and I can't say I blame you. You figure a boat gets away under a different command, you won't get it back. Well, you're wrong in this case. You'll get it back. I only need it for a week, maybe two at the outside. You have my word on it."

Carpenter was not moved. "My boys are out on an operation, and I don't know when they'll be back. That's all there is to it. However, I do have the *PT-133* available. You likely saw her tied to the dock."

"I'd prefer a boat that is actually afloat," Josh answered. "What happened to her?"

"Air raid."

"Our planes or theirs? I heard you boys recently sank Admiral Thompson's flagship."

Carpenter's smile faded. "That was an accident. Listen, Thurlow, you might have a low opinion of PT boats, but the Japanese don't. We're a thorn in their side, and they bomb us with some regularity. Anyhoo, *PT-133* could be pumped out. With a good mechanic and the necessary resupply, I'm confident you could get her going. Sorry I can't help you otherwise, old boy."

"I can use my Catalina to find your boats. I figure it will take me no more than fifteen minutes. Likely they're anchored in the next cove."

Carpenter weighed Josh's pronouncement. "You know, Colonel Burr is not in my chain of command."

"He's not in mine, either. I'm under Admiral Halsey's orders. You answer to Halsey, I'm fairly certain."

The lieutenant waved Josh's barb away. "Let me explain something, Commander. My officers are not graduates of that trade school in Annapolis. We are for the most part Harvard, Yale, and Princeton boys with the odd Dartmouth interloper. We don't like to make much of it, but most of the officers in the PTs come from, let us say, influential backgrounds. We don't have to be out here, but we are, because we love our country and we're willing to fight and die for it, if we must. But because of who we are and who our families are, we have been allowed to operate with a bit of laissez-faire from the big boys. Of course, Admiral Halsey could certainly come in here and lay waste, but he's been content to let us do what we do because he knows it's good politics for him, for us, and for everybody including you. I would advise you to tread very carefully."

When Josh didn't say anything, mainly because he knew Carpenter wasn't finished, the lieutenant went on. "Our casualty rate is high, so it isn't as if we've established a country club out here or anything. We're doing the best we can with what we have, which, as you've noticed, isn't all that much. In any case, Commander Warfield and I intend to keep our command intact and will resist with whatever means are at our disposal handing it over boat by boat to you or anybody else. Is the bull cut fine enough for you now?"

Josh contemplated grabbing the young man by his sharp lapels and lifting him out of his chair and flinging him into the side of the Quonset because he didn't have time for such horse manure. On the other hand, it probably wouldn't solve his problem, even though it might make him feel good. He searched instead for a reasonable compromise. "As I came in," Josh said, "I noticed on your chart that another boat, the *PT-59,* is listed as under repairs. Where is she?"

Carpenter rediscovered his smile. "Well, Thurlow, maybe we can do some business after all. As a matter of fact, the *PT-59*'s in Santa Cruz. An air raid cracked a few of her ribs, and she had to be towed down there to get patched up. You want her, well, that would be fine with me. Just bring her back when you're through. To be up-front with you, likely somebody's already stolen her. Every PT squadron's short of boats, you see. Any PT commander worth his salt sees a boat in the dockyard, he snags it by hook or crook. It's a game we play. Santa Cruz has always been a good place to pick off a boat. Frankly, I never expected to see the *59* again. But go rescue her for me and I'll be in your debt."

Josh thought about it. "Santa Cruz" was a hundred miles south of Guadalcanal. With *Dosie,* his boys could get down there in short order. "How about a skipper? I'll need one of those, too."

"You look like a man who could captain a PT boat yourself."

"I could, but I'll be in the Catalina, scouting ahead."

"What the hell are you up to, Thurlow?"

"That's between me and Admiral Halsey."

Carpenter switched gears. "Well, if you need a skipper, you're in luck, more or less. I've got one who's unemployed. He's a little beat up and is expecting some R&R with the medics, but if you want him, he's yours. That is, if he's willing to go."

"Where do I find him?"

"Go outside, turn right, and take the boardwalk to the top of the hill. He'll be in one of those tents up there. Tell him I'm willing to cut orders that will attach him to you."

"What's his name?"

"Just ask for Shafty. You'll find he's competent enough for a Harvard man. I'm from Princeton. What's your school, Josh?"

"Virginia Polytechnic Institute," Josh replied, "otherwise known as Virginia Tech."

"Never heard of it."

"That don't surprise me. You boys tend to call schools like mine cow colleges. By the way, do you understand how radar works?"

"Not exactly."

"Sonar?"

"A mystery."

"Internal combustion engines?"

"All I need to know about most machines is that they work."

"Well, that's fine, Lieutenant. But a few of us, even if we're officers, need to know *how* they work. That's what they taught folks like me at Tech."

Carpenter smiled. "I am duly impressed."

"Shafty, you say?"

"Shafty, indeed. 'I've been *shawfted!*' is his favorite phrase in that awful Boston accent of his. He'll stand court-martial for losing his boat, but not to worry. The court won't assemble for another month."

"Is he worth anything?"

"He's competent, but he's also through out here. The navy isn't very forgiving when it comes to losing one of their boats, even a scrap of mahogany and plywood like a PT. You might say the navy is like the world according to Aldous Huxley. It plays fair, just, and patient but never overlooks a mistake."

"It wasn't Aldous who said that," Josh informed the Ivy Leaguer. "It was Thomas."

Carpenter's smile faded. "Bring my boat back to me, Josh."

"How about Shafty?"

"Him you can keep."

7

Josh carefully climbed the slick boardwalk, peeking into each of the tents, all of which sat in a sea of brown, liquid mud. Josh finally found a tent that was occupied by a young sailor in his skivvies sitting dolefully on a cot. "Got the creeping crud, sir," he said when Josh asked him how he was getting along.

"You know an officer called Shafty?"

"Just follow the music, sir. Can't miss him."

Josh cocked his ear and heard Frank Sinatra somewhere higher on the slope. He climbed until he came to a mud-stained four-man tent, its flaps thrown open. Inside, a thin young man with knobby knees, a large Adam's apple, and a bush of brown hair sat in his undershorts on a cot. He was reading a book. Around the cot were more books, green mold discoloring their covers. Nearby was a windup record player on an overturned ammo crate, the Sinatra disc spinning and Sinatra happily singing. When the man looked up, Josh saw he had a square-jawed face, though it was emaciated, drawn, and the color of a lemon. "Shafty?" he asked, fearing the answer.

"That would be me," the man replied, marking his book with a string and closing it. He allowed a smile, his teeth very white against his sallow, thick lips. "New skipper, are you? Pick a bunk. As a matter of fact, take mine. I'm headed south to visit the medics."

The young officer, though it was impossible to tell his age from his skeletal face, spoke in a kind of peculiar Yankee accent that wasn't exactly Bostonian, despite Carpenter's description. Josh had heard something similar from Montauk Point fishermen who'd come south to Killakeet. "I hear you've been through some trouble," Josh said, figuring to establish some empathy with the man, not that he really cared a whit about his situation.

"I lost my boat," he replied, then gave Josh a closer look. "Your cap insignia says you're Coast Guard."

"We're part of the navy now."

"Tough luck."

"What happened out there?"

The officer lifted the needle from the record, and Sinatra's last note hung in the air. "You're part of the investigation, aren't you? Did you bring handcuffs? I'll go quietly."

"I'm not here to investigate anything. I'm here to offer you a command."

The ravaged face took on a petulant expression. "I can only presume I heard you incorrectly, Commander, or perhaps you are blind. Do you not notice that the fellow sitting in front of you is scratched and bruised, nearly from head to toe? Are you not aware that he has recently been dragged across a coral reef, explaining his wounds? Have you not been advised that he also possesses a back that I can assure you is completely sprung? I should have thought you might also have noted the jaundice that presents itself in his face. He also stands accused of losing his boat, for which the navy has no mercy. Is this the fellow to whom you offer a command?"

"Maybe. If he convinces me I should. How'd you lose your boat?"

It had started to rain, and Josh came inside the tent and had a seat on one of the adjoining cots. The raindrops pattered against the roof of the tent and splashed into the mud outside, playing insistent liquid notes in a truculent singsong.

The PT officer opened one of his books, withdrew two folded sheets of paper, and handed them over. "Here's my report, short and sweet. I wrote it with my usual attention to literary form, so, unlike most dull naval after-action reports, it's succinctly told in but four action-packed paragraphs."

Josh read the four paragraphs, which did indeed pack a lot of information into a short space. He handed the document back. "I noticed you blamed everybody but yourself."

"Oh, the court-martial will take care of blame. I've been *shawfted* ever since I came up to Lumbari and joined this chickenshit outfit."

"Shafty, I think you have a bad attitude," Josh observed.

The PT officer's faded blue eyes burned bright for an instant, then subsided. "In my opinion, it's a miracle I have an attitude at all. Now listen, Commander, this isn't going to work out between us. You say you need a

PT-boat skipper? Very well. I hope you find one. One thing for certain. It isn't going to be me."

Josh was tired of sparring with the sickly and petulant young man. "Now you listen to me, Shafty. I've made up my mind. It has to be you, mainly because I don't have time to find anybody else. Get your things together, go down to Santa Cruz, and get the *PT-59* out of the dockyard."

The PT officer's countenance changed to one of amusement. "You want me to go to Santa Cruz? That might be a horse of a different coloration! How would I make my way?"

"That's my Catalina tied to your dock. What's so great about Santa Cruz?"

"It has a hospital."

"You can forget the hospital until we get finished with our mission."

A staring match ensued. "Just for the sake of argument," Shafty said, after blinking, "let's say I go off on this little adventure. What's it all about?"

"What I'm going to tell you goes no further. We're going after a Marine Corps lieutenant named Armistead. Some say he's deserted."

A glimmer of interest registered in the PT officer's eyes. "Do you know where this jarhead officer is?"

"Last seen in New Georgia. But he may have a boat, and he's not alone. A woman's involved, wife of a coast-watcher."

"An affair of the heart!" he cried, flashing a surprisingly boyish grin. "Adventure *and* romance in the South Seas! I love it. Well, hell, Captain, let the boy have himself a fling. Likely Jap will capture him, anyway, or the cannibals will eat him. Or he'll get married. One way or the other, he's done for. Why chase him?"

"Lieutenant Armistead comes from an important family."

Still amused, Shafty raised an eyebrow. "Is that a fact?"

"His father was once ambassador to France."

"How interesting!"

"His middle name is Roosevelt."

"The plot thickens."

"Get your things together," Josh said.

The PT officer did not move from his cot. "Let me ask you a question, sport. Are you offering me a chance to avoid court-martial?"

Josh gave the question some thought. "I can't make any promises, but I have some influence," he said finally. "If you do well, I'll see what I can do. Just keep this in mind. This is an operation that never happened. No one, other than a few very select folks, will ever know about it."

The PT officer took on an expression of disbelief. "You're telling me you have influence? And you want *me* to be on a secret mission? Can you not understand how impossible all this is, considering who I am?"

"Who the hell *are* you?"

"Surely you josh, Josh. You really don't know?"

Josh was through talking. "Get your things together and let's go. That's an order."

Shafty shook his bushy head. "Add my refusal to the charges. I'm not about to risk my jaundiced hide to catch some poor lovelorn bastard. I'll take my chances with the court-martial. Sorry, sport." He reached across to the record player and put the needle back on his record, then closed his eyes and began to snap his fingers as Sinatra started to sing. It was the same song Josh had heard as he walked up: "All or Nothing at All."

"Don't you have another record?" Josh demanded.

"It reminds me of a woman I once adored," he replied without opening his eyes. "Her name was Inga. Inga-Binga, she put my heart through the wringa."

"What happened to her?"

"She found somebody else. That's what they all do, sport, when you're not around to keep them entertained."

Josh considered pummeling the aggravating young PT-boat skipper but then decided it wasn't worth the further aggravation. Let him have his court-martial and go home. Carpenter was right. The man was through out here. Josh rose and left the skinny yellow youth to his misery.

As he walked down the hill, Josh's damp shirt clung like warm glue to his chest. At least it had stopped raining. He found Once and Again fishing on the dock, although they didn't seem to be having any luck. The other boys were lounging around. "You ready to get out of this place, Skipper?" Phimble asked, getting to his feet. "Mosquitoes are so big here, one of them asked *Dosie* for a date."

"Let's go," Josh said irritably, and waved the boys into the float plane. Inside, he noticed a stack of crates that hadn't been there before. "What's this?"

"What do you mean, sir?" Ready asked, ducking through the hatch. "Oh, them boxes? Some PT mechanics had some extra beer and thought we should have it."

"Just handed it over, did they?"

Ready ran his fingers up under his tub cap and gave his head a good scratch. "Well, we let them take pictures of Pogo, so we figured they owed us something. We didn't hear any complaints."

"They'll complain plenty when they find out they're missing their beer," Josh said, then shrugged. One outfit stealing from another was the big game out here, and his boys were some of the best at it.

After the boys had cast off *Dosie*'s lines, Phimble cranked up the engines while Josh subsided into the copilot's seat. "Lucky these PT boats use avgas," Phimble said. "I topped us off from the tender. Where to now, Skipper?"

"Todd Whitman is at the Truax plantation," Josh said. "You know where that is?"

"Southwest of Munda. They still shooting around there?"

"Probably, but not as much as they were. The army finally took the airfield, but Jap's still around. He don't give up easy, as you well know."

Once stuck his head into the cockpit. "Sirs? There's a Chinaman out there waving a white flag."

Josh looked through the cockpit window and saw it was neither a Chinaman nor a white flag. "Turn around," Josh ordered Phimble, after hesitating for a long second.

Phimble turned the Catalina around and chugged back to the dock. Josh poked his head through the cockpit hatch. On the dock stood Shafty, dressed in officer's khakis, which appeared to be a size too large for him, and holding a skivvy shirt that he'd been waving. "What do you want?" Josh demanded.

"I've decided to go with you," he said.

"Why?"

He lifted his bony shoulders, grimacing as he let them down. "Let's just say my conscience got the better of me." When Josh looked dubious, he added, "I know Armistead or, I should say, I used to know him. We were in the Spee together."

"What the hell is the Spee?"

"It's a club at Harvard. Except it's more than a club. You have to swear allegiance to one another for all time. I've got to help you find Armistead because of my oath, more's the pity."

"Is that the only reason?"

"I'd like the chance to pay Jap back for killing two of my men."

Josh dropped back into his seat, sorted through his misgivings, then called over his shoulder. "Ready, send a couple of the boys across to give that navy lieutenant on the dock a hand with his traps."

Phimble looked askance. "Jesus, Skipper, that bastard looks like he's about to keel over. Look how yellow he is. Jaundiced, for sartain, and probably malaria, too. And what's this about paying back Jap? He's got his mind FUBAR'd."

"I need him."

"Why?"

"Because I don't have time to find somebody better."

Phimble, watching the PT officer flinch when he did nothing more than lean over to lift a small satchel off the dock, shook his head. "Nothing but trouble, that's all he's going to be," he predicted.

"He can join you in that category, then," Josh replied.

Shafty clambered inside the Catalina. At the sight of Dave, he asked, "What is that thing?"

"A megapode," Josh answered, ducking through the hatch from the cockpit. "His name is Dave. He won't peck you too often if you stay away from him."

"And that creature?" He nodded toward Pogo, who was asleep in one of the blister wells, apparently worn out from having his picture taken.

"That would be our bushman. He joined us on Guadalcanal."

"Is he a headhunter?"

"I don't know. I never asked him. Come forward. I want you to meet Ensign Phimble."

Shafty tripped over Marvin, who growled a low warning. "The inevitable Coast Guard mascot dog," he marveled. "Does he bite?"

"If you provoke him enough, he'll take off your leg."

In the cockpit, Phimble would scarcely turn around to shake the officer's hand. "Pleased to meet you" was the best he could do, but it was clear he wasn't, particularly.

Josh frowned at the quantity of suitcases, duffel bags, and crates coming aboard. "How'd you collect all this stuff?"

"A gentleman needs a change of clothes or two, not to mention books to keep his mind alert," Shafty replied with no apparent concern.

"Books are heavy," Josh worried.

"Yes, they are, in more ways than one," he replied. He selected a tome from one of the crates. "I happened to write this one."

Josh glanced at the book, which he presumed was a dime novel. "What else is there about you I should know?"

"I suppose you should know that Armistead and I are both sons of ambassadors. His pater was assigned to France, mine to Great Britain. How about those apples?"

"Can you drive a PT boat?" Josh asked.

"With alacrity."

"Then, assuming alacrity means what I think it means, that's good enough. Otherwise, I don't care whose son you are or what nooky novel you wrote."

Deflated, the PT officer replied, "Righty-o."

"I suppose I should know your actual name," Josh relented.

Frowning, Shafty studied Josh's face. "Am I to understand you really and truly don't know who I am?"

"Why does everything have to be so difficult with you?" Josh demanded. *"What the hell is your name?"*

"Well, sport, I am Kennedy, the terror of the Solomons. John Fitzgerald Kennedy is the entire moniker, but my friends like to call me simply Jack."

Josh pondered the frail-appearing, skinny, sallow, and thoroughly miserable-looking creature. "How about I just call you simply Shafty until I figure you deserve better?"

"Around here, I'm used to it."

"Let's get something straight, Shafty. Whatever you did back in the world and who the hell your daddy is don't mean crap to me. You and me, we've got jobs to do. My job is to tell you what to do. Your job is to do it. Just don't forget that and we'll get along fine. Understand?"

"I understand," Kennedy said. "And I will do my best."

Josh gave Kennedy a penetrating stare. "I expect better than your best. Now, find yourself a spot and hang on. Mister Phimble ain't quite learned how to fly."

8

"Missus," Colonel Burr said in his most solicitous voice, as he rose from behind his desk.

"Colonel," Felicity answered, and took her usual chair while the colonel snapped his fingers. His clerk entered with a steaming pot of tea and dainty porcelain cups, all on a tray. Felicity smiled at the clerk as he tried to act the proper servant in his heavy boots and camouflage utilities. "Aw, shit," he said, as he spilled the tea from her cup into a saucer. "You can drink it outa the saucer, ma'am," he said. "Won't hurt nothin'."

"That will be quite all, Sergeant Stipich," Burr said with an implied threat in his tone, and the man made a hasty exit.

Burr took his cup, pinky out, and raised it to Felicity. "Here's to you, missus. A creditable day, is it not?"

"I daresay, Colonel," Felicity answered, sipping the tea, which tasted terrible, entirely too sweet and thick. God only knew where the Yanks had gotten the awful stuff. Try as she might, her face screwed up a little.

"Not to your liking?" Burr asked, alarmed. "I'll have the man who made it horsewhipped! Sergeant, tear off them stripes!"

"Aye, aye, sir," came the resigned but stoic reply from the parlor.

"No, no. The tea is quite good," Felicity lied. "If you are reading my face, I fear you are merely reading my general homesickness. Colonel, please help me and John return to our island home. It is within your power. All your men tell me that if there is any officer in the Solomon Islands who knows how to get a thing done, it's Colonel Montague Burr."

Burr was susceptible to flattery, and he took what Felicity had just told him as the absolute truth. "Of course I could arrange it, missus," he answered in his grand style, "but it is not yet safe to go north. The Japanese, for all I know, occupy your island. I would not consider letting you and little John-Bull risk your lives until I'm absolutely certain you would be as safe as you are here on Melagi."

Felicity lowered her eyes, and even batted them in what she hoped was a provocative manner. "If I do not return and make my copra, I will be ruined, Colonel. You must let me go."

"Do you not like it here, missus? I have done everything I can to make certain you and the boy are comfortable. Do the men harass you? I notice them lining up to watch you each day."

"No, they are all very kind and attentive."

"Yes," Burr said. "They respect and admire your person, missus, and, of course, little John-Bull."

Felicity rested the cup and saucer gently on Burr's great desk. "Colonel, for what purpose do you imprison me here?"

Burr allowed an expression of astonishment to cross his ugly mug. "Imprison? Why, missus, I desire only your safety and comfort!" He rose once more from his chair and crossed to stand beside her. His hand briefly touched her shoulder. "Tell me what I can do to make you happy. You know I would do anything. Anything at all."

Felicity impulsively took Burr's hand. "Colonel, the only thing that will make me happy is to be allowed to go home."

Burr let her hold his hand for a long second, then withdrew it. "I can't, Felicity," he said. "I . . . I think I would be lost without seeing you each and every day."

Felicity folded her hands in her lap. "Montague, you are a dear, dear man."

Burr cleared his throat. "I have a jeep. If you'd like to go with me one afternoon, perhaps this very one, I would be pleased to take you on a picnic. There is quite a beautiful waterfall on the south side of the island, so I'm told."

"Yes. Morissette Falls. I know it well. The owner of this plantation used to organize trips to it on horseback. I've been several times."

"With your husband. I'm sorry. Sometimes I feel as if I am struggling with a ghost."

Felicity smiled. "With many ghosts, Colonel. I see these islands as they once were, not as you see them now. Oh, what fun we had! Parties like you wouldn't know, with good food and fine drink and dancing. But now, this war, this terrible war. Sometimes, I fear . . ."

"You needn't fear anything as long as you are with me," Burr simpered.

Felicity was resolute. "It isn't pain or death I fear, my dear Montague. It is the fear that no matter what might happen, I shall never again stand in a room of my fellow mastahs and missuses, with our Malaitan servants standing nearby like ebony statues, and then hear once more our voices raised, proud and defiant." Felicity could almost hear them singing, and their voices echoed, on and on. "Let me go home to Noa-Noa. Please, Montague." Tears crept from the corners of her eyes and found their way down her cheeks.

Burr presented her a handkerchief, swiftly withdrawn from his hip pocket. "Dear God, but I can't. If something happened to you, I would never forgive myself." He turned abruptly when there was a knock on the door. "What the fu— What is it?"

"Sir, your scheduled company commander meeting," the clerk said, his sleeves relieved of their stripes. "They're waiting."

Burr heaved a long sigh and returned to his desk. Felicity stood, dabbing at her eyes. "I should be going in any case," she said, returning the handkerchief. "I am sorry to be such a bother."

"My dear Felicity!" Burr cried. "A bother to me you will never be. Will you at least consider my offer for the picnic? It needn't be the waterfall. Anywhere you like. A pretty beach, perhaps?"

Felicity smiled, her eyes downcast. "You are such a dear man."

Burr puffed up. "I would do anything for you, I swear, anything but let you go."

"Would you be a planter? After the war, I mean? Do you see yourself in this life, this terrible yet remarkable life of the colonial planter of the South Seas?"

"My people have always been farmers. My grandparents even lived in a sod house on the Kansas prairie. But I would ask you to think of a different life. A woman such as yourself deserves to live in comfort, with the finest things available to her. A well-appointed house, an automobile, bridge on Thursdays with the other women of her station. I should like to see you away from this place. For your own good and, of course, for the good of little John-Bull."

"Your kindness sometimes overwhelms me," Felicity whispered.

"Tomorrow, then? I shall drive the jeep myself. Pick you up at eleven hundred hours sharp?"

"All right, Montague. All right."

Felicity left Burr's office, startling the young Raider officers assembled in the parlor. They leapt to their feet and tore off their helmets. "Gentlemen," she said, acting very much the grand lady as she swept through the gaping assembly.

"Get your friggin' asses in here!" she heard Burr bellow as she made her way outside and down the steps and thence along the path back to the beach. She had played the gentlewoman to the hilt but now was prepared to yell at Captain McQuaid, just for the sport of it.

But Captain McQuaid was nowhere to be found. Instead, she discovered three young men without shirts working on his boat. They were so muscular and handsome, they quite took her breath away. The men stopped what they were doing and watched her approach with equally appreciative eyes. One of them walked brazenly up to her, though he took off his tub cap and held it over his belly button as a sign of respect. He was a tall and rough-featured man, with a shaven head. By the alchemy of the feminine mind, she was immediately able to deduce he was American navy, and not a marine Raider. "Ma'am," the sailor said by way of a greeting.

"So you're working to get the old *Minerva* afloat, are you?"

"Yes, ma'am. We've rented her for the week."

"May I ask why?"

The man looked around at his fellows, who all looked away. "Well, you see, ma'am . . . we heard there were islands out there that had maybe . . . other people on them, like."

"Other people? Women, you mean?"

"Well, yes, ma'am. It's been a powerfully long time since we seed one, you know, not counting yourself. Only you're much too high-flown for the likes of us. Nothing meant by that, ma'am, as you can imagine. Cap'n Mc-Quaid, he said he knows where a bevy of what he calls Maries be. We don't mean them Maries no harm, of course. We just want to look at 'em, that's all, talk to 'em maybe some. We ain't bad, ma'am. Honest we ain't. Just lonely, like all the men out here."

Felicity touched the man on his arm. "I don't believe you're bad," she said while feeling a bit light-headed at the firmness of his muscles. "Nor any of you boys. But let me tell you the truth. Captain McQuaid may know where some ugly old pickaninnies might be, but for comely maidens, there is but one place, an island to the north. Its name is Noa-Noa. Perhaps you have heard of it?"

The sailor took on a worried aspect. "Ma'am, would you tell us how to find this island?"

"I will do better than that. Noa-Noa happens to be my home. If you are willing, I will let you take me there, and you may stay as long as you like. I'm certain the pretty Maries of Noa-Noa will be more than pleased to entertain you."

The sailor gave her proposal some thought. "How long would it take to get there, ma'am? We're shipping out next week."

"Oh, it's only a day sail. If we get an early start, you can spend three or four days courting Noa-Noa Maries before you have to get back."

The sailor looked around at the other two men, both of whom looked back with faces creased by eager grins. He smacked his fist into his hand. "We'll take the chance. Hell, we've missed the boat before. They just yell at us for a while, then put us aboard another one. Noa-Noa. Yes, ma'am. I reckon we'd be glad to take you there."

9

When the boys completed stowing the lieutenant's things, Josh told them to listen up. "This here's Mister Kennedy. He's going to be with us for a while. He gives you an order, it's like it's from me. Any questions?"

Once raised his hand. "How do I get out of this chickenshit outfit?"

Josh glared at him. "You can get out right now if you don't mind swimming back to Melagi."

Once hung his head. "I was just funning, sir."

Josh was clearly in no mood for fun. "Each one of you boys come up here and introduce yourself," he demanded.

The boys did as they were told except for Marvin, who was using one of his hind feet to scratch at a flea behind his ear, and Dave, who was still fast asleep. Pogo studied the PT officer for a long second. "Kennedy fella sick too much," he said to himself, then touched his lucky shark tooth and went to sit with Marvin, where he plucked the offending flea from the dog's ear, snapped it between his long fingernails, and ate it.

After the other boys had finished their introductions, Millie lingered for a word with Kennedy. "What else do you have besides jaundice, sir? I'm the medic of the outfit."

"My back might have gotten a bit sprung when my boat was sunk," Kennedy said in a low voice. "And my feet and legs are scratched from dragging them across a coral reef."

"Anything else?"

Kennedy touched his stomach. "Low-grade fever much of the time. My bowels need a bit of work. I was hoping to get them some attention until your Commander Thurlow came along."

Millie beckoned Kennedy aft, so as to get away from the other boys. "Peel

off your uniform and let me take a look at those coral scrapes . . . Uh-
huh . . . They got you good, didn't they? . . . But they seem to be healing,
though they'll certainly leave scars . . . Are they itchy? I've got some salve
here that might help some . . . Let me know if any of these scratches start to
smell funny or you get some red lines that sort of streak out from them. OK,
Lieutenant, you can get dressed. What exactly is wrong with your bowels?"

Kennedy tucked in his shirt. "Sometimes they're too loose, and sometimes I'm plugged up like I've, uh, got sand packed in there."

"Which way are they now."

"Sand."

"When I had trouble like that, my mama used to give me a good dose of
cod liver oil."

Kennedy shook his big head. "I've taken cod liver oil until I nearly looked
like a fish. I've tried every remedy known to mankind. You see, I've had this
problem all my life."

Millie gave the lieutenant's bowels some thought. "Doc Folsom—he was
the doc on Killakeet Island, where most of us is from—used to say the bowels and the brain are connected closer than any two other organs. Maybe,
beg your pardon, sir, it's your brain that needs some work."

A sad smile slid across Kennedy's tired face. "My brain's about all I've ever
been able to depend on, Millie."

Now that the lieutenant had his pants back on and his shirt buttoned up,
Ready came over for a word, sending Millie away with a jerk of his chin.
"You ever rode in a Catalina, Mister Kennedy?"

"No," Kennedy replied, then leaned in. "Is that Negro really our pilot?"

"Negro? If you mean Ensign Phimble, yes, he's our pilot all right, and I
reckon he can fly this plane as good as you can skipper a torpedo boat. As a
matter of fact, reckon he can do anything as good or better'n you . . . sir."

"No offense meant," Kennedy said.

"No offense taken," Ready answered, although it was clear there was.

Phimble pushed *Dosie* up on her step, drove her to altitude, then called the
lookouts to stay awake. "We might not be alone up here, fellas," he told them.

Blanche Channel between Rendova and New Georgia was indeed a dangerous stretch of water. A Japanese fighter plane could lift off from its base
on the big round island of Kolombangara and be over the channel in minutes, diving out of the sun or popping out of puffy white clouds. And it
wasn't only Jap that was the problem. American ships spying an aircraft sil-

houetted against the sky would often shoot first and ask questions later. One screaming chunk of lead or steel, no matter where it came from, could kill you just as dead as any other.

Sure enough, as New Georgia coalesced out of the afternoon steam, Phimble caught sight of a cluster of American landing craft in the process of carrying troops and supplies toward a long, narrow beach. If he could see them, he knew, they could see him, and their crews were most likely racing to their guns. Phimble jinked away only to discover he'd turned toward a pair of destroyers racing in to protect the landing party. He saw the telltale red blinks of antiaircraft fire lighting up their turrets followed by a streak of tracers flashing past the cockpit. Phimble threw the Catalina into a hard turn and, though she shook and complained, *Dosie* came about and left the destroyers shaking their fists behind.

"If you're finished playing around, how about taking me to see Whitman?" Josh demanded.

"You're welcome, Skipper. What a wonderful commander you are, indeed, for recognizing that I was doing my best to keep us from being shot down by our own ships."

"Just fly," Josh grumped.

"Fly it is," Phimble replied, just as grumpily, then turned the *Dosie* to line up parallel to the coast.

The Truax plantation lay between Mbanga and Lambete, two tiny settlements difficult to spot from the air since they were hidden by the overhanging bush. Phimble was focused on finding the cove he'd been told was a good landing site, and Josh was back to thinking about Armistead, when a shout startled them both. It was Again in the forward turret, and he was yelling, "Bandits at two o'clock high! They're Rufes!"

Again was right on the money. A Rufe was actually a modified Zero fighter plane with a long pontoon attached at its centerline and two smaller pontoons on its wingtips. They were a bit slower than the superb little land-based fighters but just as well armed. There were four of them, and they were coming in from the northeast, likely from Kolombangara.

"Get those guns cranking!" Josh yelled, and was rewarded by a blast from Again in the forward turret followed by a steady barrage aft from the starboard blister gun. The Rufes ignored the bullets and swept in, all barrels blazing.

Phimble put the Catalina into a howling dive, then threw the wheel hard over. Aft, the boys were yelling, and they were oddly jubilant. After a few seconds, Phimble figured out why. American fighter planes, covering the landings on New Georgia, had pounced on the Rufes while the Japanese pilots were distracted by *Dosie*. Phimble came about and hoped the American P-40s wouldn't mistake *Dosie* for a Japanese seaplane. In the heat of air combat, anything was possible.

Phimble pointed *Dosie*'s nose along the beach until Mbanga and Lambete finally crept into view. He spotted a decent-looking cove and dropped the Catalina down, not even worrying about the direction of the wind, and set her on the water. He peered through the cockpit windshield and saw three men in lap-laps standing like ebony monuments on the beach. "Looks like you got a reception."

Josh climbed out of his seat. "Head south to Santa Cruz and secure *PT-59*. Kennedy will skipper it back to Melagi. I'll meet you there tomorrow."

"How will you get back to Melagi?"

"I don't know. I'll figure something out. Maybe Whitman has a boat."

"Why don't I just drop Kennedy off, then turn around and pick you up?"

Josh couldn't find fault in the idea except that it exposed Phimble to some risk, probably including night flying. But the entire mission was a risk, any way you cut it. "All right, Eureka. Get back up here as soon as you can." He stuck out his hand. "I'm sorry for being in a foul mood."

Phimble grasped Josh's hand. "Me, too. Just take care of yourself. I don't like the looks of those black birds on the beach."

Josh climbed out of the Catalina, walked along its wing, and stepped onto its pontoon and then into the surf. The three men on the beach looked like hard men. Their eyes were sullen, and their painted faces looked to have permanent scowls, as if they had something stuck in their craws. Shell necklaces were draped around their necks, dilly bags hung from their bare shoulders, and cartridge belts were strapped around their waists. They were carrying rifles, Enfields from the looks of them. Josh raised his hand and greeted them in his best pidgin, or Bêche-de-Mer, as it was formally called in the Solomons. "Good fellas! You all right?"

The three maintained their glowering expressions, but one, a tall, majestic man with slick, oiled skin, unbent long enough to reply. "What you do along this place?"

"Look-see-talk big fella Whitman."

"What name you?"

"Thurlow."

"Whitman no say bring one fella Thurlow."

"No worry-worry," Josh replied.

"Whitman no say bring one fella Thurlow," the man insisted in a truculent tone.

"My word. Boy talk too much," Josh snapped. "You take me to Whitman, double quick! Savvy?" He put his hand on his pistol, even though he was outnumbered by three Enfields.

Josh knew the game. It was a contest of wills. His eyes bore into the man who'd spoken. Malevolent eyes probed his in return. After a long minute, the other two men shifted on their feet and started looking a bit sheepish. At last the man blinked. "We go," he said. Without another word, he turned and walked into the jungle at the edge of the beach, his fellows following.

Behind Josh, *Dosie* roared, then lifted off. Josh turned to watch her, feeling quite alone. The bushmen had completely disappeared. He hurried to catch up with them, all the while hoping they weren't waiting in ambush to take his head, though he supposed they might.

1 0

All was peaceful as the *Darlin' Dosie,* suspended between fluffy cotton clouds and an empty turquoise sea, droned down the Slot. In the Solomons, such rare moments were known as lulls, as between the deadly storms, which were surely forming, created by nature or man, but always on their way. The crew were enjoying this particular lull, mainly by sleeping, except for the pilot, Phimble, and the passenger, twenty-six-year-old John F. Kennedy, the second son of Ambassador Joe and Mrs. Rose Kennedy of Hyannis Port, Massachusetts.

Kennedy sat in the port blister, nursing a cup of coffee brewed for him by Millie before the cook/medic found a nook in the rattling airplane to take a nap. Kennedy admired the sleepy indolence of Thurlow's crew. Even the bosun, Ready O'Neal, announced that he was going to climb in the rack (which meant curling up beneath the navigator's table with Dave the megapode), leaving only Kennedy to sit behind one of the machine guns and look out for the Jap.

Kennedy was tired, terribly tired. He realized now it was the ultimate foolishness to go along with Thurlow. He started to think of a way to get out of it. Perhaps he'd simply check himself into the hospital at Santa Cruz. One look at him and the doctors would surely put him to bed.

Truth, Kennedy thought as he stared through the blister view port. *Tell the truth to yourself. The court-martial won't do it. You'll not be able to confess to it, not now, not ever.* Truth was, after all, what the priests and nuns told him Jesus the Christ had come to give: *You will know the truth, and the truth will set you free.* Kennedy had never completely understood the phrase until now.

On the first little island they'd swum to after the sinking of the *PT-109,* Kennedy had realized his crew was in a bad way. One man was horribly burned. Another had a broken leg. All were battered and bruised, and the infections of the Solomons were surely already rampant in their bloodstreams. Without water or food or medical attention, they weren't going to last long. They scarcely had energy to move as it was. In contrast, Kennedy had suddenly been infused with tremendous energy. His crew had commented on it. "Jesus, Mister Kennedy," one of them said, "you're acting like you can walk on water!"

Where had all that energy come from? *Tell the truth.* On that little island, he had seen in his mind an image of his father, and then his brother Joe, and he had imagined how they would share knowing glances when they heard for the first time that he, the second son, the younger brother, had come out to the Solomon Islands as a representative of the Kennedy family and *had royally screwed up!*

On that nasty little spit of sand, with his men dying, and Jap all around, Kennedy had panicked. The Japanese destroyer had not made him afraid. Swimming with a strap between his teeth towing one of his men across shark-infested waters had elicited no fear. Even being captured and tortured by the Japanese was not his primary concern. What concerned him most was that he'd given both his father and his older brother yet another opportunity to ridicule him and to find fault in him.

As the sun lowered itself on the horizon that day and transmogrified itself into a gigantic red ball, Kennedy felt as if it were frying his brain. He had ricocheted from hopelessness to despair. He *had* to get off that island, had to get back to his base *right now* and explain what had happened before the announcement went out to his father and brother that he'd disgraced himself, a message that would land surely like a dead, stinking fish on the desk of his ambitious, scheming father and be like a prayer answered to Joe Jr., who was always in competition with his younger brother for their father's approval.

Kennedy stared unseeing through the blister window of the Catalina and clenched his teeth, although he didn't realize it. Joe Jr., the great Joe, the literal fair-haired boy, the apple of his father's eye, a cliché that was *the truth* and always had been and always would be. Joe, the favored son who was to set the world afire with his brilliance, the favored son who had all his life made certain that the world knew how much better he was than his weak little brother. And now Kennedy had given him all the ammunition the bastard would ever need to keep braying it forever. He had screwed up the worst way an officer could in the United States Navy. *He had lost his boat!*

Kennedy remembered the night he swam alone into the darkness, the cold seeping remorselessly into his bones. Sometime during the night, a phantom had appeared before him. It was Rosemary, his sister. She was wearing a white hospital gown, and there was a scar on her forehead, throbbing as if her skull were experiencing an internal earthquake. She watched over him with a gentle, loving smile for a long time. "What is it, Rosemary?" he'd finally asked her. She'd replied with one word: *Father.* And then Rosemary had shimmered away, and Kennedy found himself staring into the blackness. He'd been staring into it ever since.

Kennedy understood now that men who are about to die have no use for falsehoods. They seek the truth because they require it to be their last thought. As the sea of the Ferguson Passage drained him of what little warmth was left in his frail, bowel-constricted body, Kennedy had looked into his soul and found it filled with darkness.

The Catalina bumped through turbulent air, and ribbons of white vapor streaked past the blister window. Thurlow's boys kept sleeping. Kennedy wished with all his might that he could join them in their peaceful, innocent state, but peace and innocence were things he knew very well he was never going to be allowed. But then he woke suddenly. To his surprise, he had fallen asleep, after all. He looked through the blister window and saw they were flying across a great mountainous island. He was awestruck by its emerald beauty, its volcanic peak rearing heavenward, and then allowed himself to be further amazed at what appeared to be a vast city covering its southern edge. He made his way forward. "That's our base on Santa Cruz," Phimble said as Kennedy climbed into the cockpit.

"My God, it's huge!" Kennedy marveled.

"If Jap could see it, he'd be smart to give up," Phimble replied. "All that stuff down there is aimed directly at him."

For a reason that he couldn't discern, Kennedy's favorite poem condensed into his mind:

> *I have a rendezvous with Death*
> *At some disputed barricade,*
> *When Spring comes back with rustling shade*
> *And apple-blossoms fill the air.*

It wasn't spring. It was never spring in the Solomons. It was always summer: hot, wet, rampant summer. But that didn't matter. What the poet, a soldier in the Great War, had meant by his words was that if a man was truly lucky, he would meet death in a state of grace, and even gratitude. He was thinking about all that when Phimble splashed the Catalina into the water. The impact was so sudden and hard, Kennedy thought it surely had knocked the fillings right out of his teeth. While Phimble taxied the aircraft toward the beach, Kennedy was suddenly infused with the idea of making the ensign his friend. He figured he could use one. "Mister Phimble, I have a favorite poem," he said. "Would you care to hear it?"

Phimble was busy nudging the throttles and steering the Catalina and didn't have the time or inclination to talk. His silence Kennedy naturally took for acquiescence, and he quoted the first stanza of the poem, adding afterward, "Very meaningful for our present situation, wouldn't you say?"

Phimble's expression was one of aggravated disbelief. "I take that poem as both shallow and ignorant of war," he said.

Kennedy felt as if the wind had been knocked out of him. He replied with sarcasm. "Thank you for listening to it, just the same."

"I told Captain Thurlow I didn't think you'd be anything but trouble," Phimble shot back.

"I'm sorry for your low opinion of me," Kennedy replied. "I'll endeavor to improve my character."

"Just don't go spouting that rendezvous with death crap around the boys. They're close enough to dying out here without a sad sack like you turning it into poetry. Savvy?"

"I savvy," Kennedy replied, his expression turned to stone.

"Good. Now, you can do one thing for me."

Kennedy's countenance softened. To provide a man a favor was often the beginning of a friendship. "What's that?"

"Get the hell off my airplane."

1 1

Whitman's men were not waiting in ambush for Josh. In fact, they were not waiting at all. They had slipped quietly through the surrounding vegetation, like fish swimming through a coral reef, and had simply disappeared. Josh plunged in the direction he thought they'd gone. Wait-a-minute vines entangled him, and catch-and-keep thorns stuck him in the arms and legs. He sweated and panted in the hot, stagnant air and pushed aside vast leaves, some as big as elephant ears, only to be blocked by huge trees, their exposed roots like the legs of gigantic octopi. The air seemed thick and nasty. Dim spokes of light filtered through the layers of canopy overhead. Dripping moisture made a staccato patter on the moss-covered floor. He fell into a vast spider's web, and the sticky strands enveloped him like a net. He tore at the tendrils of the web stuck to his face and pushed on, slogging past steaming piles of vegetation that exuded an evil stink of decay. A high-pitched scream erupted not far away, an animal with a warning or a death scream, he didn't know and couldn't tell.

If this was what the army boys had faced on New Georgia, Josh was beginning to understand why they had panicked. He wondered, too, if the jungle had somehow gotten to David Armistead, had pushed him over an edge in his mind that the lieutenant had not even known was there. It had happened before to others, and Armistead had been in combat for over a year.

Josh finally staggered into a small clearing, where he stood, his utilities soaked with sweat, and tried to figure out which direction to go. His neck felt as if something were crawling on it, and he slapped himself there, hitting something hard and knocking it down his back. He pulled out his shirttail and shook it until the thing fell into the moss, so heavy it made a thumping noise on the green cushion. He sought it out, a writhing yellow and black millipede, and stomped on it. Josh felt as if he were suffocating. Every direction he looked disappeared into green darkness. He was hopelessly lost.

But then . . .

"Cheerio, mastah," came a lilting, feminine voice.

Where a moment before there had been but a charnel house of massed vegetation, there now stood a young Marie wearing a bright blue lap-lap that started at her slim waist and ended about six inches above her pretty, dimpled knees. She walked toward him, her bare feet somehow impervious to the thorns and stickers that littered the clearing, and came so near that Josh had to lift his eyes from where they'd naturally been diverted, her round and gorgeous breasts. Her skin, black as the night sky, was oiled, and she exuded the scent of sweet coconut. There was a bright pink hibiscus pushed into her curly hair just above her left ear. She smiled at him with fulsome lips, seemingly taking delight in his openmouthed astonishment at her appearance. "You afraid good fella Marie?" she asked.

"No," he said, although for some reason, he was.

"Are you lost?" she asked, cocking her head and inspecting him with eyes that were big, brown, and intelligent, though they seemed a size too large for her round, inquisitive face. She had a correspondingly small nose, and when her lips parted, Josh saw that she had ivory-white teeth. Put all together, she was mesmerizing, and Josh couldn't tear his eyes from her. "I'm looking for the Truax plantation," he croaked.

She pointed off in a direction that seemed random. "Go this way. No worry-worry. I saw your airplane. It is a nice one, I think. Will it come back?"

"I hope so," he answered. "Why do you ask?"

Her train of thought seemed to shift. "You should give me a present," she said.

Josh was still trying to get his eyes to focus somewhere other than her breasts. "Why should I give you a present?" he asked, even though he was willing to give her most anything he had, at least at that moment. It had been a long time since he'd been near a naked female.

"I directed you to the Truax plantation, and therefore you owe me a gift for my work. That is the local custom."

"But I don't have a present."

"Look in your pockets."

Josh looked in his pockets and brought forth a small copper wire he'd picked up on the cave floor near Stobs's radio, a washer found on the deck of the Catalina, and a spool of brown thread he kept to patch tears in his uniform. He'd lost the needle. "The thread, please," the girl said.

Josh handed it over. "How do you know English so good?"

"I know English *well*," she corrected him. "I attended a missionary school."

"I see. Do you live nearby?"

"Yes," she said, then walked past him and disappeared into the bush, leaving behind her sweet scent.

Josh wondered over the encounter for a long second, and waited, hoping the girl would return. When she didn't, he headed in the direction she'd pointed. To his surprise, he almost immediately stepped through the jungle onto a lawn of short-cropped grass. Across the lawn was a rock fence overhung with bougainvillea and wild roses. The fence circled a white plantation house that had a wide front porch and dormer windows. It was a pleasant, congenial scene except for the fact that bullet holes riddled the house and its windows were shattered. What had appeared at first as the site of intensive gardening proved to be shell and bomb craters, and scattered among the flowering bushes were cartridge belts and helmets, bloody remnants of uniforms, and there, just beside a pretty oleander, a boot with a gory foot still inside it covered by a stream of ants. The Marie's fresh coconut scent had been replaced by the stink of death, and Josh's nose further directed him to a mound of bodies, all Japanese from their uniforms.

Whitman was on the porch, sitting in a swing, watching him. Josh judged him to be in his midforties, a short, thick, though imperial-looking man, bald but with a thin mustache and neatly trimmed beard, both graying. He was wearing a khaki shirt and shorts, midcalf tan socks, and brown army boots, the uniform of the coast-watchers. Despite his reputation for toughness, he looked for all the world like a kindly uncle. Josh couldn't say he knew Whitman, but he had been around the man a couple of times on Melagi when the coast-watchers had gathered for a meeting with Colonel Burr. Whitman never lacked for an opinion, and it was always to the point and without equivocation, but Josh had noticed he was a man who knew when to keep his mouth shut, too.

"Thurlow," Whitman said as Josh came up on the porch.

"Mister Whitman." Josh put out his hand. "How are you, sir?"

Whitman briefly clasped Josh's hand with a grip that felt like a bear trap. "Happy as a bastard on his father's birthday, mate. Why are you here?"

"To investigate David Armistead's disappearance," Josh replied as the pain in his overwrung hand subsided.

A bushman in a floral-patterned lap-lap with an ammunition bandolier across his chest came out of the house onto the porch. He stood at attention, chin up. "What's your pleasure?" Whitman asked. "Truax won't mind if we raid his liquor cabinet, since I doubt he'll be coming back. Man had more alcohol than a Brisbane pub. Don't know if he was ever sober." Whitman quietly chuckled to himself, then said, "I recall you're a rum man, Thurlow. Wretched drink, entirely too sweet. You need to turn to a sharper dram of rotgut out here to stay healthy. Gin's the choice of the colonists."

"Mount Gay rum, if there is any," Josh said, ignoring Whitman's advice.

"Very nice one, I think," the bushman replied, then slipped inside, easing the screen door shut so it didn't slap against the frame, even though it was splintered by bullets. Whitman made no conversation, just kept swinging in the swing, and Josh waited. The bushman soon reappeared balancing two glasses on a tray. He handed one to Josh, saying, "Sah!" then repeating the word when he presented the other glass, filled with gin, to Whitman.

"Thank you, Moru," Whitman said delicately. The bushman placed the tray on a small, curved-legged table inlaid with a design of the sun and the moon, then went down to stand in the grass.

Josh took a taste of the rum. It was the good stuff, all right, and he lolled it around his tongue before swallowing it, feeling the comfort of its warmth as it eased down his gullet. In contrast, Whitman apparently received no pleasure from his drink, downing it all in a gulp, then twisting his face as if it hurt him. He tossed his glass to the bushman, who, without moving any other part of his body, caught it with one hand. "Well, Thurlow," Whitman said, "you disappoint me. I hoped for a moment you'd come to help me kill Armistead and my wife, not for the purpose of some bloody investigation."

"If I find David," Josh answered, "I guess I'll find your missus, too. But why do you want to kill her? I thought she'd been kidnapped."

"Bloody hell. Who told you that?"

"Vickers."

"That idiot. Never could get a story straight."

"Well, that's why I'm here. To get it straight," Josh replied.

"How much of it do you need?"

"The entire thing, I reckon."

Whitman nodded. "It's a sad thing when the woman you love betrays you, ain't it, Commander?"

Josh nodded back, thinking of Dosie. It must have shown in his eyes.

"You've had the same experience? Then you understand why I have to kill her. It's the only way, though God knows, I still love her more than life." He shook his head and released a long sigh. "Do you ever wish you could turn the clock back?"

"All the time," Josh confessed, and it surprised him when he said it. He didn't want to philosophize with Whitman. He needed information and he needed it quickly. "So what happened, Mister Whitman?" he asked, allowing obvious impatience to enter his voice.

Whitman pondered Josh for a long second, then started his tale with when he had attacked the Japanese after the American army troops had landed down the coast. "I expected your Yank soldiers to keep the Japanese busy, but they apparently bogged down right away. The Japanese commander, a chap I've been fighting for over a year, took advantage and wheeled around to box me in. I managed to get one radio working long enough to yell my head off to Vickers for help. A day later, he called back. Between the static, I understood Colonel Burr was sending some of his Raiders to help out."

Whitman went on to tell of the arrival of Armistead and his men, four Raiders with two crew-served fifty-caliber machine guns. Armistead had immediately established sites for the fifties. "Armistead's plan was to simply stave Jap off," Whitman said. "He reported that the American army was finally moving, and there was a good chance they would get up here in time to save us, but he couldn't guarantee it. I told him not to let on to any of my boys that Jap might scrag us."

"You were afraid they'd run?"

Whitman gave Josh a long stare, then glanced at his servant, who still stood as straight and still as if he were a statue. "I never really know what these blokes are thinking, you know," he confessed in a lowered voice. "But that ain't here nor there. The next thing I noticed was my wife taking Armistead off to the shadows. Oh, they were having quite the conversation, about what I don't know."

"Tactics, maybe?" Josh asked. "I heard your wife is a warrior."

Whitman eyed Josh. "Kimba's been known to fire a rifle now and again, but she's no warrior. Who told you that?"

"A Missus Markham."

"Felicity?" Whitman laughed with his mouth open, showing his false teeth. "Her brain's been immersed in gin for a decade. You'll never get naught but bull fodder from the likes of that dingbat."

"Hold on," Josh interrupted. He took a small notebook and a pencil from his shirt pocket, opened the notebook to the first page, and wrote a single word: *Kimba*. "OK, go ahead."

"What did you write down?" Whitman asked suspiciously.

"Your wife's name. I just realized I never heard it before now."

Whitman continued his story. "By and by the sun went down and Jap still hadn't come, although we could hear him out there in the bush. Jap ain't the bloody jungle fighter he thinks he is. He sounded like he was having a full-dress parade. I got Kimba to the side and told her if Jap broke through, to kill herself. Jap considers it his right to rape and murder civilians, part of his pay and allowances, if you will. I impressed on her that death was the better course."

For the first time, Josh had heard something that made a little sense. David Armistead was the kind of man who might be upset with the concept of a woman killing herself. He might even want to do something about it. "When did you see your wife last?" he asked.

"Around midnight. She was sitting on this very swing. Armistead was sitting on the steps, just as you. The two of them stopped talking when I came near. I should have killed them both then and there. I knew there was something going on between them. It probably started back on Melagi. Three times in the past year, I came down the Slot by canoe to meet with your Colonel Burr and Vickers about this or that. Kimba usually came with me. Armistead met her there. My guess is he fell in love with her and probably leapt at the chance to get close to her again, even if he had to fight Jap to do it."

"I was at those meetings, too," Josh said. "I don't recall your wife."

"Oh, she knows her place, Thurlow. She camped out on the beach. But one night, I came back from a party hosted by Colonel Burr and found Armistead and Kimba sitting together down there. I had my Webley with me. A bullet to her brain right there and then, and his, too. That would have been the ticket."

"But they were just talking, right? God knows, all us Americans out here don't get the chance to talk to a woman much."

Whitman grimaced. "If you ever laid eyes on her, mate, you'd understand. Most men would bloody well lie down beneath a lorry for her. Let me give you some advice. Always marry an ugly woman. It will save you some heartache."

Josh reflected a man didn't have to marry a beautiful woman to get his share of heartache. Just loving one was enough. "What happened when the Japanese attacked?" he asked.

"We beat them back," Whitman replied, grim as a rock. "But Jap ain't never beat all the way, not unless he's dead."

"What did Armistead do during the attack?"

"Do? All right, I'll tell you. I'm not the type of man who won't give a man praise, even a man what cuckolded me. He stopped the charge cold with his bloody big fifty calibers. Then, he stepped out front and his four bloody Raiders with him, drawing out their God-awful K-bars. They went after the Japs still standing, killed every one of the blokes. It was a good example for my boys, I can tell you that. Give no quarter to the enemy. Kill them, kill them all."

"So Jap ran?"

Whitman laughed, a harsh, sharp sound like a yapping dog. "Jap don't run for long, not when he thinks he's got a ghost of a chance of winning. The next time he came, he flanked us from the beach, charging up through those palm trees right in front of us. Armistead had anticipated it and had put one of his guns down there. It bloody well chewed Jap up. He backed off after that and did what he should have from the beginning, started using his mortars. Not much you can do to defend against them. But it being night, you could see the flash of the tubes every time a bloody round was shot out of them. By then, one of the Raiders was dead. Armistead took his three remaining fellows and went out. One by one, we saw the flash of his grenades or the rattle of his guns until the mortars were put out of action. But two more of his men were killed. You'll find his Raiders buried right over there." He pointed along the lawn and Josh saw three mounds of dirt with American helmets sitting atop them.

"Where's the fourth one?"

"Half a moment. I'll get to it," Whitman answered gruffly. "A few things you need to understand first. With the mortars knocked out, things got quiet, and I decided to get some sleep. At sunrise, one of my boys woke me, said Armistead and Kimba were gone. My boys were all spooked, started mumbling something about ghosts, their usual idiocy when they can't explain a thing. Then I spotted boot prints leading down to the beach. Marine Corps issue. And small bare feet. You want to know my first thought? I figured they were down there screwing. Don't look at me that way, Commander. A jealous man can't help the way he thinks. I was going to follow them, but then Jap came at us again and I got distracted. Then your United States Army must have fallen on Jap from the rear. Anyway, he withdrew, and when I had time to clear my head, I immediately started looking to find Armistead and my wife. It didn't take me too long to find it."

"It?"

"How's your stomach?" Whitman asked.

"Empty except for the rum," Josh said.

"Let's take a walk." Surprisingly catlike in his movements, Whitman pushed out of the swing and went down the steps and headed down a path that went straight through the palm trees to the sea. Josh followed, and the three bushmen who'd met him on the beach fell in behind, their rifles slung across their shoulders. Josh found Whitman standing beside a rusting fifty-caliber machine gun set on a parapet. "The last Raider, not counting Armistead, was stationed here with a couple of my boys to help serve this gun. When I came down, it was abandoned, just as you see it."

Whitman was a fast walker and took off again, disappearing behind a line of bush that hid the beach. Josh next found him next standing with a significant look on his face beside what was evidently a war canoe. It was an ancient craft, and it was half submerged. "This is a *tomako*," he said. "Truax kept it around to remind him of the old days. Rotted out long ago, but it'll give you an idea of what one looks like."

Josh looked at the canoe. He'd seen one before, on Melagi, where some enterprising natives would paddle you around for two or three cigarettes. As a man of the sea, Josh admired the workmanship of the long, plank-sided, cigar-shaped craft, even though the one before him had seen better days. On its prow was a carving of an ugly, scowling head. "The head represents death," Whitman said, noting where Josh was looking. "A *tomako* is built for one purpose, and that's to kill people. Armistead and Kimba left in one very similar. We found the scrape marks on the beach. Couldn't be from anything else."

"It would take a lot of men to maneuver one of these," Josh said.

"At least fifty, and they were in full headhunting regalia, feathers, cockleshells, beads, tattoos, paint, all of it."

"How do you know that?"

"One of my men saw what happened."

"Can I talk to him?"

"No." Before Josh could ask why, Whitman provided the answer. "He's dead. Japanese sniper. Jap always likes to leave one or two sharpshooters behind. Don't worry. I think we've killed them all."

Josh shook his head. "To the best of my knowledge, one thing Jap doesn't do is dress up in beads and paint and paddle war canoes around. So who manned this *tomako?*"

"Renegades, led by a man named Joe Gimmee. Nasty brute, though he sometimes pretends to be a holy man. He's been trouble in the Solomons for a long time, raiding up and down the islands. He sells himself to the highest bidder. Right now, he works for Jap. I've been fighting him off and on for years. He hates white men especially. Been known to take more than one poor planter's head."

"Missus belong Joe Gimmee," one of the three coast-watchers suddenly interrupted in a low growl. The other two men let their eyes drift over to the one who had spoken, then echoed him. "Missus belong Joe Gimmee." Then all three muttered something together that sounded like a chant and stamped their feet. "We kill Joe Gimmee!" they cried.

"Keep your bloody yaps shut!" Whitman snapped. "You boys. Get!"

Sullenly the three men crept off, but only to the shade provided by an avocado tree, heavy with fruit. "First-class fighting men but so steeped with superstition they can't operate at times," Whitman said dismissively.

Josh found himself impatient. "Look, Whitman, your story's all over the farm. It sounds like now you're saying Armistead and your wife were taken prisoner by this Joe Gimmee. That's a lot different than Armistead running off with your wife."

"As I said, one of my men saw what happened. Come on back to the house and I'll explain."

"You said you'd found 'it.' What was it?"

"I've changed my mind about showing it to you. Come on. There are too many flies here."

"I don't care about the flies," Josh lied, since a big one had just savagely bitten him, leaving a bloody welt on his arm.

Whitman considered Josh for a long second, then seemed to come to a decision. "All right. You might as well see it." He beckoned Josh into a tangle of bush, over a log, and into a clearing.

A sharp, burnt odor penetrated Josh's nostrils, and he saw the remains of a fire in the sand and the greasy black residue of something in the ashes. Whatever it was, the flies were really working it over. "What is it? A pig? Somebody roast a pig down here?"

"It's not a pig," Whitman replied, his voice grinding as if he were having trouble making spit. "Though the bushmen call it long pig. It's a human."

Josh felt a chill travel up and back down his spine. He stared at the black lumps in the spent fire while Whitman used a stick to drag something out of the ashes. He picked the thing up and held it out so that Josh could see what it was, a scorched piece of green cloth, soaked in grease. "Notice the insignia?"

Josh noticed it very well. It was a scrap of uniform, a collar, and on it was the ball-and-anchor insignia of the United States Marine Corps. He felt his stomach turn over.

"This is all that remains of the last of Armistead's Raiders," Whitman said.

"Are you saying somebody *ate* him?"

Whitman tossed the collar remnant back into the horrible remains of the cooking fire. "Oh, they had themselves quite the party, they did," he mused, then stared at the sea with such intensity that Josh would not have been surprised if it had suddenly started boiling. "A man can go insane out here, Thurlow. It ain't difficult. The heat, the bloody bugs, the disease. Add in this war and the cruelty of our enemy. Armistead has probably been insane for a long time. God only knows how Kimba affected him. He wanted her, that much I know, so much he'd do anything to have her."

"I can't believe David had anything to do with this," Josh retorted.

Whitman turned toward him. "How well do you know him?"

"We were on Wilton's Ridge together."

"And he never did anything that made you wonder about him?"

Josh didn't answer, because he couldn't. Yes, there was something about David Armistead that had made him wonder, all right. But did it mean anything? He would have to think about that.

Whitman, in any case, didn't seem to expect an answer. "Oh, how I wish I had killed that girl when I had the chance," he said, repeating what had become a refrain, though Josh noticed wetness at the corners of Whitman's eyes. "I still love her, Thurlow. That's why I never did it, but now I know I must, and your David Armistead, too. Kimba's from Joe Gimmee's tribe. I captured her two years ago. I thought she loved me and would put her heathen ways behind her." He wearily shook his head. "But they say once you've had a taste of long pig, you can never stop."

"That doesn't include David Armistead."

Whitman huffed out a snort. "Doesn't it? I can't imagine Kimba would let him go with her if he didn't have a bite, too. Call it an initiation rite."

Josh said, "If you believe that, you're the one who's insane, Whitman."

"I wish I were, Commander. I wish I were. And before this is over, I suspect you'll wish you were, too."

1 2

The American encampment at Santa Cruz was covered by thousands of Quonset huts, tents, and warehouses. Wooden crates and steel containers and every imaginable kind of machinery and spare parts were piled behind barbed wire fences. Thousands of men roamed the roads and the fields, every one of them apparently on an important mission. It was America with all her industry and might and bureaucracy brought to the South Pacific.

Phimble and Kennedy climbed out on the wing of the Catalina and peered into the endless military city. "How will I find my PT boat?" Kennedy asked.

"That's not my particular problem, Mister Kennedy," Phimble replied. "It's yours. What I'm going to do now is find some avgas, then go back to New Georgia for the skipper."

Kennedy was startled. "You mean you're just going to abandon me?"

Although Phimble had developed an unreasonable dislike for the skinny yellow lieutenant, he was not so thick that he couldn't gin up at least a little sympathy, especially considering the man had just recently been run over by a Japanese destroyer. "Here's Ready," he said, snagging the bosun as he was trying to sneak past. "He'll go with you, help you find your boat. Won't you, Ready?"

"Uh, sure, Mister Phimble. If you say so."

"I do say so. And take Millie, Once, and Again to act as crew. Be in Melagi by tomorrow afternoon, no later."

Kennedy considered Phimble's plan, or lack of it, then put out his hand. He managed a twisted smile. "Don't worry, Ensign. I'll be there."

Phimble glanced at the hand but didn't reach for it. "If you're not at Melagi on time," Phimble said, "you'll answer to Captain Thurlow, not me."

Kennedy slowly lowered his hand. "Why do you dislike me so much?"

"I don't know," Phimble replied. "Sometimes I find I simply don't like a man and it doesn't go any farther than that. There's something about you that rankles me, that's all I can say."

"Is it because I'm rich? Other men have disliked me for that reason, especially since I did nothing to earn my money except being born a rich man's son."

"I told you I don't know why!" Phimble snapped. "Maybe sometimes a man don't like another man and there's no good reason."

"I want you to know," Kennedy said, in a somber tone, "that I'm proud to know you. You have made something of yourself. You are a credit to your race."

Phimble's eyes brimmed with anger. "Mister Kennedy, I know you don't mean nothing by your remark beyond a compliment. But I must tell you I'm an American, and that's all I am. Now, sir, it's time for an end to talk. Go find your boat. I'll see you in Melagi tomorrow."

Kennedy shrugged, then walked down the wing, sat on its tip, and eased down onto the pontoon and thence to the beach. There, he stood unsteadily while pushing his fist into the small of his back. Phimble watched him and felt moved to apologize, but he didn't. Ready had meanwhile accomplished a quick calculation, finishing it by counting on his fingers. "I think it ain't possible for us to get up to Melagi by tomorrow afternoon, Mister Phimble," he griped, "given what time it is right now and the miles we'd have to cover even if we was sitting on that boat this minute."

"Stop thinking," Phimble growled. "You know thinking is bad for you out here. That's the problem with Mister Kennedy. He thinks too much. Now go find his damn PT boat for him and run on up to Melagi quick as you can."

"How about Marvin? Can he go with us?"

"If he wants to."

"How about Dave?"

"He stays with me. I'm afraid one of these Santa Cruz boys would try to kidnap him."

"How about Pogo?"

"For God's sake, Ready! Do I have to do all the thinking around here? All right. Take Pogo if you want him! But if you do, put him in some utilities. Otherwise, you'll never get anywhere. All these rear area commandos would be stopping you to take pictures."

Ready eyed Kennedy, who was still forlornly pushing his fist into his back. "Poor man. He looks like he's about to keel over."

Phimble looked at Kennedy, then allowed a little charity. "Don't forget it was just last week he got his butt run over by a Jap tin can. That can tend to make a man unsteady. Now listen, Ready, I'm counting on you to take care of him and the other boys. You understand?"

Ready guessed he understood, although he didn't like it. He said "Aye, aye, sir," and sought out Pogo inside the Catalina and told him what it would take for him to go on this particular adventure. The bushman agreed and climbed into a pair of utilities but couldn't get his big, flat feet into boots. He also refused to take Dave's feathers out of his hair. "Dave, him magic," the diminutive bushman said.

"It ain't GI, Pogo," Ready said.

"Magic belong Pogo, him happy too much. GI belong Pogo, him no care."

Ready gave up and sneaked Pogo past Phimble, who was in the cockpit yelling over the radio at someone about avgas. Once, Again, Marvin, and Millie met him on the wing. "All right, boys," Ready said. "Here we go."

Ready shepherded the boys down onto the sand. Kennedy seemed genuinely delighted to see them. "Well, let's find ourselves a PT boat," he said. "Does anybody know the way?"

When Thurlow's boys just stared at him, Ready came alongside and whispered, "Never admit you don't know something even if you don't, sir. You're an officer, after all."

Kennedy looked at the boys, who were all looking back at him with dubious expressions, except Pogo, who for no apparent reason had his back turned. "I have no idea where to find this PT boat," he confessed, to Ready's obvious chagrin. "But I will do my best to figure it out with your help. Now, first, I'd like to know if anyone has an opinion as to which direction you think we should go."

Each boy, without so much as a glance at the others, pointed in a different direction, except for Pogo, who had now lain down in the sand with his hands behind his head, apparently to take a nap. "You see, Mister Kennedy?" Ready said in a low voice that could be heard by anyone who cared, "You've got them all confused. Just pick a direction."

Kennedy picked a direction, Pogo was roused, and an hour later they were a sad little retinue deep inside the endless camp. Led by the limping

Kennedy, they'd traveled across a myriad of roads and crossroads, all crowded with soldiers, sailors, marines, and airmen dressed in a variety of uniforms going this way and that. They'd even encountered some honest-to-God female nurses, dressed in their crisp, starched whites, who giggled at the dirty boys and the thin, jaundiced, but not entirely unhandsome lieutenant. They were also not fooled by Pogo's utilities and thought he was "just the cutest thing"; they made him stop and get his picture made with them, since one of the nurses was carrying around a Kodak 35 mm camera. Kennedy tried to strike up small talk with the nurses, none of whom was a knockout but who were all pleasant to look at, and was astonished when he couldn't do it. He supposed he'd lost the knack, another price of his war in the South Pacific. Instead, he served as photographer, clicked off several shots of the nurses posing with Pogo, then handed the camera back, and the nurses went on their way, their glances over their shoulders reserved entirely for the little bushman.

Kennedy's morale kept dropping. The pain in his feet and knees joined the pain in his back. His entire body was a walking torment. A marine passed, carrying a Thompson submachine gun with a cylindrical ammunition magazine. It was a tommy gun worthy of Al Capone. At the sight of it, Kennedy reflected on his father's reputation of being a bootlegger during Prohibition. Kennedy also remembered that his classmates at Choate were forever giving him the business about his father making his fortune from the illegal sale of alcohol, as if their fathers and ancestors were any better, those descendents of the *Mayflower* who'd made their fortunes in rum, molasses, and slaves. But Kennedy also recalled one of the boys who'd taken up for him: David Roosevelt Armistead.

With the pain coursing through his legs and back so intense he could scarcely stand it, Kennedy stopped and peered at a signpost with a dozen arrow-shaped boards aiming in different directions, each with numbers written on it. "There's a code to these signs," he said, "but damned if I know what they mean."

"Oh, sir," Ready said in a low, confidential voice. "Don't say that."

"Dammit, Ready!" Kennedy railed. "I did what you said. I picked a direction, and we've walked for miles. Now we're lost, and it does no good not to admit it."

Once, Millie, and Again came up alongside. Pogo sat down in the middle of the road and patted Marvin on the head. The little dog grinned and thumped his tail in the dust. "We asked a sailor about five miles back where we could find your PT boat," Once said.

Kennedy's astonishment registered on his face. "You did? Why didn't you tell me?"

"You didn't ask," Once replied while Again and Millie vaguely looked off in the distance.

Kennedy pressed his eyes closed, then said, "You're right. I didn't ask. But what did he say?"

"He said to go down to a place called Tugu Beach. Supposed to be some docks down there and boats anchored all over the place, big and small. He said you can't miss it if you go the right way. Of course, this ain't the right way."

Ready strolled by, humming. In the middle of the hum, he said, "Don't let on you didn't know that, sir."

"Are you going to yell at us, sir?" Once asked.

"I have no intention of yelling at anyone," Kennedy said, even though he felt like it. "Now, which one are you, Once or Again?"

"I'm Once, sir. You can tell me by this here little dimple in my right cheek. I got it when I fell on an end table when I was but three."

"Thank you, Once. That's good to know. Now, which is the correct way?"

Once perused the signpost. "That number right there, 4125. That's the number for Tugu Beach."

Kennedy looked at the number and wondered why it didn't just say "Tugu Beach." Oh, the navy had its ways! He just wanted to sit down for a while and take off his shoes and rub his feet and let his knees rest and brace his back up against something so maybe it would stop hurting. Instead, he said, "Let's go."

"Wait a minute, sir," Ready said.

Kennedy had taken but a single, limping step. He stopped and dropped his chin on his chest. "What is it?"

"This asking questions seems like a good idea, sir."

"Yes," Kennedy agreed. "Yes, it does. Thank you, Ready. You are a great help to me."

"Mister Phimble said I was supposed to be, sir." He snagged a passing navy chief. "Chief, if one was to go down to Tugu Beach to get oneself a boat, who should one see?"

The chief, an ancient character with a mop of longish white hair that spilled out beneath his hat, replied, "You're kidding, right? Nick, of course." He eyed Pogo. "Say, where's that man's boots, and why does he have feathers in his hair?"

"He lost his boots, and his feathers are camouflage," Kennedy explained. "Now, Chief. Help me out here. Who is this Nick?"

The chief was clearly puzzled. "Why, sir, everybody knows Nick."

"Well, pretend we don't," Kennedy replied in a voice as tired and frustrated as he felt. "How do we find him?"

The chief looked at Kennedy as if waiting for the punch line. When it didn't come, he said, "When you get to Tugu Beach, ask anybody. They'll tell you where to find Nick."

"Thank you, Chief," Kennedy said, giving up on extracting any other information from the man. "Ready, let the chief's arm go. That's good. Thank you, Chief. Good-bye, good-bye. All right, men, you heard what the chief said. Tugu Beach, just ask for Nick. We'll be there in no time and soon acquire our PT boat. Follow me."

Kennedy stepped off smartly, only to start limping again on the very next step. Ready fell in beside him, and they soldiered on. The other boys, including Marvin, watched until the lieutenant and the bosun disappeared around a turn, then slipped off on their own.

1 3

Josh Thurlow was somewhat forlorn, generally irritated, and not a little gloomy, which all added up to an unusual unhappiness besotting his mind. He sat with his arms around his knees on the narrow brown beach and decided he would not see Phimble return before the next morning. The Japanese Rufes out of Kolombangara especially liked to hunt at night, and catching a big fat American float plane lumbering around looking for a place to land in the dark would suit them just fine.

Seaward, the South Pacific was busily presenting Josh one of its patented mighty sunsets, the descending crimson orb obliterating fleets of clouds that looked as if they consisted of mercury rimmed with blood. Josh admired the heavenly glory, though he thought it a bit gaudy, and reflected that he missed the blander sunsets on Killakeet Island that somehow brought a proper calm to the end of what might have been a tumultuous day.

Not a breath of air was moving and it was still very hot, causing the sweat to run down Josh's back and soak his shirt and the waist of his utilities trousers. It was out of the question to take off his shirt. On every inch of exposed skin, there was already a squadron of bloodsucking insects competing to see who got to bite him next. He swatted at a mosquito that landed on his face and then crushed another on the back of his neck that had already bitten him, leaving behind a bloody, swollen wound, and then he initiated the Solomon Islands salute by waving a hand across his eyes to keep the no-see-ums from climbing into them.

Josh was having trouble getting the recollection of the charred, meaty hunk of human being in the ashes out of his mind. He had seen many dead men, and killed more than a few of them, some so near he could smell their breath, and the peculiar coppery odor of their sweat when they knew they were about to die. He had heard them cry for their mothers or their wives or their emperor or just themselves as their lives leaked inexorably away. These moments were horrible, but he never lost sleep over them. They were part of war. But seeing proof that a human would eat another human had so repulsed him, struck him as so savage, so *inhuman,* it was nearly beyond his ability to absorb it.

When he stopped to think about it, though, wasn't this the place for it, after all? The natives of these islands had for centuries practiced cannibalism and headhunting. It was only the arrival of the European missionaries that had stopped the barbarous custom of eating one's enemy or carrying off his head. *But was it still in the air, like a disease, waiting to enter a man too weak to resist?*

Josh was not a particularly religious man, but, like most sailors, he was prone to being more than a little superstitious. He wondered now if it was possible that angry, evil little gods inhabited some places and awaited the soft and impressionable man. Were the Solomon Islands themselves responsible for the horror he'd seen? It had been documented that starving Japanese troops on Guadalcanal had eaten their own dead. And, in at least one instance, there was evidence that a downed American pilot had been cut open and his liver cooked by a Japanese colonel on Kolombangara who'd shared the bounty with his staff. Was it possible, as Whitman had conjectured, that Armistead had gone insane, whether because of a perverted kind of obsessive love or simply the rigors of life and war in the Solomon Islands? Was any man immune to insanity, given the right balance of circumstances?

Josh recalled the long battle for Wilton's Ridge when a thousand fresh, eager troops of the Imperial Japanese Army slammed into a hundred Raiders commanded by Armistead. The result was that every one of the Japanese troops was either gunned down, bayoneted, clubbed, stomped, or strangled to death. It was a slaughter, pure and simple. The lust for blood had been high on both sides, but it had been greater on the American side. When Josh had taken off his boots after that battle, he had found them filled with a black, sticky goo. Only later did he realize it was blood. He had been literally wading in it.

Now he recalled Armistead during the battle. Josh had noticed almost immediately a reticence to do what had to be done, which was to slaughter the enemy without remorse. During the first phase of the battle, Armistead had been quick to cease fire, allowing the Japanese time to withdraw. He seemed to be surprised when Jap had come back at him. "You're going to have to kill every one of them, David," Josh had patiently explained. "They ain't going to quit."

Armistead understood. After that, he'd kept up the fire until the last Japanese had fallen. Josh had further illustrated what needed to be done by crawling out with his Aleut ax and killing the Japanese soldiers who were wounded or simply playing dead, waiting to snipe at any marine who raised his head. The next time, he'd taken Armistead out with him and taught him how to cut a throat. The lieutenant had vomited the first time he'd done it. But he'd kept cutting throats.

Yet even though Armistead had learned the hard lessons of war with an intractable enemy, it had seemed to Josh that he'd never allowed himself to do more than what needed to be done. To stay sane in a situation like that, Josh had learned, you had to allow yourself a certain temporary insanity, to detach yourself from reality so that it did not become real but was more like a dream. After the battle for Wilton's Ridge was over, and the last Imperial Japanese troop killed, the other Raiders were jubilant in their victory, but Josh recalled that Armistead was not jubilant. He seemed *self-absorbed*—that was the word for it. When Major Wilton came up to visit the line and saw all that had been done, he pumped Josh's hand, then Armistead's. "By God, boy, somebody deserves a Medal of Honor for this," Wilton told Armistead, then looked at Josh. "Captain Thurlow, if you'll co-sign my recommendation, I know Colonel Burr and Admiral Halsey will approve this fine young man his rightful due." Then he went on down the line, slapping backs and generally celebrating.

Armistead watched Wilton go, and Josh had never seen such misery on a man's face. "Me with the Medal of Honor," he said in a dull voice. "Father would be pleased." He turned to Josh. "But don't agree to it, Josh. I don't deserve it and I don't want it. Most of all, I want to forget everything that's happened here." He looked out over the battlefield where the bodies still lay. "Why wouldn't they quit? I kept giving them the opportunity."

"Jap doesn't have it in him to quit, David," Josh explained.

Armistead sat heavily on a stack of sandbags. "When I was sixteen, I visited Japan with my father. He was interested in a partnership with a small factory there. I found the Japanese to be a lovely people. When I visited their homes, I was treated with the utmost courtesy and respect."

Josh did his best to explain the difference, at least as he understood it.

"The Japanese are a stubborn people, David, and when they get a thing in their heads, they have trouble getting it out. Right now, the men in Tokyo who started this war are trying to to bloody our noses down here in the Solomons so we'll ask to parley and let them keep what they've won. It's our duty to make certain they understand that ain't a possibility by killing as many of their boys as we can."

Armistead had lowered his head then and wept. Josh did what he could to keep his men from seeing their lieutenant give in to such foolishness, but some had seen. Josh knew then that he could never agree to a Medal of Honor for Armistead. It wouldn't set a good example. Crying needed to wait until after the war. Plenty of time then to do it, if one was still alive.

Josh wished now he'd never agreed to this cockamamie assignment, but he'd had no choice after Burr had said one word: "Hypo." That was the same as hearing directly from Admiral Nimitz and Secretary Knox that the Japanese were somehow involved with Armistead's disappearance. Hypo was the secret name for the team of cryptographers in Nimitz's employ who'd cracked the Japanese code. Halsey had sent the word to Josh through Burr's mouth to let him know that there was Japanese radio traffic concerning Armistead. But what was it? Perhaps it had been unclear and that was why nothing more was passed on. Or perhaps Halsey's admonition to kill Armistead at the first opportunity told Josh all he needed to know.

Josh watched the sun continue to sink into the sea, then looked around and wondered what he should do to prepare for the night. He considered returning to the plantation, to bunk down with Whitman, but then he heard the low thrum of an engine seaward. The hairs stood up on the back of his neck as a boat slid around the northern point of the lagoon, its rakish prow identifying it clearly as a Japanese barge, one of the landing craft used to resupply or bring ashore troops.

Josh melted into the shadowy bush at the edge of the beach. The barge apparently had been skirting a reef, as it abruptly turned and headed directly toward him. He considered slipping away but then decided it was his duty to find out what the barge was doing. It might be landing troops. If so, he would need to warn Whitman. He drew his pistol. When the prow of the barge dropped onto the sand, Josh saw that it was empty. A Japanese sailor got off and proceeded to walk up and down the beach, his head cocked as if listening for something.

Josh heard it before the sailor did. Japanese troops, with that odd high-pitched natter peculiar to the Imperial Army, were headed his way.

Josh understood now that the barge had come to evacuate Japanese soldiers off New Georgia. He was caught, as it were, between the devil and the deep blue sea, and about all his pistol was good for now was to shoot himself between the eyes so as avoid the misery of certain capture, sure torture, and a slow death.

1 4

Kennedy and Ready, their morale sunk as low as the sun, continued to hike through the sprawling camp. Hundreds of soldiers, sailors, and marines passed them by with scarcely a glance. Even a few natives walked along, somewhat civilized in appearance by the absence of bones through their noses or anything stuck through their ears. They were dressed in a variety of uniform castoffs. "Hullo, Joe!" they effusively greeted any American they encountered.

Kennedy and Ready trudged past yards stacked high with generators, engines, transmissions, bulldozers, trucks, jeeps, and spare parts of every kind. They plodded past countless pallets weighted down with mounds of uniforms and helmets and mosquito nets and blankets and pistol belts and knapsacks; past piles of artillery shells and rifle ammunition and trip flares and satchel charges and blocks of TNT and a variety of specialized bombs; past ball fields and gymnasiums and outdoor movie theaters and mess halls and officer's clubs and hospitals and military police stations. They walked so far that Kennedy's limp became a painful, wrenching process of putting one foot in front of the other. "I've reached the end of my string," he finally confessed.

Ready took stock of his surroundings and was immediately encouraged by what he saw. "Look, sir!"

Kennedy looked after Ready's point and saw a sign that read NICK'S TROPICAL LAUNDRY. "So what?" he demanded. "I don't have any laundry, and neither do you."

"Nick's the guy we're supposed to see about your boat. Don't you remember?"

Kennedy guessed he did remember, but it didn't much matter.

He couldn't go any farther. "I'm done in, Bosun," he confessed. "Completely spent. My feet hurt, my legs hurt, and my back is sprung. Mister Phimble is right about me. All I'm going to do is let you down."

"Oh, no, sir!" Ready exclaimed. "You're doing a wonderful job. Here, lean on me. Come on. It's going to be fine."

Kennedy put his arm around Ready's shoulder and the two kept moving, though each step for Kennedy was misery. Finally they arrived at a big concrete dock fronting a harbor filled with rows of anchored barges, landing craft, small freighters, and a variety of other small vessels, which might, they hoped, include at least one PT boat. Kennedy, still leaning on Ready, squinted vainly into the gathering darkness to see what they had come so far to find. "I suppose my boat's out there somewhere," he said. "But how do we requisition her?"

"Nick, sir. We got to find that Nick," Ready urged.

Kennedy sat down on a stack of lumber. "Then go find him, Bosun. I'm just going to rest here for a while."

Ready could see the lieutenant was truly done in. "I'll be right back," he said, and went off looking for someone who might know something about Nick. He soon discovered a guard shack at a gate that opened into a fenced-in compound with a sign that read:

SOUTH PACIFIC COMBAT LOGISTICS COMMAND
Rear Admiral Daniel M. Klibanoff, Commanding

"Say, bub," Ready said to the guard, who was all gussied up in sailor whites, "I'm looking for a guy named Nick. You know where I might find him?"

"That's his office over there," the guard said, pointing with his truncheon to a plywood-sided building that had a deck overlooking the harbor. Men were going in and out of it, a constant stream.

"Is he there, you think?"

"Oh, yeah. Nick's pretty much always there."

"How do I get past you?"

"Getting past me ain't hard as long as you're going in. It's getting out that's the problem. You go in empty-handed and come out with anything, don't matter if it's a bullet or a tank, I'll need to see your paperwork."

Ready went after Kennedy, told him what he'd found out, and helped him through the gate to the building where Nick was supposed to be. Kennedy hobbled up the steps, then sank down on the deck, his back against the wall, his eyes closed against the pain. Ready peered through the open door into a big open area, where men were going in every direction, papers were flying, typewriters were clattering, file cabinets were being opened and closed, and adding machine handles were being pulled. There was an electric excitement about the place with the singular exception of a long line of men who stood dolefully before a closed door. Ready noticed that the line contained a mixed lot, both enlisted men and officers. One of them, Ready noticed, was even a full navy captain. He picked out a fellow bosun who looked halfway friendly. "Excuse me, Boats, but who's behind that closed door?"

The bosun, who held a sheath of forms, looked at Ready as if he were insane and replied, "Why, Nick, of course."

"Why are all these people waiting to see Nick?"

"Because we need stuff." He held up his forms. "Nick's the man what's got it and can give it to us."

"He's in charge of everything in this yard?"

"Not officially. That would be Admiral Klibanoff. But Nick's got the juice."

"The juice?"

"The power. You know."

"How long have you been waiting?"

"I got here an hour before sunup. People in front of me got here yesterday. People behind me will be here tomorrow, or maybe longer."

Ready came back outside. "We're screwed, stewed, and tattooed," he announced to Kennedy, who had dropped his forehead to rest on his knees.

"What are they doing in there?" Kennedy asked, his voice muffled since he was more or less speaking into his trousers.

"I don't know, but whatever it is, I never seen so many people doing it so hard."

"Did you see Nick?"

"There's a line about a mile long waiting for him."

Neither Kennedy nor Ready had noticed a young naval officer sitting at a bamboo table over in a far corner of the deck. The table had an excellent view of the sea into which the sun was busily setting, throwing up its usual brilliant tropical spokes of blood reds, lime greens, amber golds, and pieces-of-eight silvers in an apparent desperate attempt to be noticed. So infused were they with their own problems, they continued to not notice either the sunset or the table or the officer who sat at it until he piped up and said, "It has been my observation that work tends to expand to fill the time available. In this case, the only thing those clerks in there have in any abundance is time, and so they have learned to fill it. For instance, when one of them has an idea, he writes a note and sends it to a dozen other clerks who then read about the idea, file it, and send back their replies, with carbon copies to other possibly interested parties, all of which also have to be signed and filed and so forth. Soon, there is a veritable blizzard of notes and copies and forms going back and forth long after the original note and its purpose have been forgotten. Such is the nature of bureaucracy, gentlemen, and on which our civilization rests."

Ready helped Kennedy to his feet, and they approached the officer, who wore a crisp set of naval khakis and a wide-brimmed and thoroughly ridiculous pith helmet. Before him on the table was a bottle of actual whiskey, the kind with a label and everything, and a bucket of real, honest-to-God, impossible to ever find in the South Pacific *ice*. It was all Kennedy could do to keep from grabbing a cube and wiping it on his face.

"Pull up a chair," the officer said, and Kennedy and Ready did. The man reached into the bucket, casually dropped a few ice cubes into two glasses he took from a bamboo cabinet beside the table, poured some whiskey in them, and slid them across the table. "Be my guest, boys. Lieutenant, how'd you get so beat up?"

"Lost my boat in Blackett Strait up by Kolombangara," Kennedy answered while taking the glass. He pressed it to his forehead.

"What happened?"

"Run down by a Jap destroyer. Cut us in two. Two of my men were killed. We were castaway on an island. I managed to get cut up on the coral before we got rescued."

"Tough luck," the officer replied. "Drink up, so I can give you some more."

Kennedy drank, and the man refilled his glass and Ready's, too, seeing as how it was completely empty, including the ice, which the bosun was heavily crunching between his teeth.

"Oh, thank you, sir," Ready said, and knocked back the refreshed whiskey in one drink. He whistled out a breath. "Do you work here, sir?"

"Sure do."

"Some place."

"It is that."

"You know this guy Nick?"

"You betcha."

"He must be the busiest man in the South Pacific."

"Nick is not busy at all," he answered.

"That line inside says otherwise," Ready pointed out.

The lieutenant took on a smug countenance. "Well, you see, I happen to be Nick, and as you may notice, the sun is over the yardarm and therefore so am I." He stuck out his hand to Ready and then to Kennedy. "Charmed, I'm sure."

"Bosun O'Neal, sir," Ready said.

"Kennedy," Kennedy said, with as much energy as he could muster.

Nick had deep-set, nearly black eyes, which inspected Kennedy with intelligent interest. "I know who you are, Kennedy. There's been a lot of talk about you ever since you got out here. I am truly sorry about your boat. How might I be of service to you?"

"I'm down to pick up another one. The *PT-59*. I was told you're the man to see."

Nick raised his bushy black eyebrows. "Do you have the necessary paperwork?"

"Paperwork? No, but *PT-59* belongs to PT Squadron 1, of which I am a member. I'm sure you could look it up."

Nick peered across the harbor. The sun had finally given up and allowed the sea to swallow it for another day. The boats and barges and other vessels anchored there had turned into purple shadows. Nick shook his head and sighed a quiet sigh. "No paperwork. This is most troubling."

"I need your help," Kennedy said. "One lieutenant to another."

"We're on a mission," Ready added, in an attempt to be helpful while also covering his move to the whiskey bottle for another pour.

Nick ignored Ready's addition to his glass. "I wish I could help you, old man," he said to Kennedy, "but my hands are tied. Proper paperwork is a necessity of the supply business."

"Well, what do I have to do, Nick?" Kennedy asked.

"Do?" Nick stretched the word out about a mile. "Dooooooooooooo?"

"Yes, do. There must be something I can do to get past this paperwork thing."

"Are you suggesting a bribe of some sort, Kennedy?"

"Of course not, Nick."

"I didn't think so. Honesty is an attribute required of an effective supply officer. If the word got out I took bribes, do you think they'd be lined up at my door? No, indeed. They'd be seeking me out in my living quarters, or ambushing me on this very deck when I take a moment to admire a glorious South Pacific sunset, all the while trying to slip me greenbacks. No, without the proper paperwork, I'm afraid I could not possibly release a

PT boat to you. Oh, what's this? Wipe those unhappy frowns off your faces, you two! Look, how about some poker to take your mind off your troubles? There's a game tonight at the Tugu Beach O-Club Annex. That would be about half a mile up that way. Just follow the road. How about it, Kennedy? You look like a man who knows his way around a deck of cards."

"Actually," Kennedy answered, "I play a mean game of whist."

"I'm sure that will be helpful," Nick replied without a trace of irony. "So how about it? The game starts at nineteen thirty hours. Stakes are but a thousand dollars."

Kennedy paled, which meant he turned a lighter shade of yellow. "A thousand dollars! Too rich for my blood."

"Come, now. Do you expect me to believe a Kennedy of Massachusetts can't afford a little poker action?"

"It's my father who's got the bucks, not me. Anyway, it never occurred to me to bring a lot of cash to a combat zone. I've got maybe five dollars in my pocket, and I borrowed that."

"Well, never mind, your credit is good with me," Nick replied. "I'll front you."

Ready made a signal to Kennedy that he'd like to talk somewhere other than the table in front of Nick. His signal consisted of bobbing up and down in his chair, flapping his lips soundlessly, and jerking his head over his shoulder.

"Bosun, what the hell's wrong with you?" Kennedy demanded. "Are you having a fit?"

"I think the bosun would like a private word," Nick observed. He opened his hands. "Please feel free."

Ready helped Kennedy to a far corner of the deck. "Get in that poker game, Mister Kennedy," he advised. "You could maybe make friends with this character and he'll pony up our PT boat. Or you might win so much of his money that he'll be glad to give it to you. What's the worse could happen?"

"That I'd be out at least a thousand dollars, you twit!"

"It's our only chance, sir," Ready said.

"I think I'll go check myself into the hospital."

"Oh, please, sir, you can't do that! Play poker and I'm sure everything will be all right."

"What's wrong with you, Ready? Don't you know when you're licked?"

"No, sir. Just like you don't know it, neither."

Kennedy gave Ready a long, hard stare, then released a sigh. "Oh, all right." They went back to Nick, who had refreshed their drinks. "I'll play," Kennedy said, while mentally kicking himself for being an easily manipulated idiot.

Ready tossed back the fresh pour, then held his glass out for another one. "We should drink to it," he proposed.

Nick laughed and poured Ready another drink. He held up his glass. "To the poker game!"

"To the poker game!" Ready chorused, and he and Nick drank while Kennedy toyed with his glass. When finally he drank, he did so beneath Nick's benevolent smile.

PART II

I am black, but comely, O ye daughters of Jerusalem, as the tents of Kedar, as the curtains of Solomon.—Song of Solomon, chapter 1, verse 5

1 5

"Mastah," a feminine voice whispered, so near that it made Josh jump. Then he felt a hand in his, and he smelled the perfume of sweet coconut oil. "This way, mastah," the voice said.

He questioned the voice. "Who are you?"

"The Marie you met this morning, mastah. Come with me, please."

Josh had no choice but follow the tug of her hand. Either that or the Japanese would get him. They'd probably get him anyway. All around was the dull noise of men in boots on moss-covered rocks, the swish of fronds being pushed aside, low, mumbled curses as wait-a-minute vines tripped and thorns stabbed, the clunk of canteens.

The girl stopped suddenly, then backed into Josh and put his arms around her. He felt the velvety softness of her bare breasts against his forearms, her curly hair pushed into his chin, her warm, moist scent even greater in his nostrils. She clutched his hands insistently, a gesture meant to still him. The shadows of Japanese soldiers flitted past like phantoms. Then she took his hand and pulled him forward again. "We go up," she said after some minutes of slipping through the darkness.

Josh dropped her hand so he could clutch roots and small trees to help haul himself up a steep earthen rise. Then they were in the open. An ebony sky floated overhead, strewn with bright, twinkling stars. Thick grass brushed at Josh's waist. Her hand found his again and pulled him along. "Where are we going?" Josh asked.

"A village. It will be safe there."

"How do you know?"

"When the Japoni came, the people of this village ran away. Japoni took all their pigs and chickens, and now they have no reason to go there."

That sounded reasonable, so Josh continued to follow the woman up and down small hills, along well-trod paths and those that were overgrown. Josh had a good sense of direction and sensed they were making a circle and moving back toward the sea. Sure enough, they popped out onto a broad savannah, and in the moon's silvery light he could see straw and bamboo huts set along a white sand beach. The girl led him through the village. All was silent, not even a barking dog, and the empty doors of the huts were like gaping dark mouths. At the beach was a small round hut. In front of it, two palm trees bent toward one another; a rope hammock swayed between them, rocking gently in the light breeze. "Are you hungry?" she asked.

Josh confessed he hadn't eaten since breakfast. She bade him sit on the ground, and it wasn't long before she was cooking something in a pan over a fire in a cooking pit. It turned out to be breadfruit and yams (where she got them, he did not know), delivered up on a small banana leaf, and a drink in an earthen mug. He ate the food, which was tasteless but filling, and then sniffed the contents of the mug. It smelled terribly foul. "What is this?"

"Kava," she said. "It is very good for what ails you now. It will help you to sleep. Tomorrow we will go to Minister Clarence's mission."

"Why will we go there?"

"To see Minister Clarence," she answered as if he were daft.

To be polite, Josh drank the kava. It was bitter stuff, and slimy to the tongue. Still, once started, it seemed impossible to stop. When she saw that he had emptied the mug, the girl refilled it, and he drank that, too. Pretty soon, he discovered he wanted more kava even though it had numbed his lips and tongue. "Yes, kava does that to a man," she said when he commented on it, then added, "And a woman." That was when Josh noticed that she was also drinking kava and that her eyes had grown into large black pools.

Though he was feeling warm and fuzzy, Josh recalled that he was on a mission and then further recalled the notebook in his shirt pocket. He took it out and opened it to the first page. "My darling girl," he said, then stopped short, surprised that he would call her a darling girl. He inwardly shrugged it off as a harmless term of endearment and continued. "Do you by any chance know Kimba Whitman?"

"She is Mastah Whitman's wife," the girl said.

"Do you know where she is?"

"With Mastah Whitman, I would suppose."

Josh nodded, then went to the only other name in his notebook. "Would you happen to know a man by the name of Joe Gimmee?"

"Of course," she answered as she poured him some more kava and then topped off her own cup. "Everyone knows Joe Gimmee."

Josh peered at the woman, this lovely creature of soft curves who had about her a scent that was musk and coconut and sweet fruit and—*never mind*—he struggled with his thoughts, which seemed to be draped in a gauzy veil. He felt that perhaps, to help him think, he should put away his notebook and drink some more kava, which he did. But then he thought he was being derelict in his duty, so he worked hard to ask her another question, although his mind did not seem to want to cooperate. Still, with great difficulty, he managed it. "So who is this Joe Gimmee everybody knows?"

"Joe Gimmee is Joe Gimmee," she answered in a tone that said that settled the issue. She put down her mug and came crawling over to Josh on her hands and knees and then snuggled into his arms. He put down his mug, too, and thought that there was never a more darling girl than this, no, never in the entire history of the world. *Except for Dosie Crossan, of course,* a little voice said in his head. *Dosie. Dosie.* The name rang like a distant bell, like the one in the steeple of the old Killakeet Church of the Mariner. He thought he actually heard that very same church bell ring, and then he thought that he also saw his father's lighthouse. He watched its great sweep of light into the darkness like spokes of fire, letting all who sailed by those awful shoals know that there was a family on guard for them, the Thurlows of Killakeet Island. And there, standing at the rail of the lighthouse cupola, was a man and a woman. The woman's hat was caught by the wind and sent flying. *Oh,* she cried. *Hold me, Josh. Hold me and never let me go. I'm so frightened.*

"My darling girl," Josh whispered, taking Dosie into his arms. "My darling, darling girl."

"Yes, mastah," Dosie answered, only it wasn't Dosie but a beautiful black woman, and the tropical wind was picking up, near to a breeze. Josh was glad that there was a breeze, but wait, it was the woman blowing across his face with her pursed lips, a strange gesture, difficult to interpret, but then she leaned back on a mat of woven palm fronds and drew him down on top of her, a gesture that needed no interpretation at all. Josh wondered where his utilities were. He did not appear to be wearing them, although he didn't recall taking them off, either. Yet another strange dream overtook him, of him removing the woman's lap-lap, and her wrapping her legs around him, and then he concluded that since it was only a dream, he should go ahead and enjoy it.

He also noticed that he was happy.

Kava did that to a man.

1 6

Darkness had settled over Santa Cruz but powerful generators were humming, keeping the camp brightly lit. There seemed to be no fear of Japanese bombing raids. To pass the time while waiting for the poker game to begin, Kennedy used the five bucks he had in his pocket to treat Ready to a meal at a roadside stand. The stand was identified by a sign that read NICK'S TROPICAL HAMBURGER JOINT.

"What's in these?" Ready asked after he'd been served a cheeseburger that didn't much look like a cheeseburger at all. It was a slab of unidentifiable brown meat brushed with a pale yellow substance that had the consistency of lard, all served up between two slices of limp, doughy white bread.

"You don't like it, don't eat it, that's my advice," the short-order cook replied. He was a burly fat creature with a cigarette dangling from his lips and a dirty apron around his neck. A tattoo of Betty Boop was on his hairy shoulder. Betty was wearing a grass skirt and a garland of flowers that just barely covered her breasts.

Kennedy also ordered a "cheeseburger" and a beer. He took a sip from the long-necked bottle. "Not bad," he announced, and then inspected the label: CASTLEMAINE XXXX BITTER ALE, PRODUCT OF AUSTRALIA. "How'd you get Castlemaine all the way out here?"

"Nick got it, all's I know," the cook replied. "Nick can get anything."

"This the same Nick that runs the supply outfit down by the beach?"

"Ain't no other Nick on this island, bub. Nick's Nick and that's an end to it."

Kennedy drained his beer and, noticing that Ready had long since emptied his, paid for two more. "I'm curious," he said to the cook. "What do you do besides work here?"

"Nothing else," he said.

"You're paid by the navy?"

"I'm in it, ain't I?"

"This stand make money?"

"Sure does."

"Who do you give it to?"

"Nick. See his name on the sign?"

"What does he do with it?"

The cook shrugged. "He slips me a little. Otherwise, I never asked him. It's his money."

Kennedy and Ready carried their food and drink to the next stand, this one with a sign that read NICK'S SOUVENIRS OF THE SOUTH PACIFIC. It didn't look very prosperous. A fat brown woman in a flowery gown peered at them from behind the counter displaying a sorry collection of carved coconut heads, a few uninspired bead and shell necklaces, and a couple of wilted grass skirts. "You like?" she asked while grinning at them with black, broken teeth.

A tall, balding man wearing wire-rimmed glasses and dressed in the khakis of a naval lieutenant commander was also inspecting the goods. "Mostly junk," he pronounced.

"You no like, you no buy," the woman snapped.

"Oh, come on, Mary," the commander replied. "Nobody wants this stuff. When are you going to get some decent souvenirs?"

"Ask Nick," she said. "You think you so damned smart. You asshole, that's what."

"Now, Mary," the commander simpered. "You shouldn't use such language."

"Foh dollah," Mary said, ignoring the officer and focusing on Kennedy, who was fingering one of the grass skirts.

"Is this real?" Kennedy asked.

"I can tell you," the commander said. "No, it's not. Nick's got some boys who whip all this stuff up in a back room. Look here at the waistband of the grass skirt. It's GI issue, and those are GI shoelaces that keep it tied together."

"Son of a bitch," Mary growled.

The commander stuck out his hand to Kennedy. "Jim Michener. Don't let the insignia fool you. I'm a navy historian, out here to keep track of this mess for future generations. I do a little intelligence work, too, just for fun. This is Mary. She's Tonkinese. Bunch of them down here out of Hanoi and Saigon. Great merchants, but they'll cheat you if you don't stay on your toes."

"Bloody bastard!" Mary hissed.

"Bloody Mary!" Michener responded with a chuckle.

Kennedy introduced himself. "An honor to meet you," Michener responded. "It's good to see a man such as yourself out here. We're going to need men like you from important families to go back and tell the story of the South Pacific to the public. I think mostly they hear about North Africa and Italy. After we invade France, the Pacific theater will be practically ignored."

"It's understandable," Kennedy replied. "Europe is, after all, the mother of American history."

"Yes," Michener replied, "but the future of America is here in the Pacific."

"I agree, yet our path will be difficult. 'And when your goal is nearest, the end for others sought, watch Sloth and heathen Folly bring all your hope to nought.'"

"Well, I see you're up on your Kipling," Michener said in an admiring tone.

While Kennedy and Michener wandered off to discuss history, poetry, and politics, Ready, bored with their high-flown exchange, inspected Mary's display. "Foh dollah, foh dollah, foh dollah," she said, as if she were a cracked record, whenever he held anything up.

"Mary, there ain't nobody gonna pay four dollars for any of this stuff!"

"Not my plobum, GI," she answered. "It's Nick's plobum."

"An interesting man," Kennedy said after he'd finished his discussion with Michener. He and Ready were sitting on a bench beneath a fern tree, having another beer from Nick's Tropical Hamburger Joint.

Ready, hoping to avoid hearing about the surely dreary discussion between Kennedy and the articulate lieutenant commander, pointed out another of Nick's operations, this one proclaimed by a sign that read NICK'S TROPICAL JEEP WASH $1. A string of jeeps and trucks was lined up at a concrete slab where four men sprayed water out of hoses attached to a navy fire truck and scrubbed the vehicles.

"Corruption, pure and simple," Kennedy advised. "At his hamburger stand, Nick likely gets the meat from a navy freezer, the bread from a navy bakery, the beer"—he contemplated the brown bottle—"from God knows where, peels off a cook from some other corrupt officer, builds himself a stand out of scrap lumber and sells burgers and beer and puts nearly all the profit in his pockets, tax free. This jeep wash is the same. Four men working for Nick who should be on duty. God only knows how many sailors he has working for him in the laundry. Oh, quite the flimflam man, our Nick." He shook his head. "And this is the man you have me playing poker with."

Ready gave some thought to Kennedy's complaint. "You shouldn't worry about the game, Mister Kennedy," he concluded. "I'm an old hand at poker. I'll give you advice when you need it. But you'll catch on, pretty quick. You seem smart."

"Thank you," Kennedy replied in an ironic tone. "A Harvard education will always make a man seem smart, if nothing else."

"What's that Harvard like, sir?" Ready asked, wishing he could go back and get another of those beers. "Do you have to read a lot of books?"

"A lot of books," Kennedy confirmed. "Sometimes you're even required to understand a few of them."

"I'm not much for reading past comic books," Ready said. "I like Superman best of all. Batman's too dark and moody, that's my thinking."

Kennedy chuckled at Ready's childlike enthusiasm for comics. "Well, I guess we better get on to the O-Club Annex," he said. "Lead on, McDuff. That would be Shakespeare, Bosun."

"And a pretty fair version of it, sir," Ready replied and then quoted the actual line: "Lay on, Macduff, and damned be him that first cries, 'Hold, enough!' " He shrugged. "I was in a school play. Never could get the words out of my head."

After the startled expression faded from his face, Kennedy said, "I've never understood Kryptonite. If it's part of the planet where Superman was born, why would it make him so weak? Seems like he'd be used to it."

"You've got a point, sir. I never thought of that."

"I'm glad I've defended my Harvard education."

"Yes, sir, for sartain. Now, let's go win us a PT boat."

1 7

The Officer's Club Annex proved to be a small Quonset on the beach beside a shack with a sign that said NICK'S BEACH SUPPLIES, FLOATS, SURFBOARDS, SAILBOATS, AND SUCH. On the beach behind the shack were a half dozen tiny sailboats constructed from aircraft belly tanks. "Quite the inventive entrepreneur, our Nick," Kennedy said, marveling. "Too bad he's a crook."

"I'd surely like to sail around in them little boats," Ready said, nostalgically recalling his days as a boy on Killakeet Island when he and his pals built their own sailboats out of anything that would float.

Kennedy pushed open the door of the O-Club Annex, and he and Ready went in. Three men looked up from a round wooden table. Two of them were lieutenant junior grades like Kennedy, but the third was Jim Michener, who smiled and nodded at him. Nick was sitting on a bench in front of an old upright piano, playing a lively tune and singing, too:

> *Oh, there's nothing finer than a beach of sand,*
> *With a round of gin, and a girl so grand,*
> *Out here in the islands with the ocean so blue,*
> *All I want is to snuggle with you.*
>
> *Oh, be my pal, South Pacific Gal.*
> *Be my pal, South Pacific Gal.*

Nick finished the piece with a flourish. Everyone in the hut, including Kennedy and Ready, applauded. "Thank you," Nick said, clearly delighted with their appreciation. "I wrote it myself."

"What's it called?" Kennedy asked.

"Just as the chorus implies. 'Be My Pal, South Pacific Gal.' "

"Catchy."

"Sure to be a hit," Ready added. "Can I stay for the game, sir? I know I ain't no officer, but I got nowhere else to go."

Nick slapped his hands on his thighs and grinned. "Why, of course you can stay, Bosun. Can't he, boys? See, we don't stand on rank around here. This is poker, and poker is the most egalitarian of contests. Do you want in? I'll stake you."

"No, sir, don't reckon I do, you being my superiors and all in every respect. But I would like to give Mister Kennedy some advice now and again if it wouldn't be considered too much against the rules."

"Not at all, not at all," Nick said, rising from the piano and taking his place at the table. "Advise all you want. We're an easy game here, aren't we, gentlemen?"

The other officers all nodded. Nick introduced them, one by one. "This is "Duck" Hendricks, ace Tomahawk pilot with your United States Army Air Corps, that's Chris Welch, journalist, *Stars and Stripes,* and here's Jim Michener, who I'm not certain why he's here but we're glad to have him. Fellows, meet Jack Kennedy and Bosun O'Neal." There were handshakes all around.

Michener beamed at Kennedy. "I forgot to mention this earlier. Congratulations on your best seller. How'd you feel when you knew it was going to be published?"

"Deserving," Kennedy replied, with the smug expression only a published writer could attain.

"I'd like to write someday for publication," Michener confessed. "Maybe I'll write a book on the historical tensions between East and West and the deterministic factors of empire and commercialism."

"Boy, that sounds boring as hell!" Ready chirped, then clapped his hands over his mouth. He spoke between his fingers. "Sorry, sir."

Michener chuckled. "Well, what do you think I should write about, Bosun?"

Ready freed his mouth. "Well, if you wrote it right, I bet folks would like to read about all us guys out here doing our jobs."

"Oh, sure. It would be real interesting to read about a guy with the creeping crud," Welch scoffed. "Or a guy who sits around day after day waiting for a letter from his girl who's going out with some 4-F guy back home. Oh, yeah, some really interesting stories to be told out here."

"Nurses, sir!" Ready enthused, not willing to let his idea go so easily.

"How about the nurses you got down here in Santa Cruz? People like to read about a dame in a peculiar place. Maybe you could write about one of those nurses falling in love with some really special guy. You know, like Lois Lane with Superman."

"This is all fascinating, Bosun," Nick interceded. "But I believe we have a poker game to play, not a discussion of literature."

"Speaking of literature, I used to date a nurse when I was stationed at Hickman Field back in Hawaii," Hendricks said. "I laid her in the post library back in the memoir section."

"It's Hickam Field," Michener said.

"What?"

"Hickam, not Hickman."

"Who the hell cares?" Hendricks blurted. "It was the nurse I was talking about."

"Gentlemen, gentlemen," Nick interceded once more. "The poker game, yes?" He looked at Ready. "Bosun, are you finished with your quite interesting but, alas, extraneous comments?"

"Yes, sir," Ready replied, embarrassed at being so thoroughly patronized. "Sorry to all you sirs."

Michener looked at Ready with an interested expression but said nothing more. Nick announced the game was five card stud, dealt one down and four up with betting between the deals. Ready called for a side conference with Kennedy. Nick nodded agreement. They scooted their chairs back a few feet. "Do you understand how to play, sir?" Ready asked in a whisper.

"Well enough," Kennedy whispered back. "I essentially put up my money and then wait to be eaten by these sharks."

"That ain't a good attitude, sir."

"I will endeavor to improve it. What's your advice?"

"If your cards are lousy, drop out. If you have some good cards, then bet and keep raising until you think some other guy has better cards. Then drop out."

"Let me get this straight. Your advice is to ante up and then drop out unless I've got a killer hand that can't lose?"

"It's what I do, mostly," Ready confessed.

Kennedy shook his head. "There's only one way I have any chance at all with this bunch. I've got to act like I don't know what I'm doing and bet high a lot of times no matter what I've got. In other words, bluff the hell out of them."

"You do that, sir, and you're going to lose all our money and our boat, too."

"I may lose *my* money," Kennedy said, "but not *my* boat. I don't have a boat, in case you haven't noticed."

"You really ought to be more optimistic, sir, if you don't mind me saying so."

"Well, Ready, let's see if I have any reason for optimism after this game."

"Are you gentlemen of the Solomon Islands ready to play?" Nick purred.

Kennedy and Ready scooted their chairs back to the table. "Deal," Kennedy said.

Nick dealt, and the game began. During its early stages, Nick proved himself a heavy hitter who won and lost big. When he had something he apparently thought was good, he went after it as if he had chips to burn, exposing himself to ambushes from Hendricks, Michener, and Welch, who worked their hands carefully and reasonably. Kennedy, on the other hand, was completely and utterly unpredictable. With his bluffing, even when bluffing didn't make sense, he won a few hands, so his stack of chips grew. Soon the word got out across the base that there was a hot poker game, and a crowd began to gather. Kennedy immediately became the sentimental favorite, and he didn't disappoint, once taking a medium-sized pot with nothing but a pair of fours. Nick had folded early with a pair of tens showing.

"You got them all on the run, sir," Ready whispered excitedly. "But I think you ought to pay more attention to what cards you've got. For instance, you bet a lot on just that pair of fours. You could've got beat easy."

"Scoot back," Kennedy said.

"Sir?"

"Scoot back away from me."

Ready's lip went out, but he scooted back.

Kennedy, bluffing nearly every hand, took a few more pots and raked in the chips. "Kennedy, you're a damn good poker player," Nick allowed while smiling a disarming smile.

The play went on. Over the next series of hands, the stacks of chips before Hendricks, Welch, and Michener increased and decreased while Kennedy's and Nick's stayed pretty much the same. The other three officers were playing each other, it seemed, while there was a completely separate game going on between Kennedy and Nick. Pretty soon, there were bets throughout the O-Club Annex as to which of the two would end up the winner for the night. Ready was surprised to look up and see the guard from the gate, still dressed in his whites. Beside him stood Mary, the Tonk-inese woman. Then he saw the cook from Nick's Tropical Burgers. Ready wondered if anyone was still on duty in Santa Cruz but then stopped won-dering and started concentrating on what Kennedy was doing, which was crazy but so far successful, against any odds Ready could imagine.

The game was changed to seven card stud, two down, the rest up. Now the chips started to stack up in front of Kennedy, and hand after hand went his way. First, Welch dropped out after Kennedy skunked him with a full house of three jacks, two of them in the hole, and two tens. Then Michener gave up and went off to a corner, where he was seen scribbling in a little notebook. Nick, chewing on an unlit cigar, bought another thousand dol-lars of chips. The next hand, Kennedy took Hendricks to the cleaners and the Tomahawk pilot threw in the towel. Now, it was just Nick and Kennedy. Both had big stacks of chips, although Kennedy's was larger. The next hand was a small pot. Nick took it.

"Don't forget why we're here, Mister Kennedy," Ready whispered. "The PT boat. Got to get all his money, sir. Make him scream."

"Leave me alone."

"Yes, sir."

Nick's head was down, his chin on his chest. He shuffled the cards petu-lantly, then stopped. Scowling, he bought more chips, paid for with a wad of dollars from his pocket. "Five card stud," he said. He shuffled the cards, got Kennedy to cut them, then dealt one down and one up for each player. Kennedy had a jack of clubs showing. Nick had a ten of diamonds. Nick bet; Kennedy met the bet and raised him. Nick dealt Kennedy a ten of clubs and himself a queen of diamonds. Nick bet, and Kennedy raised. Nick met it, and both men got another card. This time Kennedy got a king of clubs. Nick got a jack of diamonds. Nick bet, and Kennedy quickly met it and raised. Perplexed, his face a frowning study, Nick reluctantly tossed in the necessary chips to meet Kennedy's raise.

The last cards went down, a nine of clubs to Kennedy, a king of diamonds to Nick. The pot was huge. Somebody took the time to count it. "I make it near four thousand dollars," he said, and an excited rumble went through the crowd, the kind of excited rumble that only big money can make in any au-dience. Animated whispers were exchanged as the expert poker players ex-plained what was happening. Both of the lieutenants were working flushes with a possibility of a straight flush for Kennedy and the highest ranking of all hands, known as a royal flush, for Nick. Or neither of them had a thing. Both could, after all, be bluffing.

Beads of sweat appeared on Nick's brow, and his upper lip became a swimming pool. He stared at the cards that Kennedy was showing. A flurry of side betting erupted in the assembly. "Two thousand dollars," Nick said, after a considerable time, and pushed forward the necessary chips.

Kennedy met the two thousand and raised three. "I don't think you've got a thing, Nick," he said.

Nick wiped his face with his sleeve. "Well, I'm all in," he said, pushing forward his remaining chips.

Ready whispered furiously into Kennedy's ear. Kennedy nodded and said, "You mean you're going to run away from my bet, Nick? I've got three thousand on the table to you, and all you can do is slide those few pitiful chips my way? I'm surprised at you. I thought you were a real poker player."

Nick's great eyebrows formed into an angry V. "Who'll loan it to me?" he croaked. "Come on, somebody! It's for the honor of Santa Cruz. Kennedy's bluffing!"

"Ain't nobody going to do it, Nick," a voice from the crowd answered. "It's Mister Kennedy's night. Ain't you figgered that out?"

Kennedy smiled. "Tell you what, Nick," he said reasonably. "Maybe you can meet my raise with something other than money."

"What do you mean?" Nick cried. He looked ill, and his Adam's apple bobbed as he swallowed.

"Something of value. That thing we talked about earlier in the day."

A trickle of sweat went down Nick's cheek, dark with afternoon shadow. "You mean the thing with no paperwork?"

"Yes," Kennedy answered. "That very thing."

Nick squirmed in his chair. "All right," he said heavily. "But I think we should sharpen up the pot a bit. I've lost count of what's there, but shove in all you've got and let's round it to, say, ten thousand dollars."

"Done!" Ready said before Kennedy could open his mouth.

Nick said, "Then I think we've both been called."

"Wait!" somebody spoke up from the crowd. "Before you show us your hole cards, let us all get our last bets down."

Nick and Kennedy nodded agreement, and the money flew. When the hubbub settled down, Nick's and Kennedy's eyes met. "All right, Kennedy, let's see the bad news," Nick said with a sigh.

Kennedy turned up his card, and it was the jack of clubs. He had gotten his straight flush. The crowd let go with a mighty whoop while Nick just held his head. "My oh my," he groaned.

"Show us your card, Nick!" a chief yelled. "Let's see what you got skunked with!"

Nick shrugged and turned his card over. The noise in the Quonset drained away until all that was left was a destitute silence. When Kennedy found his voice, he said, "Congratulations," and then patted Ready on the shoulder in an attempt to at least slow the boy's weeping. Nick had made his royal flush.

1 8

Kennedy, Nick, and Ready walked through the gate of the great supply area and stopped on the big concrete dock. The endless Pacific sky rolled above them, deep black, strewn with sparkling stars and studded by a bright half moon. All was quiet except for a gentle rustle of palm fronds, the scratching of perhaps a rat in the grass, and the thin gurgle of the placid harbor. The light from the moon turned the hundreds of anchored boats and ships into silvery ghosts. "You have my wife's address?" Nick asked.

"Yes, and I won't lose it," Kennedy replied in as strong a voice as he could muster. "As soon as I get stateside, she'll receive the money."

"Thank you. She needs it. It's not been easy for her. We owe some to the bank. This will help."

Kennedy was still angry at losing the game and couldn't resist a jab at the winner. "I don't get it, Nick. You shouldn't have any money problems, not with all your enterprises around here. Nick's Tropical Hamburger Stand, Nick's Jeep Wash, Nick's Whorehouse, for all I know."

Nick took off his pith helmet and ran his hand across his face to wipe the sweat from it. "You don't think much of me, do you?"

"I don't know what to think, Nick. But I'm curious. Why doesn't someone bring you up on charges?"

Nick put his pith helmet back on, and his bushy great eyebrows arched. "Why would anyone bring me up on charges? Do you think I'm a crook? Well, I'm not a crook. You see all the ballparks around here, the recreational clubs, the O-Club Annex, even the golf course? All the money I make from my enterprises goes into the morale fund that pays for all that. And why do I do it, Kennedy? I do it for these men, trapped as they are so far away from home without so much as a Jap to shoot at them to make it interesting, men who work twenty hours or more a day every day, even Christmas, and who are all mosquito-bit, and got grunge growing between their toes, and blisters and rashes in their armpits that drive them crazy. The money I make is so those men can have some place to get away and maybe listen to a record or two, or watch a Betty Grable movie, or play a game of baseball or horseshoes or even poker, anything to keep them from going nuts so that these supplies and all this equipment will be shoved up the pipeline to you charlies fighting the real war. That's what Nick's Tropical Hamburger Stand and all the rest are for, and I'm proud I have the savvy to do it."

Nick smacked his fist into his hand. "Dammit, Kennedy. I'd give my eyeteeth to get into this war, but we all have to follow orders. Here is where the navy thinks they can use me to the best advantage, so here I'll stay and do the best damn job I can!"

Chastened, Kennedy shuffled his brown shoes in the sand. "Nick, I've misjudged you. I'm sorry. By God, I truly am. Look me up when you get back to the States, why don't you? We'll share another glass of good whiskey. My father is likely to be able to provide us some."

"I just might," Nick said, partially mollified.

"Come to think of it," Kennedy said, "I never caught your full name."

"Richard Milhous Nixon." He stuck out his hand. "Of Whittier, California."

They shook hands. "See you around, Nick."

"I shouldn't wonder," Nixon replied with a shy smile beneath his ridiculous pith helmet. "Good luck up the Slot. And don't forget to duck!"

After Nixon had walked back inside his compound, Kennedy and Ready stood at the edge of the dock. In the quiet harbor, there was but a single light moving, a small boat maneuvering between the others. "Where are the other boys?" Kennedy asked, apparently just realizing they had disappeared.

"Beats me, sir. Guess they went off to loaf somewhere, and Marvin's probably found himself a lady friend. He's good at that."

"Not only did I lose a small fortune, but I lost my crew," Kennedy lamented. "I even lost the mascot."

"Marvin ain't a mascot, sir. He's crew, too."

Kennedy allowed himself a long sigh. "Does it really matter what I call your dog? Never mind. I guess we'd better find a place to sleep. Tomorrow morning we'll figure out what to do next."

"We got to get us a boat, sir."

"Dammit, Ready. That's what I've been trying to do!"

The light on the harbor flashed on them and then steadied. In a few minutes, the vessel with the light slid next to the dock. Someone jumped off and held onto a bow line. "Climb aboard, Mister Kennedy," Once said.

Again grinned from behind the wheel of the vessel, which proved to be nothing less than an eighty-eight-foot mahogany-and-plywood, sharp-bowed watercraft, otherwise known as a PT boat. Marvin stood on the middeck loading hatch. Millie came up from below with an apron tied around his neck. "I'm baking some biscuits, Mister Kennedy. We should have a fine breakfast, come morning."

Kennedy, in something of a daze, stepped aboard the boat. When he looked, the boat's number, usually painted on the splinter shield, was rubbed out. He had a lot of questions, but he didn't think he wanted to hear many of the answers. Once, pushing off and jumping back on deck with the line, answered at least one of them. "We found some boats made out of belly tanks on the beach and kind of borrowed them, sir. We started looking around the harbor until we ran across this torpedo schooner. She's got a full tank of gas, and she started right up, too. Seems a right fine craft."

"We came here for the *PT-59,*" Kennedy said. "We can't just steal any PT boat we find."

"Well, hell, sir," Again said, "one PT boat's the same as the other, ain't it? What difference does it make?"

The twin's logic was a bit overwhelming. "Well, I suppose there is no true difference. But the paperwork will be screwed up."

"No it won't, sir, because we don't have no paperwork. Can I take her to Melagi now?"

"Why not?" was Pogo's comment. The bushman, for no apparent reason, was wearing a nurse's cap.

Kennedy couldn't think of a reason why not, beyond an additional charge to his court-martial. He shrugged, which was tantamount as far as Thurlow's boys were concerned to his enthusiastic agreement. Without another word, Again gunned the throttles to the wall, and the PT boat disappeared into the night.

1 9

Phimble piloted the *Darlin' Dosie* northward while the shadows lengthened on the small islands below. Soon the light would be gone entirely and he'd be flying in the dark, which he didn't particularly like to do. He was also tired. Phimble had anticipated not doing too much that day, other than writing his wife a letter and maybe hiking down to the Raider base with Fisheye to see if the team mechanic could repair the generator used to show the only film on the base, *The Fleet's In,* starring Dorothy Lamour. Ever since the generator had broken down the week before, the Raiders had been assembling after dark in front of the empty screen, which was a sheet nailed to a scrap of plywood erected atop a bunker, and staring at it until somebody made a critical comment on the movie, which, even if it was not being shown, they all knew by heart. No matter what the remark was, it invariably provoked a fight and the fists happily flew. Phimble didn't much mind that the Raiders brawled, except their swearing tended to be loud and if the wind was just right, or wrong, he could hear them, even high on the volcano's slope at Thurlow's Cave. If Fisheye could fix the little generator that operated the projector, Phimble theorized, then maybe the Raiders would be mollified and it would guarantee a more peaceful evening.

It was while he was contemplating this idea over a cup of coffee that very morning that Phimble had observed Josh reading Dosie's fool letter. Then Captain Clooney had appeared out of the bush with the demand from Colonel Burr. After that, Phimble's day had simply gone to pieces. Josh had agreed to see Burr and then returned all in a sweat to be flown north to Lumbari and thence to New Georgia. Phimble had made Josh sit down long enough to spill what he'd heard from Burr. It wasn't a pretty tale, and Phimble's advice was to stay out of it.

But what was done was done, the mission was on, and it was going to play out, one way or the other. Phimble mostly wished that he hadn't sent Millie with that Kennedy fellow. The boy could make a fine cup of coffee. Stobs was indifferent at best in his coffeemaking, usually getting the grounds in it and never getting it hot enough. He glanced at his copilot, who was the megapode. Dave was working on his nap. Fisheye was in the forward gun turret, and Stobs was at his radio station. Like Dave, both boys were probably asleep, too.

Phimble wished now he and Josh had talked a bit more about the pickup. They hadn't actually established when it would occur, tonight or tomorrow morning. If it was night, he would have to land in the dark at the little harbor he'd only seen once. Landing at night was difficult even when a pilot knew the water. On the other hand, if he stopped at Melagi and waited until morning, the skipper would be stranded, and God only knew what foul temper that would cause! Phimble looked ahead to see Guadalcanal, a giant purple shadow rising from the sea. Tulagi and then Melagi were behind the big island, and the decision point on whether to continue north or stop for the night had arrived.

"What do you think, Dave?" Phimble asked the megapode, who woke at the sound of his name. "Go get Josh or spend the night in the cave? What's it to be?"

Dave rose and padded his feet a few times, then shook his head. "You don't want to go, Dave? But don't you think we ought to pick up the skipper?"

The megapode just stared at him while Phimble mused a little longer. "I have to go," he said finally. "Sorry, Dave. I appreciate your opinion, though." He keyed the mike. "Fisheye? Stobs? Wake up and keep your eyes open, boys. We're headed into Rufe country." Phimble was aware that by such simple whims, life-changing decisions are often made. "Hey diddle diddle," he sang, with a contrite nod to the megapode. "Right up the middle." Dave raised his wings, then went back to sleep.

The sun finally collapsed into the sea with a final spray of gaudy brilliance, and the South Pacific night moved in to cover the islands like a thick velvet cloak. The Catalina droned on.

"Fire on the water, Mister Phimble," Fisheye called from the nose turret, "about ten o'clock."

Phimble studied the area, where there should have been only open water. There was indeed a fire, and it suddenly blossomed, orange and red streaks streaming from its center, dimming to a glow. Other fires erupted nearby, these seeming to fall from the sky. Phimble puzzled over them, then realized what he was seeing. Some kind of vessel had been bombed and set afire, and the aircraft that had done it was dropping flares to make sure of the damage. Or perhaps there was more than one aircraft. It was impossible to say.

Fisheye called with a pertinent question. "Is one of our boats being attacked by Jap planes, or is it a Jap boat catching hell from our boys?"

"I dunno," Phimble answered. "But I'm turning this crate around before they see us." *I should have taken Dave's advice and landed at Melagi,* he thought to himself. He eased over the wheel, pressed the proper rudder pedal, and gave the engines a little throttle to head back south.

"But what if it's one of our boats, Mr. Phimble?" Stobs called. "We can't just fly off and leave them."

"What the hell do you expect me to do, Stobs?" Phimble demanded. "This is a Catalina, not a Corsair."

"I don't know, sir. You're the officer."

And there it was. Ensign Eureka Phimble, an officer and a gentleman according to the Congress of the United States of America, even though it had been a battlefield commission, was empowered to exercise the authority according to his rank. That meant he was in charge of the *Darlin' Dosie* and responsible to see her used to accomplish the mission. *But what was the mission?* However it might be defined, it included the protection of American sailors, soldiers, and marines and there just might be a few of them down there taking a terrible beating from a Japanese bomber.

"Hang on," Phimble said, making up his mind. He stopped the slow turn and kicked the Catalina into a spiraling dive. Seven thousand, five hundred feet they dropped in tight circles until Phimble flatted *Dosie* and swept just a few hundred feet over the fire on the sea. He glanced at it, then fire-walled the throttles and pulled up. Dave, awakened by the dive, was in a deep squat from the g-forces and emitted a mild squawk in protest. "Sorry, Dave. Did you get a look, Fisheye?"

"Sure did, Mister Phimble. It was one of ours, all right. An LCI, I'd say, most likely got caught in the dark coming back from New Georgia."

"Stobs," Phimble said, "get on the horn, give Cactus a call, tell them the situation."

"Aye, aye, sir!"

Phimble had but a brief moment to think about what to do next before a series of bright flashes flew past the cockpit. Then the Catalina hull rattled as if it had run into a hailstorm. They were under attack. "Jap float plane out there!" Fisheye called. "I saw it!"

"What'd it look like?"

"Single engine. Big float on its belly. Just like came after us this morning."

Phimble cursed. It was surely a Rufe, and Rufes rarely traveled alone. Phimble sent up a silent prayer that these Rufe pilots were inexperienced, ill trained, and short on fuel. He knew better than to expect a Tomahawk to chase them away. The night sky belonged to the Japanese. Stobs stuck his head into the cockpit. "Mister Phimble, my radio's all busted up. A slug went right past my shoulder and slammed into it. Got some glass in my face, but I'm OK. I got a call off to Cactus about the LCI. Not sure if they got it, though."

Phimble said a silent prayer of thanks that Stobs hadn't been killed. "Can you fix the radio?"

"Not sure. I'll have to open it up and see."

"All right. Do that later. Right now, get on one of the blister guns. If you see anything flying out there, and I mean *anything,* shoot at it."

Stobs snapped off an "Aye, aye, sir," and disappeared. Phimble threw the Catalina into a hard turn, aiming her nose toward Guadalcanal, and pushed the throttles to the stops, working for altitude. Getting out of the area was his only hope, one that was soon dashed when tracers again flew past the cockpit. The Rufe had found them. Aft, Phimble felt the vibration of another storm of bullets pounding the hull. "You all right, Stobs?" he called.

"Yes, sir. But we got more than a few holes back here."

A flash of light blinded Phimble, and he threw up his hands before he realized a flare had gone off within a few feet of the cockpit. He flew right through it, but more flares were popping all around. One Rufe or many, Phimble knew *Dosie* was caught in their light like a moth against a flame.

"There's one!" Fisheye yelled, and at the same time cut loose with the forward gun. Phimble's hopes started rising again as he watched Fisheye's thirty-caliber tracers streaming out from *Dosie's* nose, beautiful red streaks arcing into the blackness. Then he saw some of the tracers quit abruptly in a shower of sparks. "I got him, Eureka!" Fisheye yelled.

"Attaboy!" Phimble crowed. Then he heard the ominous sound of the starboard engine cutting in and out. He throttled back on the gas, too late, because the engine suddenly burst into flames. *Dosie's* nose began to drop as Phimble quickly feathered the engine. "Level out. Level out. Level out," Phimble chanted as he strained on the yoke. "Come on, old girl. *Level out!*"

It was as if *Dosie*'s nose had taken on a ton of lead. No matter how hard Phimble pulled back on the yoke, she kept plunging through the night toward the waiting sea. A howling devil seemed to be screaming in his ears, but it was only the skin of the Catalina shrieking through the ever denser air as it got closer to the ocean. Phimble suddenly had the oddest thought, that he was going to die sitting next to a megapode. It wasn't exactly how he might have predicted the circumstances of his death.

"Dave, first off, I'd like to apologize," Phimble said. "You were right. We should have stopped at Melagi. But Pogo says you're magic. If that's so, I sure would like to see some of your magic right now." Then, hedging his bet, Phimble cast a prayer toward the More Traditional Occupant in heaven.

The old megapode, pushed back against the seat by the force of the fall, cocked his head as if thinking about Phimble's request. And still the *Darlin' Dosie* fell, the wind tearing across her wings in a banshee cry of imminent destruction.

2 0

It was a long run north across the Coral Sea, and it lasted through the night. Kennedy, who'd never expected to be behind the wheel of a PT boat again, enjoyed the feel of the big engines, even though the pounding that came up through the deck from those engines was taking its toll on his legs and back. Ready kept offering to spell him, and finally, gritting his big teeth against the pain, he handed the controls over and stretched out on the deck beside a torpedo tube. Before long, the Jackson twins showed up and bolted a padded bench behind the wheel. Kennedy struggled to his feet and came over and sat on it. "This is good, very good," he said. "But how did you build it?"

"There's always a few strakes and stubs on any boat," Once advised.

"What does that mean?"

"We found some scrap lumber."

Throughout the night, Kennedy was aware that Thurlow's boys were roaming around the boat, fussing with this and that. Once and Again seemed to be most curious about the torpedo tubes. They queried Kennedy as to their operation and were astonished when he told them that the torpedoes were punched out of their tubes by black-powder charges that often didn't work.

"There must be a better way," Once said. The two boys went back to the tubes, scratching their heads and pondering, then came back and said, "Compressed air would work better."

Kennedy shrugged at the suggestion, and the twins went away again, puzzling more over the tubes. Then they came back and said, "We need to get rid of these tubes entirely, that's the answer. They're awful heavy. Get another three knots, maybe more, out of this boat if they were gone. Why not just roll the torpedoes in? We could rig up a rack."

Kennedy knew the answer to that one. "It won't work. Torpedoes have gyros in them, and they get confused if they're spun around. The tubes keep them in the correct position."

"But the torpedoes we see airplanes carry don't have tubes," Once pointed out.

"Maybe they don't have gyros," Kennedy answered uncertainly.

"I bet you're right, Mister Kennedy," Again said. "See, Once, I told you he was smart."

"But we don't have any torpedoes anyway," Kennedy reminded the twins. "So this is all an intellectual exercise." The two teenagers grinned at him, then each other, and went on their way.

Millie came up from below and reported to Kennedy that the biscuits were cooling and he had managed to get the galley shipshape. He also advised that he had taken a look at the trio of big Packard engines and, though he didn't have half the knowledge of Fisheye, his thought was that maybe by changing the gear ratios on the supercharger impeller, a bit more performance might be squeezed out of them. Kennedy replied that such an idea certainly sounded reasonable and plausible, though he had no idea what it meant, and told Millie to go ahead if he liked. Millie had looked at him for a long second and then said, "We'd need a quiet harbor to do it, sir. You see, it's kind of hard to work on engines while they're running."

Kennedy tried not to feel like an idiot and managed it by taking a nap. An hour later, Millie was back with a report to Kennedy that he'd fired up the radio and contacted a radioman he knew on Guadalcanal, and communications seemed to be working well and would likely get better. "Stobs will make that radio sing, sir. You'll see. He'll be talking to his folks on Killakeet afore an hour."

Then the Jackson twins swung by once more. "We've figured out what to do about the torpedoes," they said.

Kennedy reminded them once more that there was a severe lack of torpedoes, but off they went, slyly elbowing one another. When Kennedy went below to get away from the constant interruptions, he was surprised to discover the twins installing a vent in the captain's cabin. He'd never been able to spend much time in his cabin aboard the *PT-109*, since it was usually hot as an oven. But the boys invited him inside and finished up their work, and he lay and basked in the cooling air fed from the deck by their simple device. Still, he couldn't sleep, and he climbed back to the cockpit and settled on the soft bench, while Ready curled up around the base of the starboard gun tub. The bosun immediately fell asleep, the blessing, Kennedy reflected, of the innocent. Kennedy sat on the little bench and was nearly happy as the boat skimmed across the sea in the glow of the moon.

Ready, after sleeping for an hour, sat up and rubbed his eyes. He rose to stand beside Kennedy. "Have you ever heard of the *Curlew*, sir?" he asked. "That would be the CSS *Curlew*?"

"I can't say that I have," Kennedy confessed, pushing his fist into his back. "CSS? Do you mean the Confederate States?"

"Yes, sir, I do. My great-granddaddy served aboard the *Curlew* as a gunner. It was a fast little schooner before the war, but Granddaddy put every kind of cannon on her that she could carry. She was a bad'un for sartain. Sank a number of Yankee boats before they finally blew her up."

"But your granddaddy survived, I take it," Kennedy said politely.

"Oh, yes, sir, he did. He went on to become a great Killakeet fisherman, taught my daddy everything he knew about fish like daddy taught me. But I been thinking about what Granddaddy did with the *Curlew*, sir, and not so much about what he did with the fish."

"Well, that's fine, Bosun. I know you're proud of your rebellious ancestor."

"I'm more than proud, sir. I'm thinking."

"That could mean trouble," Kennedy replied, and found himself mildly alarmed.

"No trouble," Ready promised. "Not at all."

Kennedy sought to change the subject, since he had little interest in Confederate schooners or the guns placed on them. "This is the first time I've heard anything about your family, Bosun. Fishermen, you say? How many generations do you go back?"

"Oh, sir, back forever, I guess. Killakeet O'Neals have always been fishermen. My folks also own and operate the Hammerhead Hotel, but you can bet my daddy still cares about fish. A man named Cat-tail Garner is the captain of Daddy's boat."

"How many brothers and sisters do you have?"

"I'm the third son of four boys and five girls."

The revelation from Ready unaccountably pleased Kennedy. "There are nine children in my family, too!" he enthused. "I'm the second son of four boys and five girls."

"That's swell. My brothers are all scattered about. Two are in the Coast Guard, and the other, he's the oldest, works a boat down at Morehead City. He lost his hand when he was seven. Got it caught in a piece of machinery at the cannery. All my sisters are married to fishermen who are in the Coast Guard or the navy for the duration, except for Wesley, who joined the Army for no reason anybody can figure out. He's in the paratroops. How about your brothers and sisters, Mister Kennedy?"

"My older brother Joe is in the Navy," Kennedy said, trying to put a little pride into his voice but failing. "He's a pilot. Flies a B-24 and hunts U-boats out of a base in England. My sister Kathleen—we call her Kick—she's in England, too. Got herself a beau, a lord, in fact. He's divorced, so that's a problem, but Kick is tough enough to find a way around her problems. My brothers Bobby and Teddy are too young to join the armed forces, so they're still at home. My other sisters are Eunice, Pat, and Jean. They're home, too, and are just squirts."

Ready was a good counter, especially with his fingers. He toted them up and came out one short. "That's but four sisters, sir. You left one out."

"Did I? Well, there's Rosemary. She's the oldest of the girls. In fact, she's the firstborn of all the Kennedy kids."

"And what is she doing, sir? Married and with a bunch of babies, I suppose."

Kennedy shook his head. "No. Rosemary was born . . . well, not right, Bosun. She was always slow and didn't fit in with the rest of us. My father told us how important it was to always win in everything we did. But Rosemary never seemed to care about winning. She just wanted to read her books or play with her dolls, and I guess we left her out of most things. When there was a dance at the club, though, I would always dance with her, and tell her jokes and make her laugh. She loved to laugh. She had a pretty smile."

"She sounds like a girl on Killakeet. Her name is Willow. She seemed slow for the longest time, and everybody worried about her. Some said she was a hoodoo and ought to be put in a place away from everybody else. But then one day, everybody realized she was actually terribly smart, only in a different way. She's married to Captain Thurlow's brother now. Maybe Rosemary will prove to be like that, too."

"I'm afraid not," Kennedy replied stiffly. "She had an operation. It didn't turn out quite as planned."

Ready sensed Kennedy's discomfort in talking about his older sister, so it was his turn to change the subject, except he couldn't think of another one. Finally Kennedy did, asking, "When you go back to Killakeet, what will you do?"

Ready smiled. "Why, I'll fish, sir."

"Take over your daddy's boat?"

"Oh, no. Like I said, Cat-tail Garner's got that job. I'll hook on with somebody, though. I'm a good hand."

"But it's your daddy's boat. You should be able to take over, be its captain."

Ready gave Kennedy's comment some thought. "But then what would happen to Cat-tail? It would be terrible hard for him and his family if I took his job away."

Kennedy looked far away for a moment, into the darkness and beyond. "Ready, I wish I were you. I really do."

"I can't imagine why," Ready answered.

"It's because you can't imagine why," Kennedy replied with a catch in his voice. "That's the reason."

"You're hurting, sir. I can see it the way you keep squeezing your eyes and pushing into the small of your back. Why don't you lay yourself down somewheres?"

"All right," Kennedy said. "Thank you, Bosun. You are a great help."

"Like I told you, Mister Phimble said I was to be, sir."

"Then, whether he likes it or not," Kennedy replied, "I shall thank Mister Phimble the moment I see him again."

2 1

Josh's eyes fluttered open, and for a long second he wasn't absolutely certain where he was. An investigation of his immediate surroundings revealed that whatever part of the world he might be in, he was lying on a mat of plaited palm fronds in a round bamboo hut. The quality of light filtering through the walls of the hut was gentle and golden, and its warmth was comforting. Josh discovered that he felt good, a bit lazy, and thoroughly satisfied, all of which worried him. Through an open doorway he could see a placid blue sea, lapping gently against a sandy beach. A wild rooster crowed somewhere nearby, the final hint as to his location. It was morning in the Solomons, and Josh was inexplicably happy, though a little voice in the back of his mind kept telling him he had absolutely no right to be. That same voice also told him he'd better stop being happy at the first opportunity, lest disorder occur, the bane of any sailor who hoped to keep a taut ship.

Perhaps disorder had already occurred. Josh felt the curve of a woman's bare hip pressed against his bare leg, and then he perceived her smooth back, still glowing with a faint sheen of coconut oil, and the dark curls of her hair, and her head couched in her long black arms. Something of the past evening began to be recollected. Josh peered down his own length and discovered that he was naked as a mullet. He concluded that there had indeed been some disorderly business going on and that he had participated in it. He felt a mild panic.

The woman stirred, stretched languidly, then turned over. Smiling a dreamy smile, she raised up on her elbow to look at him. She had a pretty smile and vastly kissable lips. "Thank you, mastah," she said. "I needed that. I think you did, too." Then she rose in all her nakedness and took him by the hand and led him out of the hut and across the warm sand and into the sea where she began to gently bathe him by rubbing his skin with her tapered fingers, all the while singing a little song just beneath her breath. Josh accepted her ministrations and caught a wisp of her song. *Yes, Jesus loves me. The Bible tells me so.*

She turned Josh around. "Now, you me," she said, and Josh returned the favor, the sexual fever that had gripped him the night before coming on strongly, only this time without the kava. After he'd finished running his hands over her body, he realized he had been holding his breath nearly the entire time. She looked out of the tops of her eyes and gave him another smile, this one quite shy and nearly chaste, and led him back to the hut and climbed on top of him. "It is clear you need more of me, mastah, as I do of you," she said, and he found it difficult to disagree.

"I don't even know your name," he said afterward.

"My name is Penelope. And yours?"

"Josh. Josh Thurlow."

She rolled off of him, took his hand, and gave it a good shake. "I am most pleased to meet you, mastah."

"Why do you have an English name?"

She lowered her eyes, and the innocence of the gesture endeared her to Josh. "I must sadly confess to you that I am an orphan. I hope you won't think any less of me because of it. I was raised by Minister Clarence. He gave me this Christian name. Do you not like it?"

"I like it very much. I think it's a pretty name."

"Why, thank you. And I think Josh is also a pretty name, as pretty as the man who bears it."

Josh found himself all the more charmed by her sweetness. "I don't think any woman has ever called me pretty."

"Then you have not met the right kind of woman, have you?" She smiled her wonderful smile, but then her face settled and she cocked her head. "Why are you on this island by yourself, mastah?"

"Well, you see, I'm on a special assignment."

"Ah. A special assignment for a special man."

"That's true," Josh replied, enjoying her flattery. "You see, I am here to find a marine lieutenant who disappeared a few days ago from the Truax plantation. There was a big battle there, as you may know."

"Oh, yes. So much noise and smoke! But why do you search for this lieutenant? How was it he became lost?"

"Some people say he ran away with Whitman's wife." Josh said. "Did you tell me last night you knew Missus Whitman?"

"Of course. She is the famous and beautiful woman who fights the Japoni."

"Do you live in this village?"

"Sometimes, and sometimes at Minister Clarence's mission. But mostly I am alone."

Her evident sadness caused a pang in Josh's heart. "I cannot imagine why such a pretty girl as you would be alone," he said. Then he found himself lusting after her again. She was like a tonic.

Penelope kept her hands folded in her lap in a most demure fashion, then asked very quietly, "Why did you ask me last night about Joe Gimmee?"

"Mister Whitman said Lieutenant Armistead and Missus Whitman are with Joe Gimmee."

"Oh, I doubt that very much," Penelope replied.

"Why? Whitman said Kimba Whitman is from Joe Gimmee's tribe. He also said he is a renegade. That means he is very bad."

Penelope giggled. "I know what it means, Mastah Josh. But Mastah Whitman is such a silly man, I think. He is always grinning at me when he sees me in the village or at Minister Clarence's mission. My word, Joe Gimmee is not bad at all. He is a holy man, and quite peaceful. He once lived here on New Georgia, but he and his followers moved away many years ago. I have heard he lives now in Australia. But it is true Missus Whitman is from Joe Gimmee's tribe. I would certainly think so. She is his daughter, you see."

Josh was so startled by this news, his mouth dropped open. Penelope laughed. "You will catch flies that way," she said. "I think Mastah Whitman is confused. I am certain he is very busy, fighting the Japoni, and now his wife has gone off. It is very sad, I think. Perhaps I will say a prayer for him."

Josh wondered where his notebook was. When he found it, he intended to draw an arrow between the two names *Kimba* and *Joe Gimmee* and write *father and daughter*. He felt he was really getting somewhere now! Whitman had not told him this detail, and perhaps that was important. But then Josh had another thought. Maybe the girl was lying. If Joe Gimmee didn't work for the Japanese, it certainly didn't fit in with Hypo picking up radio traffic on Armistead.

"When is your airplane coming for you?" Penelope suddenly asked.

"Today, I think."

"I should very much like to go with you. May I?"

Josh hesitated, a psychological condition that he usually did not tolerate for long. Still, he allowed himself a moment to imagine Colonel Burr's reaction if he brought a half-naked black woman back to Melagi. He imagined that Burr's growl might be heard even in Frank Knox's office in Washington, D.C. But then Josh got tired of hesitating and agreed that Penelope would be very welcome to fly back to Melagi with him, indeed. Why, he said, she might even find work. "There's a Missus Markham there," he said. "She could probably use a servant."

"I would be pleased to find work," Penelope said noncommittally. "Would you like to lie atop me again?"

Josh did. He couldn't seem to help it. He rationalized it by recalling Dosie's letter and her fooling around with that damned doctor, and also by the time that had passed since he'd lain with a female. Later, Josh found his utilities near the cooking pit along with his socks and boots. His cap was hanging on the limb of a tree. The first thing he did was get his notebook from his shirt pocket and draw an arrow between the two names along with a comment about Joe Gimmee's parenthood. He also included Penelope's belief that Joe Gimmee was now in Australia. Then he dressed, and so did Penelope, although for her it was no great chore since all she had to do was wrap her lap-lap about her waist and stick a freshly plucked hibiscus in her hair. She soon had coffee boiling in a tin pot over a fire. To his question about where she got the coffee, she replied, "I brought coffee and many tins of food from Minister Clarence's mission and hid them nearby."

"Doesn't he need these things?"

"No," she answered. She used a GI can opener, which was called a P-38, to open a can of pickled pig's feet. He ate the feet, one at a time, and wiped his fingers on a banana leaf. Penelope ate a banana while waiting patiently for him to finish. Then she buried the empty can in the sand and smothered the fire and scattered the ashes. "If the Japoni come, they will not know we have been here," she said.

"I thought they didn't come to this village anymore."

"The Japoni are scattered these days. They fight, but they also try to escape. Their situation is confused. They could turn up anywhere."

"How do you know so much about the Japanese?" he asked.

"For a pickaninny girl such as myself to survive on this island requires much paying of attention. I shall be very glad to go with you elsewhere. But now, mastah, before our airplane comes, it is necessary that I take you to see Minister Clarence."

"I think we should talk about a few things first," Josh said. "One of them is I don't think you should call me mastah anymore."

"Then I shall call you Josh darling," she said, agreeably.

"That sounds OK."

"And you shall call me Penelope dear."

Josh pushed the brim of his cap up with his finger. "That seems fair," he said uncertainly.

"But why do you not want to be called mastah?"

"Well, considering what we've done . . . that is to say, our being together and all."

She smiled, most demurely. The sight of it made Josh's heart thump hard in his chest. "When we couple," she said, "don't you think it is so very much fun, Josh darling?"

Josh allowed as how he thought it was indeed fun but then said, in a stern voice, "But we shouldn't have done it."

Penelope was astonished. "Why not?"

"The Ten Commandments. Number seven on the list, as I recall."

Penelope shrugged, and the way she moved her pretty shoulders, Josh thought, was most endearing. She said, "Pickaninny people think about coupling this way. God made it feel very good for a man and a Marie to couple, so He must have wanted us to do it, and often. When I came of age, I asked Minister Clarence to tell me if it was right or wrong. He read me some Bible verses that made it sound as if God was against it. But then I read the Book of Solomon and had no doubt God thought more like a pickaninny than this reverend. Do white people think coupling feels good, Josh darling?"

"Most of them," Josh said. "At least while they're young."

"And you are most obviously one of them, though you are not too young."

"I'm only thirty-three," he replied, a bit defensively.

She displayed her wonderfully white teeth in a delighted grin, then stood and strapped a dilly bag across her shoulder. "I was only pulling your leg, Josh darling. Now that I see that it works, and makes me laugh, I may yet do it again, if only occasionally. Be forewarned! But now we must go and see Minister Clarence."

Josh didn't see any reason not to go along with her. He figured he had plenty of time. Since the Catalina hadn't arrived the night before, Phimble had surely stopped off at Melagi and would need to refuel before heading north again. By the time he raised the aviation fuel truck and got its crew moving, it would be midmorning. As long as Josh got back to the pickup beach by early afternoon, he figured, he'd be in time to catch his ride. He couldn't wait to see Phimble's face when he brought aboard Penelope. He was certain to get a lecture, Phimble being severely attached to all of the biblical strictures, but it would be worth it.

Penelope, a gleaming machete in her hand, led the way. Over hill and valley they traveled, through heavy bush and savannah, and past splintered palms, blasted by recent artillery, and past empty Japanese bunkers, the stink of dead Imperial soldiers inside wafting into the damp, morose air. They crossed a small coffee plantation, torn apart by a tank (the tracks were still visible in the mud), and then they came across the site of a recent battle where they discovered the corpses of six American and fourteen Japanese soldiers, all dead, terribly bloated, wild dogs and vultures vying for their carcasses. Josh chased the scavengers away but, for the lack of a shovel, could do little else. They continued on until they reached the Minister Clarence Mission.

The mission was actually a small village, set on a little plateau surrounded by a loya cane fence. It was a well-tended place. Neat bamboo houses surrounded a common green backed by a steep-roofed chapel. As they walked on the green, Josh expected to be met by friendly villagers and then Minister Clarence, who he imagined would be an interesting man, as most preachers are, with his own story of suffering or degradation followed by redemption. Instead, he was surprised to smell again the stomach-turning odor of death. Then he saw the reason, scores of dead people, their black skins turned gray. Wild dogs and vultures had worked the bodies over. Rib cages and other protruding bones, coated with dried blood, glittered in the white sun. "The damned Japanese!" he growled, trying not to gag.

"That is Minister Clarence," Penelope said, pointing to a mangled, headless corpse tied by hemp ropes to a mulberry tree. The corpse was wearing black pants, but its chest was bare and covered with gore and ants.

"Where were you when this happened?" Josh asked, with a catch in his throat. It seemed death was at every turn on New Georgia.

"I was at the river, getting water for a friend who was sick with fever. I hid, but then I crawled through the bush where I could watch. Minister Clarence was mocked, then stabbed many times. Then, when he called to his savior, his head was cut off."

"Jesus," Josh muttered.

"Yes," Penelope replied without irony.

"Why did you bring me here?" Josh asked.

"I wanted you to see, *to witness*. And I wanted you to also see one of the men who did this. He came back the next day."

"Where is he?"

"In the chapel."

Josh was immediately on guard. An Imperial soldier was always dangerous. He drew his pistol from its holster. "Show me," he said.

Penelope fearlessly walked into the chapel, its doors torn from their hinges. Josh crept in behind, then slipped around the periphery of the rows of wooden benches. He watched Penelope as she walked to the altar and knelt, her hands clasped in prayer. Josh saw no Japanese soldier, just dead parishioners lying in grotesque forms across the benches and on the floor. The stink was nearly overwhelming. Josh approached her. "Your soldier is gone," he said.

She shrugged. "Minister Clarence preached to be good to all men, and since this is his church, I fed the man and gave him water. We talked. He was sorry for what he had done. I witnessed to him our Lord. Then he slept."

"He must have gone away after he woke up."

"No, Josh darling," Penelope answered. "He wanted to go, but I said he couldn't. He had to atone. Atonement is what Minister Clarence said we children of the Lord must do if we sin."

"And did he atone?"

"Oh, yes, though he thought I was pulling his leg, as I am wont to do. How he laughed! I could see he wasn't going to do what was required, so I waited until he was asleep, then I let him atone." Penelope reached into a wicker basket set on a blood-streaked white cloth that covered the Communion table and drew out a human head by its short black hair. The sunlight streaming through a nearby window lit the thing very well so that Josh could clearly see its sagging mouth and its closed and peaceful eyes. Penelope cocked her head and admired the face. "He atoned very well, don't you think?"

22

Eureka Phimble did not know where he was, and that all by itself left him most unsettled. It was part and parcel of his being a seafaring man, a sailor always needing to know where he was so he'd go in the proper direction to get wherever he was going. Phimble's perception of unease ignored the fact that his direction didn't much matter because he wasn't going anywhere soon, considering the condition of his transport. The *Darlin' Dosie,* her starboard engine cooked by a Japanese bullet or some unknown mechanical problem, was pushed up next to a black sand beach on an unidentified island in the middle of the Solomon Sea. All Phimble could tell was that the island was an extinct volcano, its steep, jungle-clad slope leading up to a collapsed cone. It was also a noisy and active place, the surf booming against a headland south of the cove, and tropical birds of every stripe flitting from limb to limb in the bush and putting up an awful racket of twitters and yelps and crackling noises. No human civilization, native or otherwise, was apparent. Phimble, feeling much like Robinson Crusoe, except that he wasn't alone, stood on the Catalina's starboard wing, a chart in his hand, and puzzled over the scene. "Where do you think we are, Stobs?" he finally asked the radioman.

Stobs was sitting on the tip of the wing, his boots dangling over the shallow water, which was languidly slapping against the volcanic sand. He was in an oddly petulant mood. "How would I know?" he snapped.

Phimble ignored the radioman's petulance. "I didn't say you'd know. I was asking for your judgment, which is usually pretty good."

Mollified by the pilot's compliment, Stobs said, "The way I figure it is maybe that's New Georgia over there to the northwest. And maybe the Russells back behind us. Taken altogether, this could be Mary Island, but it might not be." He peered at a surf-washed, foam-flecked reef, more than a thousand yards long, that pushed out perpendicular to the cove. "If it's Mary, that reef ain't on our chart, that much is for sartain."

Phimble folded the map and tucked it into his hip pocket. "About all these charts are good for is toilet paper," he griped.

Fisheye was squatting beside the burned engine cowling, looking it over. Phimble asked him what he thought. "Damned thing's cooked, sir," he answered.

"Can we fly with just one engine?" Stobs asked.

"Yes, but we can't take off with one," Phimble answered.

The boys didn't reply to that, leaving unasked the question that was in both of their minds as to why Phimble had put the Catalina down if one good engine could have been used to limp *Dosie* back to Melagi.

The truth was Phimble had argued with himself all night about exactly the same thing. He had finally reached the opinion that he'd screwed up, even though it had seemed the right thing to do at the time. It was only at the last second that *Dosie* had pulled herself out of her dive, and when Phimble saw the ocean so close and so smooth, he'd made a snap decision and landed. It had proved to be a gully washer of a belly flop, but at least they'd survived it, even though Fisheye, his hatch open, had nearly drowned in the nose turret.

Afterward, Phimble had stuck his head outside and heard the rumble of surf. Fearful of drifting into a reef, he'd put out the bow anchor and discovered by the length of the line before it went slack that he was in shallow water. The morning light had revealed why. They were near the big volcano-island. Just a little jig or jag in the night and he'd have rammed right into the thing. But that was neither here nor there. It was time to take the steps needed to leave. "Listen, Fisheye," Phimble said. "I've seen you work wonders on engines other mechanics have given up on. How about it?"

Stobs had apparently infected Fisheye's mood. "I can't fix this one, Mister Phimble. It's shot. Can't you see that?"

"I can see you ain't even trying," Phimble answered tartly, before softening a bit. "Look, son, I know I FUBAR'd this thing. I should've kept flying south on the one prop that was still spinning. You and Stobs both can take a swing at me later. But right now, I need five minutes out of that engine, that's all. It should be enough to get us into the air."

Fisheye ran his hand through his greasy hair, rubbed his long nose, then nodded his head over the engine. "Least there ain't no bullet holes in her I can see. We were batting all over the sky, so maybe something pulled loose, a gas line or something. That could have set her afire. I'll pull off the cowling, take a look."

"I'd be most grateful if you would," Phimble replied, and left well enough alone.

Megapode Dave was also standing on the wing and seemed to be study-ing the island, as if considering its possibilities. Phimble in turn considered the possibilities of the bird. *Dosie* had been in an uncontrolled dive when Phimble had asked the megapode to do something about it. Within sec-onds, the Catalina's nose had risen as if a giant finger had pushed up on it. Phimble guessed they'd only been a hundred feet above the water when that had happened. "You're some bird, Dave," Phimble said. Dave didn't re-spond. He had stopped contemplating the island and was studying the sky instead.

Phimble joined him in his study. The sky was crystal clear except for the usual morning clouds on the eastern horizon, which would soon dissipate. There was only a faint breeze slipping in from the northeast. Maybe a sig-nal fire with lots of smoke was the answer. It would be seen for miles in the clear air. But then it might be the Japanese who came in to investigate. Sig-naling to anybody and everybody would be a gamble.

Phimble thought of Josh and was encouraged by the thought. When Josh wasn't picked up, he'd likely figure out some way to get back to Melagi. The search for *Dosie* would begin the moment he got there.

"What's that white thing?" Stobs asked, pointing toward the island.

Phimble studied after Stobs's point, about halfway up the volcano. "Looks for all the world like a parachute hanging in a tree."

"One of the flares the Rufe dropped?"

"Too big," Phimble answered, then something stirred inside him and he made several decisions at once. "I'm going ashore to scout out the place. Fisheye, keep at it, son. Stobs, see if you can fix the radio."

"The radio caught a round right between its eyes, Mister Phimble," Stobs answered in a doleful tone. "And I've got little bloody holes all over my face from the glass of the dials. I've been picking them out all morning. They hurt."

"I'm sorry, Stobs, but . . ."

"Sorry won't fix my radio," Stobs interrupted. "It's a *piece of junk!*"

"I got it, Stobs!" Phimble snapped back. "You can't do anything. The world's gone to hell in a handbasket. And you've decided to give up. Come over here and put your head on my shoulder and give us a good cry. Maybe you need burping."

Stobs, his lip out a mile long, glared at Phimble, and the ensign gave it back to him. "Guess Dave's going after breakfast," Fisheye said, breaking the tension between the pilot and the radioman. The megapode had hopped off the wing and was waddling down the beach.

"Dave's got his ways," Stobs said. He picked at his face and brought out a tiny, crescent-shaped shard of glass. A tiny dribble of blood made a path down his cheek. "Let me have a look at your face," Phimble said.

Stobs waved the offer aside. "Naw, it's all right. Look, Mister Phimble, you're right. I'm acting like a baby. I'll see about the radio. Might be something I can wire up."

"Thank you, Stobs," Phimble said. He climbed through the nose hatch and worked his way into the interior of the Catalina and looked around until he found a machete. The boys had outfitted it well. He also found a canteen, filled it with water from a jerry can, and clipped it to his web belt. Then he climbed back out on the wing, walked to its tip, and hopped off into the shallow water and slogged to the beach. He started off in the general direction of the parachute, or whatever it was.

"You be careful, Mr. Phimble," Fisheye called after him.

Phimble waved and trudged across the beach, finding himself facing a wide savannah of knee-high grass that seemed to go all the way to the volcano. There was nothing to do but start through it, and he did, stirring up little yellow butterflies that flitted around his legs. He had figured to reach the white object in an hour. It took him that long to reach the base of the volcano and start up it. Two hours later, he was still climbing, swinging his machete through the tangle of vegetation every step of the way. There were no paths that he could discover and no clearings at all, just solid bush entwined with wait-a-minute vines, studded with sharp thorns. When he'd nearly decided to turn around, he chanced to look up into the branches of a banyan tree and was astonished to find a man hanging there in a parachute harness. The man wore brown, full-length coveralls, and his chest was covered by a corrugated float jacket. On his head was a leather helmet with goggles covering his eyes. What appeared to be a stop watch dangled from his neck on a red cord. There was a pistol strapped in a holster to his waist. It was without a doubt a Japanese pilot.

Phimble drew his forty-five, then looked around until he found a long stick and used it to poke at the pilot's boots. The pilot jerked, as if coming out of a deep sleep, and then looked down at Phimble with a somber expression. Then he pushed the goggles up on his forehead and reached for his pistol.

"Don't try it," Phimble warned. When the pilot kept fumbling with the pistol holster, trying to open its flap, Phimble shot a warning round into the air. That did the trick. The pilot dropped his hand away. "Now throw down that pistol," Phimble demanded.

"Sorry," the pilot answered in a hoarse voice. "I cannot feel my hands."

"Your parachute harness must have cut off your blood."

"*Hai.* Yes."

"You speak good English," Phimble said, although even as he said it, he reflected it was much too conversational a thing to say to an enemy pilot swinging in a tree.

"English is a compulsory course at the Imperial Naval Academy," the pilot responded.

"You're an officer? I thought all you Nippon fighter jockeys were sergeants."

"I am the leader of our squadron," the pilot answered. "Will you please get me down?"

Phimble puzzled over the situation, then reholstered his pistol. "I'll have to climb the tree and cut you loose," he said, "but you're my prisoner. No funny stuff."

"I cannot be your prisoner," the pilot answered.

"Why not?"

"I am samurai."

"Right now you look more like a goose strung up to be plucked."

The pilot didn't respond to Phimble's remark but continued to hang from the tree while looking thoroughly miserable. Since the jungle earth beneath the pilot was hard-packed soil, Phimble looked around for something the man could land on that wouldn't break his legs. Finally he piled up some loose brush, the best he could do, then shimmied up the banyan tree, the machete between his teeth. When he got a little higher than the pilot, he used the machete to hack at the parachute shrouds. It took a while, but he finally sliced through the last critical cord, and the pilot abruptly fell into the piled-up brush, grunting loudly when he hit.

Phimble climbed down the tree, deftly removed the pilot's pistol, and tucked it in his belt. Then he withdrew his own pistol and aimed it appropriately. The pilot rolled over and sat up, rubbing his arms and flexing his hands. He kept doing that for some time until apparently he'd restored adequate circulation. "You are from the Catalina," he said, as a statement of fact.

"And you're the Rufe pilot. I wasn't sure we got you. And you were lucky to parachute onto the island, and not in the ocean. The sharks would have eaten you, otherwise."

"It was also lucky that I had a parachute. Japanese fighter pilots don't always wear them, you know. We find them too confining. But I have a . . . medical condition. I need a soft seat, so I carry mine to sit on."

"Let me guess. You have hemorrhoids."

The pilot nodded. "Yes, it comes from sitting in the cockpit for long hours. Do you have any water?"

Phimble did, and handed over his canteen, which the pilot nearly drained. Then, without asking for permission, the pilot stripped off his parachute harness, the float vest, and the heavy coveralls, leaving him wearing only a pair of loose-fitting brown boots, the peculiar boots of a Japanese pilot, a pair of white shorts, and a skivvy shirt. There was also a broad white sash tied about his waist, which had many short red threads stitched in it.

"What is that sash around your middle?" Phimble asked.

The pilot patted the sash. "It is a traditional talisman of good luck. My mother stood on a Tokyo street corner and asked nine hundred and ninety-nine women to sew a red stitch in it. When Mama-san added hers, it meant one thousand women had wished for my safety and my success against the enemy."

"One thousand women agreeing on anything is powerful medicine," Phimble acknowledged. He took another look at his prisoner. The Japanese pilot was no more than five and a half feet tall and nearly skeletal, his ribs showing clearly against his papery skin. He also had a thin, haggard face with a shock of ebony black hair that looked as if it had been a long while since it had last seen a comb. In short, he was a sorry sight, but if he was anything like most Japanese pilots who flew the Rufes and the Zeros, he was one helluva flier. And always dangerous. Still, since he held both pistols, Phimble figured it cost nothing to be friendly. "I'm Ensign Eureka Phimble, United States Coast Guard," he said. "How about you?"

The pilot bowed. "Mamoru Ichikawa, lieutenant, Imperial Japanese Navy. You may call me Ichikawa-san. Your Catalina is a tough airplane. I'm certain I struck it several hard blows, yet you were able to land safely. If you had not knocked me down with a lucky shot, I would have strafed you until you blew up."

"Good thing we got a piece of you, then."

Ichikawa allowed a quick grin which looked more like a grimace on his skeletal face. "*Hai.* You would be dead otherwise."

"Let's be clear on our present situation. Things have worked out that you're my prisoner."

"I already told you. I cannot be your prisoner."

"That's foolish talk. There's nothing dishonorable about being a prisoner. You got caught fair and square. You act like you'd rather be dead."

"Death is as light as a feather for those of us who serve our country and our emperor."

"But if you get killed, then some other poor slub has to be trained and sent all the way out here."

"I did not say it was efficient," Ichikawa replied, after thinking through Phimble's objection. "It is, however, glorious."

"Glorious don't win wars," Phimble retorted, then added, in a congenial tone, "but I have to say you fight pretty damned hard." He waved his pistol down the hill. "Now, come along and don't try to run off, or I'll have to plug you."

Ichikawa looked around. "I need to use the toilet."

"Then pick a tree."

"*Domo.* Thank you." Ichikawa stepped into the bush, went behind a tree, and then, with considerable crashing and crunching of low bushes, started running.

Phimble knew he'd been snookered. He ran after the pilot, then stopped when a limb slapped him in the face. It hurt like hell and drew blood, too. Deciding it wasn't worth the aggravation, Phimble gave up the chase. After all, the man was unarmed and practically unclothed, rendered therefore harmless. Phimble gathered up the pilot's coveralls, helmet, and goggles as proof to the boys of what he'd found.

On the way down the volcano, after being tripped a few times by slick tree roots and taking a good tumble off a low cliff, Phimble finally arrived at a small rock outcropping that gave him a nice view of the beach. Everything looked peaceful. He could see that Fisheye had the cowling off the starboard engine, which gave him some hope the boy had decided he could fix it.

Then Phimble noticed that there was someone on the beach approaching the Catalina. He was astonished to observe that it was Ichikawa, carrying a short tree limb. Phimble fired his pistol into the air to alert Fisheye, but it was too late. The Japanese pilot leapt aboard the wing, ran down it and hit Fisheye with the limb, whereupon the mechanic fell headfirst into the water.

2 3

It was early morning when land hove into sight. According to Kennedy's dead reckoning, it was Tulagi, the capital island of the Solomons, and Ready confirmed it. The bosun had the wheel and turned the PT boat to come up the island's eastern shore. Less than an hour later, Ready eased into a small lagoon and found his way to a little American base of Quonsets and a few wooden hangarlike structures, all set back from the beach in the shade of palm trees and Norfolk pines. It was a neat, orderly, and clean place. Here, obviously, were engineers. Sure enough, a sign proclaimed it as home of the 27th Naval Construction Battalion, though why his PT boat had been brought there, Kennedy had no idea. Ready eased the boat beside the dock, and the Jackson twins tied her up. "You just rest up, sir," Ready told Kennedy, who was resting his back by lying beside the starboard torpedo tube. "We got a few things we need to do."

"Such as?" Kennedy asked, raising his head up.

"Supplies, sir. You know. We trade for this and that. All the stuff we'll need for our journey north."

"We're supposed to be in Melagi by this afternoon," he reminded the bosun.

"We may not make it," Ready confessed.

"Bosun, we *have* to make it. I gave my word we'd make it."

"Yes, sir, but things change sometimes. This boat don't have what she needs to go up the Slot."

Kennedy was too tired to argue, and he was feeling a bit feverish, besides. He climbed off the boat, walked up a boardwalk lined by white rocks, and discovered a hammock strung between two Norfolk pines. Gratefully, he crawled into it. While he hovered close to sleep, he reflected that the place was amazingly free of bugs. There was the faint smell of turpentine, and he wondered if that had anything to do with it. That was the last thing he wondered until he came awake, though only barely awake, hearing Once's voice (or was it Again's?). When he opened one eye, he saw the twin, whichever one it was, walking with a trio of Seabees in dungarees and skivvy shirts. They were heading down the boardwalk to the dock. Then Kennedy fell asleep again, only to wake some time later to the hiss of an arc welder and the pounding of steel upon steel. He heard more voices and saw more Seabees and Pogo standing beneath a frangipani tree with Ready aiming a camera at them. Pogo was wearing a scarlet lap-lap. He also had on an outrageously complex necklace made of cowrie shells and glass beads and shark's teeth, and there were painted white streaks on his cheeks and forehead. He wore amulets around his biceps with tassels hanging from them and, for no reason that could be discerned, a big plaited straw plate decorated with various designs pinned to his hair. He brandished a gleaming machete and a huge, toothy grin as Ready happily clicked away, and the Seabees crowded next to him.

All day, it seemed to Kennedy as he lapsed in and out of consciousness, Thurlow's boys and the Seabees and Pogo went back and forth along the boardwalk. Once, he woke and found some of the Seabees standing beside him. One of them was holding a big banana leaf that he quickly tried to hide behind his back. Kennedy would have questioned the purpose of the leaf if he hadn't subsequently passed out.

Kennedy came fully awake when a big crane rumbled past on a road behind him. He shakily climbed out of the hammock and followed the crane and was astonished to find the torpedo tubes unbolted from the deck of his PT boat and dumped on the beach. In the place of the bow tubes were steel cradles that had, based on their shiny appearance, just been fabricated. Then a truck arrived. In its bed were what looked suspiciously like torpedoes, except they were only half the size of the Mark VIIIs generally carried aboard a PT boat. Ready came up alongside Kennedy. "Get your nap out, sir?"

"What are you doing, Bosun?" Kennedy demanded. "You can't just go around modifying a war vessel of the United States Navy. It's against regulations."

"We're Coast Guard, sir," Ready explained.

"It doesn't matter. The boat's navy."

"I guess that changes everything," Ready acknowledged, though he made no move to stop the ongoing work.

Kennedy felt the hammock call him again, and after getting Ready's promise that no more unauthorized modifications would be made on the boat, he climbed in for more rest. When he awoke, he wandered back to the dock and found two shiny new torpedoes sitting in their shiny new racks, twin fifty-caliber machine guns mounted in the starboard and port tubs, and a twenty-millimeter Oerlikon gun on the stern. An eighty-one-millimeter mortar tube was mounted on the bow. Wooden ammunition crates were stacked high on the dock, and the Seabees were going back and forth across a steel gangway, stowing the crates aboard the PT boat.

Kennedy looked for Ready but didn't find him until a jeep showed up, Ready at the wheel. "Great little vehicle, sir," he said. "Hop in and I'll take you for a spin."

"Listen, Ready, I ordered you to stop modifying my boat, didn't I?"

"Oh, it's not modifications, sir. We're adding to it, that's all."

Kennedy looked forlornly at the boat. "It's not even a PT boat anymore. I don't know what it is. I mean, without the tubes and those torpedoes just sitting out there all exposed, and those extra guns, the lines aren't the same."

"You're right," Ready said. "It's not the same at all."

"But you don't care, do you?" Kennedy accused. "Do you have any idea what the navy will do to me when they find out about this? Maybe the Coast Guard thinks it's all well and good to just trick up a vessel any time you feel like it, but that's not the way the United States Navy does business, mister!"

"I'm heartily sorry about nearly everything," Ready replied, in a sincere tone.

Kennedy allowed a sigh. "How did you get the Seabees to do all this work for you, anyway?"

"Pogo, sir. Don't you recall how them nurses down at Santa Cruz made over him? Everybody does out here. It ain't often you can get your picture taken with a real live honest-to-Pete headhunter and all. Most guys, they'll give you anything to get their picture taken with him."

"Is Pogo really a headhunter?"

"I don't know, sir. I never asked him."

"What else? You must have traded something else. They've practically turned this base over to you."

"Well, um, *you,* sir," Ready confessed.

"Me?"

"Yes, sir. Turns out they heard about you. Kennedy, the ambassador's son and all. Rich guy. We let them take pictures of you in the hammock with this guy or that standing beside you waving a banana leaf over you like he was your servant fanning you or something. The Seabees thought that was about the funniest thing."

"Until this moment, I didn't realize how much my luck had truly run out," Kennedy despaired. "Now my court-martial charges will include destruction of government property and probably misuse of government personnel."

"Mister Kennedy, I think you worry about maybe a few too many things," Ready advised, with genuine concern.

"That's easy for you to say!" Kennedy snapped. "You're not the one who's going to be held responsible."

Ready couldn't argue with that, so he didn't.

"How much longer?" Kennedy demanded, looking at his watch. "It'll be dark soon."

"I think we'll be ready to leave first thing in the morning," Ready said. "There's a few things yet to do."

"Such as?"

"Armor plating. We saved so much weight by throwing off those torpedo tubes, we think another quarter inch of steel could be added around the cockpit without slowing us down. We'll have us a real gunboat then."

"Did you say gunboat?"

"I did, sir. You recall I was telling you about my granddaddy and the *Curlew?* We've done the same thing he did. Yes, sir. She's going to be a real gunboat, why, even a gunboat from hell, as granddaddy would say."

Kennedy started to yell at Ready, but then he stopped. He looked very carefully at the PT boat, which was the wrong thing to call it since it wasn't a PT boat anymore at all. Thurlow's boys had made it into something very different. He didn't know if the aircraft torpedoes would work, but the extra firepower of the heavy machine gun in the stern and the mortar on the bow could make a world of difference. The armored plating wasn't a bad idea, either.

"What are you thinking about, sir?" Ready hazarded.

"I think I might be the navy's first gunboat captain in this war."

"With this rig, you'll be able to get back at Jap for sinking you, for sartain. Would you like to name her, sir?"

Kennedy gave it some thought, then decided. "I think I'd like to call her the *Rosemary.*"

Ready grinned. "*Rosemary* she is, sir!"

Kennedy felt something in his heart, all fuzzy and warm. He wasn't certain what it was, though it might have been the residue of the fever, which seemed to have dissipated. Nonetheless, he felt so good he started to tell the Jackson twins that he thought they'd done a good job, and he would have, too, except at that moment, Once accidentally crossed two critical wires and the starboard torpedo rolled out of its rack. It landed in the water with a splash and sped off, wearing through a mud flat and into a grove of palms, where it sought one of them out and rammed it, detonating with a mighty force that sent big palm splinters and coconuts flying into the air.

Knocked down by the force of the explosion, Kennedy picked himself up off the dock. Ready rose from behind the jeep. The Jackson twins were still standing on the deck beside the empty torpedo cradle, scratching their heads and peering at the rising column of smoke emanating from the burning palms. The Seabees crawled out of the water where they'd jumped. Then they all began to laugh. After a while, against common sense, Kennedy joined them.

2 4

Josh sat on a whitewashed rock along the path to Minister Clarence's mission. He was trying to come to terms with the head Penelope had serenely drawn from the basket in the chapel. The smile on her lips had been so sweet, her eyes filled with such gentle innocence, it was all but impossible for him to reconcile the grotesque thing she had lifted into the hot white light beaming through the open window. He had mumbled something to her and stumbled outside away from the nightmare of the misshapen but peaceful expression on the face she had swung around for him to admire. He had gotten only as far as the rock, where he'd sat himself down, holstered his pistol, and tried to reason things out. How was it that this woman, whom he had made passionate love to the night before (although, it could be argued, he'd been under the influence of a drug) and twice more that very morning (with no drug), had accomplished this horrible act, that of murdering a man while he slept and cutting his head off and putting it in a basket?

Penelope came out of the chapel and stood beside him. "Are you all right, Josh darling?"

Josh raised his eyes to her. She was so innocent. He could not lecture her and tell her what she had done was wrong. Still, he felt he needed to supply at least some sort of correction to her behavior. "I'm not certain cutting a man's head off is what Reverend Clarence had in mind for atonement. Usually, one prays for forgiveness and that kind of thing."

"Oh, are you upset with me? My word. I am so sorry!"

"Not upset, Penelope dear. Just a bit surprised. By the way, the face of your man did not look very Japanese."

"Oh, he wasn't Japoni, so that is the reason why."

"But you said—" Then Josh stopped, realizing she had never said who had accomplished the massacre. He had assumed it was the Japanese. "It was one of Joe Gimmee's renegades," he realized aloud. "But you said he was a holy man and maybe in Australia."

"And so he is, Josh darling. But now we must bury Minister Clarence, who was also a good and holy man and to be completely trusted except perhaps when alone with little boys, something his people never allowed once his weakness was discovered. I believe I spied his head over there beside that jackfruit tree. I should be grateful if you will assist me in the digging of a suitable grave and erecting a marker."

"I don't think we have the time," Josh answered. "My aircraft, you see . . ."

"Then we must make the time," she replied, and raised her eyebrows.

So compelling was Penelope's wish, Josh agreed to it without further comment. Beneath the tropical sun, he used one of Minister Clarence's garden shovels to dig into the minister's garden where the ground was soft. When it was deep enough according to Penelope's standards, Josh dragged the loathsome torso over and rolled it into the grave. Then Penelope held the minister's head by its hair and lowered it in. Josh started to cover the awful thing up, but she stopped him.

"Words," she said. "There must be words. And since I am a Marie, my words do not hold much weight with the Lord. Therefore, they must come from you. Church words and good ones, if you please. Then I would like to read from this book, one of Minister Clarence's favorites." She held up a book that she'd brought from the chapel. It was not the Bible.

Josh scratched up under his cap, then recalled the modified psalm that Captain Falcon often quoted at times when death and destruction were near, or just past:

The Lord is my Skipper, I shall not drift. He guides me across the dark waters. He steers me through the channels. He keeps my log. Yea, though I sail amidst the tempests of the sea, I shall keep my wits about me. His strength is my shelter. He prepareth a quiet harbor before me. Surely the sun and the stars shall guide me, and I will come to rest in Heaven's Port forever.

"Quite prettily done in its execution," Penelope pronounced, as if quoting someone, and Josh suspected it might have been a favorite phrase of Minister Clarence himself. Penelope opened the minister's book and read:

We live in a world of transgressions and selfishness, and no pictures that represent us otherwise can be true, though, happily, for human nature, gleamings of that pure spirit in whose likeness man has been fashioned are to be seen relieving its deformities, and mitigating if not excusing its crimes.

"That was also nicely done," Josh said, thinking he'd heard those words before but not quite placing them. He took the book from Penelope and read the title on its binder: *The Deerslayer.* "This was one of my father's favorite books," he told her.

"Toss it in with Minister Clarence," Penelope instructed him. "He will enjoy it." After Josh had done so, she smiled a sad smile. "Minister Clarence used to call me Natty Bumppo because I loved to go alone in the forest. I used to bring him snakes and frogs and any manner of bugs to identify. He would patiently look them all up in his big book and teach me their names."

Penelope had taken a mahogany cross off the chapel wall and scratched Minister Clarence's name along its horizontal crossbar. Josh finished shoveling dirt into the grave, then stuck the cross in the ground at the head of it, and the deed was done. He tossed the shovel aside, wiped his hands on his utilities, and took stock. "Well, my dear Penelope Bumppo, lead us back to the beach where you found me. That's where my Catalina will land."

"Yes, I am quite ready to quit this island forever," she said, walking away without looking back.

He followed her as down they went, winding through the bush, this way and that, the fresh smell of the sea soon reaching Josh's nostrils and, he hoped, flushing away the sickly smell of the New Georgian dead. They reached a headland by the sea, a place where the landing beach might be observed without their being seen. "You are a very smart girl to take us here first where we might have a look around," he said, lying down behind a small bush. He felt her wriggle in close to him.

"It pleases me that I please you," she said. "Might I please you more before we fly away?"

"I've no time for a Marie at the moment," Josh said, then immediately regretted his ill-chosen words. He cleared his throat and pretended he hadn't said anything, although her eyes felt hot on his cheek, and he knew he had hurt her. He scanned the beach, saw that Phimble had not yet arrived, then ducked when he saw three men suddenly appear. They were Japanese soldiers who were alternately looking out to sea and beachcombing, or so it seemed. They were nonchalant in the way they strolled, and Josh guessed that meant they were not alone. "A fine pickle," he said, thinking not only of his situation but Phimble's.

"A fine pickle," Penelope repeated.

"My Catalina's going to get shot down if it tries to land," Josh said, still thinking out loud.

"Its pilot will surely see the Japoni," Penelope replied. "He would have to be blind otherwise."

Josh gave that some thought and hoped Penelope was right. "Do you think we could get over to the Truax plantation without Jap spotting us?"

"It is not possible," Penelope said firmly. "I am certain there are many Japoni waiting along the path. We would surely be caught."

"And if we stay here, they'll soon catch us anyway. What do you think we should do?"

Penelope made a puffing noise between her pursed lips. "*Pfft!* You are asking me? But I am only a Marie, for which you have no time at present."

Josh gave his words some thought this time and said, "I am confident that you can do anything you put your mind to, Penelope dear."

Penelope studied him, as if looking for sincerity, then said, "I know a safe place."

He touched her cheek and said, "Then take me there, Penelope Bumppo," and was rewarded by her gracious and lovely smile, which he found himself quite lost within.

2 5

The likely scenario of events sped through Phimble's mind as he rushed as fast as the jungle-covered mountain would allow. Surely the Japanese pilot had killed Fisheye and had since invaded the interior of the seaplane, overcome Stobs, and taken any number of pistols, rifles, and even the Browning automatic rifle that was stowed somewhere aboard. Phimble cursed himself all the way for being a true begomer, having left the boys without a final caution to be on guard.

It was with the relief that comes only to a man spared the just results of his own folly that he emerged on the beach to see the Japanese pilot trussed up on the sand, his hands tied behind his back, and Fisheye sitting over him on the tip of the wing, his legs dangling nonchalantly. Stobs stood alongside the pilot, cradling a rifle. Dave was back from his journey and was squatting on the horizontal stabilizer. Nothing about the scene was of apparent interest to the megapode, as he was dozing.

"Hidy, Mister Phimble," Fisheye said from the Catalina's wing.

"I thought surely you was dead," Phimble replied hoarsely. "I fired my pistol, but it was too late. I saw him hit you with that big stick. Are you hurt bad?"

"I ain't hurt bad at all," Fisheye reported. "Ichikawa-san pulled his punches, don't ask me why."

"I heard Fisheye hit the water," Stobs said, shrugging, "and I thought he'd gone swimming. I was just going to tell him to stop playing around and fix the engine when Ichikawa-san tried to come through the hatch. I jumped on him and wrestled him into submission. He's so skinny, it wasn't much of a contest. Then I tied him up, and we've been talking some, got introduced and all."

Phimble used his sleeve to wipe the sweat from his brow, the mixed hot and cold sweat of exertion and anxiety. "So now there's no argument about you being our prisoner," he said to the pilot.

Ichikawa shrugged his bony shoulders. "I have been captured," he answered, "but I will try to escape."

"I was hoping we could get your word you wouldn't try to escape," Phimble said, with regret. "Then you could walk around, do anything you please."

"I wish I could give you my parole," he answered in an aggrieved tone, "but I have explained the Bushido code of the samurai to you and these boys as well. Pray do not ask me to break faith with it and my fellows. I can not and I shall not."

"Well, can we at least ask that you not try to kill one of us?"

"We are at war, and it is required that I try to kill you."

"You Japanese have the hardest heads I've ever run across," Phimble said crossly. His stomach took that moment to growl its way to his attention. "Anyway, how's about lunch?"

"I am very hungry," Ichikawa confessed.

Stobs waded out to the hatch of the Catalina and crawled inside. With Fisheye's help, he set up a portable gas-fed stove on the beach. It didn't take him long to produce grilled cheese sandwiches and a pot of coffee. Ichikawa's hands were untied so that he could eat. "I'll shoot you if you make a run for it," Fisheye advised.

"I make no promises," Ichikawa replied, though it was obvious he was going to be busy for a while, since he was devouring the sandwiches.

They ate while a gentle surf lapped at their feet. Then Phimble noticed that Dave was awake and his beak was pointing skyward. "We may have trouble coming," Phimble said.

Stobs and Fisheye looked where Dave was pointing. "I see it!" Fisheye cried.

Ichikawa looked, then smiled, saying, "My boys are looking for me. Surrender, Yankee, or die. Screw Babe Ruth. And Eleanor Roosevelt, too."

"Shut up, Ichikawa-san," Fisheye said. "That wasn't very nice at all. My mother met Mrs. Roosevelt one time when she came to Killakeet. She seemed a nice lady, or so I was told. Babe Ruth's got good qualities, too."

Ichikawa ignored Fisheye's comment. "I would suggest you move away from your aircraft," he said gleefully. "It will soon be filled with bullet holes and on fire."

Phimble was about to order his boys to do just that, but there was something about Ichikawa's attitude that made him angry enough to reconsider. "Fisheye, Stobs, bundle Ichikawa-san here aboard *Dosie,* then man the guns in the blisters. I'll take the nose gun."

Dave withdrew his neck and walked down the back of the Catalina and hopped inside the forward turret hatch, landing on Phimble's head just as he entered the cramped space. They looked at each other, pilot and bird, then Phimble took charge of the machine gun and Dave headed for cover.

2 6

Kennedy savored the golden sunlight that warmed his face as he turned the gunboat *Rosemary* into Melagi's deep harbor, which he was surprised to see bobbing with landing craft. "Looks like the balloon's going up for another landing somewhere," he said to Ready, who was maintaining vigil with him.

"I don't know about the balloon, but I'd say the Raiders are headed up the Slot in what Colonel Burr would say is *toot sweet,*" Ready answered. Even as he spoke, a group of helmeted Raiders gathered along the shore, rifles slung over their shoulders, preparatory to boarding one of the slab-sided LCI's. "Swing over there, Mister Kennedy. I know that slub at the tiller."

Kennedy eased the gunboat over as directed. The "slub" was a stocky young Coast Guardsman in denim pants, faded blue shirt, and a tub hat shoved to the back of his head. "Hey, Ready, what you got there?" he asked, his big grin not enough to mask a massive overbite. "Man oh man, lookit all them guns. And them fancy torpedoes. What do you call her?"

"She's a gunboat, Sully," Ready answered proudly. "She not only can raise hell, she can go so fast, she blows the hair right off your head. How's life in the real Coast Guard?"

"Pret' near perfect if it wasn't for carrying these jarheads hither and yon."

The Raiders all perked up at the insult and jeered in unison, calling the driver a "puddle pirate." "Pipe down, you gravel-grinders!" Sully yelled, and they did, although with much muttering through the tobacco chaws stretching their cheeks. Before long, they were singing:

Bless 'em all, bless 'em all,
The long and the short and the tall,
Bless all the sergeants and corporals, too,
Bless all the privates and above all bless you.

Then, just for fun, the Raiders changed the lyrics to substitute a not very nice word for "bless" that rhymed with "truck." It made them laugh, which Kennedy supposed was the reason they did it.

"Where you headed?" Ready asked the LCI Coast Guardsman.

"Today, just over to Florida Island. Training exercise. Next day or two, though, we're headed somewheres real. Not sure where. Up north, prob'ly."

Ready conducted a scan of the harbor. "I don't see our Catalina."

Sully looked around and agreed that there was no seaplane in evidence. "You supposed to meet up?"

"That was the plan." Ready turned to Kennedy. "It ain't like Mister Phimble not to be where he said he was going to be. It's right worrisome, that's what it is. And I reckon if Captain Thurlow was here, he'd have spotted us coming across Iron Bottom Bay and be here to greet us."

Kennedy eased the *Rosemary* alongside the dock, just kissing the bumpers. All the boys, except Ready, immediately jumped off the boat and headed inland. "They're going to our cave to collect a few things for the trip," Ready advised Kennedy. "But I still can't figure why Mister Phimble and Captain Thurlow ain't here. What do you think we ought to do, Mister Kennedy?"

Kennedy sat down on the engine hatch and tried to think his way through it. After considerable thought, he reached his conclusion. "I don't have any idea," he said.

Ready's disappointment showed on his wide face. "There you go again, sir."

"When are you going to learn that officers don't always have the answers, Ready?" Kennedy demanded.

"That ain't the point, sir. The point is you have to decide even when you ain't certain. You know, like you decided which direction we should go back at Santa Cruz."

"And you saw how wonderful that turned out," Kennedy replied. "We got lost."

"At first, we did," Ready confessed. "But we got where we was going, didn't we? That's what counts, to get where you're going, even if you're not sure where that is."

Kennedy's head was spinning from Ready's logic. "You are *vaahstly* too deep for me, Bosun."

"Well, let me put it this way. If you quit trying, people are liable to say, 'There goes a quitter.' You don't want them to say that about you, do you, sir?"

"I don't much care what they say," Kennedy lied.

A Raider sergeant appeared at the dock. "Lieutenant," he said, "Colonel Burr wants you to report in on the double."

"Who is Colonel Burr?" Kennedy asked.

"Monkey Burr, sir," Ready interjected. "The meanest bastard in the South Pacific, excuse me, Sarge, for saying so. You're his clerk, ain't you?"

"I am, Bosun, and you'll get no argument from me about him being a mean bastard. Hurry now, Lieutenant, or we're both gonna get yelled at."

"Why would Colonel Burr want to see me? How does he even know I'm here?"

"Well, dang, I forgot to ask."

"Your sarcasm is observed," Kennedy sniffed.

"Hey, Sarge, you ain't seen Captain Thurlow around, have you?" Ready asked.

The Raider clerk took on a hangdog look. "Got some bad news for you, there, Bosun. Best we know, Captain Thurlow is likely dead. Your Ensign Phimble, probably, too."

Ready's jaw dropped. "Dead? How can that be?"

"Well, that's quite a question," the sergeant said, and took on a philosophical expression. "I guess the general answer is dying is what we do out here in the Solomons, and your captain and ensign ain't no exception."

"It just can't be true!" Ready cried, a tear already carving through the salt on his cheek.

"Take it easy, Ready," Kennedy said. "We need details, Sergeant. Do you know any?"

"A few. Monkey gets all the hot skinny, and sometimes I can't help but hear what's said. That coast-watcher Whitman finally got a radio working. He told us Jap is still crawling around up there on New Georgia where he's at. He also said Thurlow was probably captured or killed by Jap, which is the same thing. As to your Ensign Phimble, Cactus got a call from his radioman last night. They were flying their Catalina up the Slot and spotted what they thought was one of our landing boats on fire. Nobody's heard nothing since. The flyboys found a burned-out LCI this morning, but it was adrift, and everybody killed aboard it. All we know for sure is there were a slew of Rufes flying around last night. Most likely they shot down your Catalina."

"But nobody knows whether Thurlow or Phimble is dead for certain. Is that correct?" Kennedy asked.

The Raider clerk shrugged. "Ain't been no bodies found, if that's what you mean."

"Is a search being conducted?"

"Flyboys over on the Canal been told to keep their eyes open. That's about it."

"Ready, I'm going to see the colonel," Kennedy said, after a moment of reflection.

"Tell him we want to go look for them, sir!" Ready cried. "Tell him it ain't right to leave the skipper and Mister Phimble out there all alone without nobody looking for them!"

"I'll be sure to tell him," Kennedy replied with a hard edge. "I happen to have some experience at being abandoned."

2 7

Kennedy followed the sergeant-clerk to the Raider headquarters and sat on the veranda for the better part of two hours waiting for Colonel Burr to receive him. He didn't mind the wait, as it gave him a chance to rest his back in a wicker chair. An observer of people by nature, Kennedy took note of the nervous body language of the various Raiders as they approached the old planter's house and went up its stoop and into Burr's office. Officer and enlisted man alike would approach with their heads up, shoulders back, all filled with the piss and vinegar that came naturally to the marines, only to have their swagger falter as they climbed the steps and crumble entirely as they approached the open double doors that led into the inner sanctum. The clerk, sitting behind a typewriter that he pounded with two fingers, sometimes solved their problem, whatever it was, and they ran off in obvious relief. But when they were told to go in to see the colonel, each instantly whipped off his headgear, helmet or utility cap, and walked inside as if treading on fresh eggs. Soon afterward, Burr's voice, nearly always at full bellow, rattled the pictures on the wall. One by one, the visitors fled, sustaining a fast pace until they were out of shouting distance. A lot of men were feeling the colonel's wrath this day.

The clerk apparently received some sort of silent signal and called to Kennedy, "Your time has come, Lieutenant." He made his advisement in much the regretful voice a guard might use to alert a prisoner that they had fixed the problem with the short circuit on the electric chair.

Kennedy slowly unbent his frame. He'd sat for too long. His back was stiff, his knees like concrete, and the coral wounds on his feet stabbed at him like needles. He stood, teetering, sweat breaking out on his forehead, until he came to terms with the pain. The clerk gave him a quick once-over, as if looking for fleas, then ushered him inside, where he was left standing before the ugliest desk Kennedy supposed he had ever seen, a big gray metal thing heaped with stacks of papers and charts. Behind the desk sat Monkey Burr, as ugly as the desk. His head snapped up from the papers and charts. "Well, Lieutenant, are you going to just stand there and continue staring, or are you going to properly report?"

Kennedy stood in as near a state of attention as his body would allow, while mumbling, "Reporting as ordered, sir."

Burr stared hard at him for a long second, then directed Kennedy to a chair, which he took gratefully. He was in agony but still managed to ask the colonel a question. "Can you tell me what you know of Captain Thurlow and Ensign Phimble?"

"Do I look like a briefing officer to you, son?" Burr asked, in a quiet though thoroughly menacing voice.

"Their boys need to know, Colonel," Kennedy replied.

"All they need to know is their gravy train is off its rails!" Burr snapped, with obvious satisfaction. "I shall see them packed off to the regular Coast Guard within a day."

"What about Lieutenant Armistead?"

"That mission no longer concerns you," Burr replied. "In fact, I was astonished when I heard Thurlow had recruited you, considering your situation."

"My situation?"

"The loss of your PT boat."

"I see."

"You're famous, son, and that can work for you, and it can work against you. Ever since you left Lumbari, your command has been trying to find you. Very soon, a launch from Guadalcanal will pull up to my dock, and in it will be a naval intelligence officer. I believe you know him. A Lieutenant Byron White."

Kennedy straightened in his chair, wincing from the pain it caused. "Whizzer White?"

"If he has a nickname, I'm not aware of it. But if that's the man, and he's a friend of yours, then maybe he can help you. Your court-martial has been moved up, and White's been appointed as the investigating officer."

Kennedy's head swam. "Why has it been moved up?"

"It is my understanding Admiral Halsey made the decision."

Kennedy understood the situation now. His father had been in the forefront of the America First movement, an organization that existed entirely to keep the United States out of the war. Halsey probably blamed Pearl Harbor on men like Joe Kennedy. Now the ambassador's second son had given the admiral the opportunity for revenge. Numbed, Kennedy asked, "What of my new boat?"

"Your squadron is sending down another officer and crew to bring it back to your Lumbari base in Rendova. Just leave the paperwork with my clerk."

"There is no paperwork. We stole it."

Burr's eyebrows shot up. "What?"

"We stole the PT boat that's tied to your dock. Actually, she's not a PT boat anymore. We converted her into a gunboat. Her name is the *Rosemary*."

"No, it's not. Nothing you just related ever happened. You may have forgotten the paperwork, but you did *not* steal a boat, nor did you illegally convert her. Do you require anything else, Lieutenant? A place to stay the night? Just let my clerk know your needs. You will find him remarkably amenable."

Kennedy stood, feeling as if the slightest breeze might blow him over. "Thank you, Colonel," he said dully.

"Good luck, Lieutenant," Burr said, in a surprisingly kind voice. "It sounds as if you could use some."

Kennedy nodded, saluted, and walked out of Burr's office. A familiar voice hailed him. "Jack, old man. There you are!"

It was indeed Byron "Whizzer" White, as Kennedy had surmised. Before the war, he and the Rhodes scholar had made an automobile tour across Germany together. Along the way, they'd managed to roll the automobile and later were stoned by a group of Nazi thugs. It had all been quite the adventure. Whizzer had gone on to become a professional football player and was now studying to be a lawyer. He had always been a sincere young man, with a blocky jaw and an expression of perpetual honesty. Kennedy supposed Whizzer was just the kind of man the ambassador wished had been his second son, rather than the screw-up he'd actually sired. Kennedy shook hands with him while White beamed his block-jaw sincerity.

White was carrying a briefcase and treating it as if it were the most important object on Melagi. "I want to go over everything that happened from the moment you left Lumbari until your rescue," White told him, in most urgent tones. He opened the briefcase and withdrew a document. "I won't sugarcoat your situation, Jack. It looks bad for you, very bad. This is the order from Admiral Halsey establishing your immediate court-martial. You're pretty much guilty, based on your own report, but perhaps your actions after you lost your boat until you were rescued will serve to ameliorate the blame. I think we might get the dereliction of duty charge reduced to simple inattentiveness. There'd be a comment on your record, but you wouldn't lose your commission. You're finished out here, of course, but maybe we can get you a desk somewhere back in the States to finish out your time."

Kennedy stared at White, and something snapped inside him. He wasn't certain why, but all of a sudden he felt free. "I was not rescued," he said while squaring his shoulders. "I saved myself."

White rubbed his jaw. "I don't think it would be wise to say it exactly that way," he advised. He looked over his shoulder, then lowered his voice. "Jack, please understand me. If you are to have any chance of avoiding a finding of guilty on some very serious charges, you must cooperate from this moment on. It is especially important that you not criticize any of your superior officers."

"My superior officers abandoned me. Don't you understand?"

"As your friend, I understand very well, but as your legal counsel, I have to tell you it doesn't matter."

Kennedy smiled, then walked away.

"Where are you going?" White called after him.

"To my boat," Kennedy said. "Don't follow me, Whizzer. Just wait right here. I'll be back."

"When?"

Kennedy did not reply, just kept walking until he reached the dock where Ready sat on a piling, his face in his hands. All the other boys had returned and were also sitting around the dock in various stages of moping. Looking at them, Kennedy thought about a number of things in swift succession, all the while feeling a fluidic strength seep into his bones. It was like electricity because he had decided what he was going to do, and it was as glorious as it was audacious. *A man should occasionally do a glorious, audacious thing,* he thought. *Or else he isn't really a man.*

"Ready," he said, and patiently waited until the bosun lifted his tear-streaked face. "Did the boys bring everything they need?"

"Yes, sir, only of course now it don't matter, Captain Thurlow and Mister Phimble and Fisheye and Stobs and Dave being dead and all. And we got told to report to Colonel Burr's clerk for reassignment, *toot sweet.*"

Kennedy stepped aboard the gunboat named after his eldest sister. "Boys, listen up. There's a chance that Captain Thurlow and Ensign Phimble and Fisheye and Stobs and your megapode aren't dead after all."

One by one, Thurlow's boys raised their eyes.

"I want you to know something else," Kennedy continued. "Just like you, I've been ordered off this boat. My squadron's sending down a new skipper and crew." He climbed into the cockpit and put his hand on the throttles. "Well," he said, "if you're waiting for a formal invitation, this is the best I can do. This is our boat. We stole her fair and square. I'm going to take her and go north. Who's going with me?"

2 8

Penelope's lap-lap danced fetchingly before Josh's eyes as she led him through the tangled bush to a place where she said they would be safe. He confessed to himself that he was quite taken with the girl all in all, even though she had demonstrated a tendency to cut off the heads of men who didn't atone to her standards. He suspected his father would make a fool of himself over her, too, if he ever got the chance. After all, the Keeper had made a habit of bringing home to the lighthouse more than a few fancy ladies from Morehead City, some even a third his age, and capering around with them. His activities had simultaneously appalled the Killakeet women and earned the secret admiration of most of the island's men.

"Women are both God's blessing to men and also His curse," the Keeper had told Josh years ago when he'd been so foolish as to ask his father for advice about a difficult girlfriend. "To keep the blessing and avoid the curse, I have memorized these words: *You know, my dear, now that I have given it some thought, you are absolutely right.* No matter the woman, no matter her consternation over some foolishness I might have perpetrated, those few and quite magical words have usually saved me. Don't ever forget them, my boy, and I predict a rosy future for you with the female class."

Josh had not forgotten the words, but he guessed he'd forgotten to use them often enough, especially with Dosie, his once and now gone forever love. He thought about Dosie as Penelope's very nicely turned rump danced before his eyes, and he reflected that he was having some difficulty recalling exactly what Dosie looked like, although he was certain that his heart must still be broken over her.

Then he thought that the only thing certain about his situation was that he surely must be an idiot, perhaps even a dangerous idiot. Here he was, stealing his way through the bush on New Georgia, likely surrounded by a thousand or more Japanese soldiers who would be happy to use him for bayonet practice or worse, and all he could think about was women. *You're an odd duck, Josh Thurlow,* he said to himself and knew it was true, for sartain, but he was blamed if he could figure out what to do about it, or if he should do anything at all.

Penelope's lap-lap stopped its mesmerizing hula. "Josh darling," she whispered over her bare shoulder. "Do you see the Japoni?"

Josh had healthy eyes of which he was most proud, but he'd seen nothing for the last hour other than a jumble of bush and trees and tall waving grass and Penelope's fetching backside. He took a long look around, recognizing that it was his peripheral vision that tended to pick out the unusual or a pattern that didn't fit. Before long, he was astonished to discern quite clearly a Japanese soldier squatting just off the path Penelope had recently started following. The soldier was the same color as the long saw grass in which he hid, a sickly brownish-green. His uniform was tattered, his bony knees poked through his trousers, and his bare arms and face were plastered with dirt. His large oval eyes rolled in their direction beneath his soft cap. He adjusted himself, a skeletal hand going to his stomach.

"Now you see him, don't you?" Penelope whispered. "I have seen him for the longest time."

"He is almost surely booby-trapped," Josh replied, ignoring Penelope's comment about the perfection of her vision. "That is why he's so near the path. From the looks of him, he's been gut-shot and left to take the first American or coast-watcher with him to Japoni heaven." Josh withdrew his pistol from its holster, meaning to take care of the situation.

Penelope stayed his hand. "Josh darling, I am certain even at this range you could drill the Japoni with your pistol, for, my word, with all your other talents, you must certainly be an extremely good shot. But the noise would only bring more Japoni for you to kill. No, it must be a silent death."

"But he will blow himself up if you get near him."

"I do not think so. I will speak to him."

"Can you speak Japanese?"

Penelope gave Josh a contemptuous glance, her first, he would later reflect. "Josh darling, there are times when I believe you do not comprehend your good fortune at falling into the company of yours very truly."

Before Josh could stop her, Penelope was striding down the path, slowing as she neared the soldier, who watched her with his huge eyes, his mouth a crooked line of pain. She knelt a dozen feet away from him, plunging the point of her machete into the soft earth. Josh could hear that she was talking to the soldier but could not understand her words or even what language she was speaking, though it was in a soft, melodious tone. The soldier replied, his voice like the snapping of small, dry twigs. Then he began to search his pockets. Josh raised his pistol, but Penelope, even though her back was to him, held up her hand as a signal for him to do nothing. Josh was wondering if she had eyes in the back of her pretty head. Nothing much about Penelope, he thought, would surprise him.

The Japanese soldier held something up to Penelope, a pouch of some kind. Penelope came closer and took the pouch from his bony hands, inspected its contents, then gave it back to him. She pulled her machete out of the ground and walked back to Josh. "He has been here for a day and a night and now a part of another day. He is in much pain and is ready to die. His fellows left him with a grenade. He hopes to use it to kill an American."

"He told you all this?" Josh asked, and though he didn't mean it to, a note of doubt crept into his tone.

"A dying person speaks so that all may understand," she answered in a quiet voice. "He showed me a photograph of his wife and children."

Josh pushed his cap to the back of his head and wiped his sweaty brow with his sleeve. The humidity was so thick, it was like breathing steam. "We can't wait all day for him to die," he said, "and I can't just leave him here. What if an American patrol should come by? He could hurt somebody."

Penelope placed a finger to the corner of her mouth as she gave the matter some thought. "I will explain this to him," she said, and headed down the path before Josh could stop her. She squatted a few feet from the soldier and started talking. His eyes grew concerned as she fluttered her hands and flung her arms around in animated conversation. He said a few words and then, to Josh's astonishment, smiled.

She returned. "He understands."

"Understands what?"

"I explained to him that you were an American but you were not a proper one for him to kill since you were not here to fight, that you were looking for a lost man and a lost woman and to kill you would be a waste of his grenade. He said it was a sad thing. He so hoped to kill an American. Then I told him that it is a lovely day, a good day to go to his ancestors, though he should let nature take its course and go quietly."

"And you think he agreed?"

"Why not?"

"Penelope dear, I think you are an optimist."

"I hope that is a compliment."

"I do, too."

Penelope's lips turned down. "Sometimes I think you are a cruel man."

"I'm sorry—get down!"

The soldier had managed somehow to get to his feet and, hunched over, was staggering in their direction. Josh pushed Penelope beneath him just as the grenade the soldier was carrying exploded. It wasn't a powerful explosion (Japanese grenades were notorious for being duds), and all it did was fling the man off the path while thoroughly making a greater mess of his stomach. A small, hot fragment of the grenade landed on Josh's hand. He flung it off while the Japanese soldier's bloody chest heaved once, then went still.

"Well, so much for him dying quietly, little miss optimist."

"It was because you're an American, even though I explained you were not a proper one," Penelope retorted, neatly transferring the blame. "Would you climb off me now? There is a sharp rock beneath me, and it hurts."

Josh climbed to his feet and helped Penelope up. He pondered the Japanese soldier. "What an idiot," he said, shaking his head.

"Why do you call him such a name?" she demanded. "He was very brave."

"Too brave. A soldier who is willing to follow orders certain to get himself killed is a bad soldier. Such soldiers make for lazy officers who throw them away at the enemy, hoping to get lucky. That's the problem with the Japanese in this war. They think dying is the answer, and it is, I suppose, if the question is *How can I lose the war?*"

"You have clearly given war a great deal of thought," Penelope said. "I think you love war. That is the only reason why you are here."

Josh was taken aback by her accusation. "That isn't true! I am here because I was ordered here. I would like nothing more than to be back home."

"Where is that?"

"A wild place off the coast of North Carolina. It's called Killakeet Island."

"Would you take me there?"

"To Killakeet? But it's on the other side of the world."

"I am not afraid to travel."

"It is often cold there. It has even been known to snow."

"Then I would wear a coat."

Josh studied her. "Have you ever worn a coat?"

"No, but I like to do new things."

Josh allowed an interval of thinking, looking for the harm of being agreeable. When he couldn't find any, he said, "I would be proud to have you visit Killakeet."

And there was that lovely smile again, which warmed Josh's heart. "We should go now," Penelope said.

"To Killakeet?"

"No, silly man. I was referring to the here and now. The sound of the grenade must surely have stirred up the Japoni."

It was a point that Josh had momentarily overlooked. "Let's go," he said, and so they did. Up a rise, around a bend, down a bank, and after that Josh lost track of where Penelope might be leading him. He was tired and hot and sweaty, and he wondered if he was coming down with a fever. He'd escaped malaria up to now, but in the Solomons, one never knew.

Penelope finally brought them to a small stream. "Here the water is clean and we can drink," she said. "And we should rest here, beneath this poison-fish tree, which allows us excellent shade and a bit of coolness."

Josh observed the shiny leaves and the white, sweetly scented blossoms of the tree and thought them poor cover for the sun or bullets, though he didn't comment. Penelope picked up one of the brown, squarish fruits littering the ground. "These are the seeds we use to poison fish. Thus the name of this tree."

"Very interesting," he said, feeling his forehead. It was surprisingly cool. Maybe he wasn't coming down with fever after all. Maybe he was just going crazy.

Penelope sat beneath the shade of the tree and patted the ground by its roots. "Sit beside me."

Josh sat and, in the waving shadow, rested and even slept. When he awoke, he found Penelope cradling his head in her lap, looking down at him with an expression he couldn't quite define. "You are a pretty girl," he observed.

"I know where he is," she replied. "Your Lieutenant Armistead. He is with Joe Gimmee."

Josh sat up. "But that's what Whitman said, and you denied it."

Penelope shrugged, her smooth shoulders rising and falling in the dappled sunlight. It was all Josh could do to keep from putting his hands on those lovely shoulders and drawing them near. "Do you know where Joe Gimmee is?" he asked. "It isn't Australia, is it?"

She ran her long fingers through his hair and to the back of his neck, while her eyes took on a dreamy look. His hands, as if outside his control, slid around her back. "He is not in Australia but he is far away," she whispered into his ear. "And Joe Gimmee demands much of those who find him."

His nostrils were filled with her wonderful scent. "Why didn't you tell me this before?" he croaked.

"I have been trying to make up my mind about you."

"In what way?"

"I want you to do something for me," she said. "I want you to kill Mastah Whitman. Then I will guide you to Joe Gimmee."

Josh was startled, and his hands dropped away from her. "Why do you want me to kill Whitman?"

Her expression of dreaminess disappeared, replaced by an expression that could only be defined as pure hatred. "Because of what he is."

Josh was thoroughly confused. "What is he?"

She studied his face. "Lie on me again."

"Stop changing the subject. Tell me. What is Whitman?"

Penelope sat back against the poisonfish tree. "Whitman boys kai-kai along Japoni, kai-kai along pickaninny, kai-kai even along Americans. I have seen them do this."

"Kai-kai?" Josh searched through his knowledge of pidgin until he thought he recalled the word. It made his stomach sink. "Penelope, are you saying what I think you're saying?"

"They are all cannibals," she replied.

"But surely not Whitman!"

"Especially he."

2 9

The Rufe pilot aimed his float plane at *Dosie,* then jinked around and cut across her at an extreme angle, so nimbly and fast neither Phimble in the nose turret nor any of the boys at the blister guns could get a bead on him. He sped off, then turned around to make another run. Once again, his acrobatics kept him out of *Dosie*'s gun sights, and he flashed so low across the Catalina that the thunder of the Rufe's engine nearly broke their ear drums. "How come he ain't firing at us?" Stobs wondered while rubbing his ears.

"He is looking for me," Ichikawa, who was tied up alongside Fisheye, explained. "The next time, he probably will shoot. We are all going to die." He said the last words with quiet satisfaction.

"Maybe not," Phimble said, crawling out of the forward turret to snatch Ichikawa by his arm. He half dragged, half pushed him through the hatch, then towed him to the beach. "Here he is!" Phimble yelled at the sky, just as the Rufe suddenly appeared out of nowhere and barreled overhead, the prop wash throwing up a storm of sand.

With a proud, fierce expression, Ichikawa said, "That is Kyushu, one of my best pilots."

The Rufe, now just a speck in the clear blue sky, turned and set up another run. On it came, growing ever larger, but then the pilot of the Rufe rocked the wings of his aircraft and gunned for altitude.

"So!" Ichikawa cried, then sucked air between his teeth. "I am disappointed in Kyushu. He should have fired his guns."

"Maybe he thinks you're more valuable than a few Americans and an old beat-up wreck of a float plane."

Ichikawa threw back his shoulders and stuck out his chin. "There is nothing less important than my life."

"You are an odd duck, Ichikawa-san," Fisheye said, as he and Stobs climbed out of the Catalina. "Such a thing to say."

"And a worse thing to believe," Stobs added.

"It is what I believe," Ichikawa replied, and then fell silent, their opinions putting him into something of a pout.

"So now what?" Stobs asked, as the Rufe grew smaller, then disappeared.

"So now we'd better get out of here," Phimble answered, executing the Solomons salute when a swarm of mosquitoes came after him. "Most likely, Jap will be back, but I'll bet next time with a boat. Stobs, keep working on your radio. Fisheye, back to work on the engine, old son."

Fisheye nodded. "I figured out the problem is a fuel line, Mister Phimble. It broke, and that's what caused the fire. But I've got no way to fix that won't allow a leak. Besides that, I think the pistons are likely scored."

"All I need is for that engine to work long enough to get us into the air."

"Even if I got it running, it couldn't be trusted. It could conk out just as you got up on the step."

Phimble studied the cone of the volcano. "We might should abandon *Dosie* and disappear up there as best we can."

"But we'd be stuck here forever," Stobs pointed out. "And Jap would likely track us down anyway."

Phimble gave it all a good think but no solution presented itself. "I'm open to suggestions," he said.

"You could let me go," Ichikawa suggested.

"What good would that do?" Phimble demanded. "Your pals will still come to rescue you."

"That is true," Ichikawa said, though in a sad tone. "And I would be duty bound to help them kill you."

"Kill us?" Fisheye was astonished. "That just knocks me on my can. Here I was, planning on inviting you to Killakeet after the war. I figure you for a man who likes to fish."

"I *do* like to fish." Ichikawa glanced away from Fisheye, as if ashamed to look the boy in the eye. "I like nothing better," he mumbled.

"Stop jawing and get to work, Fisheye," Phimble ordered. "I don't think you're going to change Ichikawa's mind about anything."

Fisheye stared at Ichikawa. "You're not much of a friend," he accused.

The pilot looked stricken, then gave the mechanic a slight bow. "I regret circumstances dictate our present relationship."

"Yeah. I'll bet." Fisheye climbed up on the wing, happy to go back to the engine even if it was beat to death and unlikely to ever work again. At least he understood the blamed thing!

Stobs took charge of Ichikawa and allowed him to use a bush for a bathroom break, then asked him politely to sit down. "I'll boil up some coffee," Stobs said, but the Japanese pilot didn't reply. His face was contorted. "What's with you?" Stobs demanded.

"Nothing," Ichikawa answered, but it was clear there was something.

"What?"

"I am struggling with my conscience," he said at length.

"Maybe you ought to get one first," Stobs suggested, then got busy making the coffee.

PART III

Ye lust, and have not: ye kill, and desire to have, and cannot obtain: ye fight and war, yet ye have not, because ye ask not. —James, chapter 4, verse 2

3 0

I have a wog fever and I am on a wog ship on a wog sea.

Thus Missus Felicity Markham summarized her situation as a snarling storm did its best to put the *Minerva* on the bottom of the Solomon Sea, and a fever to kill her. At times in her life, fever had almost been welcome as an old friend, taking her far away from the cares of the plantation to a different, fantastic dream world. It was said that the old Indians of America had done much the same in their heathen sweat boxes, and the Finns in their saunas. Now, though, the fever and the storm were misfortunes fate had placed upon her, to impede her in her return to Noa–Noa. But neither fever nor storm would keep her from going home. She cast her eyes toward the sky and studied the gathered black clouds. She raised her chin and felt the risen breeze. She bared her teeth to the pelting rain. She knew very well who had sent the filthy weather, and she laughed into the creature's wind and its black sky. *You're a wog, aren't you?* she asked God, a suspicion she'd had for a very long time. *After all, why else would you have made so many of them?* "Well, you great beastly wog, you won't beat me down. Not *this* white woman!"

"Mother, what's wrong?" John–Bull asked through the howling wind and crashing waves. He was standing beside her, a hand clutching her flailing skirt.

She resisted the fever even as God tried to force it into her brain. It was a heroic gesture and she knew it and it thrilled her. She wanted to laugh at God, the pitiful creature, but she had work to do and no time. "Get into the gig, John. Prepare for the worst whilst I try to avoid it."

"But I'd like to remain on deck!" John–Bull cried.

Felicity understood the boy's wish. The *Minerva*'s deck was pitching and rolling and if one did not have any other responsibilities, or fever, or a battle with the wog too many called God, it could be enjoyed indeed as a thrilling ride. John-Bull was protected from the driving rain by a poncho some Marine Raider had given him, or perhaps he'd pinched it on the sly. No matter. He stood absolutely fearless, a miniature version of his father. It made her pulse race to see Bryce appear so clearly through their son, that same wicked grin, eyes alight, soaking in the danger and reveling in it. *Oh, Bryce,* she thought. *For you. For us.*

"Go stand beside the gig," she ordered the boy. "If we start to go under, cut the lines and climb aboard. It should float off. I'll be along if I can."

John-Bull did as he was told, his hands held out to his sides as if on a tightrope, making a zigzag path across the rolling deck until he reached the gig. Though he made an attempt to look serious, the pitch of the deck soon elicited an excited grin, and he happily yodeled as sea water surged around his boots. *My husband, we did a very good thing in bringing this boy into the world,* Felicity thought fleetingly, before getting back to the task at hand, that of defeating God and saving the *Minerva,* tasks she was certain she could accomplish, even with fever.

She sorted out where they were. Following her suggestion, the women-crazy American sailors had run the *Minerva* north, taking the old schooner across the shallows between the Russells and Mary Island. She had anticipated that Colonel Burr, upon discovering her absence, might send aircraft and ships to look for her. That was why she had taken the *Minerva* well away from the usual flight paths and sea-lanes. After nightfall, according to her plan, they would come up north of Mary, then cross the Slot under the cover of darkness and slip in beneath the lee of Santa Isabel Island, a fortunate island that had so far escaped the war. Then they would cross over to Choiseul Island, another place so far mostly untouched by battles, and then strike back across the Slot toward Vella Lavella, and thence to Noa-Noa. According to her calculations, the route would have them on her island in two days. She had told the Americans the voyage would take but a single day, but then, of course, she had lied.

As it had turned out, only two of the sailors had elected to try the adventure, the leader, named Emmett, who confidently took the wheel, and a handsome, curly-haired boy named Rusty. Both seemed like rum chaps, willing to do just about anything for a Marie. Felicity had lied about the Maries on Noa-Noa, too, of course. Most of them had been brought over from Malaita on a blackbird expedition in 1936 and were considered even then too old and ugly for marriage. But, she told herself, these boys were desperate, and if they wanted the old girls and the old girls wanted them, who was she to deny either party? The only thing that mattered to Felicity at the moment, other than John-Bull, was getting to Noa-Noa, and that meant they had to get through the storm. Not an hour before, she'd first smelled the rise of a foul breeze off the New Georgia Sound, and knew what it meant. "See yon bank of gray clouds, low on the horizon?" she'd told Emmett. "It means a blow. Steer a bit to the east, get in the lee of the Russells, and it should skirt by us."

"Missus, you're wrong," Emmett had replied, though politely. The man, being an American, was an ignoramus, though of a typically cheerful and good heart. "I think those clouds will burn off long before they reach us. And if we go over to the Russells, we'll lose hours."

Of course, the clouds hadn't burned off. Why did some men have such a difficult time listening to her? The clouds had coalesced in a rush and swept down on them in a howl of wind and rain that struck her skin so hard it felt like sharp pebbles. Rusty had tried to stay on deck, but it turned out he wasn't much of a sailor. Holding his mouth, he had disappeared below. Her three Malaitans chose to huddle on deck near the gig, jabbering among themselves. They were no fools. The sailors had brought the lifeboat aboard, doubtlessly having stolen it from the American navy. Unlike the *Minerva,* the gig at least appeared seaworthy.

"Run into the wind, you fool, lest we broach!" Felicity cried to Emmett, but the man kept the bow stubbornly askance to the ranks of advancing white horses. His eyes were red-rimmed from blinking into the shattered waves of seawater that kept pounding them. "I'm trying to get closer to Mary Island!" he yelled. "Maybe we can find us a lee, missus! If not, I think this tub is going down. We didn't do that good a job patching her up."

"Bloody hell!" Felicity snarled. "Now, listen to me, Emmett. You must turn into the wind and head up toward the Russells."

"We'd never make it there," Emmett replied in a sorrowful tone. "Our only chance is Mary!"

Felicity allowed the truth to settle in, inserting itself between the wild meanderings of her fever-addled mind. The *Minerva* was going to sink. All right. She was going to sink. What should happen next? *The gig.* The gig was the answer. But it was not going to be so simple as getting John-Bull and her and the Americans in the thing and casting off. There were her Malaitans to consider. It was a consideration that occurred nearly every day on the Solomon Island plantations. Usually there was nothing but sullen acquiescence to the mastah and the missus, but then, on another day, there would be revolt, and revenge, and death. The storm had given her Malaitans an opportunity to take control of their own destiny. They could kill the whites and take the gig. Would they risk it?

Felicity looked at the three sullen men huddled behind the gig, and they looked back at her. Significantly, she touched the holster on her belt that held her Webley, a six-cartridge revolver. Bryce had given it to her when she'd first come out to the Solomons, and it provided her some comfort. The Webley used soft lead bullets that could instantly stop a man as if he'd been hit in the face with a hard-swung bat. She'd seen Bryce use the pistol against a Malaitan who'd murdered a fellow wog for a twist of tobacco. She and Bryce had tracked the man down and discovered him sitting on a log, smoking the tobacco. Spying them, he had jumped up and made a furious charge with his machete. Bryce had shot him but once, a bullet to the chest that struck the wog with such furious power that it lifted him into the air. She could still see the white bottoms of his feet as he fell heavily on his back. Upon inspection, it could be seen that the Malaitan's heart had literally been torn out. One moment he'd been running and screaming, the next he was profoundly, and correctly, dead.

Felicity would have allowed herself a little longer to recall the nostalgic event, except a huge wave fell upon the *Minerva*'s port side, sending a flood of foaming seawater plowing across the deck, tearing Emmett screaming from the wheel and flinging the Malaitans, their mouths opened in silent supplication, into the stern scuppers. John-Bull, smart boy, ducked through the water and swung up into the gig. Felicity hung on to a stanchion, the water clutching at her clothes and hair, until finally, just short of drowning, she pushed her face out of the water just as another huge curler fell on them.

This time the steamer rolled but did so very slowly. Rising from the water again, Felicity looked aft and saw that John-Bull had climbed out of the gig and was cutting its lines. The sky had turned bright yellow and the sea a brilliant purple and the wind-voice cried to her over and over, *Die, die, die* . . .

"Not yet!" Felicity yelled at the wind. Then she noticed the *Minerva* was scarcely rolling, even while the sea did its best to pitch her around. That could mean only one thing. The patch the Americans had placed over the hole in the bow had burst through. Tons of water were flooding in, and there was nothing that could be done. The *Minerva* was headed down into the Solomon Sea, and she would not be coming back.

Felicity saw one of the Malaitans, the huge, muscled man called Arenga, stagger back from the stern toward the gig. His lap-lap was blown tightly against his muscled legs, water dripped from his flat nose, and his eyes, yellow in the milky light, were huge. For a moment, they fixed on Felicity and then on the gig and John-Bull. The two other Malaitans, the short one called Kuro and the old one named Ramu, were also making their way toward the gig. Arenga grasped John-Bull by the poncho and flung him aside. Then Arenga noticed Felicia again, mainly because she had the Webley stuck in his ribs.

"My word!" he croaked. "Why you stick'm gun along me? Arenga good fella boy! Let gig go along water."

"I know you, Arenga. You pier-head jumper!" Felicia retorted sternly, pushing the pistol hard into his ribs. "Now Arenga steal'm boat belong me."

Arenga did not answer the charge. Felicity supposed he was thinking things over. Now she noticed that his huge hand, his fingers as big as bananas, was gripping a short knife with a stout bone handle. The other two Malaitans hung on to the remaining taut lines of the gig and watched her, apparently waiting to see what Arenga would do. John-Bull got to his feet. "Kill him, Mother," he said, and it made her proud.

But she did not kill the Malaitan. She still wanted his strong back and strong arms to make the copra on Noa-Noa. "Now, Arenga, you listen," she said in a stern tone. "All fellas belong gig. Arenga, Kuro, Ramu, me, John-Bull, Emmett, Rusty. We will forget all this. You good fella bimeby, savvy?"

The *Miranda* lurched, but Felicity kept the gun stuck hard into the big man's ribs. The hatch suddenly opened, and Rusty climbed out, followed by gushing water. "She's going down! Launch the lifeboat!" he screamed.

Ramu suddenly had a small ax in his hand. The Malaitans had stowed away weapons, no doubt stolen on Melagi. He walked toward Rusty and, without hesitating, buried the ax in the American's head, then wrenched it free amidst a spout of blood just as Arenga knocked the Webley from Felicity's hand, then pushed her away. She staggered backward, stunned by the force of his push, but John-Bull went after the gun, beating Kuro to it. He aimed it at the little man, who recoiled with his hands in front of his face. John-Bull swept the snout of the pistol toward Arenga, and the big man hesitated long enough for John-Bull to cross the deck to his mother and hand the pistol to her.

Arenga looked at the pistol pointed once more at him and lapsed into an expression of disappointment. "Now, Arenga," Felicity said, wiping away with the back of her hand the sweat from her fever and the rain from her face and the trickle of blood from her nose. "It is time for you to die."

"No," Arenga said in an arrogant tone. "Missus no kill'm Arenga. Arenga good fella, washee-washee, all time on gig. Mary Island, she many mile. You need Arenga."

"You, Ramu!" Felicity said, catching a murderous glance from the little man. "What name you kill'm Rusty?"

"Ramu no kill'm Rusty," Ramu said, even as he held his bloody ax and the little American sailor rolled on the deck in a mixture of his own blood and seawater.

"But I saw you!"

"No kill'm Rusty," Ramu replied stubbornly.

"Mother!" John-Bull warned.

It was Kuro. He had come up with a short sword, a Malayan kris with a long curved blade, and had advanced within a step of her. He sliced at her pistol hand. She drew it back, and the sharp steel swooped past. Without hesitation, she shot Kuro between his eyes, and he was flung off his feet, his face turned to pink mush. "Take the knife from Arenga, John, then climb into the gig," she said in a calm voice. "You, Ramu, toss the ax away."

Arenga allowed the knife to be taken away. Ramu, with a hiss of regret, threw his ax into the sea. The *Minerva*'s deck was awash, the water running across Felicity's ankles. John-Bull cut the remaining lines on the gig, and he, Felicity, and the two Malaitans jumped aboard, and the gig swirled off. Felicity looked over her shoulder and watched the schooner go down. The *Minerva* groaned and moaned as if afraid of her fate. Then Felicity pondered Arenga and Ramu, who sat at the oars and pondered her in return.

Felicity still wanted the Malaitans. They were the reason, after all, that she had left Noa-Noa. They could be worked very hard if properly handled. When Felicity pointed the pistol at Arenga, he cried, "Missy shoot'm Arenga along belly!"

You're wrong, Felicity thought. *I'll not shoot you in your big broad belly. I need a head shot with the likes of you.* "Arenga, you do as I say! You and Kuro, washee, washee!" She made rowing motions. "Good fella missus she no shoot'm. I give you the word of your wog god!"

The storm was playing out, and Felicity knew the worst was over. Storms in the Solomons were sudden and violent, but then they would simply evaporate and the scorching sun would blaze anew. Rain swept across the boat, then stopped as if someone had turned off a spigot. Overhead, the clouds were busily reorganizing themselves, and suddenly there was a slat of blue in the sky and a beam of hot white light burst forth, drawing steam out of Felicity's blouse. The sudden appearance of the sun seemed to give her fever new energy. It coursed through her body and covered her mind like a hot, muddy river.

Felicity forced herself to concentrate. They needed to get to land before dark, else they would be thrown against the reefs of Mary Island and surely perish. "Washee, washee!" she yelled at the Malaitans, and pointed north. Arenga and Ramu nodded and looked almost cheerful as they started pulling the oars. She took the tiller as the sky glimmered ever bluer overhead and the clouds scudded off. The gig moved past Emmett's floating body, spread-eagled on his face. Felicity could see he had a horrendous wound in his back. She realized he must have been swept into the stern with the Malaitans and they had quickly and quietly dispatched him. Felicity pretended not to notice. There was no reason to stir up more trouble.

"Emmett he moves!" Arenga suddenly cried. Felicity looked and saw that Emmett was indeed flopping around, but not of his own volition. Sharks were working him over. Now she saw several of the ugly brutes, their triangular gray fins cutting cleanly through the flattening water.

"Washee!" Felicity insisted to both the men, but they had stopped rowing and were just watching the sharks tear Emmett's body to pieces. "Washee or bad fella shark will kai-kai along you, my word!"

Arenga and Ramu looked at her, then began once more to draw on the oars. They hadn't gotten far before a big shark bumped against the gig. Arenga and Ramu stopped rowing and cringed each time the fish shoved the boat. "Boat strong," she told them. "Shark no belong boat, no kai-kai along good fellas. Washee!"

Arenga picked Ramu up and tossed him overboard. The man screamed a hideous scream, then disappeared underwater before coming back up, flailing desperately for the boat. For a moment, it appeared as if he might make it, but then Felicity saw a gray shape loom behind him and it was as if he'd been hit by an electric shock. His head flew up, his eyes rolled back into his head, his mouth turned down into a great frown, and he subsided into a bloody froth.

"Arenga, my word!" Felicity cried.

Arenga grinned broadly. "Big fella shark kai-kai Ramu. No kai-kai Arenga."

It was such a declaration of selfishness that Felicity was quite at a loss for words. Now she saw Arenga fix on her and John-Bull. "No, Arenga," she said, but he came at them anyway, his huge arms spreading open to take her. Felicity fired the pistol at his face, but she only caught his ear, tearing it clean away. Ignoring the blood streaming from the wound, he reached for her again, and to her horror she dropped the pistol. Cursing, she turned the tiller to impede him, but he swept it aside and clutched her shoulders with both hands. She felt his terrible strength and knew that he was fully capable of lifting her up and tossing her into the sea with just one fluid motion. John-Bull tried to break the big man's grip, but Arenga knocked him aside with a knee to his chin. The boy fell backward into the gig, moaning.

Felicity's hand darted for her boot, where Bryce's advice had placed her final defense: a thin blade. She slipped it out and with all her remaining strength swung it to where Bryce had told her to stick it if ever attacked by a wog. The blade was very sharp, and it went under Arenga's lap-lap and through the complicated organs there and sank very deep. Felicity felt hot blood pour like boiling water over her hand. She withdrew the knife and struck again. Arenga, a dumb expression on his flat face, staggered backward, stepping on John-Bull and raining blood down on the boy. Arenga looked at her with a kind of bemused curiosity, then clutched what remained of his manhood and fell into a sitting-up position. He started to sob, and to her surprise, Felicity felt her heart go out to him.

Another big shark chose that moment to strike the side of the boat, nearly knocking it over. Arenga tried to get up, then collapsed, gurgling into the lapping, bloody seawater in the bottom of the boat. Felicity sat down on the stern of the gig and tried to make sense of not only what had happened but what must happen next.

Then a monster like Felicity could not imagine rose at the bow, its huge triangular teeth tearing at the wood, ripping the planks away. Other, smaller sharks joined the huge creature. Together, they managed to rip a large, jagged hole through which flushed seawater and snapping jaws.

"John, get up," she commanded. "Come here. Sit beside me."

John-Bull crawled until he was beside her. His head was bleeding. "Mother, are we to be eaten by the sharks?"

Felicity's eyes fell on the last convulsions of Arenga just as a small shark pushed through the hole and grasped his foot in its nasty red mouth and twisted it off. It backed out with its prize. Another shark snapped at Arenga's bloody ankle through the hole.

"John, help me," Felicity ordered, and grabbed Arenga by an arm while John-Bull grabbed the other. Together, they drew him toward the stern, away from the hole. The sharks bumped and snapped through the opening.

All night they drifted, while Felicity gave in to the fever. She woke just as she saw John-Bull scramble out of reach of big snapping jaws erupting through the hole in the bow. Arenga's torso was jerked away. Now all she and the boy could do was huddle in the stern while the gig slowly eased lower into the water.

"Mother, give me the pistol," John-Bull said, and she gave it up and subsided into a complicated dream that had Colonel Burr and the big, stupid man named Josh Thurlow somehow hosting a party on the old plantation at Melagi. It made no sense, but then it didn't have to. It was the fever talking to her, telling her of a different place, and a different time . . .

John-Bull stood before his mother, ready to defend her against whatever came into the boat. Four times a shark pushed through the hole, and four times he fired. After the sharks were hit, the water around the gig turned a bright, phosphorescent blue that turned pink from the writhing fish cannibalizing one of their own. He had but one bullet left when a vast animal, the biggest yet, raised itself over the gig, striking the little boat hard. He fired, and the creature slithered back. The last shot provoked Felicity from her dream. She heard a voice coming from above. "John-Bull, little John-Bull," it said. "Come here."

It's God, she thought. *So it chooses now to speak while it lets its wog creatures eat us.* "You will curry no favors with me, you filthy great wog!" she shouted toward heaven. But then, to her astonishment, John-Bull raised his hands and floated aloft. The last she saw of him was his boots disappearing into the darkness above. The wog god had caused a miracle, but now, to Felicity's confusion, it chose a most peculiar thing to say. "Once, climb down and give the missus a hand. She looks like she could use one!"

3 1

Slipping through the open water between the northwest corner of Guadalcanal and Savo Island, the gunboat *Rosemary* pushed ahead into the darkness, her three big engines sending messages of their splendid power through the deck to Kennedy's feet. Kennedy had always nursed the engines of his *PT-109*. Rough treatment almost guaranteed they would sputter and die. His boys often sang the anthem that frustrated PT crews had made up about them:

> *Oh, some PTs do seventy-five,*
> *And some do sixty-nine.*
> *When we get ours to run at all,*
> *We think we're doing fine.*

Of course, no PT boat went seventy-five knots, or even sixty-nine, but they were designed to go over forty, although only a few had ever done it consistently. The *Rosemary,* however, could go that fast and probably faster. Not only was she much lighter with the heavy torpedo tubes dumped, but her engines, modified by Thurlow's boys and the Seabees, were amazingly responsive. Kennedy gloried in their raw, reliable strength, although a glance over his shoulder showed that the perfectly spinning props were leaving a huge **V**-shaped trail that pointed at them like an arrow. Any hotshot, sharp-eyed Rufe pilot looking to make a name for himself could follow that bright phosphorescent blue-white wake, even on the darkest night. Rufes were the reason Kennedy had decided to avoid the Slot, where they patrolled, and maneuver south of the Russells before turning north toward

New Georgia. Still, he occasionally turned the wheel and carved question marks on the sea, just in case a Rufe might be sniffing along his trail.

Despite his concern over the night-flying float planes, Kennedy felt free, as free as he had ever felt in the entire history of his life. He commanded a good boat and a competent, cheerful crew, and he was taking her and them into the teeth of trial and tribulation. Was there ever a better thing that could happen to a naval officer? He couldn't imagine there was. "Something out there, Mister Kennedy," Once called from his lookout position on the bow.

The something proved to be a lifeboat, nearly awash. Kennedy steered toward it. "Take the wheel," he told Ready, after he put the gunboat alongside. Millie was kneeling on the deck, apparently handling something from the lifeboat. To Kennedy's astonishment, the crewman straightened up with a boy in a green poncho hanging from his clasped hands. He swung the boy onto the deck. Kennedy leaned over the torpedo rack and saw that there was a woman in the stern of the little boat. She was breathing heavily, and her eyes were staring skyward as if in a trance. "Once, climb down and give the missus a hand," he said. "She looks like she could use one."

Once climbed down to help the woman, although he first had to kick a small shark in the face when it pushed through the hole in the bow. "I know who this is," he said. "It's Missus Markham, from Melagi. What are you doing way out here, ma'am? She feels real hot, Mister Kennedy. I think she's got fever."

Millie and Kennedy helped Once lift her aboard, and together they gently laid her on the deck.

Millie took away the pistol that John-Bull was clutching. "It was for the sharks," the boy explained.

"How many did you shoot, John-Bull?" Millie asked, since he recognized the child.

"Four. Then the others ate them because of the blood. Emmett and Rusty are dead, murdered by the wogs. They also tried to kill Mother and me, but she killed them with her pistol and the knife she keeps in her boot."

"What's wrong with her now?"

"Fever. She gets it now and again."

The woman's eyes flickered, then opened. Kennedy knelt beside her. "Oh," she said, staring up at him, "what a pretty man . . ."

"She's got fever, all right," Millie said.

"Get her and the boy below," Kennedy ordered. "Do what you can."

"Not much to be done," Millie said. "Except wait it out and hope her temperature drops."

"Oh, Mother will be fine," John-Bull said nonchalantly. "But please don't send me below. This is a PT boat, isn't it?"

"She's a gunboat now," Once said. "We converted her."

"It's too dangerous for you to stay on deck," Kennedy told the boy.

"I will stay out of the way, Captain," John-Bull promised, and stuck out his hand. "My name is John Markham, but I'm called John-Bull."

Kennedy shook the boy's hand. "Well, John-Bull, it is good to meet you. I am Lieutenant Kennedy. I shall personally give you a tour of my boat when I have a moment, but for now, I would appreciate it if you would go below with Millie and assist him in taking care of your mother."

"But I already told you it is just fever. Please, Mister Kennedy. Might I join your crew? You'll find me handy."

Kennedy said, "All right, you can join. Raise your right hand. Do you swear to uphold all the rules and regulations of the United States Navy and follow the legitimate orders of all its officers, both commissioned and non-commissioned, to the letter, bar none?"

John-Bull knew he was being tricked by the skinny naval officer, but he was in too far to turn back. "I will, sir," he promised, though dubiously.

"Very well. You can put your hand down. My first order is for you to go below with your mother and stay there with her until you receive orders to the contrary."

"But, sir—"

"No buts, Seaman Markham."

John-Bull's face clouded, but he said, "Yes, sir."

"Pretty slick," Ready said, as Millie and Once picked up the woman and carried her below. The boy followed, just as ordered, although his lip was out.

"I have two younger brothers, Ready," Kennedy said, grinning. "One thing I know is how to handle boys." He looked around to see who was on deck. Once was looking out on the bow; Pogo was doing the same on the stern. Nobody else was in evidence. "Where's the rest of the crew?" he asked.

"It's night, sir. They're asleep."

"Maybe you ought to draw up a duty bill."

"They don't need one, sir. They've worked it all out between themselves."

"That doesn't sound very navy."

"Guess that's why we're in the Coast Guard. Hark!" Ready cupped a hand to his ear and leaned to starboard. Kennedy listened, too, and heard a low beat, as if someone were thumping on a bass drum. "That's a Japanese barge, sir," Ready whispered.

"How do you know?"

"Because that's what they sound like."

"But *how* do you know?"

"I been out here for over a year. And I pay attention. The better question is *Why?* Do you know *why* that barge is out there?"

"How would I possibly know?"

"There you go again. If you don't know, sir, you really ought to at least hazard a guess."

"All right. Here's my guess. I guess they're out there to win the war for the Japanese Empire in their own small way."

"In that case, shouldn't we try to stop them?"

Kennedy stared at the bosun. "Dammit, Ready. I'm finally starting to understand you. You have a profound sense of duty."

Ready appeared startled and then confused. "Well, I guess so, Mister Kennedy," he answered. "Don't you?"

Kennedy didn't answer mainly because he didn't have an answer to give. Instead, he listened. "It appears to be a single vessel," Kennedy said. Then added, "Of some kind."

"I'm telling you it's a Jap barge, sir. Let's go mess them up."

"It would be crazy to tackle one of those things. Even you must see that."

Ready shrugged. "This is the Solomons, Mister Kennedy. Crazy kind of goes with the place."

Kennedy could see Ready's point, at least to a degree. It was very definitely the Solomons, where craziness tended to be epidemic. For confirmation, he only had to consider that there was a woman below who had recently killed three men, and a boy who had killed four sharks. It was part and parcel of the insanity of the place. "We'll sneak up on it and see what it is," Kennedy relented. "If it's a Japanese vessel, and I think we have a reasonable chance of stopping it without damage to ourselves, then that's what we'll do."

"Aye, aye, sir," Ready said. "Now, that wasn't so hard, was it?"

"What?"

"Making that decision."

"You should remember your place, Ready," Kennedy warned.

"Yes, sir. I'm really sorry, sir."

"I don't believe a word of it," Kennedy replied, and then called the boys to their guns and pushed the throttles ahead, damn the wake. Within a few minutes, they had caught up with the craft, and sure enough, just as Ready had predicted, it was a Japanese barge, its heavy round stern and flat bow clearly visible in the pale light of the silvery crescent moon. What it was doing around Mary Island was a mystery, but it could only mean trouble.

Kennedy aimed the gunboat so as to pass the barge on its port side. Its crew was apparently intent on their navigation, as they took no note of the *Rosemary*. "As soon as you can bear, you boys on the guns let them have it," Kennedy called across the deck.

"Shouldn't we use our torpedoes?" Ready asked from his position behind the twin fifties in the starboard tub.

"I think we'll save them for bigger game," Kennedy replied. "Now get cracking!"

Ready shrugged, then pulled the trigger. The big bullets from the twin-barreled gun tore into the barge, sending up a shower of sparks as they punched through its steel side. The barge turned away abruptly, but Kennedy smoothly turned the gunboat with it. The Japanese were keeping their heads down, which was probably wise, as Ready's twin fifties, and the single twenty millimeter on the stern, manned by Again, were rattling away.

"We got them on the run, sir!" Ready crowed while reloading his guns. But then the Japanese gunners suddenly started firing back, although their aim was wild. Tracers flew like sheet lightning overhead. Kennedy wore the *Rosemary* around to get away from the horde of bullets and came up on the barge's starboard side; this time it was Millie on the port twin fifties slamming it with the heavy, high-velocity rounds. Kennedy was astonished to see the barge suddenly rear up, its slanted bow thrown high into the air.

Kennedy turned the *Rosemary* away while the barge settled in a spreading circle of foam. Then he realized what had happened. "They've hit a reef!" Kennedy called. "It's damn lucky we didn't hit it, too." He drove the *Rosemary* back and forth to give all the guns some exercise. The barge, battered by the big rounds, began to burn. Men were seen jumping into the sea.

Kennedy felt duty-bound to attempt a rescue. He slowed and allowed the boys to shine their flashlights to see if any of the Japanese in the water would surrender. For their trouble, they dodged bullets from pistols some of the barge crew had taken into the drink with them. Kennedy tickled the throttles until the gunboat was out of pistol range, then eased off until the engines subsided in a low rumble. He listened carefully. Mary Island was near. He could hear the boom of her surf.

"Sir, I've been thinking," Ready said, leaving the gun tub to stand by Kennedy in the cockpit.

"That always means trouble," Kennedy replied. "But let's hear it."

"Well, sir, maybe we should wait around here until morning. Got to be something on Mary that Jap barge was after."

"We're searching for Captain Thurlow and Ensign Phimble," Kennedy reminded the bosun. "Time is of the essence."

"You're right, sir. But I think both of them would see it as our duty to stick around, just to find out what's up."

Kennedy looked over his shoulder at the burning barge. Any Rufes in the area would be attracted to it. It was best they clear the area, but not too fast because of the damned phosphorescent wake. "All right, Ready," Kennedy relented. "We'll go out to deep water and just maintain our position. It's probably better for the woman if we keep things quiet for a while, anyway. Then, come sunrise, we'll take a quick peek at Mary and be on our way. Satisfied?"

"Good decision, sir," Ready answered, and, though he was not certain why, it very much pleased Kennedy to hear him say it.

3 2

While Josh kept guard, Penelope built a hut of bamboo and banana leaves and palm fronds lashed together with braided hibiscus twine. "A little hut for two," she sang as she worked. "Just for me and you." When she was done, she led Josh to a small stream where they took a quiet bath, with their clothes dangling from an overhanging branch. The air was cool beneath a cover of stately she-oak trees. The stream gurgled, sounding like small crystal bells, while little yellow and brown lorikeets gently fussed in the branches, and gold and blue butterflies fluttered above bushy green ferns amongst the rocks. It was all so peaceful. Penelope sang while she scrubbed him and washed his hair. When the bathing was done, they lay on big flat rocks to let the sun dry their bodies. Josh wished they could lie there all day and that his mission no longer existed, but reality exerted itself. "Is Kimba Whitman a cannibal, too?" he asked.

"No," Penelope answered. "But I think it must be the reason she had to run. Kimba knew she no longer loved Mastah Whitman. She was also afraid he might someday kai-kai her."

"How do you know this?"

"Kimba often came to Minister Clarence's mission. We talked. She told me Mastah Whitman recruited his warriors from a tribe headed up by a chief named Kwaque. I know Kwaque very well, as do all the people of New Georgia. He keeps to himself in the high mountains, and he and his people are very rude. They sometimes hunt heads and eat long pig. Kimba told Minister Clarence that Whitman had become a cannibal, too, since he believed it was the only way he could get Kwaque's boys to respect him. But she said they ate more than Japoni. Sometimes they ate pickaninny, too, and Americans when they could find them, such as a pilot shot down. Whitman also murdered Minister Clarence. These are the reasons why I think you must kill him."

Josh gave it all some thought. If Penelope was telling the truth, then he supposed the man deserved killing. "Any suggestions on how I might kill him?" he asked her. "He seems to be pretty well guarded. And we have traveled far."

"I will guide you, like Natty Bumppo. He is not so far away. We could be there in perhaps six hours hard walking. As to how, I think it should be at night. I am certain you are very adept at fighting in the dark."

"But you said there were too many Japanese between us and the Truax plantation."

"That was before you agreed to kill Whitman. No worry-worry. I can get us through. After you kill him, then we will go and find Joe Gimmee and your lieutenant."

"You seem to have everything figured out," Josh observed. "But I think maybe the best thing is for us to make contact with American troops. That way I could get the word out about Whitman, and we could let the authorities handle him."

Penelope's expression took on the aspect of a pout. "Whitman will only lie his way out of it. He is a very good liar. No, you must kill him, Josh darling. It is the only way."

Josh considered this, then asked, "How do you know where Joe Gimmee is?"

"Kimba told me."

"Why did she tell you?"

"She thought I would be a good follower for Joe Gimmee. She said I was very smart and that Joe Gimmee would give me all the answers I sought. She asked me to travel with her someday to hear her father's teachings. Now that I think on it, I realize she may have been asking me to help her escape. I am sorry now that I was so silly as to not understand."

"What does Joe Gimme teach?"

"That there is this war with the Japoni, which is very important, but there is also another war, one that we cannot see. It is the war for the gods who look after these islands."

"I see," Josh said, though he did not. He added, a bit plaintively, "I just want to find Lieutenant Armistead."

Penelope smiled. "And I just want you to kill Mastah Whitman."

At an impasse in their conversation, they finished drying in the sun, then went to their naturally camouflaged hut. Penelope brought out dried bully beef from her seemingly bottomless dilly bag and darted into the bush to pick several kinds of sweet fruit. Then she opened a ripe coconut with a sure swipe of her machete. All this she cooked in a small pan over a small fire that produced virtually no smoke. She was a natural *guerrilla,* Josh realized with admiration, and thought to himself that an army of Penelopes would be a formidable enemy. For that matter, *one* was a formidable enemy.

The meal was delicious and the company charming since they did not talk about Armistead or Whitman or Joe Gimmee. They talked of other things, of her life at the mission (she'd enjoyed it but thought Minister Clarence, God rest his soul, was a bit lazy and had worked her too hard as a child), Josh's wife (murdered by renegades in Alaska, which was a long story, which Josh considerably condensed), the lighthouse where he'd been raised (a tall spire that had saved many a ship and sailor), and the people of the Solomons (whereby Penelope told the story of how the people and the animals came to be).

"Once upon a time," she said, "which, according to Minister Clarence, is the favorite way for white people to have a story begin and therefore I hope is pleasing to you, Josh darling, there was an earthquake god named Maruni. He had a tail, which he took great pains to hide. One day, his wives returned unexpectedly to his hut and caught him with his tail showing. So, ashamed, he cut his tail off and divided it into many segments from which grew people and birds and snakes and pigs and even the fishes."

With the story apparently at an end, Josh found himself a bit confused. "What does it mean?" he asked politely.

Penelope was clearly affronted by his question. "What does the story of Adam and Eve mean?" she demanded.

"Well, that story included a warning against eating from the tree of wisdom," Josh replied, after a moment's thought. "It had a moral, I guess you might say."

"So our story has a moral as well," Penelope replied. "Don't get caught with your tail hanging out."

Josh thought that was funny, so despite his best intentions he laughed. She watched him with a dark frown. "Tell me another one," he said, trying to get back into her good graces.

"I will tell it, but no laughing," she said pointedly. Josh promised to never laugh again, and she said, "There are many tales of brothers on these islands. They have many names, but all of them are mischievous, and they are always getting into trouble. Once upon a time, there were two brothers,

Tengo and Qat, and they decided to steal wives. Qat stole his wife from Malaita, which meant he would be forever unhappy. Malaitan women argue about everything and always want more than any husband could possibly provide. They also go *pffft* at their men very often. That is a sign of great disrespect from a pickaninny woman to a man. Anyway, Tengo, desiring to avoid a Malaitan wife, decided to kidnap a sky maiden instead. He found one bathing in a spring one day and hid her wings. To avoid starvation, she had no choice but to marry him. One day, her mother-in-law hit her for being lazy, and she started to cry, so much that her tears washed away the dirt hiding her wings. She put them on and flew away. This made Tengo very angry, so he tied a banyan root to an arrow and shot it into the sky, where it lodged in the sky-world. He climbed it and met a man using a machete to open coconuts and begged him not to cut the root. Then Tengo found his wife and forced her to return with him. The man with the coconuts, seeing this, cut the root, and Tengo fell to his death while his wife flew away."

Josh kept his countenance completely serious. "I suppose the moral to that story is it's better to marry a Malaitan and be unhappy than a sky-woman and be dead."

"Sometimes I believe you to be quite perverse," Penelope accused, even as she hid a smile by looking away.

"You are a good storyteller," he said, which, though she kept her head turned, he could tell pleased her, more than a little.

After the meal, when the long shadows of the waning day had turned into the infinite darkness of the jungle, they went inside the hut, and it didn't take much convincing for Josh to happily lie aboard Penelope again, which seemed to give her so much joy. Even as he was placing a leg over her, though, Josh knew that he was of one mind and she another. He had the odd thought that he would fix it all later, that explanations would be made, and when they parted, all would be well between them. But as they clung to one another, she said, "I love you, Josh darling," and Josh felt his blood run cold. Then she moved against him and it ran hot again, and he gave in to it. *I am a bad man,* he thought to himself. *I don't care* was his answer. *I'll fix it later* was his further thought when he woke during the night. The shadows of generations of other men in his situation nodded their heads with understanding.

The next morning, Josh woke to the sound of boots on the earth and the nearly inaudible clunk of canteens muffled by rags. He knew this could mean but one thing. He roused Penelope, and she led him to the edge of a clearing where they could hide in the tall grass and still have a good view of the mountain slope. There were at least thirty of them, and they were coming fast, the mist swirling off the grass from their churning boots, the bayonets attached to their rifles flashing in the morning sun. They carried no rucksacks, nothing to weigh them down except water, guns, and bandoliers of ammunition.

Josh took a moment to admire them. No other army could move as fast as the Japanese Imperial Army when it was on the attack. He watched a mortar team go by, three tiny men humping huge loads on their backs but keeping up with the others. A machine-gun team went by, similarly loaded. Then, to his surprise, a line of stragglers stumbled into view. Their uniforms hung on their scrawny bodies, and they were having to stop every hundred yards or so to lean on their rifles to catch their breaths. New Georgia had taken its toll on these men, but they were still fighting. *Jap don't give up easy.*

Josh tried to figure out where they might be going. "Jap must be after something good to be in such a hurry," he said as much to himself as Penelope.

"The village in which we stayed our first night together is at the end of this path," she advised.

"Why would they attack an empty village?"

"Perhaps it isn't empty anymore."

"How far away is it?"

"They are going the long way. This path goes down and up and around to the sea and then across a small river. Maybe three miles."

"So there's a shorter way."

"Yes. But it is a bit of a scramble."

"Then let's take the scramble. I'd like to know what they're up to."

"Of course." Penelope paused, then asked, "Do you love me, Josh darling?"

Josh was astonished by the question, though he'd expected it. "I only met you a couple of days ago," he said in his defense.

"I do not recall asking you how long we've known one another," she replied, and supplied a deep frown.

"We will talk about it later."

"We will talk about it now. Do you love me?"

Josh knew he was going to have to answer one way or the other, so he said, with neither preamble or elaboration, "Yes." It was taking the easy way out, but he was, after all, in a hurry.

Penelope threw herself into his arms, kissed him tenderly (which made him feel bad and good at the same time), then led him to a path that crossed through an abandoned orchard of coffee trees, their branches laden with berries that were likely never to be picked. The path next plunged across a meadow of saw grass and candle bush and kept going down until it arrived at the village. They stopped at a row of loya cane just above the empty pigpens. Astonishingly, music was playing over a loudspeaker, swing music, and Josh thought it might possibly be the Dorsey Brothers. Laundry flapped from lines strung between trees. Big cooking fires were cheerfully burning, their smoke curling thick and high in the sky. It looked for all the world to be a picnic outing. A few men could be seen walking about; others were lounging around the huts. Laughter drifted with the smoke on the wind.

"Who is it?" Penelope wondered.

"The United States Army, God bless 'em," Josh said, and shook his head at their foolishness. "Come on, Penelope dear. We've got to deliver some very bad news to these gentlemen."

"That the Japoni are coming?" she asked.

"Yes, that's part of it," Josh replied.

"And the rest?"

"That they're about to die."

"If we go down there, we will die, too."

Josh wavered between duty and good sense. Duty won out, as it usually did. "You stay here," he said.

"I will go with you. If you die, I die."

Josh looked at Penelope, then hugged her. "I think I really do love you," he said.

"You said you did," she answered, pushing him away. "But now you act like you just realized it."

"Can we talk about this later? We have to go get killed now."

"I trust you *not* to get us killed."

Josh considered her trust, then took her by the hand and led her down the path into the village.

3 3

Kennedy slept. No mosquitoes bit him, no blanket of heated air covered him, no sweat dripped from his armpits. A mild rocking lulled him. He was at sea, where he was happiest. When he awoke, he found himself lying in front of the splinter shield of the *Rosemary*'s cockpit. He recalled that he'd come there just to sit and think, but he hadn't thought long. Now he blinked up at a night sky filled with fading stars. Dawn was near. His first thought was to discover if Felicity Markham had survived her fever. Hurrying below, he found her sitting up in a cot, taking some soup. Millie sat at her side. John-Bull was asleep on another of the crew cots. She looked at him over the soup and said, "Lieutenant Kennedy, I presume?"

He was pleased to see her so improved. "Yes, and you're Missus Markham. The boys recognized you. It's good to see you up."

"Oh, we old Solomon hands know fever almost as a friend." She extended her hand. "I thought you were but a dream, Lieutenant. But I see you are very real."

"You called me a pretty man," he said, his toothy grin broadening. "You were obviously delirious."

"There are two aspects of fever," she replied in a scholarly tone. "One is delirium, but the other is often a clarity of thought impossible to have otherwise. It is similar, I am told, to the effects of the poppy, or perhaps the sweat houses of your American Indians. You are a very pretty man in my eyes, and I am too old to deny I said it or meant it."

"I'll just put the soup away," Millie said. Blushing, he stole away to the galley.

Kennedy and Felicity studied one another. What her actual thoughts were toward him, he had no idea, but there was real warmth in her eyes.

The last time any woman had looked at him like that had been Inga. Now Inga was gone, perhaps descended into marriage with a man who could not possibly deserve her. At least that's what she had announced in her last letter, which had been weeks ago. Kennedy's suspicion was that his father had somehow influenced Inga to stop writing. Somehow? His father's ways might be subtle, but they were always effective, especially when it came to interfering with the lives of his children. But Felicity Markham was here and now, and there was a light in her eyes, and his father knew nothing about her. "Missus Markham, what can I do to make you more comfortable?"

"You're doing it by your visit," she replied. "And I do hope you will call me Felicity. Do you have a first name, or must I address you by rank as long as we are on board a military vessel?"

"You're a civilian and can call me anything you like. Out here, I've been tagged with Shafty, but I wish you would call me Jack."

She looked at him out of the tops of her eyes, as if not quite daring to look at him directly. "So, Jack, what brings you to these waters?"

"It seems we are both on the lam," he answered, and explained that the Thurlow boys had told him that she had escaped from Colonel Burr. He also related a considerably condensed version of all that had occurred to him since Josh Thurlow had appeared at his tent in Lumbari.

"Yes, I had a discussion with Commander Thurlow prior to his departure," Felicity sniffed.

"Mister Kennedy!" Ready yelled through the galley hatch. "Sun's up and guess what?"

"I'm too tired to guess," Kennedy replied. "So just tell me." He rolled his eyes to Felicity's smile.

"We can see a Catalina parked near the beach. I think it's *Dosie!*"

"I'll be right up." He looked at Felicity. "If you need anything . . ."

"Don't be the least bit concerned. Making do is the way of life here in the Solomons."

"Mister Kennedy!" Ready bawled down through the hatch. "We can make out Mister Phimble on the beach!"

"All right, Ready!" Kennedy snapped as Felicity found his hand and squeezed it. "Must go," he said, reluctantly.

"Must let you," she replied, and off he went, climbing the ladder to the deck, her eyes never leaving him.

3 4

Josh and Penelope ran down the path into the village. A trio of soldiers were sitting on a big palm log. One of them whistled when he saw Penelope. "Mercy," he said.

"Get your rifles!" Josh snapped. "Japs are on their way in force. Where's your commander?"

"Lieutenant Carter's over there," the startled man answered, waving off toward the cooking fires. The other two men simply stared.

Josh and Penelope ran through the village, other soldiers stopping whatever they were doing at the sight of them. A few produced wolf whistles for Penelope's benefit. When Josh and Penelope reached the largest of the cooking fires, more soldiers were sitting around it, eating from mess kits. "Where's your lieutenant?" Josh demanded, and the forks and spoons of the soldiers stopped halfway between their plates and their mouths. Not one of them had a rifle.

"Right here," came the answer from a skinny young man with a mop of bright red hair. He was crossing the beach, a towel around his shoulders. He had a big loopy grin on his freckled face. "What's up?" he asked, then took a second to admire Penelope. "Quite an aide-de-camp, sir. How do I join the marines?"

"I'm Coast Guard," Josh said in an irritable tone while pointing at the insignia on his cap. "But never mind. Listen to me, Lieutenant. There's at least thirty Japanese Imperial Army troops headed your way. They'll be here in about half an hour. Do you have machine guns and mortars?"

"Of course not, sir," the lieutenant said, toweling off. He kept his loopy grin, as if he hadn't heard anything Josh had said beyond the question. "We're a platoon of special service troops. We're here to turn this village into a rest camp." When Josh looked at him with a puzzled expression, he said, "You know, a place where the boys can come and relax a bit. Swim in the ocean, play horseshoes, badminton, that kind of thing. But you say Japanese are coming here, sir? I was told this area was clear."

"You got told wrong," Josh retorted. "How many men do you have?"

"Twenty including me."

"Any of them ever seen combat?"

"I doubt it," Carter said. "I've got a comedian and a few musicians, but the rest are a mixed bag of carpenters, electricians, and handymen to help build the center. And me, of course. I used to be a radio announcer."

"Get your men rounded up. Tell them to bring their weapons. They do have weapons, don't they?"

"I think most of them have M-1s."

"Ammunition?"

The lieutenant shrugged, and Josh despaired. "Do you have a radio?"

"It got dropped when we landed. It hasn't worked since."

"Anybody supposed to check on you?"

"I asked the sailors who brought us here to tell my company commander on the Canal that we needed a radio. They said they'd be back in about three days. That was yesterday afternoon. We're in trouble, aren't we, sir?"

"Yes, but keep your head and we'll figure a way out of this. We've got a secret weapon."

"What's that?"

"You're looking at her." And it was true. The redheaded lieutenant couldn't keep his eyes off Penelope.

An hour went by and, to Josh's relief, the Japanese had not yet arrived. He thought that was odd, but he wasn't going to argue with good fortune. He took the time to organize a defense, choosing to place the soldiers behind a meadow that lay between the village and the path along the beach where he expected the Japanese to appear. The palm logs the soldiers had been using for benches he had placed end to end as a defensive position. Penelope scouted the Japanese and returned with a report that they had stopped at the river about a half mile away. An officer was apparently angry about something and was yelling and stomping around. Some of his men had run back up the path.

"It's likely the stragglers," Josh said. "They're having to wait for them to catch up. Jap on attack don't like to wait." He walked behind the line of prone entertainment soldiers, tapping every other one on his helmet with a stick. "If I tapped your helmet, you'll fire first, but only when I tell you.

The rest of you will wait. That way we won't have a pause while everybody puts in a fresh clip. Try to remember your basic training and you'll do fine. Sight in and squeeze the trigger. Aim for the body. It's a bigger target. Use the log to steady your rifle. If Jap gets in close, get on your feet and use your bayonet. Every one of you is bigger than the average son of Nippon. Use your weight and strength against him and you should kill him before he kills you. Any questions?"

A soldier, a round little man with a big nose and wide, pink lips, looked over his shoulder. "Hey, Captain Thurlow, you heard the one about the guy who grabbed his wife by the tail and said, 'If you'd firm this up, we could get rid of your girdle'? Well, she grabbed him by the jonas and said, 'You know, if you'd firm *this* up, we could get rid of the postman, the grocer, *and* your brother!' "

"Good one, Jersey Joe!" Lieutenant Carter said while the soldiers behind the log laughed and Josh, despite himself, did, too.

Penelope frowned and asked, "What is a jonas?"

"Don't you worry your pretty little head about it, dear," Jersey Joe said. He looked at Josh. "You really think a bunch of comedians like us can stop regular Japanese troops?"

"Sure you can. Just aim and fire. We'll get by."

"Boy, Captain," Jersey Joe said, "and they think I'm funny! You should go on tour!"

Josh chuckled, though he was aware they probably didn't have more than a few minutes to live. The Japanese mortars and machine guns he'd spotted that morning would surely cut them to pieces. Then, if the Japanese officer in charge had any sense, a simple flanking movement would mop up anybody still alive.

"Isn't there something we can do, sir?" the redheaded lieutenant asked, for the first time sensing Josh's gloom.

Spurred by Carter's question, Josh asked himself if there was anything tricky he might accomplish to stave off death, at least for a little while. Captain Falcon had always said to figure out an enemy's weakness and exploit it. *Well,* he thought, *Jap has one great weakness, and that's his pride.* "Do you have a way to talk through those speakers?" he asked the lieutenant.

"Sure do, sir. There's a mike back at the mess tent. Just flip a switch and you're on the air. What do you have in mind?"

Josh was warming to his idea. "Jersey Joe, do you know a few insults you could hurl at Emperor Hirohito?"

Jersey Joe grinned. "I might could come up with a few."

"Would you like them in Japanese, sir?" another soldier asked. He was a round-faced man of obvious Oriental descent.

"You know Japanese?"

"Jack Hamoru at your service, sir. I'm a trumpet player. Born and raised in Portland, Oregon, but my folks talked the old language at home."

It was the good fortune that often comes to those who form desperate plans rather than just lie down and die. Josh explained what he wanted them to do. "Go set up on that mike. I'll let you know when to start."

Jersey Joe and Jack Hamoru loped off toward the mess tent just as the first Japanese soldiers appeared on the path on the other side of the meadow. Josh saw a few of them move off to the side, probably the teams carrying the machine-gun and the mortar. He waited for a bit, watching the Japanese fan out. It was all very professionally accomplished. Then Josh sent a runner back to tell Jersey Joe and Jack Hamoru to start talking. Some squawky feedback occurred, but their voices echoed across the grassy field to the Japanese.

Hey, Tojo! Your emperor is so stupid, he has to think twice to say nothing! Hey, Tojo! Your emperor is so ugly, the doctor slapped his mother when he was born! Hey, Tojo . . . !

The Japanese stopped their preparations for battle. Some of them shook their fists and yelled back their own insults. *Babe Ruth go to hell!* was a favorite. Also, *Fug Eleanor Roosevelt!*

"God, no, *you* fug her!" Jersey Joe called back, and everybody lying along the pitiful log defense line laughed. The Japanese, however, were clearly furious. They were yelling and shaking their fists.

"Not a round will be fired until I say so," Josh told the soldiers, who, despite their nervous laughter, were wriggling anxiously around in the dirt behind their pathetic logs.

A Japanese officer stepped forward, his face pinched and nearly scarlet with rage. He marched back and forth, waving his sword and exhorting his troops. One or two of them made mock attacks, rushing forward, then falling back, yelling and waving their rifles. The officer faced his troops and spoke to them, then raised his sword. "Here it comes, boys," Josh said. "Get ready." Then, to Penelope who was kneeling beside him, "Go and hide. Save yourself."

"I will not leave you," she said, and tapped the flat side of her machete in her hand.

The Japanese officer turned toward the line of soldiers and pointed his sword at them. His men roared in unison and then charged, their rifles tipped with bayonets held horizontally at their hips. The officer led them, his sword waving over his head. *"Banzai,"* they yelled in a high-pitched wail. *"Banzai!"*

It was precisely what Josh hoped might happen. The inherent weakness of the Japanese soldier was on parade. Insult him and it was as if he were compelled to come at you, standing up. Josh walked behind the men lying behind the logs and said a single word over and over in as soothing a tone as he was able. "Wait . . . wait . . . wait . . ." When he judged the charging Japanese were less than fifty yards away, he yelled, "First group, fire *now!*" The designated men fired, and a few Japanese soldiers fell. "Aim, men!" Josh yelled. Then he ordered everybody to cut loose, and more Japanese fell. The Japanese officer kept coming like a maniac, waving his sword and screaming gibberish.

Now it was Josh's play, the only one he had remaining. "Don't shoot me in the back!" was his plea to the special services troops as he stepped out in front of them while unsheathing his Aleut ax from his belt with one hand and unholstering his pistol with the other. He began to run, his eyes un-flinchingly held on the Japanese officer. He dodged a thrust of a bayonet from an Imperial soldier, shot him with the pistol, and kept going. When he reached the officer who had taken no notice of him, Josh plunged the ax into the man's chest. The officer gave Josh an uncomprehending stare, then fell. The charging Japanese soldiers stopped to gaze dumbly at their quivering, bloody officer lying in the grass while the Americans kept shooting them. Josh wiped the blade of his ax on the officer's shirt and then waited to be killed. But the Japanese began to back slowly away, then turned and ran.

Now Josh heard the unwelcome cough of a mortar followed by an explosion and then the chatter of a machine gun. The Japanese had pulled themselves together and were fighting the way they should have from the beginning. Josh consoled himself with the thought that he had done his best. He looked across the field and saw that Penelope was still alive, though there was a stricken look on her face that was strangely at odds with the special services troops, who had stopped firing and were standing up and grinning. Jersey Joe and Jack Hamoru were even laughing and, their arms around each other's shoulders, kicking up their boots like cancan girls. This didn't make any sense to Josh at all. Why would they laugh and dance now that they were being chewed up by mortar rounds and machine-gun fire? The answer, it dawned on him, was that they weren't.

Josh turned to look at the Japanese and saw half-naked black men among them, hacking away with long knives and spears. The Japanese who tried to run away were shot down by a machine gun secreted in the bush. Mortar rounds stopped the rest. Very quickly, it was over, the last gun popped, the last Japanese fallen, and the black men in lap-laps and ornamental beads and feathers were stalking across the field toward him, only stopping to loot the dead. A white man, dressed in khakis and wearing an Australian campaign hat, also crossed the field, his bearded face wreathed with a smile. It was Whitman. He cupped his hands around his mouth. "Good show, Thurlow!" Then he looked past Josh, and his eyes widened and his mouth dropped open.

Josh was confused by Whitman's expression, but he became even more confused when he saw the special services troops leaving their rifles to greet their saviors, only to be greeted in a most unexpected manner. One by one, they were cut down with a slash of a knife or a jab of a spear or, when a few ran, a bullet in the back. Penelope appeared at his side. "I told you what Whitman is," she said. "Have you forgotten? I think we should run now."

Josh hadn't forgotten, but he hadn't entirely believed her, either. Now the proof was undeniably before him as the last American soldier was struck down. "Run, Penelope," he replied urgently. "Run and don't wait for me." And run she did, with Josh close behind, though several of Whitman's men, rifles in their hands, their beads clicking, their feathers waving, their horrible red mouths grinning in eager anticipation, followed.

3 5

Once and Again dived off the gunboat and swam to shore, then ran up the beach to where Mister Phimble, Fisheye, and Stobs stood in the shade of the *Darlin' Dosie*'s wing. There were shouts of joy while the Japanese pilot, Ichikawa, sitting with his hands tied, watched with an indifferent expression. Again, being the more voluble of the twins, told their story quickly, how they'd run a barge onto the reef the night before, and that it was Lieutenant Kennedy at the wheel of the PT boat, except it was really a gunboat and named *Rosemary* after the officer's sister, and all else was well, except that Captain Thurlow was missing on New Georgia.

The last of Again's story was stressful to Phimble, and it only got worse after Kennedy came ashore and confirmed it, adding, "Colonel Burr says Captain Thurlow is probably dead."

"No he ain't," Phimble declared. "And don't you be telling our boys he is."

Kennedy pressed his lips together, his only outward expression in response to Phimble's intemperate remark. "Don't concern yourself with what I might say to these boys," he replied evenly. "I got my boat, just as I said I would, and those boys and I have worked very well together."

"You did well to attack the barge," Phimble relented. "They were coming to rescue this Japanese pilot I captured." He led Kennedy to Ichikawa.

After an introduction, Ichikawa said, "I have sunk three of your PT boats and killed their crews."

"Then you can go to hell," Kennedy replied with some heat.

"Don't pay any attention to Ichikawa-san," Phimble advised. "He's got some screwed-up ideas about war being heroic and all. Kind of reminds me of you."

"Ensign Phimble!" Kennedy snapped. "I have been on the receiving end of what passes for your wit long enough. You don't like me. Fair enough. But keep your comments to yourself. Understand?"

Phimble eyed Kennedy, then shrugged. "Fisheye's near to fixing our starboard engine, at least good enough for me to take off. My plan is to head for New Georgia and find the skipper."

"In a crippled Catalina? The Rufes would have you for dinner. What you're going to do is to abandon your aircraft and come along with me. Together, we'll find Thurlow if he's capable of being found. That's an order, by the way."

"And I heard you loud and clear, Mister Kennedy," Phimble replied. He looked out to sea, his hands shoved in his pockets. Then he shook his head. "I'm not going to abandon *Dosie*. Josh would have my hide."

"Then take her back to Melagi and see to her repair. I'll take the *Rosemary* and go to New Georgia. You can catch up with us as soon as you can."

Phimble nodded. "Take Stobs with you. You'll need a good radioman, and he can keep me informed."

"Agreed," Kennedy said.

"If I know Josh Thurlow, and I know the big creature about as well as I do any man, he's still alive near that beach where we left him."

"What if he's not?"

"Then use all that authority you're aching to display and come up with a plan to find him."

"And Armistead, the purpose for this entire adventure?"

"You can forget Armistead until you find the skipper. Just keep my boys safe, Lieutenant. You get them killed, you'll answer to me."

Phimble went off to check on the engine work, and Kennedy was surprised and pleased to observe Felicity, dressed in a sailor's blue jeans and chambray shirt, climb off the gunboat's bow and wade ashore. Kennedy walked over to greet her. "He's a pilot," he said when she stopped to inspect the prisoner.

"I've not known too many Japanese," she responded. "There was Yodo, a merchant who owned a trading post on Choiseul. He was murdered in '37 by a saltwater boy. A nice enough man, but he played with the Maries too much, the downfall for most men here, sooner if not later."

Kennedy led Felicity away from Ichikawa. "We're going to New Georgia to see if we can find Thurlow," he advised. "Phimble's taking the Catalina back to Melagi. You and John-Bull can go with us or with him. Either way, I can't guarantee your safety."

"I'll go with you, of course. New Georgia's a lot closer to Noa-Noa than Melagi."

"We could see combat."

"Death is a constant in the Solomons even without war," she replied. "Don't worry about me and John. We can take care of ourselves."

Kennedy grinned. "You remind me of my sister Kick. Tough as nails."

"I will take that as a compliment," she replied, returning his grin.

When Fisheye told him he thought the engine was ready, Phimble came to talk with Ichikawa. "Now, Ichikawa-san, we're going to fly south, and you're going with us. Please climb aboard the Catalina."

"I will go only if you force me," Ichikawa responded.

"Let me talk to him, Mister Phimble," Fisheye said.

Phimble nodded and walked away. Fisheye sat beside Ichikawa. "Look, Ichikawa-san, we've got to go, and we can't just leave you here. Come and go with us, easy like."

Ichikawa shook his head. "No, Fisheye. It is against my Bushido code to go willingly into prison."

"I wish you'd forget that code. They only wrote it so they could order you to get killed without talking back. I don't see your old Tojo coming down here to take his lumps."

"Prime Minister Tojo is a brave man."

"But stupid to get into a war he can't win."

"We may lose in these islands," Ichikawa replied, "but we will have written a glorious chapter in our history. And you will never beat us completely. You will see."

"I don't want to see anything. I just want to go home," Fisheye said.

"Ah. In that we agree, Fisheye."

"OK, how about this? I've only put that engine together with spit and chewing gum. It's probably going to conk out when we try to take off. In that case, we'll most likely crash and die."

"Do you think so?" Ichikawa asked, perking up.

"The odds are in favor of it, I fear."

"Give me the odds."

"I'd say three to one against us surviving takeoff, and then two to one against us making it down to Melagi without crashing."

Ichikawa closed his eyes in thought, then nodded. "Help me up." When Fisheye did, he bowed. "Fisheye, I will be proud to die with you."

"Attaboy," Fisheye said, bowing back.

Kennedy, Ready, Felicity, and the crew of the *Rosemary* plus Marvin watched as the *Dosie* turned and aimed directly into the wind, which was coming offshore. Kennedy had moved the gunboat past the reef into deeper water just in case the Catalina didn't make it. That way they would be better positioned to assist in the pickup of survivors, if there were any. "May God be with them," Felicity prayed, as the Catalina's engines revved to a tortured howl.

"Dave's with them," Once said. "That's got to help in the luck department."

"He was with them when they got shot down, too," brother Again pointed out.

"Dave, he make'm *Dosie* fly," Pogo said.

Dosie plowed ahead, her nose bashing into low waves. Millie listened to the engines. "They sound good," he allowed. "I think they're going to make it."

"Then why have they stopped?" Stobs wondered.

On board *Dosie*, Phimble cursed. Fisheye had reached into the cockpit and pulled back the throttles. "What the hell are you doing, boy?"

"Sir, I've had a change of heart. We got to let Ichikawa-san go. It'll kill him to be put into prison. I lied to him, told him we'd probably crash and die. But I really think we got better than a fifty-fifty chance of making it."

Phimble pulled the headset away from his ears and stared at Fisheye. "Listen, you numb nut, he won't go to prison. Just some sort of camp."

"Same thing. He won't be able to take it. He'll find some way to kill himself. We've got to let him go."

"We don't got to do no such thing. Now, strap yourself in. We're taking off." He eyed Fisheye and saw something in his expression. "Wait a minute. Have you already let him go?"

"Not exactly. He escaped. I opened the starboard hatch and looked away and he jumped out." He added, after a short second, "I had untied him, you see. Those ropes hurt his wrists."

Phimble stared at Fisheye. "On your own, you let a prisoner of war go free?"

"I guess you could put it that way."

"They could hang you for that!"

"Well, I done what I had to do," Fisheye replied staunchly.

"You liked that Jap bastard that much?"

Fisheye shrugged. "Mister Phimble, he ain't no bastard. He's just a man like you and me. Besides that, he likes to fish."

Phimble considered turning the seaplane around and taxiing back to pick up the Japanese pilot. It would be easy enough to do, but then he realized Fisheye would probably just let him go again. "Fisheye, consider yourself busted to basic seaman."

"Yes, sir. That's my rank anyway, I think. It's been a while since I've been paid."

Phimble shook his head. "All right, boy. Strap yourself in. Let's see if we can make this old bird fly."

As the boys cheered her from the *Rosemary*, *Dosie* lifted off, as smooth a takeoff as she'd ever managed, and turned south. Soon she was a dot in the sky. And on the island known as Mary, a Japanese pilot touched sand and crawled up on the beach. He looked after the American aircraft until it disappeared south, then at the American gunboat until it disappeared north. Then he sat down and waited for rescue, which he was certain would be soon.

3 6

Penelope was scampering up the mountain slope like a rabbit, and Josh was having trouble keeping up with her. He could hear the feet of the following warriors slapping against the earthen path, and even the rush of their breath. Josh knew they were going to catch him. Like Penelope, they could slip through the bush as a fish swam through the water, while he was heavy-footed, ensnared by vines, and tripped by roots. It was tempting to simply turn and fight even though all he had was his pistol and ax, and Whitman's men were carrying Enfields.

Why the warriors hadn't shot him already was a question that formed in Josh's mind, even as he twisted and twirled through a thorny bush that tore at his utilities and scratched his skin into bloody rents. More than once, he knew, he'd presented a clear view of his back to his pursuers. Perhaps the bushmen were in competition to catch him. If that was so, that meant they were not working together. All this came to Josh in an instant, as wisdom sometimes did, and he thought to use it as an advantage and at least save Penelope, if not himself.

He made his plan and wished he could tell Penelope what he was going to do, but he lacked the breath to do it. He could only hope she would fig-ure it out. When they reached an opening in the bush, a wide meadow with waist-high grass, she dodged to the left, but he turned and faced the onrush-ing warriors. He jumped up and down and waved his arms and yelled at them, then ran to the right, away from Penelope. He didn't look back, just chugged along until he reached the edge of the bush. When he realized he couldn't hear anyone following, he looked over his shoulder and was aston-ished to find that he was alone. Whitman's men had ignored him and instead chased after Penelope.

Josh thought perhaps they had not seen him. He walked back into the meadow and yelled at them. He even fired his pistol into the air. There was no response. Penelope kept running, and Whitman's men continued to chase her. Josh followed, careful of ambushes. His ripped utilities were soaked with sweat. His knees were sore from falling. His arms were bleeding from the thorns that had scratched him. And his feelings were inexplicably hurt that he was apparently of much less importance to the mangy murderers than the girl. Finally he climbed up on a ridge to see that Penelope had stopped to make a stand.

It was going to be a pathetic stand. The three pursuers were taunting her, raising their rifles and pointing them at her, then lowering them to make gestures of cutting her head off by drawing their fingers across their throats. She was angry and frustrated and was giving them what-for in the local language, not a word of which Josh could understand.

Such was the intense focus the men had on Penelope, Josh was able to walk up behind them. He waited for a moment for them to look over their shoulders and confront him. When they didn't, he yelled at them. Still they ignored him, so he raised his pistol and shot two of them in the back. He didn't like being a back-shooter, but he was too tired to resist temptation.

This policy at least gained him some attention. The two back-shot men dropped and died, and the third, a muscular man with an angry but intelligent look on his face, turned to look with some curiosity at Josh, as if wondering what had come over the white man to make him shoot his comrades. Josh realized this was the tall man he'd seen on the beach the day he'd arrived to talk to Whitman. That meant the two men lying dead were probably the same other two he'd met that day. He was about to exercise his pidgin as best he could to discover the truth of the entire odd state of affairs, but the opportunity was cut short, to say the least, when Penelope sprang at the man with her machete, her terribly sharp machete, and slashed the man's tendons at his knees. With a shriek, he fell and clutched his bloody and useless legs, then rolled over and raised his rifle to shoot her. Penelope contemptuously kicked his rifle aside and wore her terrible blade across his face. He threw up his hands to hold his face together, blood spurting between his fingers, but she laughed and hacked his hands, one of which flew off. He rolled and cried and bled. "You belong devil," Penelope said to the bawling man. "Die same."

It is a terrible thing to see a man so horribly cut up and still be alive, but it didn't last long. Penelope hacked off the man's head with two hard cuts and then kicked it away, sending it tumbling down the hill. "Baho, Moga, and Coronga," she said, pointing at each of the three dead men. Her eyes, dilated after her furious killing, gradually refocused. "They were my cousins. More will follow when these do not return."

"Why will they follow? What does Whitman want with you?"

She studied him, as if observing him for the first time. The machete moved in her hand, and he started to raise his pistol to defend himself, but all she did was wipe the blood off the blade with a handful of grass. Then, without another word, she turned and loped up the hill.

Josh watched her, half supposing she would stop and wait for him, but she determinedly made her way through the tall grass until she disappeared. He followed her, but as soon as he stepped one foot inside the darkness of the towering trees and clutching vines and thorny bushes, he knew he would not find her. Josh did the only thing he could think to do, the thing he always did when he was lost, or confused, or unhappy in any way. He set his sights on the sea and made toward it. He did not see that there was another one of Whitman's men, a warrior who was thick around the waist with stumpy legs and a bit of an indecisive mind. He was a dogged sort, however, and had tracked along the path that had been made during the pursuit. Having gotten very tired, he'd stopped to lean up against a banyan tree for a rest and a smoke. He was sitting there, smoking and resting, when Josh came across him. Josh had his pistol up and pressed against the warrior's forehead before the man could make a move for his Enfield, which he had tossed carelessly on the ground more than an arm's length away.

"Now you will talk," Josh said. "Now you will tell me why you chase the girl."

The warrior grimaced, showing teeth filed to triangular points and blackened by betel nut. Beads of sweat erupted on his brow and rolled down his cheeks. "She belong dead" was his only comment.

"Why?" Josh demanded, and cocked the pistol and pushed his knee against the man's chest until the wind was expelled out of his nasty mouth. "Tell me or you belong dead just now."

The man's eyes were bugged out from the pressure of Josh's knee but he stubbornly shook his head. "You look'm along pistol," Josh snarled. "You look'm along me. You look'm along death in the eye. Tell'm or so help me I will pull this trigger." He pressed the pistol so hard against the man's forehead that it started to bleed, a trickle of blood running down around his nose. Yet the warrior stayed defiant.

"He wants to kill me because of who I am," Penelope said, appearing almost as if by magic at Josh's side. "You see, he believes I make Mastah Whitman weak."

The fat warrior started to rise, as if he had forgotten that Josh's heavy knee was against his chest and a pistol was indenting his forehead. Josh pushed him back against the tree. "Kill Toronga," Penelope said, nodding toward the fat warrior. "Kill him and I will take you to Armistead in short order. I know what happened to him. I know the entire story."

Josh was tempted, mightily tempted. Pull the trigger and, he supposed, Penelope would do exactly what she said she would do. But to his considerable relief, he discovered he could not kill in quite such cold blood, ignoring the fact he'd recently back-shot two men. He had always been quick to forget and forgive himself. It was a weakness, but a convenient one. Josh relaxed his knee and pulled back his pistol and took a step away from the warrior. "You tell me," he told Toronga and nodded toward Penelope. "My word, you tell me or I will let her use her machete on you."

The stream of blood from his forehead was now coursing in a rivulet down Toronga's face. He looked from Josh to Penelope. Then he said something to Penelope in their native tongue. Penelope didn't reply, although she flicked her machete, carving a little circle in the air. The hate between them was so fulsome, it felt to Josh as if it were a living thing. It was at that moment he realized that there was nothing that mattered to either Toronga or Penelope except this hatred. The Japanese and the Americans, battling across their island, were as inconsequential as the rain that, as it happened, was beginning to fall. Big drops pattered down from the canopy above, and within a few seconds it was a thundering downpour. A tree branch broke and came crashing down. It was then that Toronga made his move.

Josh would have undoubtedly shot Toronga except he was knocked senseless by the falling limb. The same limb also whipped across Toronga's outstretched arm, breaking it just below the elbow. Only Penelope stood unscathed. She stuck her machete in the earth while the rain flung itself across the small clearing in great gray sheets. She lifted the limb off Josh and knelt beside him and smoothed his hair and sang a consoling song while the forest shook from the storm. Toronga, ignored for the moment, crawled to his rifle and clutched it with his remaining good hand, then tried to wedge it in his armpit to get off a shot. Penelope saw him and pushed his rifle away, as if he were as inconsequential as a flea. "Run, Toronga," she said in a quiet voice.

Toronga dropped his rifle and got up and ran, only to slip on a wet root. He rose to his knees, holding his broken arm, which hurt something terrible, and then looked over his shoulder. Penelope stood watching him. She had retrieved her machete and was patting its blade in her hand. Toronga knew that if he ran, she was only going to come up behind him and slice him with that blade. He would have to kill her, or die trying.

He died trying. Josh came to his senses just in time to see Penelope standing with a bare foot on Toronga's shoulder while she kicked his head away with the other. "Penelope," he muttered through a pink haze, "you're going to have to stop cutting men's heads off if you want me to take you to Killakeet."

Penelope knelt and took Josh's head onto her lap. She sang, but it was not a song she had learned in Minister Clarence's chapel. It was a song of the ancients. "What are you singing?" he asked when she was finished.

"It was a song to Toronga. He and I were not only cousins, but once we were friends. It was to remind him that death is more certain than life, that war is more certain than peace, that unhappiness is more certain than joy."

"It is a sad song," Josh reflected.

"He was a sad man," Penelope replied with a shrug. "There are ever so many sad men these days."

"Penelope, take me to Armistead so we can get this over with."

"Armistead," she said, and it sounded to Josh as if her voice were coming from a faraway place. "He is the saddest man of all."

"Not as sad as you are going to be, dearie," came the voice of Whitman. Although the Australian could not be seen, the bush stirred and out stepped a phalanx of his warriors, their bayonet-pointed Enfields leveled, their faces painted, their hair powdered with wood ash, their grins scarlet and hideous. Whitman emerged from behind a tree and leered at Josh. "I must thank you, Commander."

"For what?" Josh demanded.

"Why, for finding *her,* of course," he replied, swinging his rifle toward Penelope. "My dear, sweet, loyal wife."

3 7

After the Catalina could no longer be seen or heard, Kennedy set the course and took the wheel of the gunboat and powered the throttles full ahead. Kennedy was energized and fixed in his determination to push forward, to rescue Josh Thurlow and perhaps even find David Armistead. It did not matter that Phimble had dismissed the mission. Kennedy, filled with vigor, was on the hunt.

In fact, Kennedy could not recall ever feeling quite so happy and free. All his aches were gone, his stomach settled, his intestines accomplishing their functions as required. And no one on board gave a damn who he was or his father was or who his brother was. *That was the finest thing!* He was truly Kennedy, the terror of the Solomons, ace gunboat skipper and armed adventurer. He felt as if he could take on the entire Japanese Imperial Fleet if it came to it. The *Rosemary* was a fine craft, swift, deadly, with an efficient crew, and perhaps even equipped with torpedoes that worked. He grinned, his bushy brown hair blown back from his bright and determined eyes. *If only,* he thought, *my pappy and brother Joe could see me now!*

Ready, standing beside Kennedy in the cockpit, watched the lieutenant out of the corner of his eye and wondered about the grinning. The other boys did, too. "Mister Kennedy must be telling himself jokes," Once said into Ready's ear.

"Wish he'd tell me one," Ready replied, just loud enough for Once to hear over the wind and the rumble of the great engines, now tuned to a fever after Fisheye had briefly laid his hands on them. Kennedy was not aware of his crew's worry over his condition. He had moved on in his thinking to Felicity Markham. He could feel her watching him, and he glanced over his shoulder and found her sitting on the galley hatch cover, her legs crossed at the ankle, a pleased expression on her heart-shaped face, and he knew it was just for him. He pressed against the throttles, though they were nearly against their jams already, and was made all the happier when the *Rosemary* responded with the same joyful abandon he felt.

All afternoon, Kennedy kept the gunboat heading generally northwest, making Vangunu Island by dusk. New Georgia was ahead, but it was fifty miles long. Josh Thurlow, if he was still alive, was likely on the northern tip. Night came, the bright, twinkling stars and the silvery crescent moon unveiled themselves, and Kennedy knew the Rufes would soon be out looking for targets. He had no choice but to find a secluded harbor to hide until sunrise. Felicity recommended the village of Tevara for their refuge, explaining that it was on the island of Tetepare, which was just south of Rendova. "An easy run from here," she said, "and well off the usual sea-lanes."

Kennedy agreed, shot across Blanche Channel to Tetepare, and there found a palm-crossed beach with no evidence of habitation, save a few burned-out huts. "This was Tevara," Felicity said in sadness and confusion. "At least three hundred people lived here."

Kennedy joined her on the bow. "Where do you think they've gone?"

She shook her head. "I don't know. Maybe inland, maybe to other islands. Everything here is being changed by this awful war. Sometimes I wonder if I will ever know happiness again." Her hand brushed against his. "Understand, Jack. I am the daughter of a Welsh coal miner. Poor as mice we were, never with a farthing to rub together with another one. Bryce was the son of the man who owned the mine. We met, we fell in love, and we were condemned for it by both families. So we ran here where no one cared who we were, and we made our own way. Is it any wonder that we fell in love with these islands and this way of life?"

"I envy you for the adventures you've had," Kennedy said. "I've always had a taste for adventure."

She took his hand. "Tell me about yourself, Jack Kennedy."

Kennedy thought about making a quip, something clever about Choate and Harvard, but instead, for a reason that wasn't clear even to himself, he told her something of his family, and of his father, and of his writing.

"Well, I must say it is a bit overwhelming to realize I am in such famous company."

"I told you because I was afraid you would hear it, anyway."

"You were afraid? Why, Jack, your accomplishments should be entirely a source of pride. Imagine. A best seller at, how old are you? Twenty-three?"

"Twenty-six."

"I am thirty-six. There. We have that out of the way."

"You are as young as anyone I have ever known." Then, when he noticed that her face was flushed, he asked, "Do you have fever?"

"In a manner of speaking," she replied, and looked up at him with her bravest smile.

Kennedy waited until sunrise, pulled anchor, and blew back across Blanche Channel, then turned west along the New Georgian coast. Felicity stood in the cockpit with Kennedy to point out the winding route that lay between the inner and outer reefs. She knew the way perfectly, having often gone to visit the various plantations of that coast. She called them off as they passed by their ruins. "There's the Wagner plantation. Oh, look how horrible. So many fine trees going to waste. And their house, burned and gutted. And there, that's the Conover place. Their house used to be just there. I can't tell if it's still there because it is all too overgrown. Ah, the poor cattle, bloated and dead. Missus Conover was so proud of her bossies. Oh, it is enough to bring me to tears."

At last, they reached the deep lagoon where Thurlow had been put ashore. They found it empty of life but filled with death. Silently the boys of the *Rosemary* lined up to watch in horror. Felicity put her arm around the shoulder of John-Bull and Kennedy eased back on the throttles to allow the gunboat to glide parallel to the beach. Staked out on it were bodies, both American and Japanese, tied to posts that were driven into the sand. Each body had been mutilated and was surrounded by masses of black flies. The stink of the bodies and the buzz of the furious insects drifted across the lagoon. Felicity said, "If I could, I believe I would destroy the world, blow it up into little pieces, so such madness could never be repeated." She turned and found Kennedy standing beside her. Impetuously she buried her face into his shoulder.

3 8

Kennedy led the party ashore. He had a Bowie knife strapped to his web belt, a forty-five pistol in his hand, his officer's cap shoved on the back of his head, and his shirt open to his waist. He felt like a character lifted out of the comic strip *"Terry and the Pirates."* Left aboard the gunboat were John-Bull, Millie, Stobs, and Again (he and Once had flipped a coin). Millie was put in charge with orders to move the *Rosemary* out of the lagoon if night came and the shore party had not returned. They were to defend themselves if attacked and to head home if it seemed prudent.

Felicity had insisted on going ashore. "Nonsense," she'd replied forcefully to Kennedy's objection. "I know this shore. I can be of great help." She patted her Webley on her hip. "And I can take care of myself, Jack. Not to worry. Now, this bushman," she nodded toward Pogo, "let him be our scout. You Pogo," she said directly to him, "you find'm bad fella boys?"

"Yes, missus," Pogo responded, looking out of the tops of his big round eyes at the colonial woman. He was wearing a green lap-lap and a simple necklace of cowrie shells, but his face was painted with white finger streaks, giving him a most warriorlike appearance. A hawk feather was stuck in his hair and what appeared to be a yellow electrical wire through his nose. What might have been chicken bones were stuck through his earlobes. He carried an M-1 Garand, just like all the boys except Ready, who carried a Browning automatic.

Kennedy eyed the diminutive native and wondered if he was up to the task. "Are you a good tracker?" he asked.

Pogo nodded. "I find'm," he said. He pointed toward the bush and said, "These fellas not too many. We chase'm. Mastah Josh belong them."

"How do you know?" Kennedy asked.

"Here Mastah Josh foot."

Ready inspected the prints in the sand. "It's a Raider boot track, and a heavy tread. It could be the skipper."

"Is Skipper," Pogo said stubbornly. "We chase'm."

Kennedy was dubious. "We're more likely to get ambushed."

Pogo said. "Pogo walk'm easy. Kennedy, boys walk'm easy. Look-see bad fellas. Look-see Mastah Josh. No see Mastah Josh? My word! Pogo, Kennedy, boys belong beach double-quick!"

Kennedy looked into Pogo's eyes and saw a reflection of self-sufficiency and confidence. Then he pondered the ghastly remains that were roped to the stakes on the beach. Whoever had done this awful deed, even if half of their victims had been Japanese, required punishment. "All right, Pogo," Kennedy relented. "Go ahead."

"Why not?" Pogo said, which gave all the boys a chuckle, the last they'd manage on that particular day.

Pogo went forward, a machete in his hand, his M-1 given over to Lieutenant Kennedy. The path ran through a slimy, rotten-smelling jungle, then onto rising ground, slippery with wet saw grass. They slipped and fell as they climbed, and gasped to find the least bit of oxygen in the hot, stagnant air. Gigantic, impossibly huge leaves of the most amazing corrugated design crowded in on them. Thick-rooted trees, with huge hairy vines hanging from their limbs like dead snakes, blocked their vision. Thousands of sleeping flying foxes hung head down on high branches like squadrons of tiny vampires. Every person in the party felt as if eyes were watching them from the deep recesses of the bush. Pogo did not just feel it. He *knew* it, for these were the eyes of the evil spirits who occupied this land.

Pogo was caught in his reverie of spirits and failed to see the phantom hiding among the many limbs of a giant tree. He jumped back from the thrown spear as it flashed past his nose and buried into the soft, moist earth between his big flat feet. The trajectory of the spear led Pogo's eyes to the shadowy figure in the tree. Pogo returned the spear with a mighty heave. The shadow, now revealed to be a man, fell from the tree, rolled, pulled the spear from his rib cage, and ran for the bush. Just a glimpse of him had revealed a fierce countenance, a face like the devil, a bone stuck through his nose, and more bones through his earlobes. Other than his hideous tattoos, he was as naked as a reptile. Before he got far, Pogo was on him, grabbing him by his towering puff of hair and jerking him to the ground and kicking his hand away from the wound, which coursed blood like a small river into the greedy black earth.

Pogo, asking rapid questions in the local dialect, pulled the man's head back. The man made low moaning sounds, and his mouth pulsed open and shut between thick, pursed lips. Pinkish foam began to form at the corners of his mouth. Pogo spoke to the man again, this time in a more soothing tone, then let him go. The man made choking noises deep in his throat. In a second, no more, he fell away, dead. "Poison," Felicity said, coming up during the last second of the man's life. "Just a scratch is all it takes."

Pogo looked over his shoulder and saw that Once had picked up the spear and was looking it over. "That fella spear alla same devil. It finish you altogether, Once!"

"Put the spear down, Once," Kennedy said. "Easy now. Don't touch the tip. That's a good lad."

Pogo was back to studying the dead man, especially the tattoos on his chest and back and arms. "Him this place fella boy. Him not fella we look-see."

Felicity translated. "This man had no part in the business on the beach."

Pogo nodded toward an all but invisible path. "This fella live there short way little bit."

"Maybe he was defending his village," Ready said.

"Then why didn't he defend it against those buggers we're following?" Felicity asked.

"Those buggers in village," Pogo explained. "Those buggers, they say fella boy you go here, watch'm, come quick you see'm other fellas."

"That makes sense," Felicity said. "This man was sent to be a lookout."

They all froze at the deep, hollow beat of a distant drum. "What does it mean?" Kennedy asked Pogo after the little bushman had kept silent for too many uncomfortable seconds.

"Drums say all ready soon kai-kai." Pogo put his fingers to his mouth.

"They're having lunch?" Ready asked.

Pogo nodded, though he kept a stubborn silence.

"They're having lunch," Ready said again, this time in a whisper as he realized the import of the word in these awful woods.

Once was sent racing back to the *Rosemary* to bring the mortar and at least a dozen shells. Pogo was sent ahead to scout the village. He soon returned with a report. "Mastah Josh belong this place."

"Tell me exactly what you saw," Felicity said.

Pogo covered the situation. He had worked his way to the ridge that overlooked the village. At least twenty men armed with rifles could be seen. Mastah Josh was tied to a post, his hands roped over his head, and a black Marie was similarly strung up beside him.

"Do you think we can get on that ridge without being seen?" Ready asked.

"Look-see boy there but Pogo cut throat." He held up his machete to show the blood on it.

Kennedy considered his options, which were three: Sit tight and wait for Once to return with the mortar, then attack the village; go up on the ridge and be prepared to attack at a moment's notice; or simply go at it straight away. "We'll go up on the ridge and have a look around," he said, taking the middle choice.

Pogo led the way through the dense bush. A few chickens gave irritated clucks, but their approach was otherwise undetected. The forest grew right up to the edge of the ridge that overlooked the village. They crawled the last few yards. The lookout Pogo had killed lay a few feet away, his throat busy with flies. Felicity, lying beside Kennedy, studied the village. "Jack, when they get ready to kill Commander Thurlow, they will do so very quickly, without ceremony, and when their victim least expects it. Less trouble for them that way."

Two men came out of one of the larger huts. One of them was a white man in khakis and an Aussie campaign hat, the other an obese native, covered only by a filthy lap-lap over which his stomach hung like a huge brown bag. The fat man waddled in front of Thurlow and apparently said something, as Thurlow replied, although what he said was too far away to hear. The Marie tied up beside him said something, too, and the fat man held his gelatinous stomach and laughed, apparently amused by the comment.

"The white man is Todd Whitman," Felicity whispered to Kennedy. "He's the guerrilla leader Thurlow came up here to interrogate. The fat rascal is the chief around these parts, a nasty brute named Kwaque. He's stirred up trouble in New Georgia for years. He's long been suspected of headhunting and cannibalism."

A shriek jerked their heads around. Kennedy feared it was Thurlow or the girl, but it proved to be one of the villagers, pointing toward the ridge with a long, trembling finger. They'd been spotted. Kwaque and Whitman looked in their direction but didn't move. "Ready," Kennedy said, "shoot the chief."

Ready fired his Browning, and Kwaque staggered back, his hand thrown to a bloody hole in his chest. He flopped against Thurlow, who kicked him away. Then Kwaque staggered some more, most theatrically, yodeling imprecations while his fellows looked at him in dumb wonder. Whitman was unmoved and kept frowning at the ridge, where a little puff of smoke rose from Ready's rifle.

"Come on!" Kennedy cried, then got to his feet and raced out of the bush and down the incline into the village. Ready, Pogo, and Felicity followed. Kennedy fired his rifle from his hip, missing his target, which was Whitman, then ducking a storm of arrows that suddenly filled the air. He dodged a man lunging at him with a spear, then shot the man in the chest. Felicity pushed Kennedy to the ground and shot another warrior in the stomach. Kennedy was astonished at the power of her pistol. A hole big enough to put his arm though appeared in the man's belly, and he flopped on the ground like a caught fish. Felicity stood over Kennedy, firing until she ran out of bullets. Then there was a series of pounding explosions, and one of the huts disintegrated.

"I do believe Once is back!" Felicity remarked cheerfully while reloading. Kennedy struggled to his feet. He looked at her and saw that her eyes were wild with excitement, her sweat-soaked hair hanging in tendrils along her cheek, her nostrils flared. She whooped and took two quick steps and fired at a black Marie trying to sneak by, her arms cradling a baby. The woman fell, and the baby, squalling in terror, rolled onto the ground. Felicity aimed at it, but her arm was caught by Kennedy. "Felicity, for God's sake!"

She looked at him, then pulled her arm away. "Don't ever stop me from my duty again, Jack. Just as I would not stop you from yours." She went charging off, firing her pistol at any villager she could see. The villagers were running hysterically in every direction. Kennedy picked up the baby. Another Marie suddenly appeared and tore it from his grasp and ran away. Kennedy watched after her and was relieved when she and the child made it safely into the bush.

Then Thurlow was there, along with the woman who'd been tied up beside him. "Stay here, keep the boys safe," Thurlow ordered, which irritated Kennedy more than a little. After all, he'd just engineered the man's rescue, and here he was barking orders to do the obvious! Before Kennedy could remark on such abuse, Thurlow and the woman left on the run. Felicity returned, her smoking Webley in her hand. The excitement drained from her face. "I'm sorry, Jack," she said. "It was the heat of battle."

"I know," Kennedy answered. "But to shoot a baby . . ."

"I don't know what came over me. All of a sudden, I just wanted to put that child out of its misery. I thought to spare it from a horrible life."

"Did you see where Thurlow went?"

"He and the girl are after Whitman, I think," she said.

"We should follow and see if he needs help," Kennedy said, which was the last thing he said for a good bit, as Kwaque, the chief he thought was dead, came up behind and struck him on the head with a stone. Felicity had a bullet in Kwaque's brain in an instant, but it was too late for Kennedy. He was down, and he was out.

3 9

Josh and Penelope raced down the path after Whitman and his men. The path was well worn and went past several pigpens, the occupants grunting nervously as they ran by. It continued through small garden plots and into a grove of Norfolk pines. Josh and Penelope loped along like tigers, looking neither left nor right but dead ahead. Josh had retrieved his Alaskan ax from Kwaque's hut, and Penelope had recovered her machete from a lately deceased warrior. The blades were their only armament, and given their fury, all they needed.

Swiftly, swiftly. Josh felt as if he were floating, borne by the wings of vengeful angels. Nothing slowed him, no root tripped him. He was astonished at the swiftness of his own feet, propelled by a blood-red anger.

The path turned at a gigantic monkeypod tree, and there, in a clearing not more than twenty paces ahead, was Whitman, walking fast with his head down, followed by three of his men. Josh and Penelope came on, silent as eagles. Josh ran past the two hindmost men, startling them so much they froze—a mistake, as Penelope was upon them in an instant with her awful blade. The man behind Whitman turned and caught Josh's ax along his ear. He fell without a sound. Whitman dropped, rolled away, and came up with his pistol, well aimed. Josh dodged, his ax thrumming through the air, knocking the pistol away.

Whitman sat on the ground, looking at his pistol hand in astonishment. Josh's swipe had also happened to carry away Whitman's thumb. He pressed the bloody stump to his shirt, a scarlet stain spreading into the khaki, while with his other hand he calmly picked up his hat, swiped the mud off it against his legs, and put it back aboard. He looked at Penelope. "Will I ever stop loving you, I wonder?"

⟩ "Yes, very soon, husband," Penelope answered, her lips rolled back to reveal an avaricious grin.

"Why did you kill our soldiers?" Josh demanded. "And why did you turn us over to Kwaque?"

"My dear commander," Whitman said, "your soldiers were killed because my boys simply had their blood up. I can't always control them. My apologies. As for Kwaque, he has been my ally against the Japanese. Most of my boys come from his tribe. I could hardly resist turning you over to him for a good kai-kai. Americans are known to be extremely tasty blokes. As for my dear but disloyal wife, I gave her to Kwaque to disfigure, not eat. You recall I remarked on the curse of being married to a beautiful woman? I sought to fix that. Now, please bind my hand."

Horrified by Whitman's calm explanation, Josh pulled a red bandana out of his hip pocket and tossed it over. "Bind it yourself."

Penelope said, "Josh, you must kill Whitman. Quickly, please."

Josh stared at Penelope and wondered where the dear, sweet girl who'd made love to him that first night beneath the bright moon had gone. He didn't know this Penelope at all.

Whitman withdrew his bloody hand from his shirt, then pushed it into the bandana in his lap, using his other hand and his teeth to wrap it tightly. "Ah, that's better. I shall miss that thumb." He eyed Josh. "Have you and my wife, by any chance . . . ? Yes, you have! I can see it in your eyes. Well, don't feel privileged, Thurlow. It ain't love, no matter what she says. She ain't capable of it."

"How would you know, Whitman?" Penelope snapped. "To you, love and pain are the same thing. My father did not know your filthy mind, or he would have never given me to you." Penelope turned to Josh. "Please understand. A Marie is loyal to her husband, even when he is cruel. But when Whitman began to kai-kai long pig, it was then I decided to run away."

"Armistead agreed to help you," Josh said.

"No. I wish for your sake it was that simple. My father, you see, finally sent my brother to see how I was doing. I had prayed for so very long for him to know my plight, and he answered my prayers, though he took long enough. Of course, Whitman thought my brother was just another warrior come to fight the Japoni."

"Such treason," Whitman sniffed. "Imagine, Thurlow! A man pretending to fight for freedom and democracy while planning on stealing a man's wife."

"Shut up, you," Josh said. "Or I'll cut off your other thumb."

"My brother and I had a canoe, just waiting our chance," Penelope explained.

"Whitman told me Joe Gimmee sent a *tomako* for you," Josh said.

"Yet another lie," Penelope replied. "But please, Josh. We must stop talking and kill Whitman to end his evil."

"We can't kill him. Colonel Burr needs to hear his story."

"Whitman will only lie, and he is oh such a very good liar."

"That makes two of us," Whitman said, though his eyes rested on Penelope longingly.

Josh pointed his ax at Whitman. "Burr will get the truth out of you, Mister Whitman, one way or another. Now, be assured I will kill you if you don't do exactly as I say from this moment on. Stand up and march back to the village."

Stand up and march back to the village Whitman might have done, too, as it was certainly likely that Josh would do exactly as he threatened. But proof that Whitman was a survivor and lucky besides came very quickly. There was a sudden whoop of murderous screams and four of Kwaque's men came rushing out of the bush. With Josh distracted, Penelope took the opportunity to swing her machete at Whitman's neck, but Whitman had anticipated her attack, and her sharp blade missed by no more than a hair's breadth. Then arrows rippled through the air, and Josh and Penelope had no choice but to run once more. And run they did.

4 0

Josh and Penelope finally slowed enough to look over their shoulders. When they saw no one following, they stopped and listened, and heard nothing but the sound of their own breathing and the usual twits and chatter of the forest. Penelope said, "I believe we are safe now." She looked long and hard at Josh. "If only you would have killed Whitman."

Josh nodded, acknowledging his error, then trudged up the path, stopping when he noticed she wasn't following. "Are you coming?" he asked.

"Is that your wish, considering who I am?"

He studied her, as if seeing her for the first time. He saw the blood of the men she'd just killed speckled across her glistening ebony skin and recalled, with some nostalgia, when he thought she was but a simple, smiling, and gorgeous Marie who'd saved him from the Japanese and then made passionate love to him by the sea. Now he knew she was Whitman's wife and had lied about nearly everything from the moment they'd met. But nothing mattered as his eyes roved across her. He was not willing to let her go. "Yes, it is my wish," he said to her, and meant it. "But tell me what happened that night. And this time the truth."

"You shame me," she replied.

"You're forgiven. I've been known to tell less than the truth from time to time, too."

"Such as when you told me you loved me?"

"That was not a lie."

She looked into his eyes carefully, and he knew she was looking for the lie. Finally she said, "When Armistead went out to silence the mortars, he told me one of the Japoni officers was still alive, and that they sat for a little while and talked before the officer died. I am not certain what was said between them, but Armistead said it affected him. On his way back to our lines, he came across Whitman's men eating Japanese long pig. This sickened him, of course, but he said it confirmed in his mind what he needed to do. By then, you see, all his men were dead. He asked me if I would help him go north. When I asked him why north, he wouldn't tell me. I told him I would talk to my brother, and so I did. My brother said it was a good time for us to go, that Whitman was plotting to kill Armistead now that the lieutenant had discovered his boys were cannibals. We had a small boat hidden away by the beach. When there was a lull in the battle, we took our chance. Unfortunately, someone saw us.

"They were trying to capture us alive, I think, so they did not shoot us but came at us with spears. When Armistead was stabbed, we had to drag him to the canoe. I am much the better fighter, so I asked my brother to have my father pray for me and stayed behind to hold off Whitman's killers. I expected to die, but then a cloud passed over the moon, and after seeing my brother and Armistead were well out on the water, I slipped away into the bush."

"Then Armistead could be dead," Josh realized, half hoping that it was true. But if he was dead, how would that square with Halsey's reference to Hypo, unless . . . "Or is it possible the Japanese captured him?"

"Either or both is possible," Penelope agreed. "I have no way of knowing, although my brother is strong, and smart, too. If anyone could have carried Armistead to safety, it would have been he."

Once, Again, and Pogo came running down the path from the village. "Oh, sir!" Again cried at the sight of his commander. "We have saved you!"

"I knew you would come," Josh said. "Although I have to admit you had me worried when you ran a bit late. How are things in the village?"

"The natives have all cleared out, and Mister Kennedy got knocked in the head. I think he'll be OK, though."

Josh introduced Penelope, and Once and Again fell all over themselves to be polite and to not look at her bare breasts. Pogo frowned at her but said nothing. They followed the boys back to the village, where they found Kennedy sitting against the post where Josh had recently been tied. His head was bloodied, but his eyes were clear. Josh did a double take at the woman who was tending to Kennedy. "Missus Markham?"

"Very nice to see you, Commander," she replied.

"How is it that you're here?"

"Lieutenant Kennedy rescued me and John. Our boat sank during a storm near Mary Island."

"So you tried to escape from Colonel Burr."

"More than *tried!*"

Josh introduced Penelope to Felicity. They nodded to one another during mutual arched-eyebrow inspections. "I recall seeing you at a planter's party," Felicity said.

"And I recall you as well, missus," Penelope replied. "Though from a distance, since I was most assuredly not allowed in the main house."

"I regret that you weren't," Felicity offered, though the flecks of fresh blood on the woman's body made her pause. Then she looked down at her own hand, the one that had held the Webley, and saw blood and powder marks on it. She looked up and saw Penelope was looking there, too. When their eyes met, they both smiled at the same time.

Ready appeared. "Skipper, there's something I think you need to see. It's in that big house, the one with the tall roof."

"It is called a devil-devil house," Felicity said. "If you look inside, I fear you'll discover why."

They followed Ready to the great thatched house, ornamented in front with fancy plaited mats and carved posts of obscene figures. Inside, they found a vast hall, laid out with parallel logs. "All-same fellas not belong Marie sleep-sleep," Pogo said, pointing at the logs with a sweep of his hand.

Felicity translated. "The bachelors sleep on those logs."

Even though his head ached, Kennedy had joined them. He ducked his head when it brushed against something dangling from a string. "Jesus, Mary, mother of God," he said when he saw it was a dried fetus.

"Quite," Felicity said.

Past the benches was a circle of stones containing a smoldering fire. Behind the fire was a table of stacked flat rocks, and on it was a line of mummified heads, blackened by soot. Felicity peered at them. "I recognize this one. Cunningham, a trader. He disappeared five years ago."

Kennedy came near, curious about the heads and repulsed at the same time. It was with a start that he recognized one of them, too. It wore an expression of dismay. "My God, that's Paul Grant. His boat went out about six months ago and was attacked by a Jap bomber. We thought he and his crew had drowned."

"He likely made it to shore only to run into Kwaque and his merry men," Felicity said.

Kennedy lurched from the devil-devil house while clutching his mouth. Felicity followed him. "It is the manner of these people, Jack," she said, standing above him as he knelt on the ground. "There is nothing to be done save stealing their children and educating them."

Kennedy dropped his face into his hands. His head ached and he needed something for it. He recalled briefly the joy he had so recently felt on the deck of his gunboat, but that was all gone now. The stink of the devil-devil house seemed lodged in his nostrils. He felt sick to his stomach and worried that he might throw up. In seconds, he was no longer worried. Felicity made Kennedy lie down in the shade and took his head into her lap, the blood oozing from his wound onto her shirt. "Rest, Jack," she said.

"Mustn't rest," he answered, though his voice was dull and unconvincing.

Pogo led Josh into the shadows behind the stone altar and pointed at dozens of other heads, stacked in several pyramids like gray and black cannonballs. The stink was overwhelming. "Kwaque kill'm Japoni, Americans, pickaninny, no matter," Pogo said. "This place belong devil."

"Not anymore," Josh said. "Ready, take the head of that PT-boat skipper and put it in a sack or something. We'll bury it at sea. Then burn this place. Not just the devil-devil house. The entire village."

Felicity looked up to see the first flames licking from the roof of the devil-devil house. Once and Again helped her with Kennedy, and they walked him to the pigpens just below the village. There was a roar as the entire structure of the devil-devil house became a great mass of flame, then collapsed. The huts surrounding it were on fire, too, columns of flames rising in superheated boils of crimson and gray smoke. The little band retreated, the moist heat of the burning village scalding their backs.

Josh led the way. Kennedy, supported by Once and Again, lurched along. As they neared the beach, one of Kwaque's men unexpectedly erupted from behind a tree and charged with a spear. Felicity was his target, but Pogo leapt in front of her and took the spear in his stomach. Felicity blew the top of the man's skull away with one well-aimed bullet. Pogo, still standing, pulled the spear from his guts and threw it down. Josh rushed to Pogo, but there was nothing he could do. Pogo looked at Josh and smiled. Pink foam appeared at the corners of his lips. "Pogo finish altogether," he said, then died.

"There lies as fine a man as ever lived in these islands." It was Pogo's epitaph, and it was Felicity who said it. She holstered her pistol and walked into the clear, fresh air of the beach.

PART IV

The LORD will be terrible unto them: for He will famish all the gods of the earth; and men shall worship Him, every one from his place, even all the isles of the heathen.—Zephaniah, chapter 2, verse 11

4 1

Kennedy awoke to find himself in a large room with bamboo walls that creaked in the wind. It was night, and an open window revealed a bright crescent moon and a trillion stars that flooded the interior with their silvery light. It was bright enough that a table in a corner could be discerned, and a chest of drawers near it, and another table on which sat an unlit kerosene lantern. He realized he was in a bed, a real bed with a mattress and sheets and a pillow. A mosquito net, suspended from a hook drilled into a heavy, dark beam, tented the bed. He could see now that the beam was a component of a vaulted thatched roof. A cloud crossed the face of the moon, and the room darkened, just before a sudden heavy rain rattled the roof. Then the rain stopped suddenly, followed by a steady drip-drip from the edges of the roof onto the ground. The moon and stars popped out again, and Kennedy could make out the tops of palms through the window, and beyond the trees a glittering sea. He sat up, and his head pounded, and he recalled that he had been struck on the head by the filthy chief named Kwaque. He felt along his skull and found a bandage tied around it. He explored beneath the bandage until he discovered a sore spot on the back of his head. It hurt but wasn't too bad. He knew he'd been lucky. The blow could have cracked his skull.

He heard the singsong chant of geckos, leavened by the eerie cry of a distant bird. Kennedy listened to the odd symphony for a little while, then fell asleep, only to be startled awake by something climbing the mosquito netting. It was a rat, hanging like a sailor on mast shrouds. It peered at Kennedy with inquisitive beady eyes, its twitching nose poked through one of the squares of the netting, then clambered on up to the rafters, where it ran along a horizontal beam, disappearing somewhere. Kennedy fell asleep once more. When next he woke, he heard the full cry of a rooster, which sounded as if it were under the hut. Hot, white sunlight streamed through the window. There was a fluttering sound, and a big hen appeared on the window's ledge and hopped down on the floor of the hut, which was covered by a straw mat. It pecked distractedly and then clucked with pleasure when it discovered a pile of dead insects beneath the table that held the lantern.

Kennedy rolled over and lifted the edge of the mosquito netting and looked directly into a pair of eyes. They belonged in a black face, the very black face of a young boy who scrambled backward as if he had seen a devil. Kennedy realized the boy must have spent the night beside his bed. The boy jumped up and darted to the door of plaited straw, flung it open, and disappeared through it. The boy shouted something in pidgin that Kennedy couldn't understand. To his considerable relief, he heard Felicity's voice yelling back and her footsteps shaking the hut as she climbed the steps that apparently led to a porch just outside the door. She appeared at the door dressed in a nightgown, her hair tied in braids that draped over her shoulders, Heidi-style. "I see Mumba told the truth for a change. You're awake. Let's have a look at your skull."

Without further preamble, she sat on the bed, gently removed the bandage, and inspected the wound. "Healing nicely, I think," she said, and wadded the bandage up and pitched it expertly through the window, bawling at the same time, "Mumba, you lazy creature! Pick up the trash around Mastah Jack's hut, if you please!"

"Felicity," Kennedy said, "where are we?"

"You are on the island of Noa-Noa. This is my plantation."

"Thurlow . . ."

"Thurlow and his men sailed on to find Joe Gimmee, a local holy man. They have reason to believe that Lieutenant Armistead is with him."

"The last thing I remember we were leaving that village. It was on fire . . ."

"It exists no more, thanks to Commander Thurlow. He is a decisive sort, I will give him that." Her expression changed to one of melancholy. "The little bushman, Pogo, was killed on the way back to your boat. It happened very quickly. Poisonous spear. It was meant for me, but Pogo stepped in front of it."

Kennedy absorbed the terrible news, then said, "Thurlow just took my boat and left me here? Without asking me what I thought of it?"

"Is it so horrid?" Felicity responded. "You were—*are*—hurt. You lost consciousness, hardly in shape for a sea voyage. It was at my request Commander Thurlow left you here where I could tend to you. I hoped you would be pleased."

"I am, Felicity. I didn't mean to sound ungrateful. It's just . . . dammit all. The *Rosemary* is my boat, not Thurlow's!"

There was a shuffling at the door, and the boy who'd slept in his room came inside, carefully balancing a tray containing a steaming pot and twin sets of cups and saucers. "Tea, missus," he said.

"Well, set it down. Not there, Mumba. How many times must I instruct you? Yes, there on that table. Now get out. Don't look at me with those big eyes. Out!"

"I pour," the little boy replied stubbornly, his lower lip stuck out.

"You will pour with a bloody nose if you aren't careful," Felicity warned. "I will not tell you again. Get out!"

Mumba left, though with a resentful glance over his shoulder. Felicity poured the tea, a very strong, nearly black tea. She offered neither sugar nor cream, and Kennedy supposed neither was available.

Kennedy was dressed only in his skivvies, but since it didn't seem to bother Felicity, he didn't apologize. Together in silence they drank the hot, bitter tea. Then Felicity rose and picked up the tray. "Now, Jack, I will leave you. Mumba will come back and instruct you as to your toilet. I fear in my absence the plumbing has gone to hell. I am washing in the sea until further notice, and you will have to do the same. I have the boys working on all that they have left undone. They should have the old place up to snuff in a few days."

"Might I help?" Kennedy asked. "I'm not much of a plumber, or carpenter, or much else in that line, I'm afraid, but I'm willing to add to the effort."

"Perhaps you might be more valuable in the fields," she answered with a twinkle in her eye. "But that is for tomorrow. Today, you must rest."

Kennedy saw no more of Felicity for the remainder of the day. Mutely the little houseboy Mumba showed Kennedy his toilet, an outhouse near his hut, and then led him to the sea. There Mumba stood, his chin raised proudly, a snowy white towel draped over his arm, while Kennedy bathed. Then he led Kennedy back to his hut, which sat beside the main house. The main house was set on a ridge within a cluster of hardwood trees. The placement allowed an excellent view of the front lawn of short-cropped very green grass and the white sand beach and the glittering blue sea. When Kennedy asked Mumba about Felicity, he said, "Missus go along Delight, go along fields."

"Delight?"

"Horse, mastah."

Kennedy was given a rather tattered maroon silk robe to wear, along with threadbare house slippers, then was shown to the east veranda of the main house and there served a breakfast of boiled fish, breadfruit fritters, and an ancient pot of jam that was so crusted over he had to use his spoon to break through it. It spread nicely on the fritter, however, and had a surprisingly good taste. The fish was hideous, having been boiled with the skin and not a few scales still on it. Still, he ate it, all but the head. Afterward, he wandered into the parlor and found a book of poetry on the table. He opened it at its marker and discovered a poem by Emily Dickinson:

Wild Nights! Wild Nights!
Were I with thee,
Wild Nights should be
Our luxury!

Futile the winds
To a heart in port,—
Done with the compass,
Done with the chart!

Rowing in Eden!
Ah! the sea!
Might I but moor
To-night in Thee!

When he returned to his hut, which was built up on four stout stilts, Kennedy discovered that his khakis had been washed and pressed via some unseen magic. The creases on his trousers were as sharp as he'd ever known them to be. He dressed and went back to the main house, entering accidentally through the kitchen. There a boy, actually a man of about forty, worked at the sink, washing dishes. He looked over his shoulder at Kennedy, and his face changed from surprise to disgust. "Kitchen not for you, mastah!" he exclaimed in an angry voice.

Kennedy retreated to the veranda and entered the next set of double doors. Inside he found a vaulted ceiling, much like the one in his hut, only steeper. The great room beneath it was light and airy, with cushioned wicker and cane chairs along with great, sagging shelves of books, so many books.

Kennedy was excited to inspect them but was disappointed to find few novels. Most of the books had to do with horticulture or hydrology or the many other aspects of farming in the tropics, even an entire volume dedicated to the coconut and all its components down to the last molecule. There was also a variety of medical texts, the kind that people who have to self-doctor might require. *How to Pull Teeth* was the title of a pamphlet, complete with photographs.

The chairs, he noted, were in a poor way, most of them dry-rotted and bound up in cord to hold them together. He chose one carefully, eased into it, and began to read a few selected texts, including the one about pulling teeth. He didn't last long before he fell away into a light sleep. He was waked by the cook, who roughly shook him by the shoulder. "Mastah, here is food," he said, then trudged back to his kitchen.

Food proved to be a bowl of rice with a thin, dark sauce, apparently of beef stock. A tin cup of water sat beside it. Felicity's plantation clearly was not wealthy, nor a place where a man was likely to get a good meal.

Toward evening, there was a great commotion. Kennedy had fallen asleep in a chair on the veranda and awoke to see that Felicity had returned. She was riding a great brown stallion, and John-Bull a black, stumpy-legged gelding. Smoothly she leapt from her saddle and thumped up the steps. She wore jodhpurs, tucked into knee-high leather riding boots, and a white blouse that was wet with her sweat and clinging to her breasts. Her hair was tied back in a braided bun. "Well, Jack," she said, a bit breathlessly, "you look refreshed. Mumba, we'll have our tea here, if you please. Don't just stand there looking at me, you ugly creature. And tell cook not to burn the toast again!"

She watched the houseboy scurry into the kitchen, and then she pulled off her sweaty gloves. John-Bull was seeing to the horses, leading them to a corral, which was a rickety fence draped with bougainvillea. Jack rose to greet her, and a book on rare tropical flowers fell to the veranda floor. Felicity took his hand. "Sit. I can tell you have been sleeping. It is exactly what you need." She stooped to pick up the book. "Bryce and I considered raising exotic flowers, perhaps shipping them overseas. But we couldn't solve the refrigeration problem. Mumba, where are you? We need our tea!"

She fell back into one of the sturdier chairs, wiping her forehead with her sleeve. "I must say the day has been a revelation. I fully expected the plantation to be falling down around our ears, but Gogoomey has been industrious in my absence. He's my overseer. Bryce always liked him, but I have long suspected he plotted against us. It appears I am wrong. He has managed to round up several local villagers. The village is a place called Lahana about five miles down the coast—we will go there tomorrow or the next day if you're up to it. In any case, he has recruited three men, surprisingly willing to work, and together they have laid in quite a harvest. The drying shed is laden with coconut flesh, and they already have quite a great number of sacks of copra ready for shipment. I tell you, Jack, if I can get transport for my copra, I may be able to not only make up the interest owed on my loan but perhaps dent the principal more than a little!"

"I am glad to hear it," Kennedy said. "But tell me. I've never understood what copra is. I've heard much about it, but it's always been a mystery. What's it used for?"

"Ah, here you are, Mumba. Well, stop staring and put the tray down. Would you like cream for your tea, Jack? I understand most Americans require it. And also sugar? Off you go, Mumba, cream and sugar for our brave and handsome naval officer! You ask what is copra? Here, do you like margarine on your breadfruit toast? It's very good, isn't it? Margarine, Jack, is made almost entirely of copra. Copra is the source of coconut oil. Most commercial soaps are predominantly derived from copra. So what is it? Simply the nearly dried meat of raw coconuts, but the moisture content is critical. Drying has to be done before shipment and is as much an art as a science. There, you are now an expert on copra."

"I had no idea," Kennedy confessed, as the little houseboy poured cream into his cup and then ladled in sugar with a tarnished spoon. "The cream has a coconut taste to it," Kennedy said, after giving it a sip.

"That would be because it is made from coconut milk. The coconut palm is the most magnificent and beneficent of plants, Jack. Its fruit can feed and clothe and clean us. Its trunks are nearly indestructible, perfect construction materials, as I observed the marine Raiders had discovered on Melagi for their air raid dugouts. Its bark can be woven into baskets, the hulls of its nuts fashioned into bowls and cups and further carved into eating utensils. Without the coconut, life here in these islands would be untenable, not only for the planter but the natives as well. It is a wonder the palm is not worshipped as a god."

Kennedy sampled the margarine-slathered toasted breadfruit and discovered the spread made all the difference. The coconut-cream-diluted tea was also nearly palatable, especially saturated as it was with raw sugar. "Very good," he pronounced. He studied her over the rim of his cup. "I must say you look happy. You are obviously filled with energy."

"Yes. This place has that effect on me. There has been tragedy here, and much hardship. That is part and parcel of the planter's life. But it is also a good life, a life where a man and a woman can make their way within the folds of raw, unforgiving nature, owing nothing to anyone, save the usual mortgage."

They were joined by an old black man with an intelligent face and worried eyes who stood patiently on the packed brown earth below the veranda until Felicity acknowledged his presence with an imperious nod of her head. He wore a battered, floppy-brimmed hat, a lap-lap, and a checkered shirt three times too large for him. Kennedy couldn't understand the pidgin that rapidly transpired between him and Felicity but he presumed this was Gogoomey, the overseer. Whatever the problem was, it demanded the immediate attention of the missus, and off she went without explanation. Kennedy sat on the veranda and finished the breadfruit, although the tea had turned cold. The houseboy appeared like a puff of smoke. "Mastah, he finish tea?"

"Yes," Kennedy said. "Thank you, Mumba."

The houseboy took up the tray and retreated to the kitchen. Soon there was an explosion of pidgin from that quarter, apparently Mumba and the cook disagreeing about something. It was followed by the sound of breaking crockery, then a long period of silence, before the argument began anew. Kennedy felt at loose ends. He wanted to go into the kitchen and see what the problem was but knew his presence would be most unwelcome. And he wanted to follow Felicity and Gogoomey (to whom she had pointedly not introduced him) but wasn't exactly certain where they had gone. He was saved by the return of John-Bull, fresh from cooling down the horses and seeing to their feed. The boy sat on the steps. "I should ever so much like to go to America," he said without so much as a greeting. "Are there really still cowboys and wild Indians there?"

"Not as many as they show in the movies," Kennedy replied with a smile. "But certainly, here and there. The western states, Texas, Arizona, Montana, and the like, have their share of cowboys. The Indians live on reservations."

"I would love to see them!" John-Bull cried. "I believe I would make a very good cowboy, and to live with the Indians would be fun!"

"You seem to have the same spark of adventure as your mother," Kennedy said.

John-Bull nodded. "That is very nice of you to say, sir. My mother is a most remarkable woman. My father used to say that he was glad I took after her and not him."

"Why would he say that?" Kennedy asked.

"I do not know exactly, sir," the boy answered. "Unless it is the manner in which she runs the plantation. Father also said that he had no need of an overseer as long as he had his wife. He was terribly proud of her. He used to read to me at night while Mother was still in the fields, and he would often remark how hard she worked for us. He taught me my books, too, you know. Every day, I was required to learn something new. Do you miss your father, sir?"

Kennedy managed a smile. "I miss my sister Kick more than anyone else in my family. She and I are alike."

"How so?"

"We see ourselves as individuals, I suppose. That may sound strange, but in my family, we are supposed to be part of a structure, a great ambitious enterprise. Everything we do must lend itself to the family fortune, in one way or another. It is difficult to explain."

"Yet I understand it fully," John-Bull replied, with a maturity Kennedy found surprising. "All the hopes and dreams of my mother rest in me. I doubt that I will ever make her fully happy, no matter what I accomplish."

"I think she will be happy just to see you grow up into a responsible young man."

John-Bull nodded, though doubtfully, then lowered his face into his hands.

"What's this?"

John-Bull rose and threw himself into Kennedy's arms. His little body shook with sobs. Kennedy stroked the boy's hair. "What is it, John?"

"I didn't want to come back here," John-Bull said in a quaking voice. "It reminds me of my father. I miss him so."

Kennedy held the boy, patting and rubbing him gently on his back. "It is a good thing to miss your father," he said. "It is a very good thing." And to his surprise, a tear leaked down Kennedy's cheek, though for what purpose, or for whom, he could not say.

4 2

Pogo was dressed in his best lap-lap, the bright blue one with the Raider patch stitched to it, and he wore his lucky shark's tooth necklace. Penelope knelt beside him, her head bowed, and sang a song of farewell. Though it was in her native language and not understood by anyone else on board, its words seemed to be filled with remorse and a longing for better times. Then the boys wrapped short lengths of fifty-caliber machine-gun bullets to his ankles and draped him in an American flag and laid him out on deck. It was sunrise, and they were over a deep trench in the sea. The head of Grant, the PT officer, was buried first. Tied up in a cloth sack, appropriately weighted with ammunition, his remains were eased overboard with all the ceremony that could be mustered, considering the circumstances. Millie played taps on his harmonica, and Josh commended the man's soul to the deep and said the Lord's Prayer. Then Ready got out his fiddle and played while they all sang the old song of home, and going home:

> *Oh, Shenandoah, I long to hear you*
> *Look away, you rollin' river . . .*

As Josh intoned his maritime version of the Twenty-third Psalm, Once and Again solemnly folded the flag, lifted Pogo over the stern, and gently lowered him into the sea. Salutes were rendered; then the *Rosemary*'s great engines thrummed with their power and energy, and the gunboat moved off.

Josh was taking the long way around to get to Vella Lavella, which was the island, according to Penelope, where Joe Gimmee and his followers lived. He didn't want to get caught out in the open by a Rufe, and anything near

Kolombangara was definitely prime Rufe country. It would take him an extra day by heading southwest from Noa-Noa, turning north around Pomaria Point on the island of Ranongga, and coming up the west side of that island, but he was fairly certain to avoid both Japanese and American eyes. Needing to conserve fuel, he also kept the throttles pulled back. There was nowhere north of Rendova he could get avgas.

All night Josh, spelled by Ready, piloted the *Rosemary* along the chosen course. The clouds were thick in the morning, obscuring the sunrise, and Vella Lavella, still well to the north, was shrouded in a gray mist. Josh eased the *Rosemary* across the limpid water. The rumble of the gunboat's engines masked all other sounds, but Josh sensed they were not alone. He idled the engines and listened and was not surprised when he heard the noise of a big diesel. Ready was in the cockpit with him. "Sailor Jap is on the move this morning," Josh said to the bosun. "What do you think? A barge?"

"No, sir. Something different. What are we gonna do, Skipper?"

"We're here to find Armistead, not get in a battle with Jap," Josh answered. He looked over his shoulder at the starboard torpedo. "But I confess to wanting to use our fish."

Penelope, who'd been sleeping on the galley hatch, rose and came forward. In deference to the crew, who kept walking into things when she was around, she had taken to wearing a chambray shirt. That had only helped a little, since the shirt was damp much of the time and tended to cling to her perfect breasts. Now she touched Josh's shoulder with a finger, felt him react, then withdrew, content that he knew she was there. Josh wished Penelope had stayed asleep. He had scarcely spoken to her since they'd left New Georgia.

The mist dissipated a little, and through it Josh saw the ghostly silhouette of a vessel, very low on the water, momentarily appear, then disappear into the soup. He tickled the throttles forward, creeping up on the vessel, straining to see it through the fog. Then the mist swirled away, and Josh was astonished to behold the narrow stern of a Japanese submarine, an I-boat, not more than fifty yards ahead of the *Rosemary*'s bow. "What the hell's an I-boat doing in these shallows?" Josh wondered. "It's a deep-water sub."

"Maybe it needs fuel," Ready suggested.

"On Vella? I thought Jap only had a small garrison there." Josh licked his lips, then made his decision. An I-boat could cause too much trouble in the Solomon Sea. It had to be attacked. "Prepare one torpedo," he told Ready. "When I tell you, launch it."

The torpedoes, as the boys had designed them on the fly at the Seabee base in Tulagi, were jury-rigged things. Arming them consisted of starting their alcohol-driven engines with a touch of an electrical wire leading up from batteries below, then pulling three pins that held them to their rigs to dump them overboard. Josh knew he had to position the *Rosemary* perfectly to have any chance of success. Penelope squeezed into the cockpit beside him. "What shall I do during the battle?"

For a reason he couldn't define, Josh resented her presence. "There's nothing you can do except go below. There's likely to be some shrapnel flying soon."

"No. I shall stay." She patted her machete on her hip. "If need be, I will defend you to the death."

"Skipper?" Ready called. "I got a torpedo armed and ready."

Abruptly the fog lifted, and Josh saw, with a sinking sensation, that there was a destroyer mothering the I-boat to starboard. To hesitate was to invite disaster, so he threw the wheel hard over to port, busting out of the wake away from the destroyer, then cranked the *Rosemary* hard over again to line up a shot at the plodding I-boat. Neither the submarine nor the destroyer had seen the gunboat yet, or at least they hadn't reacted. "Let it go, Ready!" Josh yelled. Ready complied, sending the fish splashing into the sea and speeding off, its bright white wake clearly marking its progress. Josh waited a moment to make certain the torpedo was ahead of him before he turned and rammed the throttles of the three Packards to their stops. He looked over his shoulder. The I-boat and her shepherding destroyer sailed placidly along. Amazingly, they still hadn't seen the *Rosemary*.

"Should have hit by now," Ready called, just seconds before a big spout of white foam rode up the side of the destroyer, followed by a gush of yellow flame. "It missed the I-boat and hit the destroyer!" Ready cried.

Josh kept the gunboat flying away. The roar of the explosion rolling over the sea was followed by the whooping cries of the alarmed destroyer, brought tumultuously awake. Josh had completely forgotten Penelope and was startled when she cheered and clapped her hands. "Well done!" she exclaimed.

"I told you to go below," he growled.

"How could I leave when my darling man is attacking the whole damn Japoni navy?"

"You mustn't call me your darling man," he said in a low voice.

Penelope, confused, looked at him. "Why not? I asked you on New Georgia if you still wanted me with you, and you said you did."

"I wasn't thinking straight. We can't be together anymore. Not in that way."

Penelope's lush brown eyes glittered with tears. "You're ashamed of me."

"You're Whitman's wife, dammit!"

"In name only."

"Where I come from, that kind of name means a lot."

Ready squeezed in beside Penelope. "Excuse me, folks, but I think the Japanese are pretty mad at us."

"I don't blame them," Josh retorted.

"Yes, sir. But the I-boat's chasing us."

"I shall go below, *mastah,*" Penelope said in an icy voice. "So that I will not be a distraction."

"Good idea," Josh said, then instantly regretted it. "Penelope, look—" But it was too late. She had disappeared down the galley hatch. "Dammit," he swore.

"Sir, that I-boat—"

Josh turned on his gunner's mate. "What do you want me to do, Ready? I'm running from the damned thing as fast as I can."

"I was just going to point out that fog bank over there, sir. We might have a chance if you kind of pointed the boat in its direction."

Josh looked after Ready's point and saw a bank of dense gray fog sitting heavily on the sea.

"Quickly now, sir," Ready urged. "If you please."

It did please, and Josh turned the *Rosemary* toward the protective mist just as the Japanese I-boat began to toss heavy, vengeful shells from its deck gun after them.

4 3

Kennedy was roused early, Felicity hallooing him from the bottom step of the guest house. Mumba soon delivered a tray of the inevitable breadfruit fritters and crusted, lumpy jelly, but this time with a dish of margarine on the side and a bowl of raw sugar. The bitter tea was also accompanied with a bowl of coconut milk, though it smelled a little sour. Two teaspoons of sugar made the stuff barely drinkable. When he finished the meal, such as it was, the stamping of hooves outside his hut caused him to rise and look through the door. The big stallion Felicity had ridden the day before was being held by Gogoomey. The old man's face was grim, his lip well out. "Mastah, you go along missus," he said gruffly to Kennedy, handing over the reins and retreating.

Felicity appeared, riding John-Bull's small black horse. "Well, come on," she said. "I presume you know how to ride."

"A little," Kennedy said, putting a tentative toe in a stirrup, testing his strength. It was then he noticed his head no longer ached. He pulled himself aboard the great stallion, which did not so much as flinch, even though he turned his head to ponder his missus, as if asking her why she had allowed such an outrage.

Felicity laughed when she saw the stallion's question in his eyes. "I forgot to tell Delight a stranger would be riding him today." She reached down and let the stallion sniff her hand, then stroked his nose. "Be gentle, my Delight. You hold a precious cargo."

"Of all the things I've been called in my life," Kennedy said, "precious cargo has not been one of them. And how is it I rate such a title?"

"Because you, Jack, are destined for great things, whether you are aware of it or not."

"My brother is the one with the destiny in my family," he said, then regretted his words since they sounded like a retort. Felicity clicked her tongue and aimed the little black horse toward the beach. Delight obediently followed with Kennedy simply holding the reins, careful not to tug on the bit. There was no use upsetting the animal further.

"Would you rather be happy or great, Jack?" Felicity asked as Delight chose to come alongside his mistress, nickering to her in a low voice.

"Happy," Kennedy replied instantly. "Because I have no illusions about greatness."

"I almost believe you," she said.

"Why almost?"

Felicity looked at him with a sudden longing. "Dear Jack, how is it you have found your way to this terrible place of sand, coconuts, disease, and mosquitoes?"

"For the same reason as Josh Thurlow and his boys. To do some good for my country."

"Posh! Thurlow fights this war because his country fights it, nothing else. He neither understands its larger purpose nor cares. You, however, see all its ins and outs and understand that what happens in this war is the direct result of all that has gone on before and will affect all that will occur afterward."

"I think you give Thurlow too little credit," Kennedy replied, although he was of much the same opinion.

During their discussion, Delight and John-Bull's horse, who proved to be named Blackie, had followed a path that paralleled the beach and then wound through some low bush. Cooing birds within were described as fruit doves. "A great nuisance," Felicity summarized her opinion of them. They next rode onto a great green plain studded with coconut palms that, in contrast to the graceful lean of their wild cousins along the beach, grew as straight as telephone poles. When asked about it, Felicity explained, "For the best bearing, the tree trunks must be exactly straight. It depends on how the nut is placed in the ground. Haphazardly, as nature does it, the tree will grow at an angle. The rows of the trees, as you will notice, are also straight, precisely thirty feet apart, so that each receives the same amount of sun."

It seemed to Kennedy that they had entered a great open-air temple, the alignment of the palms creating perfect aisles that led straight ahead, sideways, and at diagonals. The sound of the hooves on the clover that lay between the trees was as soft as the padding of a bishop's slippers on a cathedral carpet. Kennedy looked up and saw clusters of brown nuts hugging sheltering fronds that swept out to meet their neighbors, crisscrossing into a vast green, undulating ceiling. With the white sky filtering through the interstices, it was as if he were peering vertically into a kaleidoscope of varying shades of translucent green with brilliant whites and dull taupe as contrast. Squadrons of little yellow butterflies wafted between the palms, along with the occasional bright blue interloper, its wings as big as a bird. In some places, spiderwebs, still wet with dew, stretched between the palms. Kennedy stopped and inspected one of them, a vast net. The creature that had constructed it was not in evidence, apparently nocturnal, but the strands she had left behind were amazingly thick. He touched one and found that it stuck to his finger.

"The natives use them to bind wounds," Felicity informed him. "They are as strong as silk yet are elastic and, as you've discovered, quite sticky. Amazing stuff, really. I wish I could find a way to sell it. I'm sure it would have its application in medicine."

At last they came to the plantation's drying shed, which was the altar for which the temple of palms had been created. It seemed unworthy for such an edifice, being nothing more than a small tin structure with a flat roof. Inside, Felicity proudly showed off the drying oven, consisting of a big iron grate over a wood fire with an opening in the roof to vent the smoke. Three men were busily prying coconut meat out of hacked-open nuts, then chopping the meat into wedges and tossing them onto the grate. Gogoomey used a rake to move the coconut meat around until the sections turned into yellowish, greasy lumps, then dragged them off onto a plaited palm mat to cool. The smell of the drying copra was sweet and lush. When the lumps began to pile up, one of the cutting boys would put aside his blade to load them into cloth sacks and then haul them to the end of the building used for storage. A pile of sacks, neatly stacked, was evidence of the morning's work.

"At the end of the day, the copra is carried to the warehouse down by the dock," Felicity explained. "Part of my astonishment upon arrival was to discover it all but full. Gogoomey has been most industrious. Another several days' work and it will be completely filled. After that, I either charter the construction of another warehouse or we will have to stop."

Gogoomey said, with a shy smile, "Missus, she is happy?"

"Yes, very happy, Gogoomey. You have accomplished a miracle. I am going to give you a case of tobacco to share with your boys."

The three helpers instantly broke into grins, apparently understanding and appreciating the compliment the missus had given the overseer, not to mention the tobacco that might soon come their way. Gogoomey said with majestic dignity, "Missus savvy these good fellas. Gogoomey happy."

"They are very good fellas, indeed," Felicity answered, although then she frowned. "Gogoomey, are you certain these fellas belong Lahana?"

"Yes, missus. Belong Lahana altogether."

Felicity led Kennedy out into the fresh air. "Why did you ask Gogoomey if his boys were from Lahana?" Kennedy asked. "It sounded as if you didn't believe him."

"I'm not sure I do. In all the years I've been here, I have never been able to recruit labor from Lahana. Yet these boys seem happy, even eager, to work." She shook her head. "Perhaps this afternoon I will ride up there. Something's afoot, but I have no idea what it might be."

"I'd like to go with you," Kennedy said.

"After lunch, then," she said, distractedly looking over her shoulder. Gogoomey was standing in the doorway of the drying shed watching her. When her eyes landed on him, he made a little bow to his missus, then turned back to his work. The three boys within had also been watching her, and now they waved. Surprised, she waved back. Felicity could not recall any copra boy ever waving to her before.

4 4

Safe harbor for the *Rosemary* was the edge of a dank mangrove swamp. Josh had aimed for shore in the dense fog, hoping for refuge from the pursuing I-boat. When he saw the swamp, he didn't hesitate to run at it, then throw the rudder hard over, sliding into the mush beneath an overhanging jungle canopy. He immediately killed the engines, and the boys jumped overboard and splattered the hull with mud for camouflage. As the sun rose and the mist swirled away, a plume of smoke to the south told them that the destroyer they'd hit by mistake was still burning. There was no sign of the I-boat. Either they had made good their escape or the Japanese submarine had stopped searching. "That Dave's a miracle worker," Stobs said, coming up on deck. "He got us out of this jam."

"Dave's not even on board," Ready reminded him as Josh looked on.

"I got one of his feathers," Stobs replied, withdrawing same from his shirt to show the bosun. He also had something to report. "I contacted Mister Phimble," he said. "He made it to Henderson Field, and Fisheye's already found them a new engine."

Josh was relieved to hear his old friend was safely on Guadalcanal. "Tell Eureka to stay where he is," he told Stobs. "No use him coming up here. Did you get through to Colonel Burr?"

"No, sir," Stobs reported. "And I wasn't able to talk to Mister Phimble for very long. I think Vella's mountain is blocking our signals."

"Keep trying, and also get out the word on this damned I-boat if you can," Josh told the radioman. Stobs nodded, then went back to his set.

In the early afternoon, when a horde of mosquitoes and biting flies descended on them, Josh was forced to move the *Rosemary*. With lookouts keeping a sharp eye, he set their course northward, working up the eastern side of the island. They were heading for the village of Karaka, where Penelope said her father presently lived. According to intelligence reports Josh had seen, Vella Lavella was at least partially occupied by Japanese troops, though only along the southern shore, and Karaka was well north. But he also knew intelligence reports were often wrong, or wrong-headed.

Vella Lavella was a lovely island, its beaches sugar white and framed by towering coconut palms. An inviting grassy savannah stretched back from the sand to a steep blue-green volcano that climbed into the clouds. The sea seemed unusually, luxuriously rich. Flocks of seabirds followed the gunboat, dolphins rode her bow wave, and flying fish scurried out of her way. It was all lovely, and peaceful, and wonderful, and therefore very dangerous according to Josh's way of thinking. The Jackson twins requested permission to fish, but he wouldn't allow it. He feared a curious Rufe or Zero might descend on them at any moment, not to mention that unhappy submarine, probably still on the scout for the little boat that had torpedoed its destroyer escort. But despite Josh's concern, the seas and skies and land stayed empty of Jap. It was early afternoon when Penelope walked up to the bow and began to point at the next cove. She did not turn to look at Josh, just pointed the way.

With the Jackson twins calling out directions, Josh steered the *Rosemary* between two sharp coral outcrops and into a wide lagoon where the peaks of a number of thatched-roof houses could be seen poking above a fringe of palms and other trees. A group of people came through the village gate and began to wave. Penelope excitedly waved back. Suddenly the people on the beach burst into song, the grand singsong of the South Pacific islander, the lower male notes insistent and harsh, yet somehow merging perfectly with the higher, sweeter notes of the Maries. The songs rose and fell, and the people swayed together, their arms linked. Penelope clasped her arms around herself and twirled on the bow in her excitement, all but dancing on her toes. Josh called down to her, "Why are they singing?"

"They know I'm here," she answered, and turned away from him.

"Do you, by chance, see your father?"

Penelope spoke over her shoulder. "No, I do not see him, *mastah,* but that is not unusual. He is, I'm certain, resting for all that he must do."

Although Josh suspected the reply would not likely be informative, he couldn't resist asking, "And what must he do?"

Penelope didn't disappoint. "What there is to be done," she answered. "Is mastah displeased by my answer?"

"Don't call me mastah," Josh muttered.

"But why not?" Penelope asked. "You think I am your slave."

"You are not my slave!" he roared. When he saw the Jackson twins grin, he yelled, "Wipe them grins off your faces, you two, and keep your eyes forward!"

Penelope shrugged and said to the Jacksons, "I think Mastah Josh missed his calling. He would have been a very content slave master."

The twins wisely refused comment and kept their eyes locked straight ahead.

Josh, fuming over Penelope's attitude but glad to have reached what he hoped was the final destination of his mission, gently nosed the gunboat's bow into the sand, then called Ready over. "You see any aircraft or that damn destroyer or anything else, maneuver out of this lagoon and get the boys cracking on the guns. Don't worry about me, just protect yourself."

Penelope cast off her chambray shirt, dived off the bow, and swam to the beach. As she scampered up to the crowd of people, their singing swelled. Men, women, and children crowded around her. Josh dropped into the surf and sloshed onto the beach, stopping to listen as the people continued to sing. On board, Marvin suddenly bristled and began to growl. His jowls curled back, displaying every sharp tooth in his mouth, and before the twins could stop him, he launched himself overboard, flashed through the crowd, and raced through the village gate. Josh ran after him, but the little dog was too fast. He darted inside a hut. There was much snarling and growling, and also some screams. Josh was astonished when two Japanese sailors, wearing ragged white uniforms, suddenly burst out of the hut and went scurrying past him to the nearest tree, a huge banyan in the center of the village. They climbed it like monkeys, there to sit on its massive limbs, while Marvin leapt at them, his jaws snapping. Josh pondered the treed men, who pondered him back with wide, scared eyes. "Ease up, Marvin," Josh said, although the dog clearly wasn't about to follow orders. Once and Again soon arrived and calmed the little terrier as best they could, although Marvin forgot himself and, in his excitement, nipped Once on the arm.

Josh gave the Jackson twins orders to get Marvin back to the gunboat, one way or the other, and to lock him below if that's what it took. He also ordered the Japanese down from the tree, and to his surprise, they obeyed. They bowed to him, then wordlessly went back inside their hut. Josh scratched up under his cap in wonder. Then another surprise occurred. Two skinny Americans climbed out of another hut. They were dressed in Navy denims, cut off at the knees, and ragged shirts. They were barefoot. "Hidy, sir," one of them said while the other one executed a sloppy salute. "We're

American sailors. My name's Seaman Billy Dove, and this here's Seaman Davey Gray."

"What's your story?" Josh demanded, standing with his big arms folded across his chest to hear it.

They were shipwreck victims. The sailor named Billy, who wore a golden earring, did the talking and related how their destroyer had been sunk during a battle off Vella three months before. "Those Japanese boys," Billy said, "also got themselfs washed ashore, the result of the same fight. We all got taken in by this here village. Joe Gimmee—he's the local priest or some such—said we could stay as long as we were all peaceful-like together. Davey and I didn't see no need to cause trouble with these Jap boys. We ain't soldiers, we're sailors, and now we're on dry land, so we got no beef with nobody much. We figured to stay until someone came after us. Guess someone finally did."

"Where is Joe Gimmee?" Josh asked.

"Don't know. He left yesterday. I think he's due back tomorrow, though I wouldn't swear to it. He comes and he goes."

"How about a marine lieutenant? Tall guy, kind of a long face?"

Billy and Davey looked at each other. "Well, yes, sir," Billy finally allowed, "He was wounded when he came here, stuck in the side by somethin', but Joe Gimmee fixed him up." Billy sheepishly hung his head. "He asked us not to ever talk about him to nobody, and here I've gone and done it. See, sir, he's got a plan. He says he's going to end the war."

Josh knew he should have been surprised, but he wasn't. Nothing about this mission so far had been straightforward, so why should David Armistead's plans be any different? "And how is he going to end the war?" Josh asked, as if it were a perfectly natural question.

"We don't know, sir," Davey said, finally speaking up. "I asked him a couple of times, and all he said was me and Billy and Norio and Kamejiro, that's them two Jap sailors, sir, that we was a good example of what could be done."

Josh shook his head, then went back to the beach. The villagers had finished their singing and were returning to the village, still surrounding Penelope. She was smiling until she saw him, and then her smile vanished. "Is there news of your father?" he asked.

"He isn't here, but I did learn Armistead is not only alive but healthy."

Although Josh already knew that Armistead had survived, the information was still pleasing in that Penelope had cared enough to ask. "Wonderful news. Where is he?"

"He's with my father."

"And where is your father?"

"I'm not certain. He has gone to prepare the way but will return to transport the people."

Josh didn't even bother to ask what any of that meant. "We'll wait," he said with a sigh. "And then maybe, just maybe, find out what's what, though I seriously doubt it."

"Whatever you think is best, *mastah,*" Penelope said, then walked away like a queen, her worshipful retinue following.

4 5

They rode into Lahana in the grand manner of mastah and missus of all they surveyed. Along the way, Felicity had given Kennedy fair warning not to expect a lovely tropical village by the sea. "You'll start smelling their pigpens a mile away. Then, as we get closer, you'll start to smell the village itself. The bones of fish and chickens and all manner of foul garbage will litter the path. The only thing that keeps the place habitable is that every so often it catches on fire. That's the only time you'll see them expend much energy, as new huts have to be built. But within a few months, the place is filled with garbage again."

But Kennedy did not smell the pigpens a mile away, or even as they passed them. To Felicity's astonishment, the pens were extraordinarily clean, the grounds raked and the troughs neatly filled with slices of coconut meat. The pigs were plump and grunted complacently at the horses, who, in turn, nickered their haughty response. The path that led into the village was also swept clean. Children walked along the path in clean lap-laps, waving cheerfully. Some of them carried books. The village itself consisted of what appeared to be all new huts constructed of bamboo and held together with vines plaited into artistic designs. Felicity was astonished, and her astonishment continued when she beheld a new bamboo house on stilts in the village center with a very steep thatched roof. "Missionaries," Felicity said, as if cursing. "And they've built a church. I should have known."

She reined in Blackie and dismounted while Kennedy climbed off Delight. "What name preacher man?" she demanded of a child passing by, pointing at the church. The child, a girl, stopped and stared at her with wide eyes, then went scampering off. "What name preacher man?" Felicity shouted to the village. Men and women peeked from the huts, but none came out.

"I'm going to get to the bottom of this," Felicity promised, and led Blackie to the largest of the huts. "Chief Big-Belly! I know you're in there. Come out this instant, you old reprobate!"

In a time that indicated no rush, a big face poked through the doorway. It was a wide face, with a large flat nose and thick lips and two placid black eyes. The face came slowly into the sunlight followed by what Kennedy considered a fine-looking chap, unadorned with either necklace or earrings, though there were two huge unfilled holes in his lobes. His lap-lap was made of calico and was clean. "Missus Markham," he said with a smile. "Long time you no stop along."

Felicity cocked an eye. "Big-Belly, what name you all these fine new huts? And the big house just there. What name new preacher man build'm church?"

Big-Belly peered at the building as if it were the first time he'd ever seen it. "Meeting place," he said, at last. "Not church."

"Meeting place? For what purpose? What name you meet?"

Big-Belly shrugged and sheepishly turned his toes into the dirt. "Meeting place," he said stubbornly, and no matter how much Felicity tried to gain more information, the chief refused to say anything more about it.

4 6

Eureka Phimble stood in the shadow of *Dosie*'s wing and watched the whirlwind of dust rising from the jeep speeding in his direction. His hand was clamped around a wrench, and he felt like using it on the man who was the passenger in the jeep, Colonel Montague Burr. That very morning, Burr had spent ten minutes screaming at Phimble over the radio about Kennedy taking off in a PT boat when he was supposed to be court-martialed, and about Josh Thurlow, who apparently was not keeping him properly informed. Finally Phimble got a word in sideways, enough to tell the irate colonel he didn't know much but what he knew he surely couldn't say over the radio. And no, he wasn't coming to Burr's headquarters to report. He had a sick Catalina, and he was going to see her fixed. Burr had complained for ten more minutes before saying he'd come down to the beach that afternoon.

Now here he was. His clerk, his sleeve empty of stripes, jammed on the brakes and slid the jeep in beside Phimble, stopping within a foot of his boots. Phimble didn't move nor bat an eye. Fisheye looked over the edge of the wing where an engine should have been but wasn't. That engine, recently removed from a junked Catalina on Guadalcanal, was on a stand nearby, waiting to be jacked into place. Seeing who it was, Fisheye ducked out of sight. Phimble wished he could do the same.

"Let's hear it, Ensign," Burr snarled from beneath his helmet, "and it better be good."

Phimble lowered the salute he knew the colonel expected and said, "I don't know whether it's good or not, sir, but I'll tell you what I know. I got a call from Stobs, he's our radioman, and he told me the situation."

"How can you know anything if it can't be said over the radio?" Burr demanded.

Phimble smiled. "Me and the skipper and the other boys, we've all been together long enough to know how to talk around things. For instance, Stobs says to me he guessed there ain't no use making out a piss-and-moan list on board no more, and I know that means the skipper's there. He don't hold with complaining, you see, rips up any list the boys make. Then Stobs said Pogo went swimming, and I knew by the tone in his voice that meant he was dead, buried at sea."

"Your bushman's been killed?" Burr pursed his lips, then shook his head. "I always liked that little guy. Did Stobs say anything cryptic about Kennedy, like that Irish potato-head's been french-fried?"

"No, but I saw him on Mary Island when he brought in his boat to rescue us. By the way, Missus Markham was on board. Seems her boat sank nearby."

Burr almost dropped his teeth into the sand. "Felicity is safe? Good God, man! You could have told me sooner! I've had a dozen boats out looking for her. All we found were some planks and a shark-chewed swabbie. So she's safe. And John-Bull?"

"He was with her."

"That incredible woman," Burr admired, shaking his head in wonder. "They don't make 'em like that anymore, Mister Phimble, you hear me?"

"I hear you, sir. But the radio was full of static. I think the skipper's still on the hunt for Lieutenant Armistead. Stobs said they'd heard the silversides was running up around Corolla and they were heading up there to go fishing. Corolla's a northern island on the Outer Banks. Silversides is like a minnow, but I think what Stobs meant was the silver bar of a first lieutenant. You know, like Armistead."

"Armistead's on an island up north? Did they happen to say in your special code which one?"

"That's all I know, colonel," Phimble replied. "But you know Missus Markham was in a sweat to get to Noa-Noa. Could be they've gone there or stopped along the way."

Burr frowned, then took off his helmet and wiped away the sweat on his brow with his sleeve. "Now, Mister Phimble, this is very important. You hear from Thurlow again, you tell him the billboard writer—that's Admiral Halsey, but don't say that, right?—still wants this matter taken care of, *toot sweet.*"

"You mean he still wants the skipper to kill Armistead?"

"I didn't say that." Burr glared at Phimble. "Did Thurlow tell you?"

"He didn't have to. After a while, you just know a man, even what he's thinking. But I wish you'd tell bloody old Halsey that it ain't right what he sent the skipper off to do. Josh Thurlow ain't no hired assassin."

"Neither am I," Burr growled, "but Thurlow knew the situation when he agreed to take on this thing." He plopped on his helmet. "Call me if you hear anything more. By the way, what are you doing with this aircraft? Are those bombs attached beneath its wing?"

"They are, sir. Five hundred pounders, general purpose. I decided to give *Dosie* a few more teeth while I had the chance."

"How'd you get this Catalina, anyway?"

"We stole it, sir. The bombs, too."

Burr pondered Phimble's answer, then waved his clerk on. The man jammed his foot to the floor, the jeep spinning wheels in the sand for about twenty feet, then skidded to a stop. Burr turned back, his arm over the seat and one hand on top of his helmet. "By the way, you talk to him again, tell Thurlow to duck. There's something big coming his way." With this ominous admonition hanging in the air, the clerk jammed the accelerator to the floor again, throwing a sandy rooster tail twenty feet high.

Phimble watched the jeep boil up the road for a long second, then called quietly to Fisheye. Fisheye's head popped out over the wing. He said, "I know what you want, Mister Phimble. You want to know when *Dosie* can fly. Well, it don't matter if I say a day, a week, or a month, you'll say you want her ready in a few hours. The truth is I don't know when she'll fly again, if ever."

"How about tomorrow?" Phimble asked. "The skipper needs us."

"Tomorrow it is," Fisheye replied without hesitation.

4 7

Kennedy and Felicity sat on the veranda and toasted one another with gin and tonic. The clear alcohol filled Kennedy's stomach with warmth, and then the warmth expanded outward to his extremities. "A man could work up a taste for this stuff," he said, admiring his empty glass, which Mumba was quick to refill, appearing out of nowhere and disappearing back the same.

Felicity propped her boots on the veranda railing and leaned back into her wicker chair. "It cushions the day," she said. "It alleviates the worry, dampens the concerns, and makes small the fear. This, dear Jack, is the drink of the Solomons. Brain-numbing gin, the planter's best friend."

"I should have thought it would be something local," Kennedy said, putting his legs up on the railing beside hers. "Rum, perhaps, or something made from coconut."

"Etheridge of the Kananambo plantation on Choiseul experimented with making alcohol from coconuts," Felicity said. "I visited his place back in '39 to find out about it. He had such great hopes for the concept, as did we all. Unfortunately, try as he might, the best he could do turned out to be nasty stuff, oily, unfit for human consumption. Missus Etheridge reported that it was a fine liniment, however."

The sun had turned into a fat red ball squashed against the sea and seemed balanced there, as if resisting being dragged over the edge. Finally it fell into the darkness with a splash of bright green light. Kennedy grinned and raised his glass to the sight. "I've never seen a green flash before, although I've heard of them."

Felicity smiled over the lip of her glass. "They happen every night on Noa-Noa, as long as there are no clouds on the horizon. It's said you have to be in love to see a green flash, so I guess everyone on this island is a lover."

Kennedy took a moment to reflect and was pleased to discover an opinion. "I've read that romantic love, that which requires roses and candy, is actually a rather recent invention. Some say it is a product of the industrial age. A stable relationship, with the woman keeping the house, is required for men to get up and go to work according to the factory schedule. The Bible, interestingly enough, at least as far as I've read it, doesn't seem to have much need for romantic love at all. Arranged marriages seem to be the rule."

Energized by nightfall, the mosquitoes began to buzz about their faces. In obligatory fashion, they both performed the Solomon Islands salute.

"Apparently, you haven't read the Song of Solomon," Felicity remarked slyly. "It is but one long love poem."

"Or an ode to lust," Kennedy suggested.

"And what of other kinds of love?" Felicity probed. "What of the love between parents and their children?"

"I'm not sure I take your meaning," Kennedy confessed, which prompted him to hold up his empty glass, rewarded by Mumba's quick action to refill it. The evening star had popped out, so bright it appeared to be burning a hole into the purple sky. There was also a squadron of fox bats swooping and turning, mosquitoes their prey. Kennedy felt like cheering them.

"I believe a mother's love is in her blood," Felicity said. "I only had to hold John in my arms for an instant, and I would have gladly died for him. In fact, I would have died for him even while he was in my womb. I'm certain Bryce would have done the same."

Kennedy finished his glass, rewarded once more by the glug-glug sound of Mambo refilling it. Kennedy studied the evening star, now joined by its twinkling neighbors. Soon the Southern Cross would make its nightly appearance. He put his glass to his lips. Felicity had touched on a subject that made him nervous and in need of strong drink. Felicity could feel his unease. "What is it?"

"May I tell you about my sister Rosemary?" he asked quietly.

"Yes," Felicity answered, in her smallest voice.

"I believe my father hated her so much he destroyed her."

"Why, Jack!"

Kennedy was as astonished as Felicity. He brought his legs off the veranda railing and thumped his shoes squarely on its floor. "That was a foolish and untrue thing for me to say," he said in an abashed voice. "I don't know where it came from. The gin, I guess. My father did all he could for Rosemary."

Felicity leaned toward Kennedy. "You must tell me what happened," she said. "Not so much for me but for yourself."

"No. It was just a stupid thing for me to say."

Felicity clutched his shirt and drew his face close to hers. He could smell the sweet alcohol on her breath. "Listen, Jack. Get this off your chest. Call me morbidly curious, I don't care. I want to know why you said that your father destroyed your sister. There's something inside you that needs to be talked out. So tell me, then you may yell at me, call me a nosy old bitch afterward. But tell me what you think happened to Rosemary."

Kennedy looked away, but Felicity gripped her handful of his shirt even tighter. Finally he nodded, and Felicity released him and curled up in her chair, her eyes fastened on him.

"Rosemary was always a bit slow about things," he said. "She had trouble learning in school, although she worked hard and became an excellent reader. She wasn't much good at tennis or touch football or sailing, but she tried. She was, I don't know, clumsy, you might say. But I always thought she had a good heart, and I never thought she was stupid, not at all. I always enjoyed being around her. We had lots of great talks. I think she enjoyed being around me, too."

Kennedy gripped his glass with both hands. "Looking back, I don't think there was anything wrong with her, except she wasn't like the rest of us. In any other family, she probably would have grown up, gotten married, had children, and nobody would have ever noticed that she was any different. Likely she would have been thought of as sweet, rather than slow. Hell, I've run across men out here who are doing their jobs just swell who are much like Rosemary. They're simple, but good boys."

"Once and Again," Felicity said, smiling as she thought of the twins.

"Exactly! When Rosemary got older, it seemed to me that my father, who'd tended to ignore her until then, became preoccupied with her. I heard him say once that he was afraid that people would take advantage of her, especially men. Mother insisted that Rosemary enter a convent, and so they found one that would take her in Washington. There were stories of her going out at night, wandering the streets, looking for boys to meet. I'm not sure if the stories were true, but Pappy thought they were. He went on and on about how dangerous it was and how she needed to be better protected."

Kennedy drank, then held out his glass and heard the necessary glug-glugs from Mumba. "Without letting anyone else in the family know, he decided to have Rosemary lobotomized. That means a section of her brain, the part that controls emotions, was removed. She survived the operation, but her personality was taken away. My father had turned my sister, who'd never hurt anyone, into a vegetable. That's why I said he destroyed her. She was left breathing, her heart beating, but the Rosemary I knew, that sweet, simple girl, was gone forever."

Felicity saw that Kennedy had finished his tale, by the way he raised his chin, but she refused to let him get away with it. The important part had yet to be told. "Why do you think your father did it, Jack?" she pressed.

Kennedy stared at her. "I had a vision of Rosemary when I swam out into Blackett Strait to flag down nonexistent PT boats. I think she was trying to tell me why."

"But you have your suspicions, don't you? It was more than just his concern for her safety, wasn't it? Something perhaps he didn't want her to tell?"

Kennedy looked away, into the night. The geckos were chirping, and somewhere high on the mountain an animal cried out in terror. "I don't know, Felicity," he said quietly. "At the time, I was stationed in Washington with the Office of Naval Intelligence. My apartment was quite near her convent. Yet I never went to see her. Not once. Maybe if I had, I could have seen what was coming and protected her."

"You had no way of knowing what your father was planning. You mustn't blame yourself."

"Who else is there to blame?" He turned pensive and looked up at the stars. "I wish sometimes I didn't have to go back. I love being on my own in the wilderness."

Felicity reached out and touched his arm. "The Solomons are a terribly tough place to live, yet certain types of men and women are attracted here. Those with a sense of adventure, I suppose, or just a bit perverse in their desire to be disconnected from the remainder of the world." Felicity dropped her hand from him, then fell into silence, reflecting, perhaps, on her own reasons for being in the islands.

"I've never felt quite so alive as I have since I've been out here," Kennedy said. "Maybe after the war, I'll come back."

"If you wish it, there will always be a place for you on Noa-Noa. Just be certain, dear Jack, you are here because you want to be, not because you can't face your father. I think he may be an evil man, but I know you are a good one. You are not him, always remember that."

"Thank God for my brother," Kennedy said. "At least it's him Pappy wants to make into a senator or even president. That leaves me with some choices. Poor, poor Joe. I always envied him. Now I feel sorry for him."

The mosquitoes, given impetus by a falling breeze, made another run, and Felicity and Kennedy accomplished the Solomons salute once more, then had another glass of gin, falling into a contented confusion that even the mosquitoes couldn't dent until Mumba slithered out of some hole and announced, "Cook say damn fool dinner ready, missus!"

Felicity chuckled, a throaty, gin-soaked chuckle. "Shall we dine, Lieutenant Kennedy, the terror of the Solomons, and a man with a universe of choices?"

Even though he knew he was quite soused, and therefore his opinion not completely reliable, Kennedy thought the evening meal was actually nearly good, the cook apparently challenging himself to create something edible. He and Felicity were each served an entire chicken stuffed with shredded coconut. It was moist, flavorful, and only a little tough. Dessert was a baked mash of sugary bananas. Kennedy and Felicity dwelled at the table, raising their glasses to toast the king, the president of the United States, and Josh Thurlow in turn. "I wunner . . . *won-der* . . . where the bloody bas . . . *bastard* and his black girlfriend are even as I speak," Felicity said, pleased with herself that she had managed a cogent, if somewhat slurred, thought.

"I hope he's taking care of my boat," Kennedy replied, carefully articulating since his lips had gone numb. "Girlfriend? That gorgeous Marie? Surely you don't mean it!"

Felicity covered her mouth, unsuccessfully stifling her mirth. "Oh, my dear Jack. Of course! They make *pashun* too much long time, as they say in these parts. Her eyes scarcely left Thurlow once we got aboard your boat."

Kennedy tried to form a question. He was intrigued by the concept of Thurlow finding romance with a wild black woman of the Solomons, but he was also very tired. He longed for his bed and he longed for . . . "Felicity?"

She smiled at him above her glass. Her response was a purr that ended on the upswing. Then she said, "I don't believe I have been this *jolly* in years."

"You know what we should do?" Kennedy asked.

"Yes, my dear, but I would prefer that we were both sober when we did it."

Felicity rose, gave Kennedy a firm hug, then wandered off to her bed. Disappointed, Kennedy moved back to the veranda. He sat in the chair he favored and contemplated the darkness. Then he thought he saw a movement, a shadow on the grass. "Mumba?" he called out.

The dark form moved again, this time back into the shadows, before reappearing again, as if deciding to reveal itself after all. It approached, growing in size until the shadow turned into a tall man, naked except for a lap-lap. He stopped and leaned in until his face was caught in the glow of the lantern shining from the parlor window. Tattoos began on his neck and went down his arms. Bone rings dangled from his ears. "Hello, Jack," he said. "You remember me from school, don't you? It's David. David Armistead."

4 8

Josh spent the night aboard the gunboat, and Penelope on shore. The two sailors, Billy and Davey, visited with the Jackson twins and met the rest of the boys and decided to stay aboard, too. "Can we join your crew?" they asked when the two caught Josh on the stern with his morning coffee.

"You may," Josh answered. "What was your ship? We'll need to let them know you got through."

They named their ship, and Josh told them to tell it to Stobs to signal on to Guadalcanal, if and when he made contact, so that their family could be apprised. "We'd just soon not, sir, if you don't mind," Billy said. "Likely our families have already been told we're dead. There's every chance we still might get ourselves dead before we get back down south, no use having them cry over us a second time."

Josh pushed his cap brim up with his index finger. "What makes you think you might get yourselves dead? I thought Lieutenant Armistead was going to end the war."

"Well, sir, maybe so. But Joe Gimmee's got something in the works that sure looks like there's yet to be some fighting. He's real interested in the way military things are done, you see, saluting and marching and all that. Davey here and I taught him what little we know about it. You think knowing how to drill in a straight line would help out in a battle?"

"Not since Napoleon's time," Josh replied in an ironic tone. "Well, whatever you boys think best, but I believe your families would like to know you lived at least this long."

Billy and Davey promised to give it all some thought and went off, leaving Josh to wonder about Joe Gimmee's interest in things military, or at least the formalities. Those thoughts were interrupted by a low note from shore, which proved to be a big, muscular man in a flowery lap-lap blowing on a conch shell. Josh had always heard about such things, even seen it in the movies, but could never figure out how in the world anyone ever got a sound out of a shell. He'd handled many a conch, and eaten more than a few, too, since they occasionally got tossed up on Killakeet, but using one as a horn never seemed an obvious thing to do.

Josh looked at the village and saw no apparent reason for the conch trumpeting, but then he looked out to sea and saw the reason, indeed. There was a large war canoe, a *tomako* much like the one he'd seen on Whitman's beach (which, now that he gave it some thought, had actually been but been six days ago). At least thirty big men were pulling on sets of great, long oars, with a man sitting in the middle of the boat on a kind of throne. His arms were crossed, his chin held high. As the canoe came nearer, Josh saw that the seated man was naked, save a garland of flowers around his head. He had a patrician face, black as coal, with a sunken lower jaw, as if he were missing teeth. His eyes were hooded, and neither he nor any of his oarsmen so much as glanced at the gunboat, which was, after all, the most unique and prominent feature presently in the lagoon. The canoe pushed past, then its bow slid onto the sand in front of the conch trumpeter, and the seated man rose and stepped regally ashore. The moment his foot went down on the sand, the villagers waiting at the village gate rushed down to the beach. There, they surrounded the man and draped his neck with more flower necklaces. The conch blower finally stopped, and the singing began, just as it had the day before, only even louder and more joyous. The man walked ahead, his big hands atop the heads of children who walked beside him, and went through the village gate with the singing throng behind.

Josh assumed this was Joe Gimmee and went ashore to meet him. His way was barred at the gate. The guards were firm but polite, so Josh asked for Penelope. It was over an hour later that she finally appeared. "I need to talk to your father," Josh told her impatiently.

"But does he need to talk to you?" she asked.

Josh took off his cap, fiddled with it, then plopped it back aboard. Penelope smiled, knowing full well it was his gesture when he was unhappy or confused or uncertain. "I need to see him," he said. "You know that's the reason I'm here."

She arched her eyebrows. "Oh? Well, I suppose that's true, since it is certainly not *me* that you might want to be near. It must have amused you so very much that time when you told me you loved me. My word, you tell a very convincing lie."

"I didn't lie." Josh took off his cap again. "But that's neither here nor there."

"Yes, yes, you wish to find Lieutenant Armistead," Penelope replied in a bored fashion. "He is not here."

"But I need to find out where he might be," Josh said, all but gritting his teeth. "Your father surely knows."

She cocked her head in an expression of wonder, as if Josh were saying a very curious thing. "He might, but he is very busy."

"Doing what?"

"Preparing himself. The time is near."

"For what?"

"I don't know."

Josh looked at the guards, looked at Penelope, looked at the bamboo gate that held him back. "Will you help me?" he asked for what he knew was going to be the last time.

"Help you?" she asked. "To do what?"

Josh nodded, then put on his cap. He gripped the gate and, with a mighty pull, tore it loose from its leather hinges. He tossed it on the beach while the two guards stared at him. "I wouldn't get in my way," Josh warned them, then walked through the opening where there had once been a gate and kept going until he reached the banyan tree, where he started yelling, "Joe Gimmee, come out! Joe Gimmee, come out!"

Josh found himself surrounded by angry villagers, all shouting at him at the top of their lungs, though wisely keeping their distance considering that his anger seemed to make him grow twice his size. Then, abruptly, they fell silent, and the man Josh had seen sitting on the throne aboard the *tomako* walked through an opening in the crowd. He had covered his nakedness with a lap-lap. He looked upon Josh with a benign smile, then said something Josh couldn't understand. Josh looked around for Penelope and found her right where she'd been all along, at his side. "What did he say?"

By the expression on her face, it was clear Penelope was somewhat less than pleased with Josh. "He wonders why you are causing so much commotion in his village."

"I take it this is Joe Gimmee."

"Who else?"

"Tell him who I am."

"And who would that be?" Penelope demanded in a snide tone.

"Tell him I am Commander Josh Thurlow of the United States Coast Guard."

Penelope rolled her eyes. "I am certain he will be impressed."

Joe Gimmee, with an amused expression, was watching the back-and-forth between Josh and Penelope. He said something to Penelope, who listened and then said, "My father says he can tell we are lovers because we argue so much."

Josh worked to remain calm. "Tell him, if you please, who I am, as I have already asked you to do too many times."

"He knows who you are. I have fully informed him."

Joe Gimmee smiled, then spoke. Penelope said, "He says he has never seen a man and a woman so clearly in love as we. Sadly, my father is not always free from error."

"Ask him about Armistead," Josh insisted, then looked directly at Joe Gimmee and did it himself. "David Armistead? A marine lieutenant? Lieutenant Armistead? Do you know that name?"

Joe Gimmee looked into Josh's eyes, and it seemed to Josh that he had never seen eyes so filled with curiosity and wonder in the entire history of his life. "I know David Armistead," Joe Gimmee said, and Josh caught the hint of an Australian accent.

"Do you know where he is?"

"Yes," Joe Gimmee answered.

"And where might that be?"

"Where I told him to go, mate."

"And that would be?"

"I am going there tomorrow."

"Can I go, too?"

"Yes. Although we must not travel together. If the Japoni see you with me, they will try to kill us all. There is a Japanese submarine that is after you."

"How do you know that?"

"Its captain stopped my *tomako* and told me to be on the scout."

"You work for the Japanese?"

"Never. But the Japanese like to tell me what to do anyway. They like to tell everybody what to do, just as the British and the Americans. It is odd since this is our country, not theirs."

"Please tell me where you are going so that I can look on my chart and find my way."

"I know the way. You can follow, although you must stay far back."

"I still need to know where I'm going. It is a rule in the navy."

Joe Gimmee raised his wispy eyebrows. "Penelope said you were in the Coast Guard."

"The Coast Guard is part of the navy for the duration of the war."

"Which war?"

"The big war. The war that is being fought in these islands."

"Oh, *that* war."

Josh impatiently ran his hand across his face. Joe Gimmee watched him serenely. "Look, Joe," Josh said, "what's your game? Talk to me. Make me understand and maybe I can help you."

Joe Gimmee chuckled when he heard Josh's plea, then answered. "Life is a game, but my people do not know how to play it. That is why I have come, to teach them the rules."

"And what are the rules?"

Joe Gimmee said, "All we haf to fee-yah, is fee-yah itself."

Josh stared at the old man, who grinned back at him with only his upper teeth. "I don't understand what you're getting at," Josh confessed.

"A day that will live in in-fummy," Joe Gimmee said, and then turned on his heel and walked back to his hut, the people, including Penelope, gathering in behind him. Josh was blocked from following, left standing alone in ignorance and the dust beneath the old banyan tree.

4 9

Kennedy was subdued as he and Felicity ate breakfast on the veranda while John-Bull gave Blackie a run on the beach. At last Felicity said, "What's the matter, Jack? I can almost hear the wheels turning in your head."

"I had a visitor last night."

"A tree rat, I'll wager! I'll have Mumba put out the traps."

"It wasn't a tree rat. It was David Armistead. He stood on the grass, just there in front of the veranda."

Felicity smiled, thinking Kennedy was joking, but then saw that he was serious. "How could that be?"

"I don't know. He said he couldn't tell me, not without a great deal of explanation. He asked if he might come again tonight. Do you have a working radio?"

"Not anymore. The cockroaches ate the wiring some years ago."

"I wish there was some way I could contact Thurlow. I don't know what to do. I suppose I should try to capture David, knock him in the head or something and tie him up."

"How did he know you were here?"

"He said he heard that a navy lieutenant named Kennedy was visiting you, and he thought to slip up to the house to see if it was me. You see, we've known each other for years, first at prep school, then at Harvard. He said once he saw it was me, he couldn't resist saying hello. It seemed to me the idea just formed in his mind. I don't think he meant for me to recognize him from the shadows. Then, as we were talking, he said he had so much to tell me. I'm afraid I invited him to dinner. I saw no harm in it."

"I suppose there is none, other than cook will be displeased," Felicity replied. "He worked ever so hard on last night's meal, now he'll have to accomplish another miracle, and we have so little . . ."

"I overstepped my bounds," Kennedy said by way of an apology.

"It's all right, Jack," Felicity said, although she was clearly puzzled and upset. She rose from the breakfast table and went inside, yelling for Mumba, who had disappeared like a puff of smoke at the first hint of the missus's displeasure.

Kennedy finished his tea and walked to the new warehouse construction site. He had promised Felicity a day of work, helping Gogoomey to build it. No one was there, so he idled about, swatting mosquitoes, until John-Bull arrived after putting Blackie to pasture. "Have you seen Gogoomey or the other boys this morning?" Kennedy asked.

"I saw them talking to a tall white man near Lahana," John-Bull answered. "He was dressed in a lap-lap, which I thought was very odd. More peculiar still, he was covered in tattoos. When he saw me, he stepped back into the bush. Gogoomey and the others waved to me and then started off in this direction. I suppose they will be along presently."

Kennedy waited for Gogoomey and then took him aside. "Gogoomey, what is going on between you and Lieutenant Armistead?"

Gogoomey feigned surprise. "Gogoomey no savvy Arm-stead."

"Yes, you savvy Armistead very well." Kennedy raised his hand over his head. "Very tall white man, this tall. Long face, big chin."

Gogoomey looked embarrassed. "My word, much work-work. Gogoomey no stop along."

"Yes, you will stop along," Kennedy insisted. "What did Armistead tell you this morning? John-Bull saw you talking to him."

Gogoomey stubbornly shook his head.

"I will tell the missus," Kennedy warned.

Kennedy had turned the correct key. "Arm-stead want Gogoomey, all Lahana go Chuma. Joe Gimmee be there."

The name rang a faint bell. "Joe Gimmee?"

"Big time holy man, mastah Jack."

Now Kennedy remembered. Thurlow was looking for this very same man. It was the reason he'd gone to Vella Lavella.

"When will Joe Gimmee come?"

"On the morrow."

"Where is Chuma?"

Gogoomey pointed to the north. "Many palms, altogether finish. Chief Big-Belly altogether finish palms."

Kennedy salted away the information, though he didn't understand it entirely, and patted the old man on his shoulder, letting him go to work on the warehouse. Then he called over John-Bull. "Where and what is Chuma?"

"It's an abandoned plantation we leased some years back. It's on the north shore."

"What does 'altogether finish' mean in pidgin?"

"It depends on how it's used. Most of the time if one of the boys says somebody is altogether finished, it means he's dead."

"How about 'Many palms, altogether finished. Chief Big-Belly altogether finish palms.'"

John-Bull scratched his head. "It might mean Big-Belly has killed some trees, or it might mean he picked some coconuts."

"When was the last time you or your mother visited Chuma?"

"Not for several months. Mother was wondering if the trees were bearing early, and we rode the horses to take a look. They were, wonderfully so. It was one of the reasons she decided to go to Malaita, to get extra workers to harvest Chuma as well as down here."

Kennedy walked back to the house and found Felicity deep into her accounting books at the parlor table. She gave him an unwelcome glance when he sat across the table from her. Apparently, she was still upset over Kennedy's invitation to Armistead. "I told Gogoomey I would keep this from you, but I don't think I should hold it back. He was seen talking to Armistead this morning. I questioned him, and I believe I understood that there is something that has occurred at Chuma. What it is, I'm not certain, but Chief Big-Belly is involved."

"Tell me exactly what Gogoomey said," Felicity replied. When he told her, including that Joe Gimmee was also involved in some manner, she closed her books, then whistled for Mumba. When the boy appeared, she said, "Saddle Delight and Blackie. Go quick!" She leveled her gaze at Kennedy. "I should put a rope around Gogoomey's neck and drag him to Chuma. He has allowed somebody to damage my palms."

"You don't know if anything has happened at all," Kennedy said. "And please don't say a word to Gogoomey. I promised him I wouldn't tell you. Let's go to Chuma, see what's what, and then decide what's to be done, if anything."

There was the sound of hooves outside. "Horsesmissus!" Mumba shouted.

Felicity pulled on her riding gloves and went striding through the parlor's double doors. She hopped up on Delight and spurred off. Kennedy followed on Blackie. He caught up with her in Lahana. She had stopped in front of Chief Big-Belly's hut. "Get out here, Big-Belly!"

"Felicity, calm down," Kennedy pleaded.

Chief Big-Belly slowly made an appearance, his head first, looking around as if unsure someone had called his name, then slowly the rest of his body on his big flat feet. He looked up at Felicity and scratched his belly, then walked in front of Delight, out of range of Felicity's riding crop. "What for you want Big-Belly?"

Felicity used the crop to point at the big house. "You built this for Joe Gimmee, didn't you?"

"Meeting house, all same."

"Don't lie to me, you savage! You've joined Joe Gimmee's religion."

"Not lie. Big-Belly good fella boy. You go now. Leave me be."

"What about Chuma? You savvy Chuma?"

Chief Big-Belly stubbornly shook his head. "Chuma long way. Big-Belly here."

"You miserable fat bastard!" Felicity yelled, then kicked Delight forward. The big stallion reared, his front hooves knocking Big-Belly to the ground. He scrambled to get out of the way as Felicity spurred the stallion on.

Kennedy dismounted and helped the fat old man to his feet. "I'm sorry, sport. Missus Markham, she's too much angry."

"She too much crazy!" Big-Belly sputtered. Two women came out of his hut to watch. He started screaming at them. *Pfft,* they puffed at him. *Pfft, pfft.* The chief was getting no more respect from his wives than he had from Felicity.

Kennedy hid his smile, got aboard Blackie, and rode off. Felicity had slowed Delight to a walk after the path turned inland. He came up behind her and silently fell into line. She didn't acknowledge his presence. The trail wound through low brush, savannah, and hardwoods, then back down to the beach before turning once more into a broad plain. The first palm trees appeared, obviously plantation palms, as they pointed skyward, straight as arrows. The horse's hooves padded on the clover beneath the great trees laden with coconuts. Kennedy eased Blackie beside Delight. "Is this Chuma?"

"Yes." Felicity's voice was subdued, her anxiety apparently somewhat alleviated by the sight of the healthy trees. "It's glorious, isn't it? The Peterson brothers managed it for an Australian company, but they were terrible businessmen and ran the place into the ground. The problem was they spent too freely. Everything had to be the best money could buy. They had a concrete drying shed. Concrete! And gas-fed drying ovens. Of course, they couldn't get the gas to operate them, so it was all a wasted effort. Bryce took it over on a lease."

Felicity surveyed the plantation. "But, oh, they were glorious farmers, I will give them that. Look at these magnificent trees! I tell you, Jack, here is the future of Noa-Noa! And to think—" Her thought was cut short as she spied three men stepping out from behind a row of palms. When they realized she'd seen them, they ran off, disappearing into the palm diagonals.

Felicity spurred Delight after them but then reined the stallion in. When Kennedy came up alongside, she pointed at a two-man saw and two axes that the men had apparently dropped. "I recognize the saw," she said. "It was Bryce's. He had in mind harvesting mahogany and ordered it from Australia. Nothing ever came of the idea, and I had nearly forgotten about it. I thought it was stored beneath the house. Now I see it's been stolen."

Kennedy looked around. "I don't see any signs of trees being cut."

Felicity peered upward into the fronds. "That's strange . . . Do you see that vine, Jack? It stretches to that tree there. And then to that tree, and that one, too. A series of them, branching out. And look, those trees there, they're all connected." She eased Delight ahead, searching the tops of the trees. "What do you suppose they're for?"

Kennedy rode along, following the network of vines. "Beats me. Transportation, perhaps? You know, crawling along them? Maybe even walking on them?"

"I don't think so. Why bother? All these boys can climb a tree as easily as you and I can walk a path." She sighted down a line of trees. "This row seems to be the end of the vines."

Kennedy dismounted and scanned the palm fronds and the intertwined vines, trying to make some sense of it. He put out his arm and leaned on one of the inner trees while scratching up under his hat. To his surprise, the tree moved. "Hey!"

"What?"

"This tree moved!"

"Yes, Jack, coconut palms are always moving. Their fronds are like sails in the wind."

"No! I mean it moved at its base."

"You mean at its bole? That's impossible"

"Base, bole, whatever you want to call it. I tell you it moved!"

Felicity climbed off Delight and put her shoulder to the swollen bole of the tree. To her amazement, it *did* move. She looked up into the fronds.

"I think it's been sawn off at the base. The vines are holding it up. Jack, the vines must be holding all of them up!"

Kennedy began rapidly walking back and forth, following the network of vines, shoving trees as he went. He was able to move most of them, and now he could see saw marks at their bottoms. "Sawn off perfectly level with the ground," he said. "I think they form a big rectangle." He stared upward, scrutinizing the waving fronds. "Felicity, the fronds. How long will they stay green?"

"Coconut palm fronds? For a very long time. They're mostly pulp. It takes quite a bit of drying before they start to turn yellow."

"But how long?"

"A month. Maybe longer."

Kennedy looked around. "I know it's crazy, but I think this might be . . ."

"What?" Felicity demanded when Kennedy hesitated.

"Felicity, listen. I'm not certain, but I'm sure David knows. And he might just tell me with a little booze under his belt."

Felicity stared at Kennedy until she understood he was asking her to help him. "All right, Jack," she relented with a sigh. "We'll give it a go."

5 0

Josh sat on the cushioned bench the Jackson twins had built for Kennedy in the cockpit and contemplated the torches in Joe Gimmee's village. All day, canoes had arrived filled with people who excitedly piled ashore. The canoes, he discovered from a friendly villager, came from all over, some as far south as Guadalcanal. Josh even ran across a fisherman he recognized who worked the reef off Melagi. When Josh tracked down Penelope, he found her with a dozen other women, all of them squatting with big wooden pestles in their hands and pounding taro root. "We must feed the people," she explained in between exertions. "Every island in the Solomons has sent a delegation."

"Why?" he asked, with little hope of a straight answer.

Her answer didn't disappoint. "Because my father has invited them here, of course," she said. "Do you desire more information, mastah? As you know, I only live to serve you."

Josh went away, grumbling to himself. The people bustling around him paid scant attention, having become used to the big American who "make'm gate fly along beach." The women were busy building sleeping huts or carrying baskets of bananas, plums, taro root, and breadfruit and laying it all up in a central storage hut. Sharp squeals in the distance were evidence that pigs were being slaughtered. Josh went looking for his boys and found them helping to bury the pigs in a big fire pit. "This is going to be a great celebration, sir," Ready said, practically licking his lips at the thought of barbecued pig.

"You do understand we're on a Japanese-occupied island, don't you, Bosun?" Josh demanded. "And our gunboat is undefended?"

Ready blinked a couple of times. "I get your meaning, sir. I'll put some-one on the guns."

Josh wandered back to the village and stood in the shade of the banyan tree, trying to decide what to do. Before he came to any conclusion, a handsome young man dressed in a clean white lap-lap and a shark's tooth necklace approached him. "I am Ogomo," he said. "Joe Gimmee's son. My father would like to speak with you."

"Then you're Penelope's brother. Are you the one who brought Lieu-tenant Armistead here?"

"I am, indeed. It was a long distance, and it was necessary I hide from the Japoni, who were everywhere, but it still took me only five days. I am a very strong paddler."

"Did you and Armistead talk very much on the way?"

"Alas, he was too weak from his wound. So I mostly sang my little songs while I paddled and he listened. He is a good listener, for an American."

"Your accent is Australian," Josh observed.

"Yes. I was born there. My father and I lived in Sydney until I was ten. Please. He wishes to see you now."

Josh followed Ogomo to a small hut. The young man drew back its cloth door flap and indicated Josh should enter. In the cool darkness within, Josh found Joe Gimmee sitting serenely on the wooden throne that had been aboard the *tomako*. Joe wore no ornamentation, save a hibiscus in his hair. He smiled at the youth. "Thank you, Ogomo. You may leave us."

"Yes, Father," Ogomo said, and backed out of the hut, closing the flap.

"I'm afraid I have no chair to offer you," Joe Gimmee said. "But please take a seat on those blankets, if you like."

Josh liked, and he sat down and crossed his legs. "Are you going to tell me where I can find David Armistead?" he asked.

Joe Gimmee cocked his head. "I think you have a one-track mind, Commander. Sometimes I do, too. Tell me, what do you think of Penelope? Before you answer, I am wondering if I should I get out my shotgun. A fa-ther gets upset when his daughter is tipped by a man without a proposal of marriage."

"She's already married, Joe."

"Not in a way recognized by your government. Whitman bought her from me."

"Then I'm even less concerned about your shotgun," Josh replied. "I understand you abandoned her when she was a child to Minister Clarence.

And now you're telling me you sold her? That doesn't exactly make you father of the year."

Joe Gimmee nodded. "You have me there. But when I handed her over to Minister Clarence, her mother was recently deceased. Her cousin Kwaque had kai-kai'ed her, I regret to say. And since I was leaving for a long sojourn in Australia, I thought it best to find a safe home for my daughter, and Minister Clarence was willing to take her in. Then when I returned, Whitman asked to buy her, and I needed the pigs he offered. I thought he'd make a good husband. I have never claimed to always be right about everything."

"Joe," Josh said tiredly, "this is all interesting, but how about telling me what you want to tell me?"

"It's not what I want to tell you," he said, "but what I want to ask you. How do you get your treasure?"

"What do you mean?" Josh asked, taking his cap off and placing it on the blanket beside him.

"Your boat, the food you eat, the clothes you wear. How do you get those things?"

Josh scratched his head. "Well, it's all government issue."

"Explain government issue, please."

"That means the government gave it to me."

"Did you pray for it first?"

Josh stared at the old man, trying to figure him out. But then he remembered that Joe Gimmee was Penelope's father, and the likelihood of figuring anyone out in that particular family was probably going to be remote. "Praying ain't required, Joe," Josh finally answered. "Paperwork, that's the ticket if you want the government to issue you anything."

"Do you think I could get this paperwork?" he asked.

"I suppose you could, but it wouldn't do you any good. You have to be authorized to make a requisition from the government."

"How do I get authorized?"

"Well, you'd have to be in one of the armed services of the United States."

"May I join one of those services?"

Josh rubbed the old polar bear scar on his chin. "I doubt it. With all due respect, you've got a few too many years on you."

"How about Ogomo? He is young and healthy."

Josh shrugged. "I don't think we're recruiting Solomon Islanders just yet."

"He's Australian. His mother was a white woman who entered my life for a brief time."

"Sorry, Joe. It don't matter. He can't join."

Joe Gimmee chuckled, then looked slyly at Josh. "I knew you would not allow him, for he might discover the great secret if he did. For many years, the people of the Solomons have watched the English receive many treasures, and we have asked them again and again how this occurs. They always lie. For instance, when I asked Minister Clarence where his tins of food and his metal cooking pots and his Bibles came from, he said he prayed and God provided. But I knew that was false. The people of the Solomons have prayed for many years, but the gods have never provided anything for us, save the hot sun and rain. Or perhaps those things that were meant for us were intercepted by the English. I stole a cooking pot from Minister Clarence, just to see if that was true. I knew the gods had meant for me to have it as soon as one of my wives used it for cooking."

"That's crazy talk, Joe," Josh said.

"Is it? I traveled to Australia to see for myself. I took a job on the docks moving cargo here and there. Sometimes, it was stacked in warehouses. Other times, on trucks or ships. It went here, it went there. I asked the English blokes and Aussie mates where did all these things come from, and how do you know where it goes, and who gets it? They showed me paper, or simply waved their arms and talked very fast. Once, a crate was dropped and from it spilled many very fine dishes and cups, all with wonderful designs on them. I asked those blokes how these dishes and cups were made, and how the designs were put on them that could not be rubbed off no matter how hard I tried. But they could not tell me. I knew then that the gods must have made these dishes and cups. How do I know for certain? Because the men who are given them do not know how they are made. For instance, do you know how the uniform you wear is made? How did it get that color and that tight, perfect weave, impossible for even the most talented woman to sew? Tell me exactly, please."

Josh looked at Joe Gimmee and considered telling him a lie, but the old man's eyes, deep and luminous and intelligent, were unsettling. He was certain that he'd be caught in any fib he tried. "Joe, I don't know much about cloth," he confessed. "There are sewing machines, but I'm not sure how they work. That don't mean the gods made my uniform."

Joe Gimmee laughed good-naturedly. "White people are all excellent liars. But I don't blame you. If I knew the great secret, I would keep it to myself, too. Yet when I was in Australia, I began to divine the truth, and then one day it came to me. First, special places must be constructed to receive treasure. Then proper ceremonies must be performed. All this is done, of course, to please the gods. Then, and only then, will the treasure be delivered." Joe Gimmee leaned forward and inspected Josh's expression. "I am very close to the great secret, aren't I?"

"Joe, you're not even in the ballpark," Josh said, shaking his head. "You want cooking pots, or even a truck? Get yourself some money and you can buy anything you want. That's all it takes."

"How do I get money?"

"For money, you have to work."

"I wondered when you would mention money and work in the same breath. The English always got to that, eventually. It was their way of making the Solomon Islanders do their bidding. But you have already admitted you get your treasure without money *or* work."

"Joe, I work for the federal government, don't you see? It's like this big man gives me stuff, and working ain't always required." Josh thought about what he'd said, then added, "Forget that last part."

"How can I forget it when you nearly told me the truth? By the way, I saw many times treasure delivered to the plantations without ever seeing any money handed over."

"They'd likely paid in advance," Josh muttered. He was glad he'd taken his cap off, though he was ready to throw it across the hut. Joe Gimmee had him all tied up in knots.

"I believe I have figured out one of the ceremonies that works especially well these days," Joe Gimmee said. "All that is required is a special place."

Josh perked up. "Is Lieutenant Armistead at that place?"

Joe Gimmee chuckled. "There is that one-track mind of yours again. Yes. He is there, but he is about his own business."

"It's very important that I find him and take him home. I think he is sick in the head."

"He seems perfectly sane to me."

"What did Armistead have to say when you asked him about the great secret?"

"Nothing much. Sadly, he also has a one-track mind. He has a plan to stop the war between you and the Japoni."

"Did he say how?"

Joe Gimmee smiled. "He did, but I can't tell you. I have enjoyed this conversation, Commander Thurlow. I sense that you are a good man, though a bit rough around the edges. I would like to have you around, but I suppose I'll have to settle for being the grandfather to your child."

"I have known your daughter for only one week," Josh said. "She ain't pregnant, or at least I don't think she is."

"But you coupled with her, didn't you?"

Josh reddened but kept silent.

"I shall enjoy bouncing your child on my knee," Joe Gimmee said, then clapped his hands, and the door flap was pulled back.

"Commander?" Ogomo said, by way of an invitation for Josh to leave his father.

Josh came outside. "Ogomo," he said, "you seem a bright lad. I say this with all due respect, you understand, but I believe your father has a screw loose. Nobody's going to give him treasure, no matter how many ceremonies he performs or special places he goes."

"Do not underestimate my father," Ogomo advised. "By the way, what are you going to do about my sister? She's pregnant with your child."

Josh sighed and trotted out his defense once more, though he supposed it wouldn't help with the brother any more than the father. "I've known your sister for only one week," he said.

"You could do worse than Penelope," Ogomo replied, as if Josh hadn't said a word. "Like any good woman of these islands, she would live only to bear your children and to keep you pleased all the days of your life, in every respect."

Josh considered Ogomo's appraisal of Solomon Islands womanhood. "The women out here are already the best treasure a man could have, Ogomo. I don't understand why you and your daddy think you need anything more."

"If you really believed that, Commander," Ogomo answered with a smile, "you would turn heaven and earth to keep Penelope at your side forever."

Ogomo had him dead to rights and Josh knew it. He shook his head and walked away.

5 1

Armistead came to the plantation after dark, appearing from the starlit shadows of the bush near the beach. Surprisingly, he was accompanied by a young woman. Mumba, a red hibiscus blossom stuck in the perfect black ball of his hair, ran up to them holding a lantern aloft, then escorted them to the veranda, where a table had been set, complete with candles. Armistead wore a flowery blue lap-lap and combat boots. His tattoos went from his neck down along his arms and were a stream of linked symbols, stars, crescents, and some designs that reminded Kennedy of barbed wire. He had traded the large bone earrings he'd worn the night before for smaller ones, and around his neck hung a necklace with a carved fish pendant. String amulets around his arms held colorful tassels that hung down to his elbows. The woman wore only a pale green lap-lap and a garland of flowers on her head. Armistead introduced her. "This is Victoria, the daughter of a holy man named Joe Gimmee."

Kennedy reached to shake her hand, but she leaned in and nuzzled his cheek with hers, first on one side and then the other. Her scent was of musk and coconut. She also nuzzled Felicity, then stepped back into the light of the lantern that Mumba held high, his arm rigid as a statue, his face an expressionless mask.

Kennedy made a quick study of Victoria. Her face was rather plain with a high forehead that glistened in the lantern's light, and she had a small nose and thin lips. Her cheeks were full, and her eyes were a bit too far apart. Her sun-streaked black hair was shoulder length and a bit limp. She had wide shoulders, which were her most attractive feature, but small breasts and thin hips. Her bare feet were a little large for her size. She was not black, but more nearly a light tan. Put all together, Kennedy thought, she was a fine-looking woman, though certainly not as attractive as Penelope, who apparently was her sister. He broke the ice with a comment that he and Felicity were most fortunate to have met Penelope, and Victoria replied, in a wispy, shy voice, "My sister is very beautiful and knows how to kill a man, if she has to." Kennedy thought that was a comment one would not hear too often in Massachusetts regarding one's sister.

Armistead was clearly surprised that Kennedy and Felicity knew Penelope. "I see we have more to discuss than I imagined," he said.

Mumba was jarred from his frozen posture by a sharp order from Felicity. He raced off after placing the lantern on a nearby table, enthusiastic squadrons of fluttering moths and buzzing mosquitoes instantly clustering about it. Soon afterward, he reappeared with a tray of drinks, the inevitable gin and tonic. Armistead handed Victoria her glass, and she took it and held it against her chest, as if unsure what to do with it. Kennedy proposed a toast. "To our hostess, Missus Felicity Markham," he said.

Armistead raised his glass. "With many thanks for your kind hospitality."

Kennedy drank, eyeing Armistead over the rim of his glass. The incongruity of the boy he'd known at Choate and Harvard now dressed and tattooed as a savage was a bit difficult to absorb.

They sat on the wicker chairs on the veranda, and the women fell silent, though attentive, while Kennedy and Armistead indulged in small talk, including a discussion of Harvard classmate Richard Tregaskis, who had written a best seller titled *Guadalcanal Diary*. "Richard always had a book in him," Armistead said. "But he missed the true meaning of Wilton's Ridge."

"Which was?" Kennedy prompted.

"That some men carry within themselves a predilection for killing, and it is like an infectious disease, especially in battle." Armistead sipped his drink, then asked, "Did you hear about Georgie Mead?"

"Yes, I visited his grave when I first got out here. There was a mess kit on it with a scratched epitaph that said 'A Great Leader of Men—God Bless Him.' Kick called me when the news came of his death. I was in Palm Beach at the time. I told her I hoped to get out here and punish the Japanese for killing him." Kennedy shook his head. "I'm afraid I was pretty naive."

"Georgie got it on the beach," Armistead said, as if to himself. "He never even got a football field's length onto the island. My God, what a waste."

"He loved his youth, and his youth has become eternal," Kennedy said.

"Pilgrim's Way," Armistead replied, and continued the quotation. " 'Deb-

onair and brilliant and brave, he is now part of that immortal England which knows not age or weariness or defeat.' Substitute America for England, and there you have it. America, after all, is the understudy for England on the world's stage."

"Oh, I sincerely hope not!" Felicity exclaimed, then lapsed back into silence.

"Were you on Guadalcanal for the entire battle, David?" Kennedy asked.

"I came in immediately after the first landing. At the time, it looked like it was going to be a cakewalk. But the day after I arrived, Jap hit us with a brigade that came out of nowhere, and the fighting never stopped for seven months. Finally Jap sent his barges to pick up the few of his fellows who were left, and it was over." He mused over his glass. "They wanted to give me the Medal of Honor for what I did on Wilton's Ridge, but I told them I didn't want it."

"A Medal of Honor would look awfully good on your record," Kennedy said. "Especially since, as I recall, you were interested in politics. I suspect our fathers hope both you and Joe will serve in the Senate someday."

"Politics," Armistead mused, while absently performing the salute against the no-see-ums trying to drink from his eyes. "Yes, I'm still interested, but in a different way from my father. He has not seen what I have seen, or done what I have done."

"The war, you mean," Kennedy said.

"I mean wading in blood up to my ankles," Armistead replied in a distant voice, which Kennedy thought odd, considering the subject. "I mean my hands around another man's throat, choking him, smelling his last breath in my nostrils. Call it war, if you will. It is but murder by another name."

"Dinnerisservedpleasemissus!" Mumba yelled from the kitchen door, and behind him came the two Lahana villagers who worked with Gogoomey, hired for the evening to be the servers. Their bodies were glistening with sweat. The heat in the kitchen was apparently overwhelming with the cook turning the stove into a blast furnace.

Kennedy seated Victoria, and Armistead handled the chair for Felicity. Victoria's thanks were whispered. Felicity thanked Armistead with a nod while growling, "Your thumb out of the soup, Mumba!" She looked around. "That goes for all you boys!"

The soup was something white—Kennedy guessed potato soup but decided not to ask for a clarification as he might not like the answer. Felicity picked up her spoon only to have a fruit bat suddenly drop into her bowl.

The dazed bat flapped its black wings, then staggered out of the soup onto the table. Armistead, his tassels flying, grabbed it with his long arms and flung it into the sky. The bat took off, leaving behind a little rain of white droplets. Everyone at the table dabbed daintily at the dampness on their clothes and in their hair. Kennedy said, "Apparently a Jap bat." And everyone laughed, even Felicity, whose lap was soaked with soup.

Before the next course, there was a disagreement in the kitchen marked by the breakage of china, the clang of pots, pans, and kettles, and the stamp of bare feet on the kitchen floor that shook the veranda. Cook's voice could be heard in a solid stream of complaints interrupted occasionally by little yips from Mumba. From this battleground, the kitchen door slammed open, and once more Mumba and the boys appeared, their expressions betraying nothing. The plates delivered up had a kind of fish on them, complete with head and tail, grilled a golden brown in every place it wasn't burned black. Each fish had a baleful eye that seemed to accuse from its plate. "Dig in," Kennedy said, taking the role of Mastah.

It was a very fishy fish, full of bones, but Kennedy ate it as if were nectar and ambrosia, smiling and chewing and picking bones from his mouth, and wishing all the while for more gin. Every few seconds, he leaned over to swipe at the mosquitoes that were furiously biting him on his legs, even through his trousers. Armistead was doing the same. Felicity held back until she couldn't stand it any longer, a minute at most, before furiously scratching her legs. Victoria, if being bitten, serenely ignored the assault.

The next plate delivered from the kitchen was a side plate of mashed breadfruit covered with chunks of unmelted margarine. That apparently completed the dinner offerings of cook, who could still be heard nattering at the boys, although the crashing of china and banging of pots seemed to have come to an end, perhaps because they had all been broken or dented beyond repair. Felicity remained calm throughout as if nothing untoward were happening.

After it was apparent no more food was coming, Kennedy called Mumba and asked for cigars. The boy thumped off, soon to return with one fresh cigar and another half smoked. Kennedy recognized the stump as one he had flipped off the veranda last night before bed. He took it without complaint.

"Victoria, would you like to see the house?" Felicity asked.

Victoria sat up very straight in her chair. "Yes, missus," she said. "I would like that very much."

"Please call me Felicity," Felicity said.

"Oh, thank you, Felicity," she simpered. Armistead rushed to her chair to slide it back. Kennedy, not to be left out, did the same for Felicity. After giving Kennedy a look that was indecipherable but full of meaning, Felicity led Victoria through the double doors of the parlor.

Armistead and Kennedy retired to the cane-backed chairs at the rail of the veranda while Mumba, abandoned by the temporary help, cleared the dining table. Kennedy produced a Zippo lighter from his shirt pocket and offered its flame to Armistead, then lit his own short cigar. They both enjoyed a few quiet puffs, the blue haze somewhat slowing the mosquito attack, at least around their faces.

"It is very nice of Felicity to treat Victoria with such kindness," Armistead said. "Most colonial women would not allow her in their homes even though she is half white."

Kennedy waved his cigar. "Perhaps the war has changed such attitudes," he said, and dropped the subject. He didn't much want to discuss colonial racism, especially since he feared Armistead might begin a long, scholarly discourse, a tendency he'd observed in the man at school. To get down to cases, he asked, "David, why are you here?"

Armistead shrugged. "I wanted to see my old classmate."

"My real question is, why are you on Noa-Noa?"

Armistead rocked in his chair, one big boot pushing on the rail, the other hanging over. "I could ask you the same thing," he said.

"I'm happy to provide the answer. I'm on a special assignment. It required me to go to Santa Cruz for a new boat—the one I had got sunk, run over by a Jap destroyer, you see. On my way north, I found Felicity paddling around off Mary Island with her son aboard a lifeboat after her schooner went down in a storm. Then I went up to New Georgia, where I managed to get knocked in the head by an old cannibal chief. Felicity brought me here to recuperate."

Armistead looked at Kennedy to see if he was joking. "Quite a tale. But where's your new boat?"

"It kept going north, still on that assignment. A Coast Guard officer named Thurlow is her present skipper."

"Not Josh Thurlow!" Armistead exclaimed. "He was with me on Wilton's Ridge! How is the son of a bitch?"

"Very much in charge of this operation."

"Which is to accomplish what, if you may say?"

"To find you and bring you back to Melagi for court-martial."

Armistead didn't immediately react to Kennedy's stark response. His cigar glowed in the darkness as he continued to rock in the wicker chair. Finally he said, "Thurlow is a hard case. He will find me or die trying."

"He has a guide. Penelope Whitman, or as you may know her, Kimba. They went to find you on Vella Lavella."

"You know, I thought surely they had killed her," he said. "She is a remarkable woman. Worthy of the Amazons."

"But why aren't you on Vella, David?"

"I was there until two days ago. Then I had business over here."

"Can you tell me what that business is?"

"It would be better for you if you didn't know. Can you tell me the charge against me?"

"Desertion. Dereliction of duty. AWOL. I would imagine they'll think up a few more."

Armistead shook his head. "While I was recuperating, I wondered if anybody would look for me. After a while, I thought they would assume I was killed in action and would keep thinking that until . . ." He puffed his cigar, blew smoke, then lapsed into silence.

"Whitman reported you had deserted and stolen his wife."

"Both lies, but it doesn't matter."

"David, it does matter. You need to wait here with me until Thurlow gets back. Then you can go into Melagi and explain everything, except perhaps those tattoos and the earrings. I would imagine your family will be a bit surprised to see them."

"Father would likely have a heart attack!" Armistead laughed. "I think Mother, if she were still alive, might be a bit more understanding. She was quite the wild child before marriage, so I hear."

"Have you turned Turk, David? Is that it?"

Armistead's lips twitched and his eyes crinkled, as if he were recalling a joyful thing. " 'From whence ariseth this? Are we turn'd Turks, and to ourselves do that which heaven hath forbid the Ottomites?' " He threw back his head and laughed. "I have become Othello, the Moor!" He wiped away a mirthful tear from his eye. "No, Jack, I haven't gone completely native, though it has crossed my mind. There would be worse things than to stay in this wild and lovely place. Certainly I have never known quite so much happiness as I have with Victoria."

"Come back with me, David. We'll get you out of this. Then you can choose any life you want."

Armistead's smile gradually faded. "I can't," he said finally. "It's too late. I have to do this thing."

Kennedy didn't say anything. He knew it was time to listen.

"What I am going to do may not do any good," Armistead said quietly, "but I have to try."

Kennedy smoked his cigar.

"I would appreciate it if you would look after Victoria. Make sure she is returned safely to her father. He's coming to Noa-Noa tomorrow, up at Chuma. Do you know where it is?"

"Felicity and I visited it yesterday. We saw something very odd there, sawn palm trees held up by a network of vines. What's that all about?"

"I have nothing to do with that. It has to do with Joe Gimmee's search for what he calls the great secret."

"What is the great secret?"

"I couldn't begin to describe it to you. I fear I slept through most of my economics classes. I don't blame you for looking puzzled. You'll just have to come up to Chuma and see what transpires."

"And *your* secret, David? This thing you have to try. Can't you tell me something of it?"

"I have come to hate this war," Armistead replied in a stony voice. "And I hate murder in the name of it. That is all I will say except I hope I will be judged by my intention, if not the result."

Felicity and Victoria chose that moment to join them. To Kennedy's surprise, they were laughing gaily, having apparently made copious use of the remaining gin. Armistead rose. "Victoria, it's time we went home." He nodded to Felicity. "Thank you very much, Missus Markham. The evening was delightful."

Felicity's smile faded. "May I ask where home is, Lieutenant?"

"We're being put up in Lahana."

Victoria extended her hand to Felicity. "I will never forget your kindness, missus."

"You are a dear child," Felicity said, taking her hand.

Victoria hugged Felicity, then stepped back, embarrassed. "I forget myself," she whispered.

Armistead and Victoria walked down the steps and across the grass and into the shadows and then disappeared, leaving Felicity and Kennedy watching after them. "I truly like her very much," Felicity said. "She is bright and quick. John could do far worse than to find such a woman for his wife someday."

"David said Joe Gimmee was coming to Chuma tomorrow," Kennedy said.

"Did he say why?"

"Something about a great secret, but he said he wasn't part of it, that his purpose in being here had to do with the war. Then he said he hoped to be judged by his intention, if not the result."

Felicity was silent for a moment, then said, "Something terrible is going to happen, Jack. I can feel it."

Kennedy impulsively took her into his arms and was astonished to discover she was trembling. She shook her head, then pushed him away. "I'm sorry, Jack. I'm frightened, and when I'm frightened, I crave solitude. It may seem perverse, but a woman of the Solomon Islands learns not to show weakness. I'll bid you a good night."

"Good night, Felicity," Kennedy said, letting her go. "My mother used to say things will always look better in the morning."

"That might be true in Massachusetts, dear Jack," Felicity answered. "But not in these bloody islands! A morning here can kill you just as surely as the night."

5 2

When the sun went down and the feast began, with much laughing and dancing, Josh returned to the gunboat and sent Once and Again, who were on the guns, off with the admonition to come back on the run if they saw a flare or heard gunfire. Later, as the party on shore was getting ever more boisterous, with much chanting and the beating of drums, Josh heard splashing in the water, then the thump of someone crawling aboard. It was Penelope, looking fetching in a white lap-lap, turned transparent by the water, and flowers in her hair. She was also wearing a dilly bag and carrying a plaited palm frond. She sat beside him, very close. "Hello, mastah," she said. "I have come to serve you. The food I bring you is quite delicious, and I have managed to keep it perfectly dry, since I am a marvelous swimmer."

Josh was hungry, very hungry, so he took the offered frond wrapping and opened it. From it came the wonderful fragrance of roast pig. He ate with his hands, island style, then wiped his hands on his pants. Penelope snuggled in close. "I thought you were mad at me," he said.

"How could a mere Marie be mad at her mastah?"

"Please don't call me that," Josh said. "I liked it most of all when you called me Josh darling. Do you think you could do that again?"

"Perhaps," she said, "but only if I can be your Penelope dear. Or even Penelope Bumppo."

"You are my dearest Penelope Bumppo."

"And . . . ?" she asked slyly.

"And you are my woman," Josh said, pleased with himself that he could recall the last endearment she had desired.

"You have pleased me beyond measure!" she cried, then graced him with one of her perfect smiles. "I shall therefore please you, I hope." She opened her dilly bag and brought forth a bottle and held it in front of Josh's nose. It was, miraculously, a full bottle of Mount Gay rum. He snatched it. "Where did you get that?"

"From my father."

Josh knew it was useless to ask any more questions, so he uncorked the rum and drank it full bore from the bottle, then wiped his mouth with the back of his hand. "God, that is good stuff!" He handed it over. "Try it."

Penelope more than tried it. She tossed the bottle to her lips and took two glugs. Josh took it away from her, lest she drain the thing. "It requires a little more sipping to get the taste," he explained, then took a glug himself that turned into two.

Penelope laughed. "You are such a fool, Josh."

"I've always been a fool for two things, women and Mount Gay rum," he confessed.

"Women are not things," Penelope pointed out, though not churlishly. "My father says that after the people of the Solomons learn how to gain treasure, women will be thought of as nearly equal to men, just as white people think, although we Maries should still follow the commands of our husbands."

Josh took another drink, then handed over the bottle for Penelope to do the same. "Quite the prophet, your daddy," he said.

"He sends you a message with the rum," Penelope said. "Tomorrow, he goes to the special place he has prepared to receive treasure. All these people will go with him. He advises you to leave early, as the many, many canoes will surely attract attention from the Japoni."

"I thought I was supposed to follow him."

"He changed his mind. Now he thinks you should go first. He fears the Japanese submarine, I think, which is looking very hard for you."

"Where is he going? I can't go there if I don't know."

"I will tell you, but only if you come into the village and dance. I would so love to see you dance."

Josh was feeling pretty warm inside, the Mount Gay kind of warm. "All right, Penelope, my girl, I'll do it. I'll dance the night away with you."

Penelope joyfully clapped her hands. "I'll bring the bottle!"

Once in the village, Josh sought out Ready, who was leaning against the banyan tree with his arms around the waists of two smiling young Maries. "I'm going to be busy for a bit," Josh said. "Send someone to the *Rosemary* to man a gun and keep lookout."

Ready confirmed he'd heard the order, although all he did in response was hug the girls closer. Kava had done its work on him. Josh and Penelope walked, though a bit unsteadily, to the fire circled by dancing people. Before they reached it, Josh was astonished to see that a white sheet had been strung between two short palm trees and a movie projector was busily projecting moving images on it. It was a newsreel. President Roosevelt flickered on the sheet, then Churchill making his V-for-victory sign with his second and third fingers. Davey, one of the stranded sailors, sidled up next to him. "They had that film when I got here, sir, and the projector and that little generator, too. Only thing was they didn't know how to hook it all together. Billy and I did it for them. Joe Gimmee loves this newsreel. He's watched it at least a thousand times since I've been here. Like to wore it out."

"Where'd this stuff come from?"

Davey shrugged. "Beats me. The projector and generator's got GI serial numbers on them, though."

Penelope pulled Josh away and started wiggling her hips in rhythm with a band of flutes and drums. In fact, Penelope wiggled her hips like no one Josh ever imagined could. Sweat poured off his face, and it was not entirely because of the heat of the fire, or the exertion of the dance, or even the effects of the rum. He couldn't keep his eyes off Penelope's exotic and erotic movements. He had quite forgotten that she owed him information concerning Joe Gimmee's special place to which he needed to go. Penelope hadn't forgotten, however. Late in the night, she whispered the place into his ear, along with a lick of her tongue, and Josh stopped his own awkward gyrations to absorb the information.

"What an odd turn life sometimes takes," he said. Then he shrugged and started dancing again, a happy man with his woman.

5 3

High over the sea beneath the stars, the great frigate bird flew, its giant wings spread to catch the mildest wafting breeze. Others of its fellows soared with it, their dark feathers making them all but invisible. The sharp night eyes of the ancient bird watched all that was below and took note of the gray boat that coughed awake on the gray beach, then, churning white froth, withdrew into the deeper waters. A ball of sardines was disrupted and sparkled enticingly as they tried to come back together. The frigate bird dived for them taking the opportunity for a night feeding. Since its feathers were not waterproof, it had to skim along the surface of the black sea, dipping its beak to snatch a meal, then rising once more. Others of its fellows made similar snatches, and pelicans, startled awake, came over to see what the fuss was all about.

The gray boat grumbled ahead, the man at the wheel bare-chested and not entirely steady on his feet. The giant wake of the boat stirred up phosphorescence and there came whooshing sounds as the pelicans began to dive into the sea, again and again, only to meet the frigate birds who slammed into them until they dropped their fish. Triumphantly, the frigate birds caught the fish in midair and flapped away.

At the entrance to the harbor, another watercraft sat there, waiting. It was painted white, clearly visible even in the light of the false dawn, and was long and thin. Men could be seen running on its deck, and a tarp was flung off a big gun. The man at the wheel of the gray boat crouched down. There were other men on the boat, but they were all asleep, their prostrate forms draped here and there. The gray boat's bow raised high into the air, and it began to race toward the open sea. The long white boat also began to make way, and there came a loud thud and a ring of smoke from the deck gun. The ancient frigate bird shuddered when the noise of the blast reached it. It turned away while the boats below began to race through the water. The thud of the deck gun sounded again, and then again, echoing into the harbor, and into the village that lay behind it.

5 4

The sun had burned its way above the pink clouds on the horizon when Penelope walked to the beach with Joe Gimmee. "I am afraid, Father," she said. "Do you think the Japoni submarine caught Josh Thurlow?"

Joe Gimmee smiled. "While you slept, I watched from that bluff over there. The Japoni submarine did not catch the father of your child, but it was drawn away as I hoped. Josh Thurlow has an odd kind of luck, I think. He is often in trouble, yet he seems to have a knack for survival. Perhaps he is loved by the gods, or at least he amuses them. The good thing is that the Japoni are gone and will not keep us from our treasure."

"I am also confused, Father," she said. "Why do we need treasure? Don't we have plenty to eat and drink in these islands? Don't we have homes and our canoes? And here, a man and a woman might find love easily enough. What else is required?"

Joe Gimmee stopped to answer Penelope's question. "It is not the treasure that is important," he explained. "It is the regard of the gods. They make the treasure and give it to those who show them the proper respect. Since we don't know how to show that respect, I fear they will think we hate them. I'm certain this has caused them to be angry and is why we have lived in servitude to the white people for all these years."

"But the white people do not seem to be happy, even though they receive the treasure of the gods."

"Yes, that is puzzling," Joe Gimmee confessed. "I shall want to ask the great Joe about this."

"Who is the great Joe, Father?"

"The one from which I take my worshipful name, dear." Joe Gimmee stopped to inspect his daughter. "Are you happy, little one?"

"I am happy," Penelope said. "Though I already miss my sailor boy so very much." She patted her flat stomach. "But I suppose I will always have him through our child. Once, when Josh Thurlow lay on top of me, I looked up into the trees and saw a bird of many colors. He was watching us. I think it was a god, blessing our act."

"Or perhaps only a parrot," Joe Gimmee replied, picking up his pace again. "Since the gods deserted us after the British came, it has been difficult to tell when one is around."

Penelope followed her father to the beach, where the people were gathered before a big fleet of canoes. He nodded to his captains, fierce warriors dressed in their finest lap-laps and shell necklaces with feathers in their hair and bones through their noses and ears. "All is in readiness," they told him. "Today, we will see the great Joe, after whom you are named."

Joe Gimmee peered at a man named Billeebo, who was from the far south. "Billeebo, are you certain the great Joe will come?"

"Yes," Billeebo answered. "We need only prepare for him."

Joe Gimmee smiled, displaying his upper teeth and lower gums. "Then it is time for us to go."

The people climbed into their canoes, and soon they were all at sea. The only people left in the village were three people who had fallen ill and the two Japanese sailors.

Kennedy was astonished by the sight he beheld from the veranda. During the night, he thought he'd had a dream, that he'd heard the *Rosemary* come to take him home. Now he saw it had been no dream. The *Rosemary* was there, her bow pushed up on the sand, although there appeared to be no one alive aboard her.

He roused Mumba to come and help him. Seeing the bodies on the deck, Mumba refused to climb aboard. The first man Kennedy came to was Ready, slumped over the starboard machine gun. He touched the man's neck, afraid that he wouldn't feel a heartbeat, but was pleased when there was a strong throb against his fingers. He also got a whiff of the man's breath. It was sour and suspicious. "I think he's drunk," Kennedy said, though on what he couldn't imagine since it didn't smell like alcohol. He left Ready and inspected all the other bodies. "Hell, they're all drunk! Mumba, come aboard and help me carry these men to shore. You savvy?"

"Not finished altogether?" Mumba asked nervously.

"Not quite," Kennedy said. "You savvy all same drink'm too much?"

A light came into Mumba's eyes. He clambered aboard, only to be met by a suddenly awake Marvin in full mouth-foaming fury. Mumba went screaming for the missus with Marvin at his heels. "Bloody hell," Kennedy sighed, and started going from man to man. One by one, at his urging, they sat up, some only to crawl to the side to disgorge the contents of their stomachs into the sea. Thurlow was found curled in the cockpit, his hands tucked between his knees. His breath was pure alcohol. When Kennedy touched him, he said, "Not now, Penelope."

"I'm not Penelope, you great fool!" Kennedy snapped.

After some blinking and smacking of his lips, Josh finally crawled out of the cockpit to lean against the starboard machine-gun cupola. "Where are we?"

"Noa-Noa," Kennedy answered. "Where did you think? You must have come in this morning, just after sunrise."

"I think I remember now," Josh said, holding his head. "I drove through the night straight across the Vella Gulf, dead reckoning for Noa-Noa all the way. There was a Jap submarine after us. All I could do was run from it. I couldn't keep any of the boys awake long enough to fight. Too much kava. I kept going to sleep myself. Then I woke and I was headed straight for the plantation. I almost ran into the dock. Best I could do was push up into the sand. But look, Kennedy, it don't matter. What matters is we found Joe Gimmee. He told me Armistead is here, on Noa-Noa. There's supposed to be some kind of ceremony today, and Armistead will show up."

"I know all about it," Kennedy replied, to Josh's astonishment.

Felicity came running down the path from the house with John-Bull and Mumba. Mumba was carrying a bucket of water and a ladle. John-Bull was carrying a jar filled with white pills. Marvin was trotting along most happily beside them, apparently having decided the houseboy wasn't the enemy after all. All came on board. "Mumba, give these boys water," Felicity said. "John, two aspirin, no more."

Mumba and John-Bull picked a crewman at random and offered him the ladle. It was Once, and he took it greedily. Then John-Bull silently handed over the two aspirin, which were also devoured. They moved to the next boy, who happened to be brother Again.

"Water is the only thing for a hangover, no matter what they say," Felicity announced. "It dilutes the blood. Drink as much as you can! And aspirin, of course." She knelt beside Josh. "Well, Commander Thurlow. Aren't we the sight?"

"Stop shouting," Josh answered, pressing his fingers into his temples.

"I am talking in a most reasonable tone of voice. I'm afraid you are a bit sensitive today. What happened?"

Kennedy answered for him. "He met Joe Gimmee, who told him Armistead was on the island. I haven't told him that we had dinner with Armistead last night."

Josh raised his head. "What? Did you grab him?"

"Grab him?" Felicity asked. "Oh, I see what you mean. No, we are fresh out of chains and shackles here on the old plantation. Sorry, Commander. In fact, we had a very pleasant evening with them."

"Them?"

"Penelope, it turns out, has a half sister. Her name is Victoria."

"Where is Armistead?" Josh demanded, while trying to not rattle his skull too much.

"Listen, Josh, take two aspirin and water, lots of water. Then, when you are feeling better, come up to the house and we will discuss all this like civilized people. Jack, you come with me. You need your breakfast. Victoria told me Joe Gimmee will not arrive until some time after noon. We will feed you all. There is fish left from the evening. Cook will prepare it."

At the sound of the proposed breakfast, Kennedy tried not to screw up his face, but he did, and Felicity saw it. "You didn't care for the fish?"

"It was delicious," Kennedy lied. "And served cold for breakfast, I'm certain it will be only better."

The cold, bony fish wasn't any better, although neither Kennedy nor Josh was willing to confess it to Felicity or John-Bull, who happily devoured it and washed it down with the bitter tea. The conversation over breakfast included what Armistead had said the evening before and what Josh had learned on Vella Lavella. Kennedy's additional news about the palms at Chuma hanging by vines left Josh scratching his head. "How far is Chuma?" he asked Felicity.

"It's on the northern end of the island," Felicity answered. "About six miles from here."

Josh checked his watch. It was already nearly ten o'clock. "We'd best get going as soon as we can. I don't intend to take the gunboat. Joe Gimmee thought it would attract Japanese, and I think he's right, especially that damned sub. I'll have the boys tuck her away."

"There's a river outflow just south of here with plenty of overhanging trees. Might be a good place," Felicity said.

With breakfast finished, Josh went off to search for life among his boys.

They had dragged themselves to the beach, where they lay, ignoring the mosquitoes chewing on them. "Ready! Get up, son. You can do it. Now, listen. Take the boat—stand up straight now, stop wobbling—take the boat and ease her into that river over there. Beneath those trees. Camouflage her as best you can. Then you stay with her, understand? Keep the boys on board, too. Make sure they get sobered up. Coffee. Lots of coffee. Get Stobs up, too, and tell him to crank up his radio. Tell him to call Eureka, tell him the entire situation. Without Vella's mountain in the way, he should be able to get through. I'm going to take the Very gun. Keep a lookout for a flare from the north end of the island. You see one, come running, and be prepared to fight your way through to me. I don't know what's going to happen, so that's about all I can tell you. And whatever you do, watch out for that I-boat!"

Felicity, having come down to the beach, asked, "Josh, do you think you might consent to transporting my copra back to Melagi? I might find a boat there to carry it the rest of the way to Australia."

"I'll give it some thought, Missus," Josh said formally. "But I can't promise. First, we've got to get this day done and see what's what."

"Oh, posh," she said. "I have been thinking about what's going to happen. If all this has to do with Joe Gimmee, it is some kind of animist religious rite. I think we are going to see some ridiculous chanting and dancing and then it will be over. What else, after all, could it be?"

A sudden din of banging pans and cursing emanated from the kitchen, and Felicity excused herself. Kennedy, coming down the path from the house, passed her. "What now?" he asked Josh.

"We grab Armistead," Josh said with grim determination. "And then deliver him to Colonel Burr on Melagi. After that, I guess you go back to Lumbari."

"Not Lumbari. Probably Australia. They've pushed up my court-martial, and Admiral Halsey is running the show."

"Are you worried?"

"Guilty men usually are. I don't have much of a defense. How could that destroyer have run me down if I hadn't been inattentive? Two other PT boat captains saw the damned thing heading my way. Why didn't I?"

"They saw it because they were running away."

"What do you mean?"

"They were south of you, heading toward Lumbari as fast as they could go. That's why they saw the destroyer and you didn't. It was coming at you from the south."

"You've got it wrong. I was hit by a destroyer coming down from the north toward New Georgia. The other two boats must have been north of me."

"No, they weren't, you lunkhead. What were you doing when you got struck?"

"Well, I was patrolling back and forth west of Kolombangara."

"What was your heading?"

Kennedy gave the question some thought. "Southwesterly, as I recall. Due west would have taken me into some reefs."

"And where were the Japanese destroyers?"

"North of me, of course."

"North? Think about it, Jack. You were going more or less west to south. If the destroyer had been north of you heading south, it would have appeared on your stern quarter but instead it sliced along your bow. Don't you get it? You were run over by a destroyer coming *back* from New Georgia, probably while it was turning toward Kolombangara! I knew it the instant I read your report. You see, I have access to intelligence reports that others don't. That night, the Tokyo Express came through earlier than usual to support an evacuation off New Georgia. They went right past your flotilla, and none of you saw them, not even the boats with radar. Then all the other PT's ran for home, but not you, Jack. You stayed out there in the dark all by yourself. That makes you a damn hero! Don't worry. I'll make sure everybody knows it, too, including Admiral Halsey. I've got some powerful sway with him."

Kennedy's mouth had slowly fallen open during Josh's discourse. "You son of a bitch. Why did you wait until now to tell me this?"

Josh grinned. "Call it an exercise in motivation."

Kennedy balled his fists. "Well, call this an exercise in getting your lights knocked out. Put your dukes up, Thurlow."

Josh did not put up his dukes, and he easily dodged the small, hard fist that was swung at his nose. He caught the next one in his big ham hand. "That'll be enough of that, Jack. You've proved yourself during this operation, not only to me, but Ready, too. So thank you for a job well done, and don't worry about that court-martial. It won't happen. Now, let's go collect Armistead and end this thing."

The canoes were at sea, hundreds of them. It didn't take long before three Rufes, patrolling out of Bougainville, spotted them. Their leader, one Lieutenant Mamoru Ichikawa, recently rescued from Mary Island, hand-signaled the other two Rufes and they dropped out of the sky to an altitude of one hundred feet, flashing across the wooden fleet. Out of the corner of his eye, Ichikawa saw a net being cast and hands raised in friendly waves. He pulled up, his men following him in perfect formation. After they came up to his wingtips, Ichikwawa shrugged, and his pilots responded the same. He signaled to keep going south, in search of American targets.

Joe Gimmee sat serenely on his throne in the great *tomako*. His paddlers were chanting with each dip of their paddles into the sea. The sky was breathtakingly clear. Noa-Noa rose in the east. The heavens and the earth and the sea were coming together just as he was certain they would. "All we have to fea-yah," he said in a whisper to himself, "is fea-yah itself."

Joe Gimmee had no fear, not today, the day when the secret of treasure would finally be revealed to him, and to all the people of the Solomon Islands.

5 5

Josh and Kennedy walked, Felicity rode on Delight, and John-Bull was on Blackie. Felicity had ordered John-Bull to stay home, but once the boy got a whiff of something extraordinary happening, he made it clear he was going to Chuma, even if it meant he had to sneak through the bush to get there. His sense of adventure made Felicity proud, but she tempered her pride by insisting to the boy, "You'll stay near me at all times, understand?" John-Bull understood very well, but he was not afraid. He was packing an M-1 carbine Ready had given him and was ready to use it to defend his mother. For her part, Felicity carried her Webley, and Josh and Kennedy had their forty-fives strapped aboard their web belts. They were ready to fight but hoped they wouldn't have to.

The village of Lahana proved to be completely empty of people. They kept going until the path turned down to the beach, and there they stopped to see what they could see. The first of what they presumed were Joe Gimmee's canoes were being paddled ashore, about a mile ahead. "The sand's too hot for us to take the beach," Felicity counseled. "Not to mention the sand flies will devour the horses. Let's stay on the path. It'll take a bit longer, but there appear to be many canoes still well out to sea."

Felicity was correct. It took another two hours before all of the canoes, including the big *tomako* carrying Joe Gimmee, pushed up onto the sand. By then, Josh, Kennedy, John-Bull, and Felicity were waiting for them. Penelope leapt from the war canoe and splashed through the water onto the beach until she stood before Josh. "I am so glad to see you," she said. "The Japoni can't sink my man, can they? But if they had, I would have found that submarine somehow and taken the heads of all aboard."

Josh was astonished all over again at the depth of feeling Penelope had for him. He couldn't imagine it, but then he knew himself better than she did. "I'm sorry I left without saying good-bye," he offered, "but I hoped to see you today, and now here you are." Then, even though it embarrassed him to do it in front of Kennedy and Felicity, he folded her into his arms.

Penelope took him by the hand and walked a little way away from the others. "Whitman will hear of this gathering and will come here today," she confided. "He will not be able to stay away, because he knows I will be here. This time, I will kill him."

"I'll kill him for you, but it's David Armistead I'm after."

"You should let Armistead go," she said. "He means to do good. Why not let him try?"

"Because I have orders to the contrary."

"I love you, Josh darling."

"And I love you, Penelope dear."

They looked into each other's eyes, and it seemed as if something were joined between them. Penelope understood it, but Josh did not. "What is to become of us?" she asked without hope, though he did not catch her opinion.

"Let's get this day behind us," he answered, which was to say he didn't know, and that she was not his greatest priority. She also understood that very well, and he also not at all. Love stood before him, but Josh did not recognize how gossamer it was, or care. He left her and went back to the others, his hand on his pistol. Penelope watched after him. "You are a great fool, Josh Thurlow," she said to herself, though her heart yearned for him more than life.

The people of the canoes unloaded plaited palm frond and bamboo crates and carried them inland on their shoulders while Joe Gimmee stayed on the beach. He was being ministered to by a number of women, and it was difficult to see what they were doing. When they backed away, a transformation had occurred. His face was painted completely white, a straw Panama hat sat on his puff of frizzy hair, and he wore a crude, Western-style suit, complete down to the lapels, although it had the appearance of being sewn together from at least a dozen different-colored lap-laps. Between his upper teeth and lower gums, he had placed a straight twig, pushed up at a jaunty angle. He sat on his throne, which was picked up and carried inland on the shoulders of four huge men, fierce in their demeanor. They trudged into the forest, taking the path that led to the interior of the Chuma plantation.

"What a lot of foolishness all this is," Josh said to Kennedy. "But it don't matter. As long as it brings Armistead in."

"What are you going to do with him?"

"Exactly what I promised Burr. Deliver him to Melagi."

"It's odd. I've always had the feeling you were going to kill him."

Josh said nothing, and his face betrayed nothing, which Kennedy took as an answer. "I don't think he'll come easily," Kennedy said.

"David's always been a good marine," Josh replied, still betraying nothing. "He'll understand what I have to do."

"I'm not sure he thinks he's a marine anymore," Kennedy replied.

Josh gave that some thought and then wished that Eureka Phimble were with him. Eureka always knew the right thing to do, and Josh, despite all his bravado and confident ways, knew he didn't. He suddenly felt very alone and needful of unconditional support for what he had to do. He looked around the beach for Penelope, but she was gone.

David Armistead was found, along with Victoria, beside the inner edge of the network of vine-connected palm trees. He was wearing a lap-lap with a dilly bag across his shoulder, and on his waist a web belt with a K-bar strapped aboard, and a holster, filled with a forty-five pistol. The tattoos down his arms were bright blue in the sun, and bone rings dangled in his ears. Josh walked up to him. "Well, David, you've given me a run for my money," he said. "Come along, now. They want you back on Melagi."

Armistead nodded to Josh. "Have you met Victoria?" he asked.

Josh touched the brim of his cap, though he didn't take his eyes off Armistead. "I lost one of my boys looking for you."

"I regret that more than you can possibly know," Armistead replied, his eyes telling as much. "But I think I know how to stop all the killing."

"You're coming with me," Josh said, and was about to make his move to grab him when Victoria stepped between them. "Not now, please," she begged in her wispy voice. "Let my father's miracle occur first."

Josh eyed her without mercy. "I'm sorry, ma'am. This is between David and me. There's no time for miracles." Josh reached past Victoria to put his hand on Armistead's arm but found himself surrounded by Joe Gimmee's men armed with spears. Josh stepped back. "You're making a mistake, David. No amount of spears will keep me from my duty. You can lay to that."

Victoria hugged Armistead's arm. "Leave us alone for now, Commander Thurlow. Let my father have his moment, then you and David can talk." She led Armistead away while talking low into his ear. He put his arm around her waist.

Josh watched them go, then admonished the spear holders still surrounding him. "Get on! I don't have no fight with you." He pushed their spears aside and found Kennedy, Felicity, and John-Bull. They were standing in a small clearing watching men build some sort of structure out of bamboo. It had all apparently been worked out in advance, and it was going up quickly, a platform on four tall, rickety legs. Plaited palm fronds woven into rectangles of bamboo were hoisted onto the platform and joined together with vines to form low walls. A vine was stretched from the platform into the trees, tied off somewhere out of sight. Two men climbed the platform and placed halves of small coconuts over their ears, tied on their skulls with strings.

"What the hell are they up to?" Josh wondered. There was no answer from his companions, who were as mystified as he.

Men next came carrying a long pole. They stuck it in a hole beside the platform, and Josh saw attached to it a crude version of the American flag. There weren't enough stars in its blue field or enough red and white stripes, but it was recognizable as Old Glory. Stones were brought and piled around the base to make the pole and its flag stable in the light breeze.

Then came the sound of stamping bare feet, and, lo, a formation of men came marching, each dressed in at least a scrap of military uniform. Some men wore utility shirts, some utility pants, others khaki shirts and pants. They were remnants of authentic American uniforms, although all were threadbare. On the shoulders of the men were short poles being carried as if they were rifles. Josh realized that he was seeing a parade much like the one accomplished on most of the American-occupied islands every morning across the South Pacific. They were reenacting the raising of the flag at reveille. Three conch blowers managed an oddly effective version of the bugle call.

The formation marched around and around the flagpole. One man marched to the side, acting as a cadence counter. "Hup, hup, hup!" he cried. He wore the khaki shirt and pants of an American naval officer although he had the stripes of Marine Corps noncommissioned officers sewn up and down his sleeves. He also wore half of a large coconut on his head like a helmet, a string holding it in place beneath his chin. Finally he yelled something incomprehensible, and the formation halted, more or less. Some kept marching, only to turn around and sheepishly steal their way back into formation. Then they all turned and faced the flag.

The men on the platform began touching the small coconuts attached to their ears. They mumbled something, then began to point at the sky. Penelope slid next to him. "What are they doing?" he asked her.

"They are talking to the great Joe," she answered.

Josh shook his head. "Why won't you ever give me a straight answer?"

Penelope looked at him. "I simply told you the truth."

Josh sorted through his situation and discovered he was hot, angry, and thoroughly rattled by Armistead's refusal to come along. He took it out on Penelope. "The truth don't ever seem to come out of your mouth."

"Here's a truth, very much to the point," she said. "I am pregnant."

Josh closed his mouth, but after a moment of work, he opened it to demand, "Who's the father?"

Penelope slapped him then, with all her might. Josh couldn't recall ever being hit quite so hard, at least by a woman, and he was knocked back an entire step. "How is it possible you know you're pregnant?" he asked, while rubbing his jaw. "We've only known each other for a little over a week."

"A woman knows these things," she answered. "No worry-worry. I will raise our son to be big and strong and, unlike you, Josh Thurlow, also smart and good."

Penelope walked away. When Josh caught up with her, she made disparaging hissing sounds in his direction. *Pfft,* she hissed at him. *Pfft, pfft.* "Stop hissing at me, you crazy girl," Josh pleaded. "We have to talk about this."

"Does that mean you will marry me?"

"You're already married."

"I intend to be a widow very soon. Then will you marry me?"

"Well . . . you'll have to give me time to think about it."

"That would be a *no* in the language of men," Penelope sniffed, and kept walking. This time, Josh didn't follow her, as he was distracted by another blast of the conch-shell trumpeters.

Now came Joe Gimmee on his throne. He was carried into the clearing and set down in front of what appeared to be a crude bamboo lectern. He rose from his throne and stiffly walked to it. The people all sat down, wearing expressions of hopeful anticipation. The men on the platform stood at attention, their hands over the coconuts on their ears. They were still looking at the sky.

Joe Gimmee removed the jaunty twig from his mouth, tapped it as if it held ashes, and handed it to one of the men who'd carried him. He gripped the bamboo lectern on its side with his big hands and said, "Yesterday, December seventh, nineteen-forty-one—a date which will live in infummy—the United States of America was suddenly and deliberately attacked by naval and air forces of the Empire of Japoni." He paused to allow the people to applaud, which they did politely. There were even a few wolf whistles.

They sounded to Josh like a GI audience at a USO show. Joe Gimmee raised his hand and formed a *V* with his fingers, just as Winston Churchill did in the newsreel. He continued, "All we have to fea-yah is fea-yah itself."

Josh stood beside Kennedy, and the two men looked at one another. "That's the second time I've heard Joe Gimmee deliver that line," Josh said. "He does a pretty fair FDR."

"Is this a show?" Kennedy wondered. "Theater of a type?"

Josh shrugged, then scouted the crowd for Armistead. He found him watching the proceedings, a sad smile on his face. Victoria was clinging to his arm. To his disgust, Josh discovered he had sympathy for the couple. He knew something of lost love, after all. This made him think of Naanni, his deceased Aleut wife, and Dosie, his no-longer girlfriend, and Penelope, his—whatever she was, all at the same time, which made him even sadder, though he forced sadness in short order into anger. Armistead was going to go back to Melagi, that was the only certain thing Josh knew at that moment. Either that or . . . Halsey's words as quoted by Colonel Burr flickered into Josh's mind: *In my opinion, any American officer who deserts his men in combat is already dead. Some bastard should find Armistead and make it official.* Josh knew his duty, and he would do it.

The men on the tower started yelling, shaking Josh from his grim thoughts. "Roger!" they called up to the sky. "Wilco! Able! Baker! Charlie! Niner zero zero two four six eight! Roger! Go round!"

Twenty men ran toward the sawn-off palms, clambering up the anchor palms, where they used their machetes to chop loose the vines. All the trees fell within minutes. More men streamed onto the field, hefted the palms, and carried them off on their shoulders, revealing as they did a long open field, not quite flat, but only slightly undulating with the natural contours of the land.

Josh instantly recognized what had been created. "If that ain't an airfield!"

"That was my guess," Kennedy said.

"An airfield this far south . . . why, Jap could bring his Bettys down from Bougainville and be back in business all down the Solomons! It would be like we fought the whole battle of New Georgia for nothing."

"That's what I figured, too," Kennedy advised.

"This has got to be reported," Josh said, and turned to John-Bull. "Listen, son, I need to you to go as fast as you can and tell Ready to radio that there's an airfield on Noa-Noa. Tell him to say Jap built it. They wouldn't understand, otherwise."

John-Bull hesitated. "But I want to see what's going to happen!"

"Seaman Markham," Kennedy said in a stern voice, "I believe I swore you into the service. Do as the commander orders."

John-Bull reluctantly saluted, had a word with his mother, then climbed aboard Blackie and was off.

The men on the platform were getting ever more excited. The ersatz American soldiers, who had all lain down to rest, got up and stood in formation again. At a command from the man playing their drill sergeant, they held their "rifles" in front of them in salute. Joe Gimmee was saying something, very low, but it sounded to Josh like the same thing over and over. Gradually the crowd started to repeat what he was saying. "Joe," and then after a pause, "Gimmee."

"Joe."

"Gimmee."

"Joe."

"Gimmee."

"Joe, Gimmee. Joe, Gimmee. Joe, *Gimmee!*"

"Boy, they love their Joe Gimmee," Josh said.

"I'm not so sure," Felicity mused. "I don't think they're just saying his name. There's something else . . ."

Josh saw Penelope in the crowd. She was reaching for the sky with both hands. All the people around her were staring aloft with rapt expressions of wonderment. He looked at her and saw a savage.

"Joe! Gimmee! Joe! Gimmee! Joe! Gimmee!"

"Do you know what I think they're saying?" Kennedy asked. "Joe, *give* me. Joe, *give* me."

"Precisely," Felicity said.

"*Give* me? Give me what?" Josh demanded.

"I understand now," Felicity said, then shook her head and chuckled. "I should have guessed. It's a cargo cult, Jack! There've been cargo cults out here for years. This is just another variation. Joe Gimmee and his followers built this place for a precise purpose. That bamboo tower is supposed to be an airfield tower, and the men in it are pretending to be airfield controllers. Those coconuts on their ears are supposed to be earphones. The vine from the platform is supposed to be a telephone or telegraph wire. But they're not communicating with pilots, they're talking to . . . well, I suppose you might say the cargo gods."

"What a load of nonsense," Josh growled.

"It may be nonsense to us," Felicity acknowledged, "but it's very real to them. They believe the wealth of the English and the Americans have been given to them by the gods. So now they want to contact those gods. They think airfields are one of the places the gods use to give us the cargo they make. So, to their way of thinking, all they have to do is build one, then go through the ceremonies of an airfield, and the gods will give them cargo, too. It's like when Catholics say mass, don't you see? The priest goes through a ceremony, and God changes the bread and water into something magical."

Josh scratched up under his cap. "But they're asking for Joe to give them something, and Joe's standing right there, empty-handed."

"Recall Penelope said we are going to see the *great* Joe today. If Joe Gimmee actually means 'Joe, give me,' then our Joe here is just the conduit for the real Joe, the great Joe, who, I suppose, is a god of cargo."

Josh gave it some thought. "What's going to happen when this great Joe doesn't show up?"

The people were becoming ever more insistent in their chanting. "JOE, GIMMEE! JOE, GIMMEE! JOE, GIMMEE!"

"You know, now that I think on it, 'Joe' is what the native workers called us on Santa Cruz," Kennedy reflected. "Joe this, and Joe that. It's their nickname for Americans."

"So why an American god and not an English or even a Japanese god?" Josh wondered.

"Have you ever been on Santa Cruz and seen all that cargo piled up? The English and Japanese have nothing to match it."

"JOE, *GIMMEE!* JOE, *GIMMEE!*"

"This is going to get ugly," Kennedy predicted. "How about we take off?"

"I'm not going anywhere without Armistead," Josh swore, and prepared to go after the man. Then he noticed that Victoria was standing alone.

The chanting began to die down. Everybody was listening. And then came the distant drone of an aircraft. "It's nothing," Josh said, scanning the crowd for any sign of Armistead. "Airplanes from both sides fly around here every day."

But the drone got louder until the aircraft producing it, a United States Navy R4D twin-engine cargo aircraft, roared at treetop level down Joe Gimmee's airfield, then pulled up and turned around.

The people's chant rose so that the R4D might hear them: *"JOE, GIM-MEE! JOE, GIMMEE!"* Some of the people were laughing, and some were crying. They raised their hands, making the V for victory sign. Joe Gimmee was nearly hysterical with laughter, and so excited he had to sit down on his throne. He wiped at his tears of joy, carving finger trails through the white paint on his face.

The R4D, the navy equivalent of the commercial DC-3 airliner, came in again, this time lowering its wheels. It bounced down on the smooth carpet of clover and palm fronds, across the flat palm stumps, and rolled to a stop. Then, with a roar of its engines, it turned and taxied back to the bamboo control tower, pivoting to present its port side to Joe Gimmee on his throne. The engines wound down, the propellers stopped spinning, and the door of the R4D opened.

The assembly fell silent. Joe Gimmee stood and walked stiffly forward. Men appeared from the crowd carting bamboo stairs. Then a man appeared at the R4D door, awkwardly ducking through it, nearly knocking his pith helmet off his head. Blinking in the bright sun, he stepped out on the top step of the bamboo stairs. He was dressed in the khakis of a United States Navy lieutenant. His shoulders were hunched, as if he were uncertain of his reception, but then he seemed to sense the wave of goodwill washing over him and relaxed. He grinned and then raised both of his hands, each making the V-sign. Kennedy's mouth dropped open when he realized who the man was.

The navy lieutenant in the pith helmet with both hands making the V-sign might be called the great Joe, but Kennedy knew him by another name. "My God," he said. "It's *Nick!*"

5 6

"I played poker with that guy on Santa Cruz," an astonished Kennedy said to Josh. "He's a supply officer named Nixon. Goes by Nick. Runs all kinds of concessions like Nick's Hamburger Joint, Nick's Beach Rentals, Nick's Jeep Wash, and"—comprehension crossed Kennedy's face—"Nick's South Pacific Souvenirs."

Nixon, still grinning, walked down the bamboo steps to be greeted warmly by Joe Gimmee. An aft hatch opened up in the R4D, and two sailors hopped out and started catching cardboard boxes being tossed from the plane by two more sailors. Pretty soon, three pyramids of boxes were stacked up. A folding table was brought out, and Nixon sat down behind it and set up shop.

A queue formed, men and women carrying their bamboo and frond-plaited crates. When the crates were opened, the wealth of the Solomons was revealed, a most astonishing quantity of handiwork: bead and shell necklaces, boar's teeth, shrunken heads, spears, stone knives, bone fishhooks, miniature canoes, bamboo flutes, monkeypod bowls and cups, elaborate feather fetishes, intricate vine-woven baskets, cloth lap-laps dyed in bright patterns, shell neck disks, wooden masks, *tomako* figureheads, carved kerosene-wood sharks and dolphins inlaid with nautilus shell and mother-of-pearl, shell money, rattles, and woven dilly bags. There were also headbands, earrings, nose and ear plugs, pendants, breastplates, and armbands. Any piece of it was certain to be coveted by South Pacific souvenir hunters, which included every American GI, marine, and sailor in the region.

As each Solomon Islander stepped forward with his or her work of art, he or she would say, "Joe, gimmee." Nixon took his time, contemplating the objet d'art, turning it this way and that, all the while mentally calculating.

After he'd made up his mind, he'd say, "Joe gives you your choice from . . ." and then he would specify stack one, which contained tools such as knives, hatchets, shovels, or picks; or stack two, which consisted of cooking pots and spoons, and also food, including cans of peaches or pears or Spam; or stack three, which was a variety of paperback books, including navy-issue Bibles with an introduction by the real, authentic President Franklin Delano Roosevelt himself. The man or woman meekly went to the designated stack and chose from it the item he or she desired the most. There were no arguments. All went away with cheerful grins.

Kennedy sidled up next to Nixon and said out of the corner of his mouth, "What do you think you're doing, Nick?"

Nixon was inspecting a coconut that had been carved into the likeness of a monkey's head. He considered it delicately done but not very original. Still, it made its own quiet statement. "Hullo, Jack. How goes the war?"

"You may find out. Do you realize this airfield could be used by the Japanese?"

"Stack number two," Nixon finally said to the man who had presented the coconut head. Then, to Kennedy, "What are you talking about?"

"The Japanese. You know, the enemy? The defeat of whom is the reason we're here? They could use this airfield to attack us."

Nixon gave that some thought. "But it's not theirs," he said reasonably. "It belongs to my friend Joe Gimmee."

"How did this get arranged?" Kennedy asked. "How did you know when to come here?"

"Oh, that." Nixon nearly giggled. "I've been putting out the word to every native I saw that I was looking for souvenirs. The word got back to me about Joe Gimmee and that all I had to do was show up on Noa-Noa today and bring trade goods. Now, don't you worry about me. I'll have my business wrapped up within the hour and be out of here."

"I wasn't worried about you, Nick. If the Japanese find this airfield and start using it, it'll mean they can reach a lot farther south, maybe even to Santa Cruz. It'll mean we fought the battle of New Georgia for nothing."

"Well, it's not like the folks made this airfield just for me," Nixon responded defensively.

"But they did! At least, it's for who you represent."

"Who's that?"

"The cargo gods."

Nixon frowned while he absorbed Kennedy's advisory, but his grin returned when he was presented with a particularly fine boar's tooth bracelet. "Stack number one, my good man!" he cried to the artist.

Then Nixon said, "Well, Jack, the main thing is these fine folks are getting some nice cooking pots and Bibles and such, and I'm going to raise a fortune for my activities. In fact, I think I might well expand beyond Santa Cruz and start building recreational facilities all over the Pacific." He pondered a crudely carved fish. "Stack number three. Ah, a shark's tooth necklace. Stack number one, my sweet girl!"

Kennedy, shaking his head, wandered away to stand beside Felicity, who was watching the proceedings. "I wonder if Nick could transport my copra," she said.

"Nick can do anything," Kennedy replied in a sardonic tone, "as long as he perceives a profit."

"A most fascinating man," Felicity said in obvious admiration. "I think I'll ask him if he might stay for dinner."

Kennedy took her aside and said, "If he doesn't leave soon, he might never leave."

"What does that mean?"

"If Thurlow's radioman is able to get through, my guess is bombers will soon be on their way. They'll want this place wiped off the map before Jap can get down and take advantage of it."

"Bombers over Chuma?" Felicity was aghast. "They'll knock down these magnificent palms!"

"A few, I would imagine," Kennedy replied.

"You *damned* Americans!" Felicity spat. "You come here and destroy everything, as if a lifetime of work isn't as important as you frustrating your Japanese for a week or two. Well, damn all you Yanks and your bloody war, that's what I've got to say!"

"It's not our war," Kennedy replied defensively. "The Japanese forced it on us."

"Maybe if you hadn't tried to cut off their oil supplies, they might not have felt the need."

Kennedy couldn't believe his ears. "Your opinion surprises me."

Felicity turned away from him, grumbling. "Damned fool," she said to herself. "I love him, but he'll never figure that out, or care."

Just as he predicted, Nixon completed his trading within an hour. By then, the R4D was filled with every type and description of South Pacific knickknack, doodad, and souvenir. He rose from the table, looked over the remaining trade goods in his three stacks, which wasn't much, and asked for someone to send Joe Gimmee to see him. Joe, his face washed clean, and back to being essentially naked, allowed Nixon to shake his hand. "It was good to do business with you, Joe," Nixon said.

Joe replied, "When I heard of you, I knew you were especially loved by the gods."

"Oh, yes, indeed. They love me like a son."

"I did as you asked," Joe said. "I brought the people together with all the things they make."

"Yes. Well, thank you."

"And now I would ask you to do something for me."

"Anything, Joe. You just name it."

"You brought us treasure from the gods because we built this airfield. But others of my people have built airfields and nothing has come. And they have built docks with the same result. And they have built warehouses, yet they were not filled. What is the great secret? What do you do to get your treasure? Tell me, so that we may have treasure, too."

Nixon gave it all a good think, then wiped the sweat from his face with a handkerchief produced from his hip pocket. "I think I see where you're coming from, Joe. You just want a piece of the pie. Can't blame you for that. If I were in your situation, here's what I'd do. First thing, I'd study up. Education, that's the ticket. Science, the arts, and economics. Lots on economics, Joe, you savvy? Then, I guess the next step would be to get control of your own affairs. Can't do much when somebody else is running the show, now can you? My own country used to be owned and operated by the English, too, but we finally wised up and threw them out. Didn't take us long after that before we were fat and happy. Lots of education and kick out the Johnny Bulls. That's my advice."

"Splendid!" Joe exclaimed. Then he faltered. "But how do we do that?"

Nixon gave it some more thought. "Education's easy enough," he concluded, patting his damp brow with his handkerchief. "To teach yourself, just start reading every book you can get your hands on. For the kids, start setting up schools, but make sure you hire the teachers and have them teach the importance of being free. Then you ought to form a political party and get ready to declare the Solomon Islands independent as soon as this war's over."

"Nick!" Kennedy blanched. "You're talking about a revolution!"

Nixon shrugged. "Well, we did it back in 1776. Why can't Joe and his folks?"

Joe grinned. "I should have known the great secret would be complex, but I promise to follow your advice."

"That's the style!" Nixon exclaimed, then stood and pumped Joe's hand, nodded to his pilot and air crew, and clambered aboard the R4D. At the top of the bamboo steps, he paused, looking down at Kennedy. "Take care of yourself, Jack. How's the war going, by the way?"

Kennedy stared at Nixon, then found himself laughing. "We're not losing, Nick. At least I don't think we are."

Nixon nodded thoughtfully, then ducked into the R4D, in the process knocking his pith helmet off. It rolled down the steps, but he did not return for it. The door was closed, the engines fired up, and the fully laden aircraft was soon waddling down the palm-fringed runway. Kennedy picked up the pith helmet and gave it to Joe Gimmee. "Here, Joe. You should have this. A souvenir."

Joe Gimmee happily plopped the helmet aboard his head and started walking back to the beach. Behind him, the R4D roared down the field and took off. Soon the only evidence of it consisted entirely of a low drone in the sky, and when that disappeared, the people of the Solomon Islands all stopped as one, looked over their shoulders, and made the V-sign toward the great man who had finally delivered to them the great secret of success and treasure: education and freedom.

5 7

First came Ichikawa and his two Rufe wing men, after completing their patrol down the Slot. Ichikawa had seen nothing of interest until he spotted an R4D lifting off from Noa-Noa. He signaled his pilots to follow and then dived after the cargo plane, but it flew into a low-hanging cloud and disappeared. Frustrated, Ichikawa turned back to the island, spying an airfield he'd never seen before. He became agitated. Apparently the Americans had performed one of their overnight engineering marvels. He flew down its length and then pulled up and flew across it again. It was on the return trip that he saw the American flag flapping on the tall pole. This confirmed his suspicions, but, low on fuel, Ichikawa turned his flight toward Kolombangara. Then he beheld several peculiar sights. The dozens of canoes he'd seen earlier in the day were beached on the western side of Noa-Noa. On the northern side sat a Japanese I-boat, and two men stood on a tall spire of a rock, looking at it. On the eastern side of the island, he saw another group of canoes on the beach. Warriors carrying rifles were streaming inland. He turned and made one last circle, puzzling over the situation, but then had no choice but to head back to base. His Rufes were already flying on fumes.

Kennedy was distracted by the sudden crackling of small-arms fire. He looked up and saw fifty warriors charging across the runway, led by Whitman. He drew his pistol and cracked off two shots, winging one Whitman man and knocking down another. "Get clear," he told Felicity, and was gratified when she obeyed and climbed into Delight's saddle.

"I've got to look after John," Felicity said. "You stay alive, you hear me, Jack Kennedy?"

"No worry-worry," he said, flashing his big-toothed grin. Then he slapped Delight on the rump, and the big stallion galloped off.

Kennedy fell back behind a line being formed by Joe Gimmee's people. Since they were armed only with spears, machetes, knives, and bows and arrows, the rifles of Whitman's warriors should have made easy work of them, but these were men whose families were on the beach, and they knew the reputation of Whitman's men, both as rapists and cannibals. They used a row of palm trees to their advantage, hiding until Whitman's men charged past, then leapt out and hacked them down. Rifle shots also rang out, and many of Joe Gimmee's men fell, but Whitman's men were thrown back.

The people began to load their treasure, their wounded, and their dead into their canoes. Then the *Rosemary* appeared and got into the action, Thurlow's boys manning their big twin-fifty guns and the mortar on the bow. Whitman's men were pummeled, and they retreated back across the island. Whitman, however, wasn't with them. He'd seen his real quarry and dodged away into the bush. He caught Penelope on the path to the beach. He burst from behind a crepe myrtle tree just as Felicity and Delight came pounding down the path on top of them. The great stallion reared, and his hooves struck Whitman in the chest. Stunned, the wind knocked out of him, the coast-watcher went sprawling. Penelope drew her terrible machete, knelt behind him, and drew him to her in a kind of embrace. She put her head next to his, then pulled the edge of the machete very slowly and carefully across his throat. It appeared to Felicity that Penelope was drawing a thin red line across Whitman's throat, but then the line grew.

Josh followed Armistead through the plantation, catching him finally when he could go no farther, on a rock cliff overlooking a lagoon on the north coast. There Armistead stood, the wind blowing his long hair back from his face. A quarter mile offshore sat the I-boat. A launch was being rowed in by white-suited Japanese sailors. "What are you doing, David?" Josh demanded, coming up behind him.

Armistead whirled about, his hand going to the pistol on his hip. Josh, however, already had his forty-five pointing at the lieutenant's chest. "Let me do this, Josh. I think I can make a difference."

"How? By committing treason?"

Armistead looked over his shoulder at the submarine launch, then back at Josh. He dropped his hand away from the butt of his pistol. "Do you know how many men I've killed? Thirty-eight. I've kept count. And most of them I have been close enough to smell their sweat and fear before I snuffed out their lives."

"That don't matter, David," Josh said.

"I think it does. I am a member of the family of the president of the United States. I am a cultured, educated man. Yet I have become a willing killer. I know firsthand the wrath that has been stirred in my heart, as well as the president's heart. I don't think the Japanese understand what they're up against, but they might, if I explain it. You see, I happen to believe they are a good and decent people."

"They're the enemy," Josh replied. "Until they stop fighting, it's our duty to kill them."

Armistead checked the progress of the launch again. It had made it halfway across the lagoon. "The night I left New Georgia, I had occasion to meet a Japanese officer. He was dying from grenade wounds but seemed to welcome my presence. It was the most remarkable occasion. I sat down beside him, and we began to talk. I explained the way I saw things, he told me what he thought, and then we agreed that the war made no sense for either side. He thought perhaps if the emperor apologized to the president for Pearl Harbor and made reparations, then the fighting would no longer have purpose and we would have peace. The point is, Josh, he understood the futility of the Japanese situation. If he did, others will, too. Many of them already do. That's why that submarine is here."

Josh felt very tired. He knew Armistead was talking nonsense, but it was seductive. The Japanese were a reasonable people, even if their leaders weren't. What would it hurt to talk to folks, explain things? "How did you contact them?" he asked as the men in the launch rowed steadily for the beach.

"I sent word to the Japanese detachment on Vella Lavella. Their commander visited me under the protection of Joe Gimmee. Then a few days later, he sent word that transport was coming to pick me up. I told them to meet me here because I wanted to see Joe's miracle first. I think there are powerful Japanese who know they're going to be beaten, Josh. They desperately want peace. That's why they've gone to the trouble to send a submarine for me."

"This is crazy, David," Josh said, though there was a hint of uncertainty in his voice.

"Maybe. But isn't it worth a try? After all, what's the worst thing that could happen? That they will cut off my head? That they will eat me? I discovered one of our own doing that already."

"Whitman's a madman."

"My cousin Franklin Roosevelt has a plan, Josh. He is marching island by island toward Japan until he gets his bombers close enough. Then he is going to pound every Japanese city into dust, and with them millions of innocent men, women, and children. Who is the madman?"

"We have to avenge Pearl Harbor."

"Two thousand men died there. It was an atrocity. But an apology and reparations should answer for that, not the lives of millions who had no part in it."

"If you leave on that sub, Tokyo Rose will be on the air tonight telling all our boys what you've done."

"If that happens, it won't matter. The war will grind on. But what if they're sincere? Just think of it! Your boys, all the boys, will go home, alive and unmaimed."

Josh discovered he was saddened and sickened by the vision Armistead had painted. In his mind, he saw soldiers on distant beaches, sobbing into their own curdling blood. And he saw the cities burning, the people screaming as they burned with them, their skins black and charred, as horrible as the lump in the fire pit on Whitman's beach.

"I'm going now, Josh," Armistead said. "Either shoot me or let me go."

The I-boat's launch was nearing the breakers. "They know, David," Josh said, using his last argument. "Don't you understand? They know what you're doing, and they sent me to kill you."

Armistead frowned. "How could they know?" Then the expression on his face changed to one of understanding. "They've broken the Japanese code," he said in awe. "That's the only way they could know."

Josh cursed himself. He had said too much, and now he had no choice. He took careful aim, as careful aim as ever in his life.

Whitman stayed conscious long enough to see his wife smile down on him. He wished he could tell her how beautiful he thought she was, but then he started to get very sleepy. He recalled the times when he had waked in the middle of the night and looked at her sleeping, then couldn't get back to sleep because he didn't want to lose a moment of admiring her. He had always wanted only good things for her, and he had wished others wouldn't look down on her just because of the color of her skin. Then, one night, while he was contemplating her beauty, it came to him as if it were a gift of the gods. It was the idea of forming a little army, which would be ready to take over as soon as the English gave up on the Solomons, which he knew they would after the war. He would set himself up as king, and then Kimba would be his queen, and no one would ever look down on her again.

My queen, he wanted to say to her now. *Kimba, my queen.* But he didn't say anything, because he couldn't talk with a throat cut to the neck bone. Instead, he stared up at her, willing her to understand how much he loved her. He saw by her expression that she was pleased he was bleeding to death. He was glad that he was making her happy at last. And then he went to sleep, which is to say he died, not to wake on this earth but somewhere else, the other else.

Penelope stood and wiped her bloody machete on the leaves of a philodendron. "Whitman him finish altogether," she said, with complete satisfaction.

"I do so admire your straightforward approach to handling a difficult man, Penelope," Felicity said from the saddle. She held out her hand. "Climb up. You will be safe on my plantation."

"No, Missus Markham. I shall go with my father. Please tell Josh Thurlow that I will always love him, though I know he cannot love me as I deserve."

"What man can any woman?" Felicity asked, then was startled by a noise that was very loud and deep, even greater than thunder. It grew until the entire island of Noa-Noa shook from it. Great bombers were coming in over the island, dropping load after load of bombs. "My dear God," Felicity cried, her hands to her mouth as she watched the massive spouts of smoke and earth and blasted trees stomp across her island.

Kennedy swam out to the gunboat, and Once helped him aboard. "Give me a report," he demanded.

"We're fine, sir. Where's the skipper?"

"I'm not sure." He looked out to sea. Most of Joe Gimmee's canoes were rapidly receding toward the horizon. Then came the thunder of the heavy bombers. Kennedy watched Noa-Noa being shattered before his eyes. "Why are they bombing the entire island?"

Ready shrugged. "I guess they want to make sure they get that airfield. The skipper told me to call it in and tell them it belonged to Jap. Looks like they believed me."

A canoe came around the western point of the lagoon. In it was a woman with plaited flowers circling her head. She waved at Armistead and began to paddle furiously, trying to beat the Japanese sailors to the beach. The officer in the launch frowned at the woman. Josh lowered his pistol and nodded toward the canoe. "They make good women around here, David. A man could go into the hills of Vella and be happy, live out his days, maybe even raise a family."

"Turn Turk?" Armistead looked at the canoe and then the madly rowing Japanese. "That would be a cowardly choice."

"Well, son, I'm afraid that's your choice, that or going back with me."

"I'm going with the Japanese. Or you can kill me. Those are *your* choices."

Josh sighed and shook his head. "You've been wrong about nearly everything, David, including my choices." Josh raised his pistol and shot the Japanese officer in the launch through the heart. The impact of the heavy bullet lifted him out of the boat into the water, where he sank. "A lot of men would have trouble hitting anything from this distance with a forty-five," Josh said with some satisfaction, though he resisted blowing the smoke from the pistol's barrel.

The sailors in the launch stopped rowing and stared at the froth in the water that marked their dead officer's disappearance, and then looked with startled faces at the two Americans on the beach. "Somehow, I don't think you're going to be welcome on that sub anymore, David. So let's go over your choices again. Go with Victoria, or come with me."

Armistead closed his mouth, open since Josh had displayed his skill with a pistol. "If I go with Victoria, what if I get caught?"

"You're an old hand in the jungle. You won't get caught. Look, I'm offering you a chance to get clear of all this. I never said it was logical, dammit!"

"Why aren't you going to kill me, especially now that I know about the code? It's a simple question."

Josh didn't know why. The question might be simple, but its answer surely wasn't. He got as close to it as he could, considering he only had seconds to spare. "We were on Wilton's Ridge together. That makes us brothers. Brothers don't kill brothers. Anyway, you don't know anything. You just think you do."

Victoria beached the canoe and ran up to Armistead and threw herself into his arms. He tilted her chin with his finger and gazed into her eyes. "You've done your part in this war," Josh said. "Go on with the girl. Just don't show your face again, at least until the war is over. Those are my terms."

Victoria held Armistead around the waist, burying her head in his chest while he stroked her hair. "Maybe I haven't been thinking straight for a while," he said.

"Who the hell can in these islands? Somebody once told me the heat and the bugs out here are enough to drive a man insane. Throw in Wilton's Ridge and one of your own men made into long pig . . . Hell, David, look at you with them tattoos and earrings. You've already gone oriental. You're the only one who don't know it."

The deep worry lines on Armistead's face seemed to smooth. He smiled. "I'm going to run, Josh. I'm going to get clear."

"I envy you, David. More than you could possibly know."

Armistead took Victoria's hand and walked rapidly with her to the canoe. Josh watched after them, failing to notice that the crewmen on the I-boat had been busily cranking around its deck gun. Josh noticed it soon afterward, because it was fired in his direction. After that, he had to struggle back to consciousness, and discovered he had blood and sand in his eyes. Then he tried to get to his feet but found that difficult, since his right leg didn't seem to work very well. He peered through the pink haze to see if the canoe with Armistead and Victoria had gotten away but couldn't see it.

Then he sensed someone's presence. He wiped his eyes again, this time managing to dislodge a remnant of sodden grit, enough so that a small, clear window opened, and enough that he saw combat boots and bare legs. "David, what are you doing? Get clear!"

Armistead said nothing, but Josh saw now why he had returned. The Japanese sailors had beached their boat and were racing toward them. Armistead had his pistol out and began to fire. Victoria was nearby, weeping, pleading to Armistead to get in the canoe. Then a roar filled Josh's ears, and he was astonished to see a Catalina flying low over the I-boat. Something small and black dropped from the aircraft, and the conning tower of the submarine disappeared in a spray of smoke and flame. The men firing the deck gun began to burn.

Armistead's pistol clip was empty. The Japanese sailors had stopped their charge to gawk at the disaster that had visited their boat. Armistead drew his K-bar. They took one look at him coming at them and ran, all but one small sailor with a big rifle. Panicked, he fell backward, the rifle butt striking the sand just as Armistead reached him. The rifle went off, and Victoria screamed a tattered wail that trailed off into sobs. Then she knelt on the beach and repeatedly struck herself in the face. That was the last thing Josh remembered for a while.

After refueling, Ichikawa returned to Noa-Noa alone on a recon mission and beheld a terrible sight. The entire island was burning. He looked aloft and saw the vapor trails of four-engined American bombers. It was all most strange. Why would the Americans bomb their own airfield? Then he spotted the gunboat and lined up on it. But before he could make his run, big tracers flew past his nose. He pulled up and saw that a Catalina had made a run on him. He recognized it as *Dosie*. Of course, no Catalina was capable of dogfighting with a Rufe, not with an ace pilot like Ichikawa at the controls. But before he destroyed it, Ichikawa slid up beside *Dosie* and looked into its blister window and saw Fisheye. He waved at his friend.

After the first wave of bombers had passed, Kennedy hurried into the shattered plantation to find Josh. He found him, finally, on the northern beach. He was unconscious, his chest and face peppered with small wounds and his right leg obviously broken. Kennedy, without even thinking about his back, lifted Josh up and threw one of his big arms across his shoulders and somehow dragged him through the burning plantation to the beach. Once and Again saw them and dived in to swim their skipper to the gunboat. Ready pushed the throttles full ahead to get away from the next wave of falling bombs. It appeared the big bombers were determined to knock down every tree on the island.

Phimble called to Fisheye over the intercom. "Fisheye, blast that bastard out of the sky. Do it now, while he's just sitting there!"

"I can't do it!" Fisheye cried. "It's Ichikawa-san!"

"Yes, and in a second, he's going to fall back, get on our tail, and that'll be the end of us."

Fisheye knew Phimble was right. Ichikawa was still waving at him, nodding, and smiling. Fisheye swiveled his gun around, sighted along its long snout, and pulled the trigger.

Three big slugs slammed into Ichikawa's engine. It sputtered a few times, then died. Ichikawa was surprised, but then grateful that his friend

Fisheye had become such a fierce warrior that he would unleash a surprise attack, even on a friend. He was proud that he was such a good teacher. He had turned the simple American into a true samurai! He waved to Fisheye in salute; then he could no longer hold his Rufe level, mainly because Fisheye had fired again, this time directly into the Rufe's canopy. The Rufe fell away, spiraling into the sea. There was no parachute.

Josh came awake, lying in front of the gunboat splinter shield. Kennedy and Phimble hovered over him. He saw his company and said, "Well, Eureka, what brings you up this way?"

"Colonel Burr said you needed to duck," Phimble replied. "Since I knew you wouldn't, I thought I'd better come up and help you out." Then he told him about bombing the I-boat and Fisheye shooting down the Rufe.

"What were you doing on that beach?" Kennedy asked Josh.

"I followed Armistead there."

"Where is he?"

"You didn't see him? Or the girl?"

"No. Just you and some dead Japanese sailors."

Josh gave it some thought, then said, "He was killed in action, brave to the last."

"We should collect his body," Kennedy said.

Josh shook his head. "He caught a slug. I guess he fell into the water. Likely the sharks have seen to him by now."

Kennedy studied Josh for a long second. "Quite the coincidence that you found Armistead on the same beach where the submarine was."

"Coincidences ain't your concern, Jack," Josh growled, then grimaced as the pain in his leg reannounced itself. Millie appeared and unceremoniously pulled down Josh's pants and stuck a morphine syrette into his hip. Josh welcomed the warm rush that coursed through his veins. Before he lowered himself to sleep, he said, "Just remember this, all of you. David Armistead was kidnapped and did his best to get home. He was a good marine to the end."

"Sirs, something to see," Ready said from the bow.

Kennedy stood up to see whatever fool thing Ready wanted them to see. It turned out there were actually two things. One was Felicity's plantation, which was on fire, every structure and every palm. The copra warehouses were especially glorious as they produced beautiful, white-hot flames, which in turn created dazzling yellow clouds, billowing toward heaven. The other thing to see was all the boats. They were actually landing craft, and the bobbing helmets of the men within them told their story. The 5th Marine Raiders, led by Colonel Monkey Burr, were coming ashore on poor burning Noa-Noa, and *toot sweet.*

PART V

LORD, make me to know mine end, and the measure of my days, what it is; that I may know how frail I am.—Psalms, chapter 39, verse 4

5 8

The landings on Noa-Noa, reads the official history of the 5th Marine Raider Battalion, *were characterized by an unusual use of heavy bombers in a support role to destroy a small Japanese airfield which headquarters feared might be expanded. Enemy opposition was lighter than anticipated and the commander of the Raiders, Colonel Montague Singleton Burr, messaged Regimental Headquarters that the island was secured within a single day after taking his men ashore. The battalion subsequently turned over Noa-Noa to Seabee elements for the construction of logistics facilities, and retired to its base on Melagi for refit. Its next action, as an element in the invasion of Bougainville, would prove to be a bit more difficult.*

Melagi sat beneath the rain, the blood-warm rain, her great volcano covered by steam that ran down her sides like ghostly rivers. On the old plantation, the Raiders, most of them fortified by drink from various applejack stills, took shelter in their miserable little tents. Soon, above the steady beating of the deluge, their voices were raised in song.

> *We sent for the nurses to come to Me-soggy,*
> *The nurses they made it with ease,*
> *Their asses on the table each bearing this label:*
> *Reserved for the officers please.*
>
> *Bless 'em all, bless 'em all . . .*

Felicity Markham stood in the rain on the beach and looked across the sea, across the terrible tragedy of Iron Bottom Bay and the distant, faded blue-green island of Guadalcanal where so many had died and were already nearly forgotten. There would yet be so many islands where men would fight and then would be lost in the memory of history as the remorseless years ground by.

Before her, anchored in the sand, was an old steamer, come across from Australia to carry away the wounded brought down from Bougainville, as well as the lost and the destitute, which was how she characterized herself and her son. A lighter, a small power boat, was going back and forth to the steamer with the stretchers holding the wounded. Nurses from the steamer did their best to keep their patients dry, holding ponchos over them, but all were soaked to the skin.

Felicity looked around for John-Bull and was startled by the appearance of Jack Kennedy. "The terror of the Solomons," she said, extending her damp hand. "When did you pull in?"

Kennedy, wearing a Raider poncho, took her hand. "This morning. I wasn't sure you were still here, but then I saw John-Bull. The Raiders are having a softball game in the mud, and he's cheering them on. He said it would be for the last time."

"We are leaving within the hour," Felicity confirmed. She nodded toward the tired old ship. "There is our transport. Let us hope she might have an easy sea. She is rocking even in this placid water."

"She appears seaworthy," Kennedy said, in a voice that was suddenly weak.

"You are well?" she asked.

"I've never felt better in my life."

She interrupted him. "And Thurlow? What of that big oaf?"

Kennedy smiled. "We came in together. He was anxious to get back to his cave and see his boys." Kennedy's smile faded. "Will you forward me your address when you know it? I'm heading back up to Lumbari. All the PTs are being converted to gunboats since they got a look at the *Rosemary*. She's still mine if I want her, and I do."

"Why? Haven't you done enough out here?"

"How can any man do enough when so many other men have given everything they have?"

"Dear Jack."

"Felicity," Kennedy began, but he stopped when she turned her head away.

"No good-byes," she said. "Not between us. Allow me to savor this fantasy all my days, Jack. We are still in Noa-Noa. We are forever there. It wasn't burned over. It yet thrives. Don't you see us, Jack?"

"Yes," he said, gently. "I see."

Felicity knew he didn't see at all, but that he at least said he did warmed her. "Ah, John," she said, proudly taking her lad under her arm as he came up. He was also protected by a poncho. But not Felicity. She stood in the rain, her shoulders squared, her chin up, the picture of the undaunted Englishwoman. "I would imagine you have much to do," she said to Kennedy. "As I have," she added pointedly.

Kennedy touched John-Bull's cheek. "Take good care of your mother, sport."

"I will, sir. Give Jap a kick for me, won't you?"

"You know I will," he said, and walked away. Felicity's arms ached because they felt so terribly empty, but she did not call out to him. She only watched him, searing his image into her mind, before turning toward the old steamer and an uncertain future.

5 9

The boys erupted from the cave at the sight of Josh, struggling off the steep path that led up through the bush from the collapsed punch bowl valley. They were so glad to see him, they were nearly speechless, which was fine with Josh, since he had nothing much to say in return. Although the broken bones in his leg were healed, he was a man whose heart was troubled. He sought a moment alone with Ensign Phimble. "What news?" he asked.

"Nothing, Skipper. Not of Joe Gimmee or Penelope. I did as you asked and put the word out to everyone heading up the Slot to be on the lookout for either one. But nothing. I'm sorry."

"She should have at least said good-bye," he said.

"Missus Markham said she got away, at least to the beach. She must have caught one of the canoes. Skipper, it's hard for me to say this, but maybe she got from you all that she wanted. She didn't need to say good-bye."

"Nothing else from up north?"

"Like what?"

"Armistead?"

Phimble stared at him. "You do recall that he's dead, don't you?"

Josh stared back. "Sure I do," he said. "I just wondered if they found his body." Then he asked, "Any mail?"

"You have a letter from Dosie," Phimble answered, knowing what the real question was, and handed the envelope to him just as it stopped raining. The clouds blew away and the sun beat down and the steam began to rise.

Far to the north, a woman stirred inside her hut. She listened to the gentle lapping of the surf, then rolled over on her back and touched her stomach.

She stared at the golden light coming through the slats of bamboo, and a tear rolled down her cheek.

Josh turned the letter over and tried to discern its contents by looking at the manner in which Dosie had written his name, but there was nothing in her handwriting that was much different. Phimble walked away, and Josh went to Look-it Rock and sat down. It had only been a little over two months since he'd sat at that very same place and read Dosie's last letter, the one that had been so hurtful, the one that had made him so angry that he needed to hurt her in return.

The woman rose and went outside. The sea was warm and blue, and her sister was bathing in it. The woman entered the sea and walked until the water lapped just beneath her breasts. She smiled at her sister, who was also touching her stomach, for the same reason she did. It made her smile, and imagine what might have been, and yet could be. "Josh darling," she whispered, and was happy for the moment.

Josh tore open the envelope, and as he did, he felt something feathery at his side. It was Dave the megapode, hunkering down for a nap. He patted the bird on his bony head, then opened up Dosie's note, which had been written on a single page. He read, and as he read, a frown formed, then deepened before gradually fading as if gentle hands had smoothed it away. The letter from Dosie was a love letter. She was in one of her moods, she wrote, when she was reminded by the sand of the Killakeet shore, and its great, violent ocean, and the flashing light of his father's lighthouse, of the adoration she had for him, and how her love would never die, no, not ever, no matter until the ends of the earth and time. She lived, she wrote, only to see him safely home. At the end of her letter, she begged for news from him, reminding him that it had been three months and more since she'd last heard any news at all.

The old man sat at his table. He had gone into the forest alone, and there built himself a house in the trees. After a triumph, a man sometimes needs time alone to sort through in his mind what really happened, and the importance of it, and what it all meant. He had writing paper, taken from an abandoned plantation house he'd come across on his solitary journey, and several pencils. He wrote a little more each day. It was a love letter to the people of the Solomon Islands. He did not know when he would finish the letter, or if he ever would, but it would not much matter. This was a matter for the gods, and they would know what was in his heart, and they would take the message of education and freedom to his people in their own good time. "Joe Gimmee," he said aloud, just to savor the sound of his once and future name. Far away, and all around, others said his name every day, too, and it also made them smile. They trusted, and they believed. Trust is always a thing of beauty, and belief always a thing of joy.

Josh rose from the rock, went inside the cave, and sought out Stobs. Stobs looked up from his radio. "A couple of months back," Josh said, "as you may recall since it was just before I went down to see Colonel Burr, I wrote a letter to Dosie Crossan and gave it to you to put in with my reports. I know the folks in Washington received those reports, but Dosie ain't got her letter yet."

Stobs blushed. "That don't surprise me much, Skipper."

"And why not?"

"Mister Phimble."

"Mister Phimble?"

"He told me to burn your letter."

"Phimble told you to burn my letter?"

"Yes, sir. And I did, too."

Josh stared at the embarrassed boy for a long second, then walked back to Look-it Rock, after first stopping by the box where such was held and retrieving a bottle of Mount Gay rum. He settled down, holding the bottle in his big hands. Then he noticed that Dave the megapode had climbed off the rock and was looking at him. When Josh looked back, the megapode's hard little black eyes seemed to grow until Josh found himself lost within their darkness until there was a tiny light, a blue-green pinprick that grew larger, as if it were a hole in reality. Josh understood that if he wished, he could look through it, and he did. He saw the woman in the water, and her glistening ebony body, and when she turned, he saw her smile, and the reason for it. Then Josh saw another woman, who was looking at someone on the beach. Josh strained to see who it was, this shimmering, ghostly figure, but then a strange weariness came over him, and he closed his eyes. When he opened them again, he found himself alone, the opening gone, replaced by an endless expanse of island, and sea, and time.

A FURTHER HISTORICAL NOTE AND A FEW ACKNOWLEDGMENTS

When Josh Thurlow and his boys moved from Killakeet to the Solomon Islands, it was incumbent upon me, as their chronicler, to read up on the new location. Pretty soon, books on these fascinating islands were stacked to the ceiling in my study. I've hung around a few Pacific islands and figured I already knew all there was to know, but it wasn't long before I realized how wrong I was. The Solomons are unique. Since my focus was on the effect of World War II on these islands as well as the prewar colonial experience, my reading gradually coalesced to those two arenas. For readers interested in the war in the Solomons, among the best references are *The Solomons Campaigns, 1942–1943* by William L. McGee, *Touched With Fire: The Land War in the South Pacific,* by Eric Bergerud, *Alone on Guadalcanal: A Coast-watcher's Story* by Martin Clemens, and *Samurai!* by Saburo Sakai. For those who would like to learn more about the colonial experience, as well as a little about how copra is made, the wonderful memoir *Headhunting in the Solomon Islands, Around the Coral Sea* by Caroline Mytinger is about all that is required. The "headhunting" in the title, by the way, refers to Miss Mytinger's quest for portrait subjects. *Bad Colonists* by Nicholas Thomas and Richard Eves is another take on the European men and women who tried to make the Solomons their home. For a look at the modern Solomons, reflecting the aftereffects of the war and colonialism, I recommend the clever and amusing *Solomon Time* by Will Randall.

It didn't take long, as I read through these and other reference works, before I began to discern the spirituality of the people of the Solomons, and especially the fascinating cargo cults that have grown up there and on nearby islands. Joe Gimmee and his movement were not unique to the war era. Cargo cults were around for decades prior to the war and still exist today. In fact, most of us are a member, one way or another, of a cargo cult. Richard Feynman wrote an interesting essay on that subject in his book *Surely You're Joking, Mr. Feynman!* where he suggested that nearly all advertising depends on our predilection to reach the wrong conclusions based on a limited amount of evidence. For good reading on the cults as they exist in the South Pacific, I recommend *John Frum He Come* by Edward Rice, *Mambu: A Melanesian Millennium* by Kenelm Burridge, and *Cargo Cult: Strange Stories of Desire From Melanesia and Beyond* by Lamont Lindstrom.

Of course, many readers will wonder how I learned about the experiences of John F. "Shafty" Kennedy, Richard "Nick" Nixon, and James "Jim" Michener that I relate in this book, especially since none of these men chose to write about their experiences with Josh Thurlow or with one another. It's difficult to explain this lapse, but perhaps they were sensitive to the memory of David Armistead, whose disappearance remains a mystery to this day. In any case, to discover for yourself John Kennedy's experiences in the South Pacific, as well as his family life just prior, you need go no further than the magnificently researched *JFK: Reckless Youth* by Nigel Hamilton. *The Kennedys at War* by Edward J. Renehan Jr. will provide further insight as to the fate of older brother Joe and why John F. became his political stand-in after the war. For Richard Nixon's experiences in the South Pacific, including his ability to play world-class poker, one might want to selectively read *RN: The Memoirs of Richard Nixon*. Although he fails to mention his trading with Joe Gimmee in this hefty autobiography, I was fortunately able to read between the lines. Utilizing a blend of fact and fiction, James Michener's *Tales of the South Pacific* tells much about him and others he met during his time around the Solomons during the war. His failure to mention Kennedy and Nixon or their famous poker game in his book was probably due to when he wrote it (first published in 1946), well before either of those two gentlemen decided to be involved in national and international politics. I suspect an overzealous editor or legal adviser deleted Michener's acknowledgement to our own Bosun Ready O'Neal, who, as I have written herein, first suggested the work that became *South Pacific*.

In writing this book, I also depended on firsthand accounts of men and women who experienced the Solomons during the war. Sadly, every day we lose more of these magnificent folks, time taking its inevitable toll. Many of them wished to remain anonymous, but Quartermaster Chet Williams, who served with Kennedy and the PT boats in the Solomons, was a great source of vital information. He recalled very well seeing Kennedy's boat burning the night the *PT-109* was run over by that Japanese destroyer. He and others who knew the future president wondered what happened to him in the weeks after his "rescue." I am proud to reveal here for the first time the adventure that saw him north to Noa-Noa. I suspect it was very nearly the last time John F. Kennedy was truly a happy man.

Others, as always, were required to help me along the way. My wonderful wife, Linda, did her usual fine job of digging through the initial manuscript and pointing out my various follies. She also keeps our Web site (http://www.homerhickam.com) up to date and answers most of the fan mail. Sean Desmond, the best editor in the world, accomplishes his usual magic with his keen eye for plot, characterization, and detail. This book is dedicated to Captain Pat Stadt and the crew of the U.S. Coast Guard cutter *RUSH*. While I was in the midst of writing this book, they provided me with a breathtaking adventure in the Pacific. I learned more with them about life aboard a small ship at sea in three weeks than years of research could have otherwise provided. Finally, thanks to Frank Weimann and Mickey Freiberg, my agents, who somehow, against all odds, have so far kept me gainfully employed. As for Josh Thurlow, his adventures are far from complete, and he will sail again along exotic shores.